The Humanarium

The Humanarium by C.W Tickner.

Published by Humanarium Publishing Ltd.

© 2018 C.W Tickner

Available in ebook on Amazon

First edition: 2018
Editor: Andrew Turpin
Cover designer: Dane at Ebook launch

Thank you for opening this copy of The Humanarium. Just to let you know, reviews are the life blood of an author and the chance of sequels stem from honest reviews.

Thank you Andrew Turpin for having the patience to teach a novice how to use his creative mind.

Thanks to Ms S Walker for starting something that became this book.

Now sit back and enjoy the story.

THE HUMANARIUM.

Prologue.

Wind whipped against Harl Eriksson's face as he sped across the fields. He leapt over a rotting fence and landed at a run, his feet pounding clouds of dust into the air. Troy raced at his side and glanced back over his shoulder at the town the moment he landed.

'Guards!' he yelled.

Both men threw themselves into a gully and splashed through the water as they scrambled out of sight.

'Damn!' Harl groaned. 'How close?'

Troy was holding his side and breathing hard.

'Just... leaving... the barracks,' he said, collapsing against the clay bank.

'And the boys?'

'Far edge of the forest,' Troy jerked a thumb over his shoulder in the direction they had been running, 'right where it breaks against the barrier.'

Harl risked a quick look back at the town. The guards were marching along the road towards them. Their spears glinted in the harsh light thrown down from the roof of the world. Harl slid back into the gulley and grabbed Troy. He hauled him up and they stumbled along until a curve in the wrong direction forced them to scramble up out of hiding.

A dark tangle of forest sprawled ahead of them, but it was a haven of light compared to the barrier that rose up behind it. Smooth and unmarked, a vast black wall spread along the horizon and climbed up to the roof of the world. It marked the end of everything. Impenetrable. Unknowable. It was the edge of their world and surrounded them on all four sides, like the shell of a giant cube slammed down around them.

This was their world, their prison. Harl couldn't think of it any other way, no matter what the priests claimed.

'Oh Gods.' Troy whispered.

Harl glanced over his shoulder to find the guards much nearer than he'd thought.

'We can get to them in time,' he said, clenching his jaw in determination.

Troy looked at him as though he was mad.

They scrambled across the rolling grassland in a crouch and stumbled into the dark mass of trees that backed against the barrier. Harl found a narrow animal trail leading in the right direction and the two men followed it.

They ran on. When they burst out of the forest, the black barrier rose up before them as though the gods had struck them blind. The two boys were hacking into the soil at its base. Both their black-haired heads popped up over the edge of the hole at the sound of Troy and Harl charging towards them. Fear clouded their muddy faces and they scrambled out of the hole, dragging a pair of shovels with them as they sprinted for the nearest trees.

Harl jumped on top of them before either could get away.

'What do you think you're doing, Luke?' Harl demanded as he dragged one of the boys across the clearing towards the trees.

'Digging,' Luke said, as though tunnelling under the barrier was a common occurrence.

'You daft buggers,' Harl said.

Troy snatched the shovels from their hands and tossed them into the hole.

'What were you thinking?' he hissed.

'Please mister!' Luke pleaded, 'We don't want trouble.'

'It's not us you need to worry about,' Harl said as they reached the first tree.

'But, father's tools...' Luke said, looking back at the shovel handles poking up out of the small pit.

'It's too late,' Harl said. 'The Elders know you're here. Just run. Run!'

The four of them plunged deeper into the woods, before crouching in a thicket to look back.

Moments later the guards surrounded the hole. Their uniform was simple padded leather and covered by a dark grey tabard. The leader wore bright white robes and carried no weapons. He crouched on the rim of the pit and scanned the edge of the forest. His robe flickered in the light as he twisted to face them, reflecting the ornate gold patterns that marked him as an Elderman.

'Rufus,' Harl hissed, recognizing the man, 'the pious vulture.'

The Elderman jumped down into the pit. He kicked at a few loose stones, shaking with rage, before climbing back out holding a shovel in either hand.

'Find them!' he screamed. 'Search the woods. They'll be lifted for such heresy.'

'Move!' Troy said, forcing the boys into a run as the guards spread out along the tree line.

'Take the long route,' Harl said. 'If we make it back to your pa's before Rufus, then no one can prove that you were trying to tunnel out.'

The boy's home was on the northern edge of the forest bordering the town. Manicured flower beds lined the wide garden leading to the cottage. As they approached the rear garden raised voices drifted across through the night. They were too late. Rufus and the guards stood in a semicircle around the back door.

The Elderman was shouting at the boy's father, Earl, who was standing in the doorway, scratching at the stubble coating his chin in confusion. Earl cocked his head to one side when he noticed Harl holding the children inside the tree line at the end of the garden.

'The tools have your initials on them Earl,' Rufus shouted as he brandished a shovel under the man's nose. 'And you expect me to believe they were stolen this morning? Fool. The evidence clearly points at someone from this house.'

'My wife was lifted,' Earl said, placing an open palm on his chest to ward off lifting. 'It's just me and my boys now.'

'Somebody must be guilty,' Rufus continued, 'and I'm going to find out who would dare-'

'Who are you accusing?' Earl barked, cutting Rufus off. His eyes flicked past Rufus to the boys and back. He stepped forward to stand over the shorter Elderman.

Rufus shook with rage. 'Where are your children? They were overheard plotting to break into the realm of the Gods. Blasphemy! Pure and simple.'

Earl looked at Harl before standing straighter and staring the Elderman down. 'It was not my boys, Rufus. *I* dared the wrath of the Gods. I've no wish to live in this prison any longer.'

'Blasphemy!' Rufus screamed. 'Seize him.'

Two of the guards grabbed an arm each, and Harl watched, helplessly, as the soldiers marched Earl towards the town. Both boys made a start towards their father, but Harl kept a hand on Luke's shoulder while Troy did the same with the other. Rufus turned to see the four of them standing beneath the trees. A nasty smile formed on his lips and then he laughed as he turned to follow his men.

'It's not fair,' Luke wailed, his face buried in his hands as he sobbed. 'Pa didn't do nothing wrong.'

'There's nothing you can do,' Harl said, 'he'll serve his time in the quarries and be back soon enough.'

But even as he said it, he knew that the words were hollow. He watched the guards drag Earl away. Luke was right. But what could he do about it?

'Bastard,' Harl said as they marched a short distance behind Rufus and his men. They had fallen into step behind the procession as it took the main road back to town. Rufus must have heard as he looked back sneering and drew a finger across his neck making Luke sob and grab Harl's hand.

'He knows,' Troy said. 'Earl's just another heretic to add to his list when he reports to the other Eldermen.'

The road led through the cobbled streets, past half timbered houses and shops until they reached the Elderman's chamber. The building was a large round stone structure set with stained-glass windows. Pillars lined the curved wall, propping up the overhanging roof that covered a walkway around the building. Its domed roof dominated the area and eclipsed the smaller buildings that filled the rest of the town centre.

Harl suspected that Rufus had deliberately chosen to parade Earl down the busiest road through town. Dark-haired men and women lined the street and frowned at the spectacle, whether at the lawbreaker or at Rufus's actions, Harl couldn't tell.

'Hey,' one man said, stepping out of a butcher's shop. 'What's Earl done?'

'Keep your questions to yourself, Pinkleton,' Rufus snapped.

'What about his lil ones?' a woman asked from a doorway.

'Not my concern,' Rufus said, looking back at Harl, Troy, and the boys, a smirk on his face.

'Come 'ere lads,' the woman said, scowling at Rufus. 'You're gonna be stayin' with me for a while.'

'Go on,' Harl said and then watched them run to her.

He decided he'd follow Rufus and Earl until they were swallowed into the council chambers. It was the least he could do.

As he turned away a shadow loomed over them all. Screams broke out along the street. Harl looked up and saw the god's hand reaching down. It was the size of a house, its four fingers outstretched as it descended. It smashed into a roof and tiles rained down onto the cobbles. Those nearest threw themselves into doorways and the guards scattered, leaving Earl and Rufus alone in the centre of a deserted road.

Rufus fell to the ground wailing, hands raised above his head as if to ward off the titanic limb.

The god's fingers spread above Earl and snapped shut, sealing him inside. His terrified scream filled the air. And then the hand was gone, rising towards the roof of the world as more tiles and masonry thundered down.

Harl watched it all, terrified and frozen by the horror of what he was seeing. The colossal fist swept out through a hinged opening near the back of the world and vanished

Not again, Harl thought as he fell to his knees. *Not again.*

Chapter 1

When I first discovered them, it was, ironically, in my own garden.
Of all the lands I had travelled across to find new species, the creatures
that brought me fame and fortune were under my very feet the whole time.

The only light in the dusty workshop came from the red glow of the forge. Sweating, but focused, Harl beat the metal ingot into the rough shape of an axe head. Each hammer blow rang out in the hot, enclosed space. He paused mid-strike, his toned arm raised. How many times had he watched his father working the forge? The ringing hammer was like the heartbeat of his youth. So many instructions and words of wisdom were hammered into him during those precious days, but now he worked the forge alone. He let the hammer fall and cringed at the jarring tone.

'A rushed job is a hasty job,' his father would have said. 'A man should work at the speed his skill allows, not batter the metal into submission. Patience is a skill to be cherished.'

Harl raised the ingot to eye-level. It was supposed to be an axe head, but the balance was all wrong, and there were too many impurities in the metal to provide a lasting edge. He sighed and dropped it back onto the anvil.

The jingle of the shop bell came from the other room. He rubbed a hand across his damp face. As he stepped away, he slid the cooling ingot back into the forge and then headed into the shop.

The shop itself wasn't that big. A counter ran the width of it, and tools of all kinds lined the wooden shelves, from hoes and axes to spades and spears. One of the Pewter brothers was standing by the door brushing the dust off himself after coming in from the busy street outside.

'Bren, is it?' Harl asked the young lad.

'Yes, sir.'

'Sorry,' Harl said, 'you three look so alike.'

'So what? No one's different, mister,' Bren said. His eager eyes strayed to the case of pocket knives standing on the counter. 'Even you could pass as me brother.'

'You're right, but what can we do?' Harl sighed. He flopped down on a stool and then propped his elbows on the counter and cupped his head in his hands. 'Our world is too small, Bren, and there are too few of us in it. There's never any new blood, so our children end up looking the same. But I guess that means we're pretty much family.'

Bren looked a bit confused at Harl's words, so he gave the boy a sad smile.

'Don' worry about it. You'll understand when you grow up. So what can I do for you, Bren?'

'My Pa needs a new shovel,' Bren said, glancing around the shop.

Harl pushed himself up off the stool.

'Okay. What has he given you to trade?'

'No trade,' the boy said, yanking out a loop of leather cord from his belt. Small metal discs were threaded along it, each one engraved with the rough outline of the god's stern face.

'Pa gave me twenty credits, but five are for food from the market.' He untied the knot in the cord and slipped five credits free before placing the rest on the counter in front of Harl.

'Looks like your Pa wants one of the better shovels this time around,' Harl said.

'He's digging a well. Been at it for cycles and the old one wore out.'

'Good luck to him,' Harl said, walking around the scratched counter to lift a shovel down from a rack on the plaster wall. 'Just pray he doesn't hit the bottom.'

'It's not that deep,' Bren said, rolling his eyes as he grabbed the tool.

'Tell him that if this one doesn't last at least ten giftings then I'll replace it,' Harl said.

'Will do,' Bren said as he made for the door.

Harl turned back to the workshop. He still had a dozen or so axe heads to fit for the Cutters' order, but his mind wasn't on the task. Easier to close up for the rest of the cycle and get his thoughts in order.

He stepped out onto Main Street and paused to take in the sights and sounds. Three story buildings loomed over him, their thatched roofs steaming as the rain from the dark cycle evaporated. Wooden signs overhung the wide, cobbled street, advertising dozens of merchants and craft shops. The gifting was only a cycle away and there was a buzz of excitement in the air.

A plump, dark-haired woman whistled a jaunty tune as she strolled past. She blew Harl a kiss and then laughed when he blushed. Flustered, he locked the shop door and turned away. A fletcher sat opposite, tying flights to the shafts of hunting arrows as he watched the people walk by. The barbed tips gleamed in the light.

The fletcher noticed Harl and frowned. It was only for a moment, and then he sighted along a finished arrow and turned away, but it unnerved Harl.

Why had he frowned?

Two boys dragged a goat passed and Harl found himself following them. He looked back over his shoulder, but the fletcher was just concentrating on his work. Harl ran the fingers of one hand through his hair. Was it because of what had happened to Earl? Or did the fletcher know something else?

The rush and gurgle of water broke into Harl's thoughts. The boys had led him down the street to where a bridge of weathered stone crossed the river. Two large arches held it above the fast-flowing water. Harl stopped at the edge of the bridge and stared down into the clear water. His thoughts swirled around as he watched the water flow by.

What had been the reason for the fletcher's frown? Could it have been Earl? People were ghosts on the edge of his perception as he replayed Earl's lifting in his mind. He could still hear the man's scream, could still see his arms reaching out for help between the cracks in the god's hand. It had only happened one other time in the last thirty cycles, but why did it? Why were people lifted? Why were so many taken? Earl, Anni, countless others, but it was his parents that cut deepest. Their lifting had ripped his simple world apart when he was a boy, and now Earl's death had stripped all of the time away to leave the memory of that cycle raw within him. He had felt like that same frightened boy again as the god's immense hand had reached down from above, only this time it had been Earl that had been snatched away, not his parents. But it was their harrowing screams that tore at his thoughts, like a claw raking painfully through his mind, not Earl's.

In truth he blamed himself. All he had wanted to do was play with the other kids, not help out in the workshop. But his father had said no, so he had fled in a tantrum and hidden under a market stall in the square. He remembered enjoying his parents confusion as they sought him out. It had made him laugh. But then someone had screamed, and there had been no hiding from the sight of the four-fingered hand coming down, or the giant face of the god as it peered through the Sight into the world, grabbed his parents and lifted them away. Their screams were a torture that echoed over and over in his dreams.

But why did the god take such innocents? His parents had been god-respecting people. He could not think of a reason for them to be lifted. They had contributed to the gatherings and attended the feasts. No one had ever accused them of heresy or a lack of worship. Why else would the god lift them? But there was something more, something intangible that Harl couldn't quite grasp. He gripped the cold stone bridge for support and lowered his head. There simply *had* to be a reason for the liftings.

A shout from below brought him back to the present. A pile of barrels had somehow tumbled down from the road into the water below the bridge. Two men were arguing about it on the far side, while other workmen scrambled around trying to nudge the barrels back to shore with long poles before they bumped and jostled their way down-river.

Harl turned away.

If only his memories could go with them.

The walk to Gifting Square didn't take long. Crossing the entire world, from his house on one side to the quarry on the other, took less than half a cycle, and all the time the immense black walls of the barrier dominated the horizon. It was something that Harl just couldn't understand. Why should their world end at the walls? No one knew the answer, and no hammer, axe, or chisel had ever managed to scratch them.

He shielded his eyes with a hand and squinted up at the strip of light that blazed across the roof of the world. Perhaps it was more vulnerable up there? But even if they did manage to reach it, they would probably go blind so close to the light.

No, the barrier was the end of their world during life. The priests promised more, but their words were hollow. *Only the pure of heart can live in a land without barriers. You must suffer the burdens of*

existence. Then, when your soul breaks free at the end of life, there will be no
barrier. Purity is its own reward.

Harl didn't believe a word of it.

He strolled onto the worn cobbles of Gifting Square. The town had grown around Gifting Square in a rough horseshoe, with only a flat, grazed field separating it from the Sight. The vendors and market stalls that normally crowded it had been cleared away for the upcoming gifting. Contributions for the feast lined the perimeter, while tethered sheep and goats wandered as far as their neck ropes allowed, creating a cacophony of animal noises. A team of workmen were stacking wood into an immense pile in the centre of the square ready for the bonfire. They sang and swapped jokes as they worked, while excited children scuttled around them and trailed their every move. The fire wouldn't be lit until the gifting ceremony began and its blaze invited the god to drop the precious supplies into the field.

As Harl walked around the square his eyes locked on Rufus. He had set up a small table at the side of the bonfire. It was covered with scrolls of paper and musty old ledgers, a chaotic mess that was threatening to spill off onto the floor. Dressed in his white Elderman's robes, he was a pale beacon of hate. His sunken, hawked face tracked anyone nearby with an accusing stare.

The youngest of the ten Eldermen, Rufus had been on the council for the last two giftings after inheriting the position from his father. It was rare to be given such a privileged position, but the Elders had deemed him capable of finishing his father's term after the old man passed away. Their sympathy had blinded them though. Rufus was merciless. No one was ever pious enough for

19

him and no sacrifice to the gods seemed to satisfy his rabid zealotry.

Rufus' snivelling voice drifting over the square towards Harl. He clenched his hands into fists. Rufus was berating an old lady for only giving a half-filled sack of goods for the feast. She was cowering before him to his obvious delight.

A flush of anger swept over Harl. He took a deep breath and tried to steady his feelings. He had to report to Rufus himself, but he knew that if he confronted the man now it wouldn't end well, so he paced to the far edge of the square and gazed across the wide field that opened out in front of him. This was where the god graced them with bounty while the faithful prayed in the square. It gave an unobstructed view all the way to the Sight at the edge of the world. He walked across the field to the transparent glass barrier and stared out into the void.

The god was moving around out there. It was only a shadow in the dark, too far away to make out any detail, but it was there... Waiting. Everything behind it faded into a dim blur. Instead of a world full of trees and valleys, people and places, there were just the ghosts of things. It wasn't always like that. Sometimes the light grew stronger and the ghosts became real. Once, long ago, Harl had seen a giant doorway, but it had made no sense. Why would the god need doors? The thought still made him shiver. And then there were the other gods, sometimes one, other times groups of them, drifting in and out of view or leaning down to cast critical eyes over the world. It was like looking out an epic window into a vast space that no man had ever reached, except those who had been lifted.

The god faded from view and Harl closed his eyes. His parents were out there somewhere, dead and forgotten by the revellers around him. It was the same for Earl and all of the poor souls who had been lifted. What happened to them beyond the Sight? Were they judged by the god before being turned to dust and left to float in the void? It was too much. He couldn't bare to think about all those who had been taken. Feeling sick, he backed away from the Sight and retreated to the square.

Rufus was still bellowing at the old woman. She bowed as she backed away, almost tripping over her tattered dress.

'Off with you,' he said at last, brandishing a scruffy quill, 'and bring the rest before lights out.' He looked up from his parchment lists and saw Harl. He scowled, but then a cold smile spread across his face.

'Late again, Harl Eriksson? Or perhaps you've been helping others lie about their children's whereabouts?' His smile faded and he snatched a parchment list from the table and hovered his quill over it. 'Your tribute's overdue. The One True God does not smile kindly on those who avoid their responsibilities. Or do you believe yourself above others?'

'Well, not all of us are gifted our position, Elderman.' Harl said, 'And not all of us lust after power. Some of us prefer the honesty of hard work. But I'll offer my share and gladly. Is three cows enough?'

'It'll have to do,' Rufus snapped. He threw Harl a vicious look as he scribbled a note, and then slammed the parchment down onto the table. The inkwell tipped over and ink splashed across the list. Rufus cursed and began to mop the liquid up with his sleeve. 'Get out of here, you idiot, before you damage something else.'

Harl turned away and for the first time since seeing the fletcher a grin found its way onto his face. Three cows were far more than some people contributed; it was a full quarter of his livestock. But seeing Rufus mop up ink with his precious Elderman's robe was worth the price.

As Harl wound his way through the melee of animals, he spotted Troy jogging into the square, a knobbly sack of produce balanced on one skinny shoulder. Troy winked at a pretty herbalist as he dumped the sack on the pile and then exchanged a few curt words with Rufus. Seeing Harl at the side of the square, he hurried over, yelling something rude back at Rufus as he stopped in front of Harl.

'Well,' Troy said, 'will we be getting as drunk this gifting as the last?'

'I'm in no mood for drinking, my friend. I need to get my tribute to Rufus before the light disappears. He'll have me breaking stone in the quarry if he gets his way.'

'I could arrange a diversion,' Troy said, glancing at the tethered animals. 'One quick cut and the goats will win freedom. Wouldn't look good under Screwfus's watch. Whadda you say?'

Harl shook his head. 'He'd just order them killed and I don't have the stomach for it.'

'You look fine to me,' Troy said, inspecting him from head to toe like a cattle merchant, before prodding Harl's muscular chest with one finger. 'On second thought you could do with feeding up a bit.' He shrugged and put an arm around Harl's shoulder.

'You just need time, Harl. And a drink. Definitely a drink. I've heard tell,' Troy said, leaning in to whisper, 'that the Harkens have brewed a particularly potent ale this gifting, and I wouldn't want to miss the fun when they break open a barrel or three. Have you got time for a quick one now at the Spear?'

'I can't,' Harl said, slumping against an animal stake 'I just want to get home by the fire, but even that'll have to wait. I'm duty bound to bring my cows here by lights end.'

'Don't worry, my friend,' Troy said. 'I'm sure You'll get more in the gifting to replace them. I'm hoping for crop seed myself. The farm's been running out and, although I get some back from the harvest, the bloody mice have been at them again. Still, you never know what we'll get. Perhaps the god will gift us some beautiful ladies.'

Troy rubbed his hands together, grinning, but Harl just frowned.

'Alright, alright!' Troy flung his hands up. 'Maybe dropping people into the world would be a bit weird, but it'll do you good to drown your sorrows, and I can make sure you get rid of that foul temper.'

Harl offered a reluctant smile that seemed to satisfy Troy, who swivelled around as a pretty girl strolled into the Golden Spear.

'Ho, ho! What have we here?' Troy said, making for the tavern as well. He winked back at Harl. 'Come find me afterwards for a drink. We can have a catch up before it all starts on the next cycle,'

'You should grow hops instead of corn,' Harl called after him, 'and start your own tavern, then the women might come to you instead of the other way around.'

Chapter 2

They are a fascinating species. Bipedal, with complex language and social interactions. In a bizarre way they are like micro versions of us.

Harl sat staring out into the half-light of the god's realm. He had returned home, selected the cattle for Rufus, and then wandered towards the Sight, hoping to clear his mind from the cycle's worries. Now he was sitting on a bench with the Sight five paces in front of him, its thick, clear glass the only thing barring him from the realm of the gods. It soared up to the very top of the world, a window looking out from the box of their world into the void.

He watched the darkness until he thought it would consume him, but there was nothing out there, no sign of the gods, no sign of his parents.

The gods were a mystery. They lived their lives beyond the barrier and only revealed themselves when they chose. He had even seen one sitting at a table eating once. The thought still made him shiver. It had seemed so strange that a god would have such needs, but he was sure that's what it had been doing. But it had only been a blur in the distant gloom, and he'd never seen the like again.

A thought struck him as if he had run into the barrier. Could the God have eaten his parents? He tried to dismiss it, but the image of the god's hand tossing them up into its vast, open maw would not pass. Their screams rolled over and over through his thoughts. Why hadn't it looked into their souls and seen their innocence? It must have known that they were faithful and honest. Why had it taken them?

He took a long, deep breath and tried to let the thoughts slip away. The scent of roses wafted over him. Blooms trailed up the young trees that surrounded the bench. They had crawled up the thickening trunks and coiled around the lowest branches long ago before blooming into a colourful red canopy. He looked down and traced the carvings across the wooden planks. It had taken cycles to hew the wood and plane it into shape; it had taken twice as long to carve his parents' faces into the timber. He ran his fingers over the carvings. It was hard to remember them sometimes. But here, in this place, this was where he could still come to find them. And yet looking at the calm faces grew more painful each time he came. He had planted the flowers and saplings around the bench to create a small beauty spot to get lost in, anything to just blunt the edge off the pain he kept feeling. But it didn't feel so beautiful now; it was just a constant reminder that they were dead and all he could do was watch the gods go about their incomprehensible work.

A god stepped into view on the other side of the Sight.

Harl lurched to his feet as something snapped inside. He scooped a handful of mud off the ground and hurled it onto the Sight before him, roaring as it splattered across the barrier to mar his view of the god as it lumbered past. Harl smashed his fists against the image, hammering at it until mud smeared across his arms, his face, his clothes, but still the god was there, mocking him, teasing him. He rained blows against the glass until his fists were raw and bleeding, and then screamed in fury and despair as he staggered back to the bench and collapsed, his face hidden in the muddied palms of his hands.

Shuddering, he wiped the exhausted tears from his face and then rose from the bench and walked away.

There was no one here for him; there were only gods.

Harl caught the scent of beer on the air as he navigated the narrow alleyway. Buildings rose up on either side of him, but there was no one in sight. Not even rats scuttled across the cobbles. The dark cycle had forced everyone inside well before he had arrived back in town. Walking through the empty, torch-lit streets was like being a lost soul. Was this what it felt like to be dead? He gazed at the glowing windows around him. It gave him no sense of warmth. Instead he felt cold and alone.

He walked out of the alley onto the edge of Gifting Square, which was quiet and deserted, aside from the dozing animals. Light from the Golden Spear spilled out through its windows and cast a harsh glare across the cobbles. It was a squat, two-story building, thatched and whitewashed, and had a ghostly hue in the darkness. Harl shied away from it at first. The Spear was normally a snug and friendly place, but the light from it made him shiver. Earl's lifting was just too recent.

Laughter echoed from inside. How could they all sit around laughing like that? Didn't they remember what had just happened? Earl's screams seemed to haunt the streets and dog his steps. Was he the only one who still heard them? He stalked back the way he had come. When he reached the alley, he stopped and laid his brow against the cool stone building.

Troy was waiting for him in the Spear. Troy would understand.

He sighed and tried to stop the anger coursing through him. Perhaps getting drunk was the answer? He could blot out the world and fall into oblivion for a while. So many people had lost loved ones to the liftings and yet they all seemed to move on, but the scar of losing his parents ran too deep. It marked him as different. Walking among the others made him feel like a fake. Their smiles and laughter just clawed at his wound. He shook himself. Troy was in there, and it was the thought of his friendly face that finally got Harl moving.

He stepped through the open doorway into the Golden Spear, his senses overwhelmed in comparison to the emptiness outside. The chaos of cheerful voices, sights and smells was almost enough to force him back outside. A blazing fire pit stretched away from him along the centre of the long, busy room. The air smelled of the brews on offer and the sawdust covering the floor. A beer-stained bar nestled to Harl's left, tucked into the corner where a balding barman passed trays of foam-topped mugs over to the pretty girls serving the bustling tables. Judging by the mass of people, the tavern was doing a roaring trade. Everyone chattered amiably to each other amid jeers and laughter.

Harl cast his gaze across the patrons. The crowd of dark-haired people made it difficult to pick anyone out, but he spotted Troy seated at his usual table in the centre of the room. His face was red with effort as his hand clasped the butcher's meaty fist, their eyes locked in a battle of wills as they arm-wrestled. Harl had seen it all before. He had no idea why anyone still tried their luck against Troy. His skinny frame belied the strength gained from a lifetime of hard labour on the farm. No one ever beat him. The credits he won usually paid the bar tab he racked up during the process, and the barman would sometimes encourage him by gifting a free ale or two, knowing that the entertainment would keep his customers drinking and spending. And, of course, Troy revelled in the attention it got him with the ladies. It was a win-win situation.

Harl squeezed past a group of merchants boasting of the money to be made at the festival. They stepped aside with a nod, seeing a fellow shopkeeper among them. An old greybeard at a nearby table was regaling some young drunks with the legend of the three men, his voice hoarse and serious as he held them in thrall.

'And when the three were placed in the world, they came from above, dropped inside by the hand of God,' the old man said. 'But within a cycle they were dead un's. They struggled to breathe and couldn't speak a word when the healers tried to help.'

Harl had heard the story so many times he knew it word for word, but the drunken men gasped and murmured to each other as the old man spoke, their tankards frozen halfway to their mouths..

'Aye, it's a long and worrisome tale, boys,' the old man said, looking at his empty mug, 'and it's thirsty work in the telling. How about another drink to set me right?'

Leaving them, Harl approached the packed bar and beckoned the barman for a drink.

'Good evening, young master,' the rotund man said, stacking a dozen beers on one plate and balancing it all on a pudgy hand. 'Looking forward to the gifting? I know I am. I've turned half my stock over to that blood-sucker Rufus, and it galls me, lad, galls me.'

Harl nodded. 'I know the feeling. I just left some of my herd in his joyous company. But I'm expecting that and more in return.'

'We can only hope so,' the barman said, as though speaking from experience.

'Do you doubt the fair division?'

The barman mopped his brow with a handkerchief and flicked his gaze to a group of priests in the far corner of the Spear. He lowered his voice even further and placed an open palm on his chest. 'Not so much the division, lad. I just remember a long way back when the gifting was poor. Almost put me out of business it did.' He slid a mug across the bar.

'We shall see, I suppose,' Harl said, placing a credit down and nodding farewell. He headed for the cheering crowd around Troy.

Troy had just finished arm-wrestling the butcher and, as the crowd moved away, Troy scooped up a handful of credits from the table before taking a celebratory swig of ale.

'Hello again, my friend,' Harl said. He placed his flagon on the stained wooden table and sat down. 'Can't you wait for the real drinking when the festivities start up?'

'Ha!' Troy said, 'I'm just warming up. The drink will be flowing early this gifting, what with all the entertainments setting up this dark cycle. And I hear there's to be juggling and fire breathing. Can't say how much of the fire liquid is left, though, but the gifting should provide more.'

'True,' Harl said. 'There's plenty of liquid each time, but never enough containers to satisfy everyone. Remember last gifting when Jonfry swapped his cow for three empty cans? I hear Ilsa made a set of pans from them.'

'I wondered why her soup tasted so bad,' Troy said as he counted his winnings. He looked up and grinned. 'But I sometimes think the god would prefer us to use it in a more productive way, say burning Rufus' house to the ground. But I doubt I could get away with it, and if half of what he preaches about the god protecting the faithful is true, then I wouldn't last long afterwards. Did you hear he actually asked for a sacrifice this gifting?'

'I didn't,' Harl said. 'What happened?'

'He said that if someone was willing to be lifted, it would prove our faith to the god and we'd be repaid for the sacrifice.'

'What did the other Eldermen say?' Harl asked.

Troy laughed. 'They told him to shove it. They know we lose more people to the liftings than we gain from births. How long until we're all lifted and there's no one left to appease the gods? It's insane, Harl. Crazy. Too many are taken as it is. What's to become of us? Earl was lifted for no reason, Harl. Why didn't the god see the truth and leave him be?'

'Shh,' Harl hushed. 'I understand what you're saying, but you don't know who's listening. That sort of talk will get us in trouble if it finds its way back to an Elderman, and I don't want to end up doing penance.'

'Okay, okay,' Troy said, raising his hands in surrender. 'It's just that I don't like where Rufus is taking us. I know he's inexperienced and young for the job, but what if the next Elderman elected shares his views? What happens when all ten of them start demanding a sacrifice and twenty prayer sessions each cycle?'

Harl sipped his drink. 'We must pray that they see sense before then. We're on a rocky road, Troy. The priests and Eldermen preach that the One True God is kind and benevolent, despite how it lifts people on a whim and holds the threat of starvation over our heads. Why can't they see the truth? The older I get, the more their words seem like lies. The god seems evil. I don't think we should be so eager to squander resources just before a gifting. Think what would happen if nothing was Gifted and we'd just thrown away half of our food. How long would we last?'

Troy looked at him with a dark eyebrow raised, 'You make a lot of sense. Why not stand for Elderman next time they hold elections? You'd get my vote.'

'Why? Those Eldermen are far too greedy and pious for my liking. Why would I want to join them? They sit back and do nothing while good people, like my parents, are lifted. And instead of helping the bereaved after a lifting, they pretend the lifted person was in the wrong. No, I don't want to be one of those crooked charlatans.'

The sound of a clinking glass drew their attention. Harl looked up and saw that the man at the next table had spilled his drink. He stared at them with a look of shock and outrage on his wrinkled face. His robes marked him as a man of the gods. He scrambled to his feet, knocking his chair over, and then stormed from the tavern.

'Damn!' Harl exclaimed.

Troy gave him a worried look and they both knew that there was trouble ahead.

Chapter 3

I have been observing them for some time now but I cannot place
their origin. I must attempt to communicate with them.

Although worried, Harl didn't find any guards waiting for him when he arrived home. The cottage was silent and lonely. Shadows from the dark cycle clung to the walls like unwelcome guests and the only light seeping in through the windows came from the torches in town reflecting in the Sight.

Troy's family had taken Harl in after his parents were lifted, so no one had cared for the cottage until he came of age. The passing cycles had taken a toll, leaving the place desperate for repair. Rain had rotted the exterior, while wood worm had gnawed at the roof beams until the timbers had fallen in on themselves to leave a gaping hole. It looked as though the One True God had smashed his fist down into Harl's home.

He had intended to rebuild it, but the more time he spent there, the more the crumbling walls and rotting timbers seemed to whisper of his past life. He saw ghosts everywhere, ghosts of his parents, ghosts of himself, ghosts of the man he might have been if his parents had lived. The pain was too much for him and he had no wish to haunt the place until the end of his time.

He collapsed on the porch and cradled his head in his hands. Troy had tricked him into drinking far too much again. The world was a distorted mess and his fragile mind was struggling to make sense of it, but his thoughts kept running over events at the Spear. What would the priest tell the Eldermen? Would he tell them everything? It wasn't hard to picture him running to them and relating his tale in a breathless rant hoping to curry some favour. It seemed much more likely than him staying silent.

Or would a guard pay Harl a visit in the dark cycle and silence him forever? A quick slice from a cold knife and he'd no longer trouble the Eldermen.

Something rustled in the nearby shrubs. He stood, wobbling on drunken legs as he tried to see through the darkness and then staggered down from the porch, plucked a stone from the ground and hurled it at the bushes. A chicken squawked, flapping out from the shrubbery in a panic as it fled into the darkness. He sighed and retreated to the bedroom, tripping on a loose floorboard as he stumbled into bed. He lay there panting as the room spun around him.

It was too late to take his words back now. It was in the hands of the gods. Let them judge him and be damned.

Light was already beaming down on the world when he woke on the next cycle. He clamped his eyes shut as the light lanced through him and then dragged the covers over his head, moaning against the agony of his hangover. His mouth felt like it was coated with coarse grit. Why had they continued to drink?

It was gifting day. He could hear the sounds of the feast in the distant town, the lively music and laughter ricocheting around inside his skull like a thousand discordant bells. He pressed a pillow against his head and lay there as the muffled sounds continued to assault him.

When he staggered out onto the porch some time later, he found Troy waiting for him.

Troy was leaning back in a rocking chair with his legs propped up on the handrail that ran along the edge of the porch. He waved and grinned. When he saw Harl wince at the light, he laughed and pointed to a small earthenware jug on a table next to him.

'I brought you a cure,' he said, tapping his head with one finger. 'A mug of Harkins will soon ease that delicate head of yours.'

Harl slumped onto a bench next to him and shook his head. Troy ignored him, poured some ale into the mug and shoved it across the table.

'It's good to see you,' Troy said, raising his own cup and taking a draught.

'Why so? I don't owe you credits for last nights drink do I?'

'No. Nothing like that. I was worried that you might have been arrested in the dark cycle or something.'

Harl groaned. 'You mean the priest?'

Troy nodded.

'Well as you can see, I'm fine,' Harl said.

Troy snorted on his drink and lowered the cup, laughing as he wiped froth from his nose.

Harl frowned, looking down at his mug, but then sighed and lifted it from the table and tipped it at Troy in salute. 'But why would they take me and forget a scoundrel like Troy Everett?'

'What?' Troy said. 'They wouldn't arrest me. What would all the women do if I wasn't around to entertain them?'

Harl groaned as he took a sip. 'The men might not mind you out of the way for once.'

Troy laughed and sprang to his feet.

'You're going to drag me to the gifting, aren't you?' Harl said.

'What else?' Troy said as he pulled Harl from his seat. 'Come on. We may as well go. You need something decent to eat. Besides, how long do we have before the guards drag us off to the quarry?' he added with a wink.

'That's not funny,' Harl said, peering around for any guards waiting in ambush among the bushes as they followed the path to town.

The streets around Gifting Square were packed with stalls and entertainment. Bare-chested men juggled flame sticks as they walked through the crowds and dozens of merchants hampered Harl and Troy's progress with generous offerings of ale and food.

They watched the first act of a puppet show seated beside a group of cheering children and adults. Rows of benches had been set up for the audience in the field at the edge of Gifting Square, right next to a dais for the Eldermen and priests. The Sight formed a vast backdrop.

The puppets took it in turns to hit each other with small clubs to the delight of the audience. Harl laughed along with the others, but then the confines of the puppets' world began to swallow his attention. They were penned in from all sides by walls of black cloth with cardboard trees standing against them as a fake horizon. Only the front was open. The similarity to his own world was uncanny and that he was staring in at the tiny puppets as if he was their One True God. The horror of it stripped the show of any warmth and left him rattled.

When the curtain fell, Troy dragged him away for a quick ale and he sat there stewing over his thoughts while Troy looked on, baffled at his mood swing. When their stomachs began to rumble they returned to the square and feasted on the sumptuous food being gifted around them. Every type of produce was on offer, from fresh-baked loaves with mounds of butter to succulent roast meats fresh off the bone. Everyone in the land was attending but Harl had no desire to be a part of it.

He tasted the food and sipped at the wine, watching as children darted in and out between people's legs, laughing and playing. None of it touched him, though. It was all so empty, so pointless. They were all just running around with blinkers on. He looked over his shoulder to where the vast wall of the Sight stood as an open window into the realm of the gods. No one seemed to see what he did. No one realised that they were all just waiting to be lifted.

He watched a mass prayer in silence. Robed priests called upon the gods' blessing for those kneeling before them. Their piety baffled him. He understood the reverence – he had believed in the faith all of his life – but he could not understand how blind they seemed to be to the horror around them. They accepted it all, the liftings, the deaths, the risk of starvation if the gifting was poor; it was all a part of their faith and they just bowed their heads and whispered their thanks. But their soft prayers still tugged at his heart. Some part of him clung to those beliefs despite all the pain he'd endured and the doubts that were running through his mind. He was torn and he was no weaver to stitch himself back together.

A priest dismissed the congregation and then strode up the steps to where a gong sat atop the Eldermen's wooden dais. A table laden with the finest food and drinks was ringed on one side by ten gilded chairs that faced the crowd. This was for the Eldermen who would preside over the ceremony. Next to it, a smaller table had been prepared for the five highest-ranking priests. It looked spartan by comparison. There was no gilding or luxury food, just plain wood for the build and bread and water for the priests.

The priest raised a hammer and struck the gong. A hush descended and the crowd parted to allow a line of priests to march through. They climbed up onto the dais, barely glancing at the crowd as they shuffled across the platform, but, as was customary, they cast an eye over the Elderman's table, straightening the cutlery and smoothing the tablecloth, before forming into a row at the end of the table and then turning to face the steps, heads bowed as the ten Eldermen climbed onto the platform, giving small waves and nods to the assembly below.

The Eldermen and priests took a moment to speak privately, some shaking hands or exchanging small gifts as the priests went forward and bowed to each Elderman in turn. When they'd finished, the Eldermen filed into place and then took their seats.

The priests waited a respectful moment and then took their own places at the smaller table.

Rufus smoothed his robes down and stared out over the crowd with a sneer on his lips.

The High Elderman, Arlet, nodded his assent to the waiting priest and the man struck the gong a second time. The Eldermen stood up as one. In the centre, Arlet took a long swig from a delicate gold stein, wiped the foam from his grey beard, and then shuffled around the long table, resting a pale, bony hand on each Elderman's shoulder as he passed, his crooked staff clunking on the wooden boards with each step. He stopped in front of the table and turned to face the crowd.

'People!' he cried. His voice carried clearly to all present, as if the ale had magical properties.

Harl and Troy edged to the front and watched as Rufus shouldered his way closer to Arlet, nudging the older men aside until he was standing next to the High Elderman. He puffed up proudly and glanced at Harl, a trace of his usual sneer slipping through his attempt at serenity.

'It is with great honour on this fiftieth cycle since the last, that we celebrate another gifting,' Arlet continued. 'The One True God has always provided for us and this cycle will be no different.'

Turning around to face the Sight, he raised his hands and stared off into the distance.

'We, the people, thank the Lord on this cycle, as on each cycle of our lives, for he created this world to provide for us. The corn, the livestock, the trees, and the rain; each of these he has placed within the barriers so that we may thrive.'

He turned back to the crowd and proclaimed, as though the words came direct from the One True God, 'I have created this world, but only the faithful will survive, only the faithful will receive my blessing. I shall look into your hearts and your souls, and I will see the truth of your faith. I will reward the righteous. I will punish the non-believers. But I am a kind and benevolent being, so I will give wayward souls the chance for redemption.'

Arlet extended his arms upwards and yelled out into the crowd, 'Praise be to the Sight and the gods that live beyond!'

His mantra was taken up by all present, young and old alike. 'PRAISE BE TO THE SIGHT AND THE GODS THAT LIVE BEYOND!'

With that the Eldermen turned and, as if on cue, the god approached the Sight. The crowd bowed their heads in reverence, placing an open palm to chest as the god bent down close to the barrier and peered inside, his critical eyes sunk within the taut grey skin of his face. Greed and appraisal glowed in his bright yellow pupils. His gaze ran over everything in the world, but then he straightened up and his head disappeared above the roof of the world to leave only his gigantic midriff visible. A mesh of blue metal bands covered his torso like a wall of woven steel.

The roof of the world opened and the god's hand drifted inside clutching an enormous fistful of supplies.

'BEHOLD THE HAND OF PROVIDENCE!' Arlet proclaimed.

With a resounding crash that echoed through the world, the god dropped the supplies on the bare soil in the field. Guards rushed forward to surround the pile as the god's hand withdrew.

'Praise to the One True God!' someone yelled.

The murmur of excitement exploded into cheers as the crowd surged forward for a better look. The guards forced them back to a respectful distance and then retreated to form a defensive ring around the gift so that no one could pilfer items before the division.

There were metal containers of fire liquid on one side, while timber and tree trunks formed the bulk of the mass; there were even giant fruits ripe for the picking. Harl noted the lowing of cattle coming from behind the pile and knew that his herd would be up to full size, and possibly more, by the end of the division. The excitement of the gifting swept through him as he watched chickens, pigs, and sheep make a break for freedom across the field. The crowd howled with laughter and then cheered as the guards abandoned their posts to chase the animals down. Bulging sacks full of hidden treasures tumbled to the ground as the whole pile settled into place.

'It's a good one,' Troy yelled as he shouldered his way between two people for a better look. 'Bound to be some seeds in there somewhere!'

'I don't doubt it, friend,' Harl shouted back, 'but it's time for another drink'

'This way,' Troy said. 'I know where to find the best brew and the friendliest ladies. '

'You always do,' Harl said, shaking his head in amusement as he followed along behind.

Chapter 4

Where did they come from? I've seen no common ancestors for the species and only their bipedal stature links them to us. There are at least twenty four other species that walk on two legs and none of them bear any genetic resemblance to these.

Harl woke on the next cycle with no idea how he had got home. His head felt like he'd used an anvil for a pillow while someone went to work on it with a hammer. They had ended up inside the Spear for the usual drinking competition and he must have won. He plunged his head into a bucket of cold water and swore as clarity replaced the pain.

He ate a quick meal of cheese and cold beef before heading into town to claim the list stating his share of the Gift. Everyone was accounted for, including the children, whose portion would be held in trust until they came of age. When he reached Gifting Square he was surprised to find Rufus absent. Harl stood on tiptoe and craned over the black-haired heads around him, sure that he would be there somewhere lording it over everyone as he handed out the lists, but there was no sign of him. Instead, it was

Elderman Vines who faced the long queue of hungover, but cheery, people.

His robe was simple and unadorned, and his wrinkled face held a constant smile beneath the cropped white beard as he dealt with each person in turn. He had been the only Elderman who had comforted Harl after his parents' lifting, and Harl felt a connection with the cheery old man, who was always quick to lend a hand or share discomfort.

Looking about for Troy, Harl joined the end of the queue. The gift had been sorted during the dark cycle and laid out ready for delivery. Lumber and cans of fire liquid were set in vast rows across the grass, and a train of carts was waiting to be loaded. The animals had been herded to a fenced off area where they would be fed and watered until collection. Priests scrawled lists as they counted and checked the goods, and then compared them to the division lists that the council had organised through the dark cycle.

As the queue shuffled forward, Harl passed the lumber division. It was laid out in neat, head-high piles to create a series of narrow rows. He watched old lady Varnen fiddling with her shawl as she hobbled among the stockpile of wood, while Tamish, the tanner's son, strolled along the opposite edge of the heaps. Tamish pretended to retie his leather apron, glancing left and right, then took several strides into the rows. Harl had a clear view as old lady Varnen came face-to-face with the young man.

'Two carts of lumber,' she said, waving a parchment list. 'I'm far too old to make use of it.'

46

Tamish nodded and glanced over his shoulder. Harl looked away before Tamish turned back to the old lady.

'Would chickens make a better meal than lumber?' Tamish asked, checking his own list. He froze as two guards ambled past on the next row along, too engrossed in their own lists to notice the odd couple. When they had moved beyond hearing, old lady Varnen and Tamish resumed haggling, working out the ratio of chicken to lumber before holding open palms across their hearts, sealing the deal.

'What would you two be doing?' a smooth voice said, startling Harl and making the two conspirators jump and spin around.

Joedal, the guard captain, had been lurking behind a stack of huge tree trunks and strolled up to the dealers. His bright red cloak waved in the gentle breeze as he awaited an answer. A barrel of a man, tall and imposing with a stubby slick back pony tail, he was a close friend to Rufus and although Harl had never spoken to him, he'd heard of the man's crooked ways.

'S-she doesn't need the lumber,' Tamish said. 'What's an old lady going to do with it?'

'Not for you to decide,' Joedal said, prodding Tamish's grubby leather apron with his index finger. 'Dividing's complete, unless you think a mistake has been made.' The captain shrugged as if helpless to do anything.

'Surely you could do something,' the old lady said, feigning equal helplessness.

A gleam entered the captain's eye and he perked up as she proffered a bulging sackcloth pouch.

'I suppose young Tamish's house is closer,' Joedal said, plucking the bag from her bony hand. It disappeared into a larger holdall concealed under his striking red cloak. 'I'm sure the paperwork can be adjusted to fix this... error. Wouldn't want to see you in the quarries because of a mistake in the paperwork now, would we?' He let the sentence hang and held an open palm in front of Tamish, who scowled and then slipped a loop of credits into the waiting hand.

Joedal smiled and jingled the credits in his fist. 'I thought there'd been a mistake,' he said, 'but nothing I can't get sorted.' He whistled a jaunty tune as he sauntered out from the timber stacks, heading for another couple arguing the value of a case of fire liquid.

The queue shuffled forward and Harl strained to catch a glimpse of Troy through the crowd, but by the time he had reached Vines, there was still no sign of his friend. It was strange, because Troy was usually one of the first at the division. Perhaps his hangover still had him languishing in bed?

'Harl, my boy,' Vines said, grinning beneath the white hair framing his cheeks. 'Survived the post-gifting drinks then? Got your list here.' He ticked Harl's name off on a long sheet of parchment before handing him a rolled up scroll from a stack on the table beside him. 'It was a hefty gift.' He hunched forward and leaned in towards Harl as he lowered his voice. 'I had a quiet word with one of the dividers to get you a little something extra.'

'As always, Vines, you're too kind. I owe you my thanks and if you need anything...' He let the question hang in case Vines wanted something for the favour, but the Elderman shrugged and shook his head

'No need my boy,' he said giving him a wink. 'Just be careful.'

Harl read the list, then smiled back at Vines as he rolled it up and slid it into his pack. He had never received such a haul. There was a good portion of food and liquid fire, but, most importantly, he would take home five cows from the gifted herd. There was the usual lumber ration, some seeds, and even a hen. The final part of the list noted any special items. These rare luxuries were seldom part of the god's bounty, but he had received a few this time around, including a pelt from an unknown animal, a thirty-stride length of rope, and a bow and arrows.

Grinning, he nodded farewell to Vines and walked away as another man jumped the line and began arguing with the Elderman about the unfairness of his list. Two guards stepped forward and seized the man. His face grew pale.

'I didn't mean it!' he pleaded, but the guards took no notice and knocked him to the ground.

'What's going on?' Joedal roared as he strode out from behind a train of carts laden with sacks and crates.

'Nothing, nothing,' Vines said. He shuffled forward to stand between Joedal and the cowering man. 'Just the usual disagreements, that's all. We'll soon have it sorted out.'

Joedal glared at the Elderman.

'Complaining, was he? Can't have that. Haul him away boys.'

The guards dragged the man to his feet and marched him away across the square. Joedal returned to his inspection of the carts, grinning at Vines in triumph. The old man shook his head and turned back to the next in line.

Unnerved by what he'd just seen, Harl took a deep breath and headed towards the captain. Joedal turned and eyed Harl suspiciously.

'You'll have to wait like everyone else,' he snapped before Harl could speak. 'All personal deliveries are next cycle. We haven't got the manpower for you to take it now.'

'I didn't want to take it all,' Harl said. 'I just wanted to collect one of my specials, if I can.'

The captain smiled, taking in the cut of his clothes. 'What is it you're requesting?'

Harl showed him the list.

Joedal nodded. 'Very nice. I suppose it might be possible. But I'll have to divert a guard from duty to find it. He'll need paying for overtime.'

Harl should have expected this.

'I forgot...'

The captain raised an eyebrow as if Harl was wasting his time but then frowned. 'You're the tooler?'

'Yes.'

'Hmm...' Joedal said, running his hand over an ornate vase in one of the carts. 'My spear snapped after last gifting...' His eyes twitched to Harl and then back to the vase. A sly smile crept onto his face. 'The head is a family heirloom and would match my new shield nicely when the weapons master gets around to delivering it. If only it hadn't snapped...'

Harl sighed.

'Bring it over to the shop,' he said, glad it was only the handle, 'and I'll have it done in a few cycles.'

Joedal grinned. 'Wait somewhere out of the way and I'll have one of my men bring it to you, but don't go flashing it around or we'll have chaos.'

'Thanks.'

Harl moved over to a large pile of lumber and watched as the first of the carts trundled off to farms in the surrounding countryside. A guard came up to him holding the new bow and quiver of arrows. The bow was made from a silvery, light-weight alloy, while the quiver was a sleek, meshed fabric that looked as though it would take a battering and remain unscathed. Ten arrows bristled from the end of it. They were the same smooth metal as the bow.

Troy's father had been gifted a similar bow when Harl was a boy. The two boys had often borrowed it for adventures in the woods, usually once Troy's father had sunk a few ales. They had become good shots and had been immensely proud after downing a wild pig that had charged at them one cycle. They sold the carcass and took a whole cask of ale back to Troy's father. Unfortunately, he'd been forced to sell the bow after a poor harvest and it had ended up in the hands of a greedy Elderman.

Frowning at the memory, Harl checked the Spear for any sign of Troy and then jumped on a wagon heading out of town. As one of the farthest farms out, Troy's backed on to the woodlands towards no sight, and although the journey was pleasant, Troy was nowhere to be found when Harl arrived. The water buckets lay unfilled beside the well and the sheep in the nearest paddock bleated at an empty trough.

Harl had had enough. If Troy wanted to drink himself into a stupor somewhere, then he'd leave him to it. He tossed half a bale of hay into the pen and headed home.

Harl stared Sightwards at the imposing glass barrier. Reflections of the town and farmlands formed a ghost image across its surface. He leaned against the door frame of his home and sipped at a bowl of meaty stew. The image seemed to float in the void beyond the Sight as if a twin of his world had materialised out there. But if he focused on the Sight – if he ignored the image as just another mirage – then he could see out into the god's realm. It was strange to look through his world, through the fabric of his reality. There should be some hidden meaning to it all, but whatever truths it was whispering were too faint to hear. He sighed and took another sip of the stew.

The land dipped away before him down a shallow incline that led to his bench and manicured garden close to the Sight. It pulled at him like a fishing lure, drawing him there even though he knew the danger of staring out through the glass and incurring the god's wrath. It felt safer at this distance. He could stare out into the void and remain hidden, but the Sight still fascinated him. He longed to be out there, to spin around and see forever. He glanced at the pitch black barrier fifty paces to the right of his home. He didn't want to be blocked by walls and corners, or constrained by the rule of Eldermen.

But the deeper truth was the hope of seeing his parents again. Each time he faced the Sight his childhood memories played before him as if they were reflections dancing on the glass. His mother's warm embrace, his father's twinkling eyes, all the cycles and emotions, all the hope and love, but when the tears from his memories cleared there was only the darkness of the void.

He wiped a sleeve across his eyes and strolled down the incline to the bench, running his free hand along the wood as he fought against the urge to look out through the Sight again. But it pulled at him more strongly than anything he could remember. He didn't care if it made him seem odd to others. He just needed to be there. He just needed to see them.

He sank down onto the seat. The turmoil in his stomach from the previous cycle's drinking only added to the pain. He raised his eyes, hoping, dreading, but there was no sign of his parents.

The One True God laboured in the distance, stomping around on his oversized legs as he trudged first one way, then the other. Each time he passed the Sight he seemed to be carrying huge boxes, but it made no sense to Harl.

A lesser god sprang into view right in front of Harl. The bowl went flying from Harl's grasp, burning his hand as he fell off the back of the bench. He rolled to his feet and turned back to face the god. The god towered above Harl and he found himself facing the god's vast midriff. His clothing was subtly different to the woven metal worn by the One True God. It was sleeker and made from overlapping metal plates, similar to the armour worn by the town guards. Harl looked up to where the god's face lurked at the very top of the Sight. Pale bluish-grey skin pockmarked with age spots clung to the god's high cheekbones, and craggy jowls sagged under his chin, as though he was older than the One True God. But how could he be? The One True God was the creator of all things, surely it was impossible for one of the lesser gods to be older?

Harl watched the god scan the world. He looked unimpressed, as though he had seen it all before. The head tilted down to study a book resting in his weathered grey hands and then raised the house-sized object to gaze at the pages before shifting his vast bulk to peer above the world. He then leaned over to inspect the outside of the world, before returning to study Harl.

The yellow pupils bore into him, as if the god knew the fate of his parents and of all those who had been lifted. Harl had spent so many cycles staring out of the world, but he had never come face to face with a god. Fear paralysed him. He wanted to run and hide, he wanted to burrow into the soil and block the face away but all he could do was cower before it and pray that the god's hand did not reach inside to crush him.

The god slammed the book shut, making Harl jump, and then lowered it to his side before stretching up as though inspecting the light at the roof of the world. Harl's view beyond the Sight became blocked by the god's midriff. The shiny clothing rippled and, as if by magic, a startling vision appeared.

Directly in front of him, on the body of the god, was a woman. Her face was framed by long, golden hair and she had startling sapphire eyes. They held a look of wonder, which Harl was sure mirrored his own. Although her figure was distorted by the curve of the god's metallic clothing, she was still clear enough to make out some details. She wore only a pure white dress and her slender body took Harl's breath away. He had never seen anyone like her.

He stepped forward and reached out to touch her, but only the cold barrier of the Sight met his fingers. He rested his palm flat against its smooth surface as his mind blanked out everything except the woman. She took a step forward. Startled, he stepped back and tripped on the uneven ground. She laughed and raised a hand to cover her mouth as he fell to the ground. When he looked back at her, her image had grown distorted. He scrambled to his feet and she became more distinct.

Was he imagining her? Surely not. Yet, unless he was still drunk from the cycle before, he could think of no other reason for this apparition.

He almost cried out loud when the god lifted the book and blocked her from view. The god turned and strode away, leaving nothing in front of Harl but the emptiness of the gods' realm. He stared at the god's plated back and cursed the cruelty of letting him see such beauty only to steal it away. All he was left with was his own pitiful reflection gazing back.

Was she some kind of dream granted by the god? He shook his head and almost laughed at the prospect. She was a beauty beyond imagining, but she was no dream. She was real. He looked into the mirror of his own eyes and stepped forward. Her image had to be a reflection. But from where? He tried to judge the angle of the reflection so that he could trace where she had been standing. The conclusion was as simple as it was absurd.

She had been standing on the other side of the black barrier to the right of his home.

A twig cracked behind him. He spun to find Rufus sneering at him from a few steps away. Joedal and several well-armed guards fanned out around him. Rufus took a step forward.

'I have you now, Eriksson. Do you think you can curse the gods without punishment? Are you really that stupid?' Rage simmered in his eyes. He moved aside and waved the guards forward. 'Arrest him.'

Harl's mind went blank as the guards shackled him and dragged him away. He turned back to the Sight in a daze, but the only reflection there now was Rufus.

Chapter 5

On further reflection, I believe the species to be from another planet;
although how they came to be here is beyond my understanding. I am
unable to comprehend their language.

Harl woke to find himself huddled against the damp prison
wall. He groaned and rolled to a sitting position on the thin
straw mattress. The cell was in the basement of the Eldermen's
meeting hall. It was only a temporary holding area, just a squalid
hole where the prisoners could be hidden away until their trial,
but it was enough. He hated the place already.

Six stone-walled cells lined the outside of the squalid room,
with only a grill of iron bars caging the prisoners inside.

Harl looked around the cell. There was hardly anything worth
mentioning: an empty food bowl, slop bucket, and the flea-ridden
straw pile on the inside, while a water bucket rested to the side of
the door on the outside. All the other cells were the same.

A single oak door led from the prison to where a set of
crooked stone stairs climbed up to the meeting hall. There was no
fresh air in the place, no vent to the outside world or any window

to show whether it was light or dark. The only light came from a flickering lantern that hung from the damp ceiling.

Two roaches crawled across Harl's leg. He shook them off and scrambled back against the wall. There was little point, really, because the place was crawling with insects, but he just couldn't get used to the feel of them.

Harl's cell was directly opposite Troy's. He still couldn't believe that they had both been arrested. Troy was already in a cell when the guards had dragged Harl in and he'd spent the whole time since then ranting about the injustice of it.

But regardless of the dread that filled him, Harl's thought's were still with the woman he had seen. He hadn't told Troy, although he didn't really know why. Something about the place made it impossible. She was like a beacon in the darkness and he was afraid that if he told anyone about her, it might snuff out that last vestige of light. He just wanted to lie there, close his eyes, and let his dreams take him to her.

'That bloody priest,' Troy yelled. He kicked his food bowl against the cell bars as he stalked from wall to wall. 'He must have run straight to Rufus in the hope of gaining some favour or other. They got me right after the gifting and I was in no shape to stop them. Broke my door down just because I couldn't hear the banging. Poor Lisa was only in her skin when they came in the room.' He punched the wall and turned. 'I bet that pleased Rufus: probably the only unclothed female he's seen in his miserably pious life.'

'Probably,' Harl said.

'What's with you?' Troy asked. 'You've barely spoken since they threw you in here with me'.

'You mean other than being stuck in a cell with your constant whining while waiting to be tried for speaking the truth?' Harl said. 'Nothing, Troy, nothing at all.'

Footsteps echoed on the other side of the door before it creaked open. One of the Pewter brothers came in balancing a grubby tray on one hand with two bowls on top, while the other gripped a bright torch that sent the roaches scurrying. Thick black smoke from the torch coiled back through the open door and up the stairs.

'What's the word, Kyle?' Troy asked the lad before he had a chance to say anything.

'Erm,' the boy mumbled, placing the tray down on the crooked flagstones.

'Well?' Troy encouraged.

'It's not good,' Kyle said, swallowing hard. 'I heard Rufus talking about how the priest's words will guarantee a guilty verdict.'

'Guilty of what exactly?' Harl asked.

'Treason, mister,' Kyle said, passing the bowls through the rusted bars to each of them before stepping back.

He made his way out through the heavy door and heaved it closed behind him.

'Bloody priests! Troy roared, resuming his pacing.

Harl groaned and slumped back against the wall, forcing himself to ignore his friend's curses. He would soon find out what was to become of them and he knew that if Rufus had any say in the matter, then both he and Troy would be in for a hard time.

'We could make a break for it,' Troy said. 'We could persuade the boy.' He looked meaningfully at the door and cracked his knuckles. 'He could bring us the keys and claim we made him do it.'

'Leave the boy be,' Harl said. 'Where would we go? There's no real escape. Once we made it outside they would find us in no time. The world's too small for us to run forever. We'd get to the barrier and then what? Turn and go back again or hide for the rest of our lives, moving from place to place up in the woods? No, there's nowhere to go. Our only choice is to accept whatever fate they give us.'

'Then it's the quarries,' Troy said. 'Dusty, hard labour for however long they think necessary and, once we're half-starved and our lungs are full of stone powder, they might let us come home. No drink, no rest, and certainly no women.'

The last part was obviously the hardest bit for Troy, but for Harl it was the knowledge that even if they finished their sentence, they would have to live with the shame and go about their meaningless lives again. Appeasing gods, respecting Eldermen, and living in what Harl now considered a prison in itself was all he could expect.

The world was too small for him. He had realised it as soon as he'd seen the woman. The barriers and the Sight were creeping in towards him. There had to be more to life than scraping a living and facing the constant injustice. How many more people had to be lifted?

He was going to make a change. He wasn't sure how he was going to do it, but he promised himself that he would and the gods be damned.

Steps sounded again on the far side of the door, then stopped. The hinges creaked as the door eased open a fraction.

'Kyle?' Harl said, hoping the boy had come back to help them.

Laughter broke from the gap as it widened and Rufus stepped into the room.

'Looking forward to the quarry, vermin?' he said, 'It was only a matter of time before you got what you deserved, and when I give my evidence maybe they'll see that their eyes aren't as sharp as mine.'

'They'll know you're mad,' Troy said.

Rufus looked from Harl to Troy and back again as he smiled and said nothing, as if he knew more than he was telling.

Troy roared and threw himself at the bars, startling Rufus, and forcing him to step back against the bars of Harl's cell. Harl jumped forwards and thrust his arms through the bars to wrap them around Rufus. One hand grabbed his mouth to cut off the shout for help and the other held him against the rusted bars.

'If we're going to get what we're due,' Harl hissed in his ear, 'then the god will pluck you out and toss you into the void.' He let go and shoved Rufus away.

Rufus scrambled for the door and fled up the stairs.

'Well that was fun,' Troy chuckled.

Harl wasn't so sure. It might have been better if he'd just snapped Rufus' neck.

Once the third cycle had dawned, they were both led up into the council's meeting hall. Entering the high-domed chamber from a back entrance, they were marched to the centre and ordered to wait.

The layout was simple. The chamber was round, like the building, with a gallery level surrounding the council floor. A long, curved table stood a little off centre. This was where the Eldermen sat in judgement and debated the day-to-day business of the world and its people. The table was raised on a dais so that anyone standing before the Eldermen had to crane their neck to look up. It emphasised the power that the men and women held over the people. Other seating spread away to the side for townsfolk, but it was considered a high honour to be seated on the council floor during proceedings, so it was usually only the lackies and favourites who sat there. Everyone else made do with the gallery above.

Harl had been here many times before, but this was the first time he had been on the actual council floor, every other time he had been a spectator peering down from the gallery above. The parquet floor was more intricate than he had imagined. From above it was just a slow spiral of tiles sweeping out from the centre, but down on the floor, down where the judgements were passed and laws were written, the detail was staggering. Each individual tile had different gifting day words etched into them. *I have created this world. Only the faithful will survive. Only the faithful will receive my blessing. I will see the truth of your faith. I will reward the righteous. I will punish the non-believers.*

'Bloody thieves,' Troy muttered as he faced front, drawing Harl's attention away from the writing.

The Eldermen had filed in from a door on the opposite side of the chamber. They stayed silent and solemn, only the swish of their robes and occasional squeak of a shoe broke the heavy silence.

But Troy hadn't been referring to the Eldermen. On the plaster wall behind where the ten Eldermen took their seats were dozens of weapons, including the bow once owned by Troy's father. Even from this distance the old scrape down one side was visible from when they had levered a rock off Troy's broken leg. Anger flared in Harl at the greed of the Eldermen. The weapon had once been used to place food on family's table. Now it was merely a trophy to convey power for those who already had too much.

Harl eyed its new owners.

The ten Eldermen sat glaring down on them from behind polished desks and stacks of papers. A few townspeople were seated to either side of them, curving around towards the main entrance behind. Their murmurings stopped as High Elderman Arlet spoke.

'Harl Eriksson and Troy Everett,' he said, his voice carrying across the packed room. 'You are charged with heresy against the gods and conspiracy to commit dissension among the populous. We will bring forth two witnesses who will present the reasons for these charges. The first will give evidence against you both, while the second will bring your character flaws to the knowledge of those present.'

Arlet sat and beckoned for an aged priest to come forward, the same man who had fled from the tavern.

Harl waited next to Troy as the robed figure took the stand to one side of the Eldermen's desks. The priest coughed to clear his throat before staring passed them and speaking to the crowd.

'I, Eman Milleton, priest of the temple, have come here to relate all that Troy Everett and Harl Eriksson spoke of in the Golden Spear tavern two cycles ago. As a priest of the temple, I can speak only truth and honesty before the One True God.' He placed an open palm on his chest before explaining how Harl and Troy had claimed that the gods were false and that the Eldermen should be overthrown.

'That's not true,' Harl called, stepping forward.

'Silence,' Arlet said, slamming a hand down on his desk. Some of the papers dislodged on the desk in front of him and slid to the floor.

A flash of red in Harl's peripheral vision made him spin round as Joedal stepped from the line of guards behind them and slammed a wooden baton into Harl's side, knocking the wind from him.

Vines jumped up from his seat, scowling down at Joedal.

'I must protest,' he said, looking around at Arlet. 'Guilty until proven otherwise. We need not hurt these men.'

Arlet nodded and jerked his head at Joedal who tucked the baton under his cloak and took a hurried pace backwards.

The priest had finished, so Rufus stepped up to the stand.

'Typical,' Troy muttered under his breath. 'I just knew he'd be a part of this. I'd like to take the captain's baton and shove it-'

Harl dug his elbow into Troy's ribs, silencing him.

Rufus took his place on the stand and smoothed his robe, casting an angry glare in their direction before a sly smile took its place.

'Both these men are well known in the community,' Rufus said, 'not for good deeds, but for their blatant disregard of the gods. Neither attend the tenth cycle mass prayer and their debauchery in the taverns is common knowledge.' Rufus looked at Troy shaking his head as though pitying their godless ways. 'It is my opinion that these two men would continue in their attempt to corrupt the good folk, and that their talk of overthrowing the Eldermen could be construed as more than just the foolish words of drunken men. If they were more dedicated to the gods and less to the ways of tavern women and drink, then they might see salvation. But, as of this moment, I believe they pose a threat to the peaceful nature of our world. I recommend that they both be held accountable for their words, if not their actions.' With that he bowed to the other Eldermen and stepped down.

Arlet stood again.

'You may speak in your defence, but only one of you can act as advocate,' he said.

Harl looked at Troy, but his friend just shrugged and waved Harl forward. Arlet nodded his permission and sat down.

'I have worked hard in my life,' Harl said, his eyes looking over each Elderman in turn. ' I contribute to the peoples' charity to help those in need and Troy raises crops that help us all to

65

survive, as his father did before him.' He couldn't help but look at the bow hung behind the stern faces, wondering how much the Eldermen contributed. 'Since I came of age, I have never relied on anyone for help, and the same can be said of Troy Everett.'

He took a breath and watched the faces of the Eldermen. There was disinterest in most, but Rufus was leaning forward with his hands clenched beneath his chin. Harl closed his eyes and took a moment to steady himself before he continued.

'Since my parents were lifted, I have held in my heart a place of anger towards that which took them.'

Rufus and the priest leapt from their seats and started to protest, but Arlet waved at them to sit down again.

'We will hear him out,' the High Elderman warned the assembly. 'But be careful of your words, Harl Eriksson. This is a place of judgement. Your words carry a weight that you should well consider.'

Harl clenched his jaw and nodded. He took another deep breath.

'My parents are dead. They were taken from me just as surely as if they were killed. If any man or woman in this assembly had been responsible, then it would be deemed a crime.'

One or two of the Eldermen nodded at his words.

'As for Troy,' Harl added, 'he has not had the misfortune of having someone he loved lifted-'

'Misfortune?' a priest cried. 'It is a blessing!'

Other priests pounded the wooden floor with their feet until the deafening drum-roll filled the hall.

'But it was not the hand of man that committed this crime,' Harl shouted. 'It was the hand of God.'

The council room exploded as most of the Eldermen and all of the priests began shouting. Arlet raised his hand and the assembly stilled. His eyes had narrowed as he watched Harl, but he waved at him to continue.

'I stand accused of questioning the gods and I admit it. I do question them. I question why a god can take my family. I question the right of that hand to come down and snatch whoever it wants from our land. If any person here was responsible for my parents' deaths, then they would be convicted of the crime. But the One True God stands above the law. I am even expected to worship him when he has caused so much pain, not just to myself, but to so many of the faces before me. So I question. I question it all, from our blind faith in the almighty to the rule of the men before me. I question as is my right, as is the right of us all.'

He fell silent, looked at the astonished faces before him, and then stepped back next to Troy.

Harl kept his eyes on Arlet as the hall erupted with angry shouts again. The old man had his hands cupped on the top of his desk and was resting his chin on them. Harl couldn't tell what he was thinking, but the deafening roar throughout the hall left little doubt what the judgement would be.

Harl had hoped that some in the hall would have agreed with him. Far too many of them had lost loved ones to liftings. But the overwhelming reaction was fury. Only a handful of people sat contemplating his words and their silence drained whatever foolish glimmer of hope he might have had.

Arlet smiled, sadly, and then struck the floor with his walking stick until the chamber drew still.

'We will now judge,' he said. 'It is the duty of this council to weigh the evidence before us and make a decision. Let no man doubt that justice. Let no man speak against it.'

With that, the Eldermen began their deliberations.

Harl knew that even if his words had failed to sway them, the most likely outcome would be hard labour in the quarry. The Eldermen could not hang them for such an offence; the population was thinning as it was, and both he and Troy contributed through their work. But the wait while the men spoke was agonising

'Harl Eriksson and Troy Everett,' Arlet said at last, staring down at them as the other Eldermen retook their seats. 'You are judged guilty. You have shown no remorse for your crimes and have dared to question the nature of our law. But you have compounded your crimes by questioning – in this very chamber – the grace of the One True God. For these crimes you are sentenced to hard labour in the quarry.'

|Arlet sighed and shook his head.

I see before me two young men whose potential has been squandered. I have watched you grow and I've witnessed the tragedies you've had to overcome, and yet I was pleased to watch men of strong will grow before me, men I would be proud to call friends, men who I deemed worthy of taking on the role of leaders one day. But a seed of evil has taken root in your souls, a seed that only the One True God can shield us from. For this reason the sentence must be harsh. We will not stand by and see the seed of that corruption grow. It is the right and the duty of this council to act.

'You will be taken from the judgement of this council to your place of incarceration, where you will remain for five hundred cycles And may the gods grant you forgiveness.'

Rufus grinned down at them as Joedal stepped forward to grab Harl's arm while two other guards grappled with Troy.

Five hundred cycles?

Harl closed his eyes in defeat. It would be the end of them.

Chapter 6

They have an array of micro technology around their nest such as vehicles and basic communications equipment. The vehicles are used to produce agricultural land and harvest strange crops.

Harl sat on top of a massive boulder picking at the last of his meagre mid-cycle meal. The food wasn't much, but he didn't expect it to be. He was a prisoner and that meant hardship. He upended the waterskin and poured its contents over his head, scrubbing his face with both hands to try and dislodge some of the ever-present dust and dirt.

The quarry's sheer cliffs climbed up around him like a set of stairs built for the gods. Three tiers in all, they were a warren of tunnels and worn out seams that had been abandoned long ago. Now the focus was a giant boulder in the centre. The titanic rock was surrounded by a tangle of scaffolding and rickety ladders, like an egg in a nest. Crawl holes pocked its surface and wormed their way inside, as if the starving prisoners that toiled around it had eaten their way deep into the ancient rock as they searched for ore.

When they had first arrived, Troy had looked at the boulder in disgust and then dipped a damp finger into a mound of rejected slag and tasted it. 'Huh. Doesn't taste like cheese.'

Five cycles in and Harl still hadn't got over the shock of his arrest. So many questions buzzed around in his mind that he struggled to swing his pick during the cycle. Why had they been arrested? Why hadn't the Eldermen seen reason? All he and Troy had been guilty of was talk. Was speaking your mind punishable now? He shook his head. He already had an answer.

The whistle blew and the guards waved them all back to work. Harl checked his gear. There was a short length of rope, a candle, flint and tinder, a small hand spade, and a waterskin. It wasn't much to keep him alive in the tunnels. He shoved it all into a bag and slung it over his shoulder, before lifting a small hand pick off the floor. He inspected the head, pleased the previous cycles' sharpening had smoothed out the nicks.

'You can do mine later,' Troy said, hefting his own chipped pick. 'I could use it to prise the smile off that stupid guard's face.'

Harl followed Troy's gaze to the burly man. Queeg stood about a head taller than most men. A burn scar stretched along the left side of his head from where someone had tried to set him alight when he was younger. It had infected the man with a permanent distaste for people; it had also made him as ugly as sin. The rest of his hair was cropped close, but it was still thick enough to make the scar stand out an angry white against his skull. He was old, grizzled, and hated everyone. In other words he was a perfect fit for guard duty at the mine.

He noticed Harl and Troy staring at him.

'Oi, you!' he roared as he strode forward. 'Get back to your 'oles. You've given us precious little so far, so pick up the pace, or you'll feel more than a tickle.' He raised his coiled whip and gave it a flick. It cracked the air over their heads as Harl and Troy scrambled away. Queeg roared with laughter.

'If I didn't know better,' Troy grumbled as they ran for the nearest ladder, 'I'd say he has personal issues.'

'Then you don't know better,' Harl said, offering a hand to Troy and then heaving him up onto the rickety platform.

A gaping hole led deep into the boulder beside Harl. He peered inside. It was too dark to see much, but he could pick out the detail of more narrow holes cutting deep into the rock. Cracks criss-crossed the stone, like the pattern on a china cup, and threaded their way through the tunnels into the heart of the boulder. It was chilling how weak it looked. It was as if the whole thing was just waiting to crumble.

Harl sighed as he looped his satchel over his chest. The ancient planks creaked under his feet as he picked his way along the first level of scaffolding.

'Did you see who arrived last night?' Troy asked.

Harl glanced at his friend. Troy was trying to mask it, but there was a definite twinkle in his eye.

'No. Who?'

'Chloe,' Troy kept his face straight until they reached the next ladder, but then burst out laughing. 'Are you going to ask her out again? What's it now? Seven times? Eight? She'll weaken eventually.'

Harl groaned. Chloe was the daughter of Carl Rayne, the carpenter. She was petite and fiery, with eyes so dark they were bottomless pools. There was a danger about her that most men found exciting. He'd tried and tried to get something as small as a smile from her, but she had no interest in him. She'd slept with everyone else, of course, or so the rumours said. Everyone but Troy. Troy had nothing to do with her for some reason. She'd tried to seduce him, but Troy had just laughed her off.

'Not interested,' Harl grunted.

Troy launched his bag up to the next level and scampered up the ladder.

'We'll see,' he said, 'but I'll wager that the thought of her warming your mattress will win you round after a few more cycles in here.'

When Harl reached the top of the ladder he found Troy crouched near the opening of their tiny crawl hole. He was helping Ryker drag a bucket of rock out as the older man spat a constant stream of vicious curses, dragging himself from the hole.

Ryker had been at the quarry for at least twenty cycles when they arrived. He was short – barely up to Harl's chest – so he was ideal for the narrow tunnels. Tight, corded muscle rippled on his arms as he hefted the bucket up and tipped the contents over the side. He wore tattered trousers and a leather waistcoat over his bare chest. His long hair had been yanked back into a ponytail coated with rock powder.

'Below!' he shouted as the rubble tumbled away. Curses came from the lower level.

Troy grinned. 'Perhaps a little more warning next time?'

Ryker spat on the dusty planks and then started to crawl back into the hole.

'Ain't no fun if I do that, boy.'

Harl crouched down and used his flint and steel to light a candle. His hands shook when he lifted the candle up. The hole swallowed Ryker into the dark before him. It looked smaller than it had on the previous cycle.

Troy laid a hand on Harl's shoulder.

'I can go in if you want.'

Harl shook his head, took a breath, dropped to his knees and then crawled inside.

When the dark cycle fell, the guards blew a whistle to signal the end of the shift. Harl crawled out, coughing and hacking up dust, then collapsed on the scaffold. Troy handed him a skin of water to swill his mouth out.

'Any luck?' Troy asked.

Ryker wriggled out and grabbed the waterskin from Harl. He took a long draught and then wiped his mouth on the back of his hand.

'Nothing,' he said, 'not even a gleam of ore,'

Harl closed his eyes and focused on breathing the clean air. The air inside the tunnels was choked with dust. It was like breathing in bitter treacle. He looked at the scratches and bruises that covered his calloused hands. He even had blisters. He hadn't had any of those since starting in the forge, but the small tools and awkward working conditions had left him raw and bleeding. His shoulders had been scraped on either side and the scars would taint him forever as having done penance in the quarries.

They packed up and returned to camp. Small shacks circled a wide yard where an open cookhouse was preparing food for the returning shift. Workers trudged out for the next session as Harl collapsed onto his bedroll. Prisoners with a higher privilege level had a shack to themselves with bedding inside, but everyone else had to sleep on the ground. The guards had a small barracks at the head of the quarry and sentry towers ringed the pit. It was miserable, especially when the rain came during the dark cycle. The only cover was a few tanned hides folded over as a makeshift tent, but water still seeped through the holes and they ended up wet.

It was harder for those inside the tunnels. Harl had worked the dark shift a few times since arriving. It made the light shift seem easy. Rainwater filtered down through the rock to drip and flood around the workers. Miners with any sense dug at a slight incline so that water always ran back down the tunnel away from them, but more than a few had died as the water gushed through and trapped them in a small hollow. And then there was the dust. When the rain came, the dust turned to cement. Thick and sluggish, it set hard unless it was scraped away regularly.

Troy slumped down next to Harl and shoved a half-full bowl of stew into his hands. Harl shovelled it down, slurping the last remnant before staring into the empty bowl. It was barely enough to live on. Ryker had already finished his own bowl and was curled up asleep in his blankets.

'I don't know how he does it,' Troy moaned. 'He didn't even look that tired when we finished.'

Harl nodded. He looked at his own blankets as the first rain started to fall, but then climbed to his feet and stepped out from under the shelter. The rain was a cascade of relief on his face. He scrubbed the filth away and took a few steps forward.

'Where are you off to?' Troy mumbled, pulling a blanket up to his chin as he closed his eyes and yawned.

Harl considered the question. 'I need to stretch my legs. I can't stand it in those tunnels, Troy. They smother me.'

Troy began to snore.

Harl paced the perimeter of the camp letting his mind and body relax. It felt good to work his legs. Rain stung the blisters on his hands, but the taste of the clear water in his mouth was invigorating.

There was very little to see with the light out. Flickering torches smoked and sizzled under the deluge of water, but their light died quickly, falling far short of its normal reach. He looked up at the boulder behind its shroud of scaffold and ladders. Shouts and flickering candles were the only things that pierced the dark. He would be back there again come the light, but at least he could breathe fresh air until then.

In the darkness it was impossible to see the quarry rearing up around him. He imagined the steps cut into the rock. How many cycles had it taken to carve them? It seemed impossible that they had ever managed to cut so deep into the ground. No well reached this far down.

He paced back-and-forth, arms folded behind his back as the horrors of the cycle played out in his mind, but he just couldn't shake the feeling of being so far below ground level. He imagined the river breaking through from above and cascading down around them. How long would it take to fill the quarry? He didn't know, but there weren't many who could swim. He scraped a foot across the ground, drawing a line in the gravel. There wasn't even anywhere for the water to go if it flooded. It was just rock down there, hard, black, and unforgiving.

He turned away and began pacing back towards the campfire. His steps faltered. Black rock? Spinning around, he raced back to the mark he had scraped in the wet ground. He slid to a stop and fell to his knees. It was there, clear in the dirt before him.

The base of their world.

The same black glass that formed the barriers around the world stared back at him from the ground. He ran his trembling fingers over it. The base of the world. He had never heard of anyone reaching it before. It had been a running joke: if there was a roof, then there had to be a floor. He tapped it and it sounded hollow, just like the walls around them and the Sight that showed the realm of the gods. He lay down and pressed his face against it, cupping his hands either side of his eyes to block out any light from the fires flickering around the shacks above, but there was nothing there. It was just black, cold and featureless against his skin, another barrier to trap them, another wall to pen them in. He smashed a fist against it and then rolled onto his back.

It was useless. He had somehow thought that digging into the ground might be an answer. Perhaps there was a way out down there? But it was just another wall. The prison was complete.

He climbed to his feet and then scraped the gravel back over the floor with his boot. There was no point anyone else seeing it.

Perhaps they already had and had come to the same heart-breaking conclusion?

Voices came from behind him and he ducked into the deeper shadow of one of the shacks. He didn't want to see anyone just now. The pain was too fierce inside, the hatred too strong. Bracing his back against the wall, he peered out from his refuge.

Queeg appeared. He was hobbling along, slapping his coiled whip against his leg as he talked to a smaller companion. The burn scar on his head shone pale in the dark. The two figures stopped near one of the shacks. Lamplight captured them and their faces were revealed in the light. Queeg's companion was a petite woman.

Chloe.

She laughed at something the man said and ran one finger down his cheek and neck, and then slid it across his chest. Her long dark hair was slick with the rain, but her eyes seemed to catch the light and flash with fire. Her simple cotton blouse and trousers were sodden and plastered to the contours of her body. Queeg's eyes were drinking it all in. He licked his lips, took a swig from a skin and dragged the looped coil of his whip across the sodden fabric covering her breast. She laughed again and tapped his nose with her finger. He wrapped an arm around her waist and slammed her against him. She arched her back slightly to keep her face away from his as he lunged forward to bite at her ear. His eyes were wild.

Harl clenched his fists as anger flooded through him. He began to step out, but then Chloe turned her face towards him. Her lip curled into a mocking smile and she waggled one finger in his direction before pushing Queeg back into the shack and closing the door.

Harl stood frozen in the rain. He felt dirty.

Chapter 7

Who would have thought they could be so intelligent. I have decided to make them my life's work. How will my fellows react to them and how will they react to my fellows?

The cycles passed and Harl and Troy began to fall into the rhythm of the quarry. Half a cycle on, half a cycle off. It didn't matter whether it was light or dark. Those who fell ill or injured were taken away to the healers. They would return when healed to complete their penance, but when the numbers fell short, those left just had to work that much harder.

He only caught glimpses of Chloe. She had seduced her way into Queeg's favour and never worked the quarry like the others, although she paid a heavy price for it. One cycle, shortly after the rain stopped and the light came back, he caught sight of her washing her hair in a bucket outside the hut. Both wrists were bruised and an angry red welt circled her throat. She saw him, but her lip just curled up in the familiar snide smile and she wrung out her hair and turned away. He didn't see her after that.

Troy had accepted his fate grudgingly and was getting on far better than Harl. Harl kept getting assigned to the tunnels, whereas Troy worked the scaffold, carting rubble and ore away.

The tunnels began to choke Harl. The flickering candlelight played tricks on him and he began to feel the weight of all the rock pressing down above him. It didn't help that Ryker was so small. The tunnels he dug weren't big enough for Harl. Rock pressed around him on all sides until he ended up wriggling like a worm through the tunnels. But he forced himself to continue until he staggered back out into the open space of the quarry to sleep at the end of the cycle.

Like the others in the quarry, he would climb the rickety scaffolding and wriggle, head first, into the tunnels in search of the elusive ore seams that ran through the giant rock. The guards were always present, lashing out at those who were too slow, or forcing prisoners back into the rock. It felt like digging his own grave at times.

It was ironic that he was using one of his own tools for the job. It had been a large order three giftings back and the work had kept him busy at the anvil for a long time. He'd had no idea at the horror the simple tools would be a part of, and the excitement with which he'd looked at the stack of credits he'd received sickened him now. If another order came in he would refuse it. But would that condemn the prisoners to using inferior tools as well as hardship?

A loud crumble of stones focused him on the tunnel ahead, snapping him from his reverie. He tensed, ready to crawl away at the first sign of a rock fall, but it was only Ryker. He had broken through into a neighbouring tunnel, leaving a wider space than normal. A whisper of air came from the outside, but it did little to ease the unrelenting heat.

Harl wiped sweat from his brow and shoved a bucket behind him as he started to wriggle his way back towards the opening. He got a brief glimpse through the tunnel opening as the next worker grabbed the bucket. Troy had been a few steps to the side chipping away at a rock to make cobblestones for repairing the roads in town. Harl thought about calling out, but his throat was so dry that he gave up.

A guard poked his head into the hole.

'Go on, get up there. Your boyfriend won't be joining you until later. And if you don't hurry up, I'll pour some fire liquid in there after you. Now get back to work!'

Harl's candle had gone out, but he scrambled deep into the tunnel before relighting it. He lay there panting for a few moments before grabbing his tools and then wriggling further into the darkness. Maybe this time he would find something. The workers who found ore got better rations and privileges, but so far he had found next to nothing.

The candle slipped from his fingers, sputtered, and went out. He drew in deep breaths as panic started to set in. He ran his fingers across the rock ahead of him searching for the candle. Nothing. He pressed forward half a stride and his blunted nails skimmed it, but the candle skittered from his fingers and rolled away. He snatched at it and clawed it back to him, panting and screaming inside. His body strained against the rock around him. The tunnel was too small, too tight. The blackness was too extreme. He clamped his eyes shut, but it didn't help.

And then he remembered her. The woman who had been reflected in the god's clothing filled his thoughts and all of the panic flowed away. The startling clarity of her bright blue eyes was a wave of calm that washed over him. Harl clutched the candle to his body and lay there in the dark, the loneliness and fear banished by her simple existence.

Who was she? He was certain that she had been real. There was a purity about her. It was a daft thing to think about in the overwhelming darkness, but she looked so different to Chloe. This strange woman's eyes had been filled with caring. They had captured some part of him and he knew that she would be thinking about him. He leaned his head against the rock and laughed. What was he thinking? It was all impossible. She was probably a figment of his imagination. And yet somewhere deep inside he knew that she wasn't. There was a truth about her appearance that cycle, as though she was the key to his freedom. He had no idea how, but it was there and he cherished the feeling. It was his future. She was his future. He had to believe it. It was either that or go insane among the sheep. She was more vivid now than when he'd first seen her. That golden flow of hair, like staring up into the light above. Her blue eyes, more precious than the gems and ore they were mining for.

But her very existence presented far-reaching implications. If she lived somewhere beyond the black barriers that surrounded the world, it meant that their world wasn't the only place of existence. There might be other people in her world. What would they be like? Would they even speak the same language?

He opened his eyes and then relit the candle. It flickered in the narrow space and threw shadows across the walls. Harl pressed his hand against the rock and smiled. It didn't feel so bad now. The weight of it seemed less. He wriggled forward a few steps.

The thought that another world lay only a few paces from his own was staggering. Was there a way to get there? He knew the black barrier had proved impenetrable, but there had to be a way, even if it was climbing up to the roof of the world and escaping when the god opened it. But why would the gods divide the two worlds from each other and what would they gain from it? The answers didn't come to him in the sputtering candlelight. He just crawled on. But he wasn't alone any more. She was with him.

The muted shriek of a whistle reached them some time later. Ryker grunted and shoved the last bucket back to Harl and they began the slow crawl out of the boulder.

Harl slid to the ground once he'd emerged and waited as Troy poured half a waterskin over his head. Torches were being lit along the scaffold now that the dark cycle was nearing and tunnel workers were making the slow climb down the scaffold now that the shift had changed. Smoke curled into the air over the camp from where the cookhouse was preparing their meal.

Ryker grabbed the final bucket of stone and upended it over the handrail. The stone tumbled away below them.

'Below!' he called with one hand cupped to his mouth.

Curses came in answer.

Ryker leaned on the barrier and scrubbed the dust from his hair.

'Another one done,' Troy said.

Harl nodded. Thoughts of the woman still whirled around inside his head. His eyes drooped shut, but he shook himself and snapped awake.

'We'd best get back and eat,' Harl said.

Troy reached out a hand and dragged Harl to his feet. They both turned to see Ryker still leaning on the barrier. He grinned at them.

'Another two cycles-'

A boulder split from the rock above and slammed into him. Ryker tipped out over the handrail and fell from the scaffold. His scream froze most people in their tracks, but Harl and Troy rushed to the rail and peered over. Ryker was lying on the ground thirty paces below them, his body arched across the top of a large rock. One leg was twisted back underneath him.

Harl scrambled for the ladder and reached him in moments. A crowd had already formed, so he forced his way through. Ryker lay there limp and lifeless. Harl hesitated, but then stepped forward and checked for a pulse.

'He's alive,' he said.

A collective sigh ran through the crowd.

'Thank the gods,' Troy said. As soon as the words had left his mouth, he frowned and locked eyes with Harl.

They both looked up to see the One True God peering into the world.

Was this some kind of retribution?

The god yawned and walked away.

Harl clenched his fists as stretcher-bearers arrived to cart Ryker away. Had the god done this? He stepped back to let the men lift Ryker onto the stretcher, but his thoughts were still boiling with anger.

No. This wasn't the god. The god didn't have the power to do this. They were here for one reason only. The Eldermen.

Chapter 8

My illness has started to get the better of me. If I can afford the treatment then I can continue, but I need a different approach than just studying these creatures in my garden.

Harl sat staring into the fire. Word had returned that Ryker was recovering at the healers. It would take many cycles for his leg to mend and he would probably always walk with a limp. It pained Harl to think of the strong man struggling through life that way. It seemed wrong. Ryker was a strong man, stoic, grim, but there was a mirth buried deep inside, like some kind of treasure to be mined.

The shift had changed well into the dark cycle. When they returned to the camp the cooks had given them the news about Ryker. After that they had settled down to wait. Sleep seemed far off. Rain fell around them as smoke rose from the sputtering fires.

Troy poked a stick into the fire and a breath of fiery sparks erupted into the air.

'You're quiet,' he said.

Harl watched as a hot ember collapsed into the glowing coals. It was true. He hadn't spoken during their meal. His thoughts were too much in torment. It wasn't just Ryker. His accident was a horror that had cut deep, but Harl was thinking far beyond that.

The woman.

He hadn't told anyone about her yet. Part of it was selfishness. While she was locked away in his thoughts she belonged to him. She was something he could treasure, a gem gleaming with hope through all the darkness that was gathered around him. But sharing his story meant more than just sharing the fact of her existence. It meant trusting someone with the implications. To tell someone about her meant revealing that the world was bigger than they had ever believed. It would change everything they knew. Did he have the right to do that?

Troy was still waiting for an answer. He stirred the embers again and sparks soared into the air. Harl flicked his gaze up from the fire and smiled half-heartedly.

'What would you have me say?' he asked.

'Oh, I don't know. Any good jokes?' Troy winked, but there was a sadness in his voice.

Harl tossed a log on the fire and watched tongues of orange flame lick at it. The warmth was a blanket of comfort in the surrounding dark.

'I've never thanked you, you know,' he said at last.

Troy cocked his head to one side. 'What for?'

'You've always been there for me. You're my truest friend.'

Troy rolled his eyes. 'Is this a proposal? Only if it is, it's not very good. Where's the ring? Where's the flowers? I expect to be wined and dined you know.'

Harl laughed and shook his head. Troy grinned.

'There's no need for thanks. We may not be brothers by blood, but we're family, Harl.'

Harl nodded. His expression turned serious and he locked his gaze with Troy's.

'That's why you're the only one I trust in this world.'

Troy raised an eyebrow. 'This world? I've never heard anyone say that. It sounds so strange.'

Harl let the words hang and then turned back to the fire.

'I'm going to find the girl of my dreams,' he said.

'Oh yes,' Troy said with a grin. 'Now that's more like it. Women I can deal with. And which lady has the pleasure of being chased by a rogue such as yourself?'

'I've seen her only once,' Harl said.

'She must be a rare one' Troy said, interested. 'Who is she then? Chloe?' He watched Harl's expression sour. 'No, I can see that it's someone else. Interesting...'

Harl leaned back against the dusty stone wall behind him. 'I don't know her name, but even the priests would believe she is more beautiful than the Sight itself.'

'Okay,' Troy said. 'You've got me curious. What does she look like or is this just a dream girl of your own making?'

'She has golden hair, bright blue eyes, and she appeared before me at the Sight'

'Golden hair and blue eyes!' Troy exclaimed throwing his hands up. 'You're crazy. She must have been a dream girl, my friend.'

'No dream, although you may think it more of a nightmare when you know the rest.'

'The rest?'

'When I saw her she was beyond the Sight.'

He explained how he had seen her. Troy's eyes widened with each word of the tale.

'Ha!' Harl laughed, 'that's the exact same look she gave me.'

'You really are crazy, aren't you?' Troy said. 'Just how much dust did you inhale in those tunnels?'

'She's real, Troy. I speak only the truth here.'

Troy frowned and started poking at the fire again.

'But how can that be true?' he said. 'Only the gods exist beyond the Sight.'

'So we are led to believe.'

Troy's head snapped up. 'You doubt that?'

Harl shrugged. 'How much of what we've been told is a lie?'

'Do you think she didn't know either then?' Troy asked, sitting forward to keep the conversation private.

'I assume she didn't. Her surprise was as much as my own. But it does make sense, and is the only reasoning I can think of to explain why she appeared. You do believe me then?'

'I believe you,' Troy stated, 'but how, for so long, could no one have known about this other world you speak of? I mean, if it truly exists, surely there must be a way to get through to them?'

'I have thought much on it already,' Harl said, 'and no sure way presents itself to me'.

'Okay,' Troy said. 'Do we go to the elders with this?'

'No,' Harl said. 'They'd think us mad and after the stunt that landed us here, we would probably end up doing more of this bloody penance. We must try to get through ourselves.'

Troy looked dubious at this. 'The elders would find out too quickly. They're going to be keeping tabs on us from now on and we're in no position to just go smashing things at the barrier in hopes no one would see or hear us. So what can we do?'

'Maybe,' Harl said, 'we could dig under it. I can get the tools for the job.'

They talked long into the dark cycle, coming up with one extraordinary idea after the next, until they fell asleep, their dreams filled with golden-haired women.

Harl sat up when the light beamed down, the smell of the dying fire and his powder-coated jerkin in his nostrils. He looked around at the four dust-covered men hunched up close to the fire and propped against large boulders. They were thin but not starving. Even Troy's slim frame had shed weight since they got here. He supposed those going into the tunnels needed to be small-framed or risk getting stuck.

They were up on the second tier of the quarry pit where the guard housing and kitchens had been built. As the others yawned and stretched he kicked a snoring Troy.

'Get up, lazy. Time to start digging these boulders again.'

Troy stirred.

'Not the butcher's wife,' he mumbled as he turned over.

Harl crouched and shook him. 'Come on. Get up.'

Troy squinted in the full light and looked up at him, resentfully.

'I'm sick of this penance,' he said, getting to his feet. 'My back aches and no matter how many times I wash, I can't get rid of the dust.' He patted himself down, sending a cloud of dust into the air around him.

'Well there's good news to that,' Harl said, watching Troy splash the contents of a waterskin over his face. Rivulets of dirt dripped off him. 'I've been thinking and, if I'm right, then its only another cycle until we're out of here, then you can have a proper bath.'

Troy looked pleased at the news and made for his mining pick.

'Good,' he said, a smile on his thin face. 'Then we can go in search of golden-haired beauties to our heart's content.' Troy seemed to think better of it. 'After a drink, though.'

They made their way from the dingy huts shared by the workers towards the boulder. The last shift shuffled the other way, shoulders slumped with fatigue. Harl studied their faces. They all looked haggard and without hope, dust and small bloodied cuts marking their faces from the day's work. He let his eyes climb the tangle of scaffold ahead. The boulder was massive, higher than twenty men standing on each others' shoulders, and was apparently far bigger than others the god had ever placed in the world. Cracks radiated out across its surface.

Harl had never been at the mines before, so he had never witnessed the god lowering boulders into place, or watched it scrape the piles of mined slag away in its fist, but he suddenly found the whole process strange. Why did the god bother with a boulder? Why not provide the raw materials instead? They had need of iron and other useful ore, but there was no need for gold or the gems they sometimes found. Why not gift these materials in their pure form and save them all of the work? Perhaps it was yet another aspect of the god's harsh nature? Perhaps it wanted to force them to struggle for existence so that it could watch good people like Ryker as he screamed in pain? Did the god feed off their suffering?

Arriving at the first ladder, he hefted his mining gear onto his back and climbed up. A waiting guard directed him to the right along the first level of scaffold, so he threaded his way past the other workers until he reached the busy platform and his heart sank.

A cluster of guards waited near one of the tunnels several paces away. Someone was curled up in a ball on the boards at their feet. He couldn't make out who, but the figure was small. Queeg was sitting on an upturned bucket with a smug expression on his face.

Harl was ushered towards the group and gave Troy a worried glance. What was going on?

The guards peeled back and Harl got his first good look at the prone figure. It was Chloe.

She appeared to be unconscious. Her bottom lip was split open. Blood covered her mouth and chin and was dripping onto the boards. Above that, one eye was swollen shut and blackening from where she'd taken a harsh blow. Her eyes flickered open and she tried to raise her head, but then slumped back down, breathing hard.

'Well, well,' Queeg laughed as he kicked her in the back. 'Not dead yet.'

Harl glared at the man. Troy nudged Harl in the ribs. When he looked around, Troy lowered his gaze to the boards, but tapped one ear with a finger and arched his eyebrows in Queeg's direction. Harl stared at the guard, but it was a moment before he noticed what Troy meant. The lower half of Queeg's ear had been torn away. Harl snatched his eyes back to Chloe. There was too much blood on her face to have come from her split lip.

Queeg got up and pointed his coiled whip at them. 'This bitch is with you. See how she prefers grubbing around in the rock. She goes in first and comes out last. No food.'

He spat on her and then marched off with the other guards trailing in his wake.

Harl and Troy ran forward. Harl knelt next to Chloe and raised her head off the boards.

'Get some water,' he told Troy.

Her eyes flickered open. She stared at him for a moment before swatting his hands away and pushing herself upright.

'Get your hands off me,' she said. She winced as she spoke and dabbed at her split lip with the back of her hand.

Troy returned with the water and offered it to Chloe. She snorted in disgust and struggled to her feet.

'What are you expecting, pretty boy? Am I supposed to wash my face and get fancied up like one of your usual tarts?' She batted her eyelids at him and then snatched a pick off the boards. Her face blanched and she clutched her arm to her side against her ribs. There was blood on her blouse under her arm. She glared at him. 'So? What of it? You think I want to grub in these holes?'

Harl raised his hands to ward her off. She snorted again and turned to the tunnel, crawling into it before either of them could say another word. Troy took a swig of water from the waterskin. He wiped his lips with his hand.

'Well, Harl my boy, you've got her all to yourself now. Just watch your ears.'

Harl ignored him and took his place in the tunnel. Chloe's feet were barely visible ahead as she crawled out of sight. Harl wriggled after her and caught up quickly. She had been crawling blind into the rock without the candle. He shielded the light from his own candle away from his face with one hand.

'I'll show you how to dig,' he said, then dodged her foot as she kicked back at him.

'Some of us have done this before,' she snarled.

It seemed that Chloe was no stranger to the tunnels. She dug at a pace Harl struggled to keep up with. Buckets of rubble were filled quickly and each time she passed one back, she tried to kick it in his face. If he grunted in pain or complained in any way, she snorted with laughter, but other than that she said nothing.

Harl was exhausted by their mid-shift meal. Troy just sat there shaking his head with a smirk on his face, while Chloe kept to herself, bloodied and coated in dust. Each time she looked out over the quarry towards the guards there was murder in her eyes. Harl tried to broach the subject of what had happened, but she screamed and threw her spoon at him. It struck him on the forehead, but it was too blunt to do anything other than leave a bruise. The look she gave him cut much deeper.

'You okay?' Troy asked as Harl was about to follow Chloe back into the tunnel.

'Yeah, fine,' Harl said and wrenched the bucket out of Troy's hands. 'She's dangerous.'

Troy tapped his own forehead and winced. 'I can see that.'

Harl shook his head. 'I don't mean that. Have you seen the hatred in her eyes? What if she tries something against the guards?'

'She wouldn't, would she?'

Harl frowned. 'I just don't know. She's different in here. Almost feral.'

Troy lit a candle and handed it to Harl.

'Watch yourself,' he said, nodding at the tunnel.

The work was as hard as ever. Chip and scrape, then drag and shovel rubble into the buckets. Chloe kept working in silence, but she had slowed. Perhaps the fire of her anger was burning below the surface now rather than raging out of control.

He cleared rock away from the walls, consciously aware of her ahead of him. Each time she shoved a bucket back, he had to move his own out of the way and scramble back far enough to pass it out to Troy. It was slow going. The rock was unrelenting. Small chips were the only things that ever seemed to break off in this part of the boulder, despite all of the cracks threading the surface.

'Rest,' he murmured as Chloe pushed another bucket back. She slumped against the rock, her face only a shadow in the flickering candlelight.

Harl pushed the bucked aside. It scraped the side of the tunnel, taking a chip of stone with it. He looked over his shoulder at it and saw the chip split into a crack. Stone began to rain down around him.

'Rockslide!' he shouted.

He rolled onto his side, his back against the side of the tunnel as the rocks came down next to him, and pressed himself away from the fall and closed his eyes. Chloe screamed and began to kick at his head.

'Get back! Get out!' she shouted at him.

He raised his hands as a shield against her kicks. Stone tumbled around him. And then suddenly everything fell silent. Once the dust cleared he could hear Troy calling.

'Harl? Harl? You okay?'

Harl coughed.

'Yeah. We're-' Chloe kicked him in the head. 'We're fine.'

He opened his eyes and gazed at the newly exposed side of the tunnel. It gleamed at him and, shoving the fallen rock out behind him, he saw it was a seam.

'Gold,' he whispered in awe. 'We've struck gold!'

Chloe wriggled down next to him and he froze. Her back was pressed against his chest and the feel of her breath reverberated through him. She ran her fingers over the veins of gold.

'This is mine,' she murmured in a smoky voice, and then dug an elbow into his ribs. 'Mine. Right?'

'It's all of ours,' Harl said.

She snarled and then slammed her pick into the wall. A sharp crack sent a shockwave through them. They looked at each other and then scrambled backwards as stone began to rain down again.

'Out! Out!' Chloe screamed at him, wriggling around as she tried to change places.

He scrambled backwards, shuffling himself out legs first, but they were too tangled up. His belt buckle caught on her clothes and then ripped free suddenly. More rocks tumbled down around them. The cracking sound magnified, rumbling through the rock as though the boulder was venting its rage. His jerkin snagged on the tunnel's side. He tugged against it, but he was locked in place. Chloe kicked and screamed, but the tunnel was too tight for her to get by. Panic set in. He grabbed a sharp rock and started to slice his jerkin free with it. The cracking rock sounded like Queeg's whip magnified in the hands of the god. Louder now, angrier.

'It's breaking!' he yelled through the growing noise. 'Get out!'

Chloe's arms wrapped around him and she buried her head against his chest. The sound of cursing men was distant, smothered. The collapsing rock was just too loud. He tried to make sense of the sounds as the rock rumbled down on top of them.

'Get them out! Pull them back!'

And then the panic washed away. He let it all go, knowing that this was the end. He closed his eyes and focused on the golden-haired woman. Warmth swept through him and he just lay there as the boulders smashed into him. She was here. She was with him.

'Get away from it!' a voice screamed from somewhere far away.

The light vanished as the candle finally sputtered out and the only thing around him was the tumbling stone and Chloe's terrified screams. But then hands fastened on his ankles and hope surged through him.

'I've got him!' It was Troy's voice.

Harl lurched free and dragged Chloe along with him as they were pulled out. Troy's yells rose above the sound of collapsing stone.

'I've got you! I've got you!'

His feet slipped out of the tunnel and then his legs and hips. And then a crack, like the booming voice of the One True God, sounded through the rock and it all collapsed on top of him. Rock crumpled around his back and head as the boulder disintegrated and blackness took him.

Chapter 9

I have it! I've come up with a plan that will assure my health, but for it to work I must start converting my home. I will order the construction materials directly.

The collapse of the boulder was a disaster the likes of which no one had seen before. It claimed the lives of fifteen fit and healthy men and injured five more. It took three whole light and dark cycles to extract the crushed and maimed bodies. Men and women had worked around the clock to free the lifeless forms from the boulder's remains.. Afterwards, a meeting of elders was held and it was found that too many bore holes had been made in the process of extracting the ore from within. A simple fracture had spread through the entire thing and caused a cascading collapse that had left nothing but dust, rubble, and death. Rufus called it the god's retribution; others just called it a nightmare.

Troy limped slow and determined up the grass mound. Fifteen dead men lay side by side on the green sward. It glistened where the rains had caressed it through the dark cycle.

He carried a bow and a quiver of arrows in his bandaged hands and wiped tears away as he peered down at the row of bodies. He knew them all and walked the length of the row until he came to Harl.

His friend.

Harl's lifeless face had been cleaned of blood, but the cuts still seemed to bleed after death. Troy couldn't look at him without pain clenching around his heart. It was strong enough to make him cry out each time he saw Harl, but there was nothing he could do, no words he could say. It was all just so pointless now.

Harl was gone.

He'd managed to pull his friend from the hole quickly after the initial collapse, but it had not been fast enough. The rock had crumbled around both of them as he'd dragged Harl free. He had sustained severe injuries to his right leg and arms, but Harl had just slumped on the scaffold before him, lifeless and bloody. When the healers had come they had just shaken their heads and covered Harl with a pale sheet, before carrying Troy away on a stretcher.

Troy knelt down next to Harl.

'I thought you might like to take these,' he said, kneeling down and looping the bow and quiver over Harl's motionless shoulders. 'I'm so sorry,' he said, tears falling onto Harl's ceremonial lifting dress. 'I wish I'd been quicker when it happened. The elders have exonerated you from any previous convictions and have abandoned using the quarry as a punishment, but it won't help now.'

He stood once more. Pain – both physical and emotional – crossed his face as he rose. He took a final look at his friend.

'I hope now you will find the woman of your dreams, Harl' he said, and then turned and made Sightwards, heading for the Golden Spear.

It was not long before the god came to lift the dead, attracted by the usual hilltop pyre used to signal a death in the world. Before the use of the pyre it would be every gifting cycle that the god lifted the deceased, its hand descending down from No Sight at the back of the world to scoop up the bodies. One time, after several corpses had decomposed over forty whole cycles without being lifted, the Elders decided that getting the bodies lifted before they rotted was a priority. So the pyre was lit and nearly every time after that the lift happened swiftly.

Troy stood at the bottom of memorial hill looking Sightwards. The god was overseeing the world and had spotted the call to lift the dead. It seemed that whenever the One True God looked in, the world froze. The people could not help but be in awe of the size and power before them. But this time it seemed as though the God would reach in right over the land instead of from no-Sight. Troy felt a slight shudder as the world opening lifted and the god peered inside. It then lifted the roof higher and putt its hand into the world.

The hand cast a shadow over Troy as the god reached inside. It hesitated as it neared the fire, and then moved around it as though to avoid the flames. Troy frowned. Why would the god be afraid of the fire? There was no way that the flames could possibly harm it, but had it hesitated? Perhaps it just didn't want to knock the pyre off the hill?

The hand hovered over the bodies before lining up alongside the row. It slid along the soil, churning the grass and scooping up each of the bodies one by one until they were heaped in the half-closed fist. As the hand rose, he could see Harl's arms hanging limply over the side. The hand was halfway to the top, heading Sightwards over the town, when Troy saw Harl's arm rise up and his hand seemed to grasp at thin air.

Horror shot through Troy so sharply that he stood frozen for a heartbeat.

Alive! Harl was still alive!

'No! Wait! Stop!' he shouted as loud as his lungs allowed.

Despite the pain in his leg, he ran after the hand, screaming for the god to stop, but his leg gave way and he tumbled to the ground. Despair flooded him. Harl was alive and yet again Troy had failed to save him.

He lowered his face into the dirt and sobbed.

Chapter 10

The first is constructed. It will be big enough for them to start with.

My fellows have shown interest in the species, but I have yet to show them.

Everything was a dark blur when Harl opened his eyes. His thoughts were muddled in a daze and, when he tried to breathe in, he became aware of a great weight on his chest. He tried to move, but pain lanced through his body and he couldn't shift whatever was on top of him. Panicking, he shoved against the weight, barely managing to move it. *Think*, he told himself, but his thoughts eluded him. He tried to focus, but his eyes hurt and he had to shut them tight.

Reaching out, he tried to determine what was pinning him down. He'd expected rock, but it was soft and sticky instead. He ran his hands over it and then screamed when he realised that the sticky strands running through his fingers were hair.

The world came into focus and he found himself staring into the blank, lifeless eyes of a familiar face. Tom? Teddy? He couldn't remember, but the face was that of the Cutters' son, mangled and gashed on one side.

He turned his head from the boy's pale empty gaze to see more bodies, dozens of them, surrounding him and piled up on top of him. He heaved them off in desperation, clawed at them, dragged them aside, and then scrambled free of the limp arms, lifeless heads, and tangled legs. Turning to look back at the mound of death, he fought the acidic taste of bile in his throat.

The bodies were twisted together in death, arms and legs wrapped around each other. Broken. Helpless. Empty. Tom, Jorni, Chloe ... All people he knew from childhood or the quarry. They were all there before him. He knelt by the mound of bodies and pulled Chloe close, stroking her hair as the tears rolled down his cheeks. Why was she dead? He couldn't even remember why she'd been sent to the quarry. What had her crime been? A joke? A simple joke about the gods? And now she was lying there, her sightless eyes empty of everything that had once made them so alive. She was wearing the same as the rest, simple brown ceremonial robes that were reserved for those who pass from the world.

Letting the body slide from his hands, he looked down at himself and found the same robes covering his own aching body. Sudden flashes of an accident ran through his mind. The memory of the dust in his throat, a tunnel collapsing, and Troy's incessant voice yelling at him to get out. Was he dead? He couldn't be. The people around him were, that was for certain.

Looking away from the faces he knew, he finally noticed his surroundings. He was in the Sight, actually beyond the barriers of the world and inside the realm of the Gods. The distances that separated everything around him confirmed it. The metallic surface beneath him seemed to be hovering midway in the realm, dropping off to nothing on all sides. Platforms similar to the one he was standing on could be seen dotted around the edges of the enormous open space. But they were different... They looked like... gigantic cupboards?

He shook his head, confused by what he was seeing. If they were cupboards, then was he standing on a table? It was too bizarre to be true.

Never in his life had his view been unobstructed by the black walls. Only the Sight had teased at such freedom and the only time he'd experienced a view like this was when he was pressed up against the Sight looking out. It was like a room, but on a scale his mind struggled to comprehend.

Why was he out here though? The question nagged at him. The only people who were lifted were unbelievers. But he had not been condemned and sent to be lifted; he'd been sent to the quarry. But that just left the dead. They were the only ones taken to the realm of the gods.

But if he was in the Sight then so was the god. As soon as his mind conjured the thought, a deep rumbling sound confirmed it.

Shaking, he twisted around and just stood, dumbstruck, as the god walked towards him. It blocked everything from view, a vast wall of living flesh that was as big as his whole world. He was sure it would see him and swat him like some pesky insect. The vast bulk leaned over him and the rank odour of it was overwhelming. He looked up at the immense face and found it staring back down at him. The god raised its hand and Harl waited for the blow, waited for it to swipe him from existence, but it didn't come.

Instead, the god reached right over him and paid no attention to his still form.

Suddenly, the god straightened up and turned away. Harl spun around and ran. He needed cover, somewhere to hide. Anywhere. He just needed to get away from the god. He wasn't thinking, he was just stumbling along, desperate to hide. But then he tripped and crashed to his knees. Lights flickered across his vision and he shook his head to clear them, then looked up at what lay before him.

He had expected to see his own world floating out there in the void, but he could hardly take in the view before him.

In the distance a vast wall stretched across to block his line of sight. It was so big that he couldn't take it all in at once. The bricks were the size of houses and the archway in the centre of it was as big as a god. A bright light streamed out through the archway, forcing him to squint as he tried to see what lay beyond. It looked like another room, but all he could make out was a wall of glowing rectangles. He rubbed his eyes to clear the glare and after a moment patches of green materialised inside the boxes.

The more he focused on what was inside them, the more his mind reeled. The boxes undoubtedly contained hills and landscapes and even though the distance was dizzying he could clearly see a world within. He rubbed his eyes again, and then peered back towards the wall of light.

Each rectangle showed some kind of landscape, like a small, self-contained world. They must have been tiny compared to the god's perspective, but it was difficult to see because of the distance across the god's realm. Rivers flowed through them and towns or villages sat comfortably inside.

He doubled over and voided his stomach contents onto the metallic floor. After a few moments he managed to look up again.

Each world was divided from the next by a solid black barrier. There must have been dozens of worlds stacked together, one on top of the other, in a great wall that stretched as far as he could see to either side behind the arch.

He dropped to his knees and lowered his head into his hands. The sight of all those worlds was making him feel giddy. He drew a breath to steady himself, but even that was difficult. He was shaking. What was going on? The possibilities whirled around in his mind. Were they worlds? Were there people inside?

Had he come from one of those rectangles?

He raised his head and was almost sick again when everything spun. He staggered to his feet, but his legs wobbled and collapsed, and he slumped onto the ground. Staring up at a strip of light in the distant ceiling, his breathing became more and more laboured. What was happening to him? He tried to drag a breath into his lungs, but it felt like he was drowning. He choked and gagged as his vision blurred and a dark shadow fell across him.

Looking around he saw that a lesser god had come up unnoticed behind him. He froze as its enormous face stared straight down at him. Its mottled grey skin was pitted with pockmarks and its dark lips curled back to reveal blunted teeth. Staring up into those gigantic yellow eyes, Harl was shocked by the emotion he could read in them. There was no doubt in Harl's mind that it was focused on him, unlike the last one. Despite the

111

alien look of it, despite the piercing yellow eyes, he could see the look of concern it held.

Everything blurred in and out of focus as if he was suddenly drunk.

The lesser god reached out and grabbed him. Time seemed to slow as the grey hand closed in what might have been a gentle pinch, but its cold fingers almost crushed him. He could feel the strength of the grip pulsing, as though the god was figuring out how firm it should hold him, the same way a child might pick up a bone beetle.

Harl began to choke. His throat tightened like there was no air and he struggled to breathe.

The universe flipped around him as the warm fingers of the hand encased his entire body. Only his face was uncovered and, with a sudden lurch, the god lifted him towards the archway. Distance raced past as the god swept him through the archway towards the wall of worlds.

Harl struggled to see everything as they passed under the arch while the waves of darkness tried to swallow him.

The place was much bigger than he'd thought. It was a blurred wall of light spreading away to either side as far as he could see, rectangle after rectangle, world after world. How many people? How many homes? And they were all just prisons.

His thoughts clouded, but he had just enough sense to hope he was going home. For a moment it looked like he was. Through his daze, he thought he could see his bench and little grove of trees far beneath him beside the dark line separating the worlds.

He was alone and scared as if he was back under the market stall, watching his parents being lifted.

The hand swung sharply up to the left of his world. He was not going back. He struggled in terror, but his hands and feet were numb and refused to obey him. The wall of lights faded and he watched in horrified amazement as the god lifted an opening at the top of the world and moved its hand inside. A sharp downwards motion made him feel like he was falling. With a racking choke, the darkness swallowed him.

Harl dreamed of the Sight.

He was standing on the palm of the god's hand, the huge face level with his own. The god was moving him in front of the worlds, displaying them each one in turn as it bragged about how it had created them all and controlled the fate of those inside.

Scenes merged and shifted. At times he could understand the god, at others it was unknowable. It held him in front of each world and forced him to make decisions about those trapped inside. Would they live or die? Would they receive a gift or be left to starve?

Time would fast forward to show the effects of his choices. Those who Harl chose to get the gift would feast and gorge themselves until dying of gluttony. But when Harl chose not to give the gift, the people would become enraged and throw themselves at the barrier, bloodying the clear wall. As time sped up they would resort to eating each other and the land would become stained with their blood. Plants withered and died. Skeletal bodies crumbled to dust.

He was forced to choose people to be lifted and once his choice was made the hand would reach in and grab Harl's victims, pulling them from the box. Each time he picked it would be a stranger but, as the god's hand came towards him, the stranger's face formed into that of Troy's. He would beg Harl for mercy and strain against the god's hand, but then, with a sudden and violent motion, the god would roar and fling Troy full force into the vast distance of the Sight to disappear as his scream faded away.

Harl screamed his own protest at the god as it looked back at him, and, with a final deafening roar, it propelled Harl directly at the barrier of the nearest world.

Chapter 11

I have gained their trust enough to observe them more directly. I will have to be cautious not to disturb them before the opportune time.

Harl shot up in bed, grateful there was no hard surface or pain. Instead the bed was warm and soft and he sighed with relief as the nightmare faded away. Just as he was about to sink down again, he noticed that the room was unfamiliar and his eyes widened to take it in.

The walls were a solid brick and mortar construction, closer to the look of the Elderman's meeting hall than the solid logs of his own cabin. The room was decorated with ornate wooden furniture. A chair was at the end of his bed and another by the window in front of a dark wood dresser. Soft cushions rested in the chairs and the blankets covering him were thick and warm.

Faint voices drifted up from somewhere below the polished wood floor boards. Not raised voices as such, but hushed conspiratorial tones. There was a subtle difference in the accent to what he was used to, but he was unable to put it down to anything in particular. There were two voices, a female and a croaky old man's. The old man spoke knowingly.

'They have been looking for him for two turns and it's only a matter of time before they come here.'

'Alright,' the woman said. 'We shall have to tell them. Will you do it grandpa?'

'I will,' the man said. 'I'm sure they'll understand, but there will be many questions for him. Is he awake yet?'

'I shall check him again,' the woman replied.

Soft footsteps padded up the stairs, coming up to the closed door set against one wall of the room.

Unsure what to do, Harl snapped his eyes closed just as the wooden door swung open. He kept them shut, at first, as someone tiptoed towards him, then – squinting a fraction – he saw the outline of a face and around it a shimmer of gold.

'Are you awake?' It was the woman.

He opened his eyes at the question and saw the same reflection he had seen so long ago in the Sight, this time unblemished and solid. It was the woman in the white dress. Her golden hair cascaded over her slender shoulders, highlighting her pale skin, and her face was full of youthful curiosity as her sapphire eyes examined him.

'W-where am I?' he stammered, then dragged the blankets up to his chin when he realised that he was naked.

She smiled.

'This is mine and my grandfather's house. Do not be afraid. We have tended your wounds and you are safe.' She moved across the room and pulled one of the chairs up next to the bed.

'What happened?' he asked.

116

'I was hoping you would tell me,' she said, sitting down. 'All we know is you were placed here from above and beyond and, when I found you, you were unconscious in the deep woods nearby. I came upon you after seeing the great hand come down as I was heading home from picking mushrooms. And there you were lying on the grass in a grove among the trees. To be honest I was quite startled, especially with your dark complexion.' She smiled down at him, then looked quickly away to study the wooden beams that ran across the white ceiling.

'You carried me here?' he asked, examining her slender frame and trying to imagine being slumped over her shoulder.

'I got grandpa to come with me and together we managed to get you back home. He says you're the first to come down in memory, and his memory is long. We've not mentioned you to anyone else but there are some from town who will be looking for you.'

He flinched as she leaned over him to place her hand on his brow.

'So how long have I been asleep?' he asked as her cool, delicate fingers touched his forehead.

'This will be the third turn,' she said, moving her hand away, seemingly content with his temperature. 'But will you tell me your name? I've tended you for sometime and I've been anxious to know more about you and how you came to be here.'

Harl sat up with a groan, feeling a deep ache in his body.

'Please excuse my manners,' he said. 'My name's Harl Eriksson and I'm deeply grateful for your care and tenderness. It's just a big shock to me.'

He stretched and his muscles unwound then tilted his head as she nodded. How much did she know? He tried to gauge what she was thinking from the expression on her face, but it was difficult. He was entranced by the look of her and his thoughts seemed jumbled around.

She smiled at his hesitation.

'We've met before,' he said, finally.

She looked thoughtful for a moment, as if deciding to whether to acknowledge it.

'Yes, I remember seeing your face,' she said, 'which is one of the reasons I was so startled to find you in the grove.'

'And have you come to the same conclusion as I?' Harl asked.

She hesitated.

'I'm not sure. I've watched you for a while, but it seems too impossible to be true. You are the man I saw reflected in the god, I cannot deny it. I've discussed it with grandfather, but he is strangely reluctant to talk to me about it. He is a very learned man... But you must forgive me, I've not given you my name. I'm Sonora and my grandpa is Gorman, but most just call him the old man or Gorm.' She smiled at the thought. 'But come, you must meet him and tell us your tale. He's keen to meet you.'

She stood up from the chair and moved towards the door, but turned before she reached it.

'You must be hungry. If you come down there is stew on the stove,' she said, indicating a pile of clothes on the claw-footed dresser. 'I have taken the liberty of providing you with some clothes fresher than the ones we found you in. Please join us in downstairs when you are ready.'

'Thank you,' he said, and then pulled himself out of bed as she headed downstairs.

He went to the window first and pulled the heavy curtains aside, marvelling at the colour and floral patterns on them before looking out.

The house was situated in a lush clearing in a forest. He squinted as light beamed in from above. It looked like a beautiful cycle outside, but the thought surprised him. Most cycles in his own world were the same, with only slight changes to differentiate them, but the light outside here was subtly different. It shone with a warm yellow intensity and Harl had the thought that plants would grow well beneath it.

He reached for the clothes on top of the dresser. They were exceptionally crafted with a delicate weave that only the gowns of the Eldermen could compare to. They fit snugly and he assumed they must have once been this Gorman's that Sonora had mentioned.

He still felt overwhelmed in his heart from what he had seen and learnt, his mind jumping back and forward from the loss of his home and his friends to what he was going to do in this new world. He was unsure if he could even call it a world at all. The vision he had seen from out in the Sight had shattered his perception. Were they worlds? Or were they just cubes of light? It seemed a stupid thought. No they were worlds. People lived in them, ate in them, and slept in them. They had to be worlds.

But what if it was a dream?

He pinched the back of his hand and winced. No, he was definitely awake, which made the strangeness of what he'd experience even more profound. Maybe it was all just a test by the god? Perhaps it would come and lift him back out of whatever vision this was and take him back home? But would he want to after all he had seen?

He gathered himself together and made for the stairs, feeling his stomach protest at the lack of attention he'd paid it recently. The staircase was short and steep, the wood polished to a deep shine.

He opened the door at the bottom and his mouth watered at the smell coming from the stove on the far side of the room. Sonora was leaning over it and it appeared she hadn't yet heard him enter. Beside her, a grey-haired old man stooped over a cupboard as he took down bowls from a shelf. Both of them were facing away from Harl.

The room was spacious and comfortable. Solid stone lined all four sides, with a large window on his left. The windowsill was crowded with potted herbs, while under it was a kitchen counter with ceramic bowls and utensils lined neatly along it. Coals were glowing in a fireplace on the right-hand side. The floor was carpeted in rich rugs with a table and chairs sat on the largest ruby-coloured rug in the centre.

Harl took a step into the room when, without turning, the old man spoke. 'You're just in time for food, stranger, but it would be wise to announce yourself next time.'

Harl was taken aback. How had the old man heard him? He was sure he hadn't made a sound coming in. The old man must have ears like a rabbit.

He stumbled out an apology.

'I'm sorry,' he said, 'I didn't mean to be rude.'

'Gramps,' Sonora said, turning and smiling at Harl, then at the old man. 'Don't be mean to our guest, playing your games and startling him like that. Please Harl, have a seat.' She gestured towards the table. 'Food won't be long in coming.'

He moved over to the table and sat down facing the two of them as they prepared the meal. They formed a duet of coordinated movements as they worked together, Sonora filling bowls with stew as Gorman passed them to her, before taking them back and placing them on the table. He shuffled over to the table and Harl recoiled at the blank whiteness of his eyes. He was blind.

Gorman spoke before Harl could introduce himself.

'Sonora tells me that you have dark hair and eyes. Fascinating.' He was silent for a moment as though picturing it. 'Many things may lie beyond this land of ours and you've been marked by the great god as a warning to us. I wonder what you have seen? Are you a man of honour, Harl? Or has the god marked you for crimes and thrown you into our home as a warning? No need to answer,' he said as he took a seat. 'Let us eat first and I'm sure we'll find it all out soon enough. My name is Gorman. And yes,' he said with a grin, 'I am blind.'

'A pleasure to meet you, Gorman,' Harl said, 'and my thanks for your part in my rescue.'

'My part?' the old man asked and laughed. 'It was my granddaughter who tended you these past changes. She's a kind soul and has looked after me for years without complaint, despite having to put up with such a grumpy old grouch like myself.'

Harl was about to ask what a change or a year was but decided courtesy would be best in a strange land.

'Thank you both,' he said as Sonora took her seat at the table.

The meat in the stew tasted succulent, making his mouth water and he found it difficult to stop taking so much of the fresh-baked bread and butter from the basket in the centre of the table. It was truly delicious.

Harl ate much and said little as the pair talked of light matters about their town and the woods around their home. It turned out that they lived up on a hill in the forest well away from a town nestled down in the valley where most of their people dwelt. Sonora often went to the town for supplies and made her living by picking and mixing herbs into potions and ointments for the townsfolk. She sold her wares in the town's market and made a good living from it.

It seemed to Harl that although this world was similar to his own it had subtle differences, like a parallel world. They only referred to the Sight once in the conversation and Gorman had called it the "vision."

After the meal, Gorman turned his blank eyes on Harl, making him want to look away from the man's knowing gaze.

'Now we're full and relaxed,' Gorman said, 'it is time for you to tell us your story. Sonora and I have discussed this deeply and I know you saw each other's reflections on the god's clothing. I have thought much on that strange incident and what it entails. It seems that you do indeed come from the other side of the wall. But tell us everything first and then we can discuss it.'

Harl explained all he could remember, leaving out only his dreams of Sonora after seeing her for the first time. He talked of the long room where he'd seen the worlds and of the larger space though the archway where he had awoken in a pile with the dead. Throughout the tale Gorman listened intently, nodding here and there and asking Harl to clarify a few details. Sonora was enthralled by his words and sat there with her blue eyes wide open in wonder. By the time he had finished his tale it was dark outside and Sonora had topped the fire up at least twice.

'Hmm,' Gorman said, leaning back in thought. 'This is far reaching news indeed. These worlds that surround us sound almost unbelievable, but I can tell when the truth is spoken. Although it troubles me deeply, I believe I understand much of what you said, for it matches with what I know of our history. But I shall not go into detail now. It's getting late and there is much for me to think on.' With that, he stood and shuffled off to sit silently on a cushioned chair closer to the fireplace.

'Come,' Sonora said, standing, 'I'll bring some water and take you back to your room.'

'Do you believe me?' Harl asked as they reached the door to his bedroom.

She paused for a moment.

'I do. If Grandpa believes it then it must be so. It is almost too much to take in and I cannot imagine how you feel having seen all those things. But I'm worried by what you said. The new worlds and the places you have seen. But for some reason I feel less alone.'

Harl did not know if she meant his presence or the proximity of a vast number of other worlds.

'What do you think Gorman will do?' he asked. 'Will your people believe him?'

'I don't know,' she said, 'but if he's thinking on it then something will come from it.'

She wished him a good sleep and then left. Harl lay awake a long time in the unfamiliar bed, staring at the ceiling. He thought of his own land and its people, but mostly his thoughts were on Troy.

What was he doing?

Harl pictured him staring out at the Sight and grieving for a friend who was still alive, believing him to be dead. But, most likely, he thought Troy would be at a tavern somewhere, drowning his sorrows, oblivious to fact that he was in a box surrounded by a thousand very different lives.

Chapter 12

Their nest had not long been established. Testing the soil showed they have only just begun growing crops in that area.

He awoke as light streamed in through the window and it took a moment to orientate himself and remember what had happened. He dressed and washed from a basin in the room before heading downstairs.

Opening the common room door, he found Gorman sitting in his chair at the table.

'Good morning,' the old man said. 'Hungry? There's porridge in the pot if you are. Perhaps you could fill me one as well?'

Harl took two bowls and filled them with the sweet-smelling mixture.

'Here,' Harl said, placing the bowl and spoon in front of the blind man.

Gorman felt around and then picked up the spoon.

The porridge was delicious. He said as much to Gorman.

'Is Sonora's cooking always this tasty? he asked.

'Yes,' Gorman said. 'She has a gift with herbs and spicing, a blessing derived from her talent with potions. I am lucky to have her. She's a good girl and has taken care of me ever since she was a child. I am not her true grandparent, for she lost both her parents when she was a little one. I took her under my wing after that.'

He scooped another mouthful from the bowl.

'I still had my sight back then and I witnessed a great many people taken by the gods,' he said the last word with a slight mocking sneer. 'It was a harsh time. My sight started to fail from then on and Sonora looked after me in kind as I had done her. She is a clever one. I taught her much and she took strongly to the plants of the land and has grown exceptionally talented in brewing mixtures to ease the pain and suffering of the people. You're fond of her?'

Harl didn't know what to say, but under the man's blank gaze he settled on telling the truth.

'She has been kind to me,' he said, scooping out the remnants of porridge from his bowl, 'And her cooking is far better than I have ever managed. She shows a tenderness I have not experienced before. '

Gorman smiled.

'She is precious to me,' he said.

Harl was about to say something about not having any intentions, but Gorman cut him off.

'You need not explain. I have watched her grow, but there has never been anyone worthy of her. She has a heart of gold, but it is a lonely one.'

Gorman smiled sadly and then finished the last of the porridge in his bowl. Harl picked it up and moved over to place it on the kitchen sideboard.

'There are people in our land looking for you, Harl,' the old man warned. 'You will need to answer their questions about how you came to be here. Sonora and I will vouch for your words and look after your needs in the meantime, but I would suggest you tell them only a little. Many in this land are suspicious of the vision and anything that involves the gods. From what you have said of your own land, it is similar there, and I'd advise caution about what is told to the leaders here. They have seen the hand come down and they know full well that you're here. Sonora sent a message and we have permission to let you heal before taking you to see them. If you tell them all that you told us then trouble will arise from it.'

Harl understood and he knew that he'd have to formulate a convincing story.

'So what should I say?'

'I'll think on it some more,' Gorman said, 'but in the meantime Sonora is outside in the woods. Head left of the vision from the house and you will find her in a small clearing where she grows her herbs. It will be good to have a strong pair of hands around for a while. Come see me later and we can discuss what to say to the leaders on the next change.'

Harl noted the word "change" and realized that Gorman meant the time between light and dark. He left the house and stepped out into forest surrounding it. Dappled light shone down from above and, when he looked up, he watched it dazzle and dance against the leaves as they shifted in the breeze. But the light of this world was a subtly different hue to his own. He had noticed how much more yellow it was straight away, but now, standing outside, the difference was even more obvious. When he looked around he could see that the forest and grasses were a brighter green than the same ones in his own world. They looked far more lush and fertile. It was beautiful.

He made for the clearing where Gorman had said Sonora would be. Spotting a gap in the trees, he drew closer and walked out into the open.

Sonora was there. She wore a soft white gown that highlighted the curves of her body. Its low neckline highlighted the pale flesh of her neck and he was amazed to see that she was barefoot. She sang while she worked, picking flowers and leaves from the herb plants clustered within the clearing's magical light. From where he stood, she looked a picture of beauty more profound than any found in his dreams.

She stopped short and looked up at him.

'Don't stop, please', he said, reaching out towards her with one hand.

She smiled slightly. 'Have you come to help?'

'I have. What can I do?'

'First,' she said, flicking her gaze to his feet, 'it might be best if you didn't step on my plants.'

He looked down and his heart sunk. He had stepped right on top of some of her well-tended herbs. He leapt backwards, wobbling from his injuries.

'I'm so sorry,' he said as he struggled to regain his balance.

She laughed at his clumsy hop.

'It is no matter,' she said, grinning. 'They will recover, as will you. But, in the meantime, if you're able to bring some water from the well it will help. '

Throughout the morning they worked together carrying buckets of water to the house and gardens. He helped her bring her herbs back and they walked together under the trees and talked of their friends and lands.

Harl learned much about the world he was now trapped in. It didn't sound that much different from his own. They received a gifting, just like his own people, and shared it in much the same way. Although they did not give offering for it, they did hold a feast each time it happened. From their talks he found that many people worked fields and small holdings and held growing things in great stead. It was a fertile land and the people made the most of it.

The following cycle, Harl woke early. He was nervous. They had decided over supper that they would go to town and make Harl's recovery known to the leaders there. It would be a fair walk through the forest down into the valley. Sonora had told him that the road led over a cobbled bridge as it wound out of the hills into town, but everything else was the dense, soft darkness of the forest.

The scent of herbs floated in the air as they walked and Harl marvelled at how different everything was. The trees were tall and vibrant, as though this land was somehow more alive than his own homeland. He could clearly see the Sight and it was odd yet refreshing to see something so familiar yet slightly askew from what he knew.

When they finally emerged from the forest Harl found himself standing on the rim of a large valley. Fields lined its slopes and off in the distance a wall of stones surrounded a cluster of grey buildings. It was a town.

They had been walking for some time with Sonora chatting amiably to Gorman about her exploits in the garden and of the new mixtures she had created, when a group of people came over a large stone bridge ahead. It arched over a wide river that meandered along the base of the valley to the gates of the town.

'There is a group of men approaching,' Harl said.

'Tell me of them,' Gorman asked, handing his stick to Sonora.

Harl described the cluster of men ahead and, by the time he had finished, they were close enough to see the light shining on their armour.

Fair blond hair was visible under their gleaming helmets and each man carried a spear. They surrounded a captain or general and Harl couldn't decide which of the dozen medals he wore marked the man as one or the other. The soldiers stopped a few paces in front of them and the leader stepped forward.

'Is this the one who was placed up in the forest, Sonora?' he asked.

The man's face was like a half-rotten fruit, spotted with several boils and wrinkled before its time. Harl guessed he was close to his own age. The man's eyes, though, were full of arrogant youthfulness and, as his gaze roamed over Sonora and Harl, a frown crossed his face.

A stir of dislike for the man nagged at Harl. It was not that he gave any inclination towards trouble, but it was obvious from the way Sonora refused to meet the man's gaze that she was uncomfortable. She shuffled back beside Gorman.

'Yes, Felmar, he is,' she replied.

'He has a lot to answer,' Felmar said, staring at Harl, 'and the leaders sent me up to find him. It is good that you have brought him down. I assume that is what you were doing?'

'It is,' she said.

'Good,' he said, his voice firm. 'I am glad you know your duties. We'll take him from here.'

Harl didn't like the snide look on Felmar's face.

'We intend to take him ourselves, Felmar,' Sonora said.

'There is no need. We'll deal with him from now on,' Felmar said.

He strode forward as if to make for Harl, but Harl stepped back a pace.

'No, you can't!' Sonora said before Harl could do more.

'Do not assume to tell me what I can and cannot do,' Felmar said, moving closer to Harl. 'It is not your place. He is coming with me as my orders dictate.'

Harl was saved by Gorman. As Felmar moved forward, Gorman side-stepped to stand directly in front of him.

'What is the meaning of this?' Felmar asked, staring down at the old man.

'He will not be a prisoner,' Gorman said. 'He is a guest in our house and I have promised him safety, such as I can give. '

'And what protection can you give him, old man?' Felmar asked, amused. 'The woman has your stick, much good it would do you.'

The men with Felmar laughed.

'I may be blind,' Gorman said, 'but I would fancy my chances against a bully such as yourself, Felmar son of Orvel.'

Sonora stood stock still as this played out, as did Harl. He wanted no trouble with the laws of this land, but it seemed that Gorman was not in the least worried.

Felmar took a pace forward. His men stood ready although it was plain that not all agreed with how Felmar was dealing with the situation. Felmar began to draw the short sword that hung on his hip, but before the first ringing of the sword as it left the scabbard was heard, Gorman stepped forward and whipped a knife out from inside his jerkin.

Holding it steady, he pointed the knife directly at Felmar's chest, as if seeing perfectly clearly. Such was the accuracy of his hand that the knife was just pricking the pale man's row of medals. Felmar stood deathly still.

The old man spoke clear and proud. 'I'm not one to be tested, Felmar, and I do not intend to do you harm. I am merely using this-' He twitched the hand with the knife, making Felmar suck in his stomach.'-to emphasise my point, which is that this man is a guest in my house and a guest in our land. The first for as long as memory holds true. I do not think your masters would want you to treat him poorly and give a bad first impression.'

Gorman lowered the knife and Felmar spoke up, his voice uncertain as his eyes flicked to the knife.

'Maybe it would be best if you two, as people of the land, take him there. I'll be waiting for you in the high building. But old man,' he said scowling at Gorman, 'do not assume I'll forget your actions on this bridge.'

With that he turned and, with his men following, strode away towards the town.

'That went well,' Gorman chuckled.

Harl glanced at the knife in Gorman's hand. It had a strange blue hue to the blade and its angular design was unlike anything he'd seen, either in this world or his own. Gorman stowed the blade away unseen again before Harl could ask about it and took back his stick.

'Shall we proceed?' Gorman asked, sticking his elbow out. 'Your arm, my dear?'

Sonora let out a laugh as she took his seemingly frail arm and led him on.

'Grandpa, you're full of surprises,' she said, although to Harl it seemed as if she had expected a similar reaction.

He hesitated before following, unnerved.

Just who was Gorman?

Chapter 13

It is time to take action and implement my plan.

They reached the open gates to the town and as they passed under the great stone arch, Harl's breath was taken away.

The town was vast and imposing. Great spires jutted up in to the air and it seemed that instead of spreading outwards, they had built upwards. Moss covered the once pale stonework that had been cut and set long ago by skilled craftsmen. All around them carts, driven by large oxen, wheeled towards the bustling market place in the town's centre. Canvas-covered merchant stalls were packed into the central road through town, hemmed in on all sides by tall buildings. Harl was surprised to see so many food stalls, each selling a variety of produce that he had never seen before. He ran his eyes over the stalls packed with brightly-coloured fruits and his mouth watered at the prospect of tasting so many new flavours.

They stopped en route and Sonora spoke with one of the traders, handing over one of her potions as they talked. The man offered them some of the fruits and meats he had on his stall, smiling as he stowed the bottle in his coat. Gorman took two of the fruits and offered one to Harl. It was bright red and small enough to hold in his palm. When he bit into it, he cried out in surprise. It was juicy and soft, but the sweetness of it made him grin and slap Gorman on the back.

'Strawberries,' Gorman laughed, and then popped a whole one into his mouth.

As they moved on, Harl noticed people staring at him. At first it was just eyes flicking in his direction, but then people began to point at him and a murmur of conversation spread. A small boy even ran into a shop and dragged his mother outside, shouting, 'Look! Look! His hair's a funny colour.'

Excitement burned through the crowd like a wildfire. Soon a small band of children was trailing them through the market. One of them bumped into Gorman's stick and the blind man swatted at the child, causing the rest of them to scamper away.

Gorman placed his hand on Harl's arm. 'Come, it's time we made for the council tower.'

They walked a short way until they reached the bottom of the largest tower in the city. The clean marble structure stood white and imposing over the three of them, its sides decorated with god-shaped carvings. Two guards stood outside and, after a look at Harl, ushered them inside.

The foyer was dark and oppressive. The only light came from dull torches guttering on the wall opposite the door they had come in through. An arched door stood twenty paces in front of them, hemmed in on either side by two more ceremonial guards, their armour bedecked in jewels and gold plating. The room had carved wooden benches lining the sides, seating patient petitioners who stared at the three of them.

A thick warm breeze encased Harl as the door opposite opened. A greying man entered and hobbled over to them. His gold embroidered robe marked him out amongst the others in the room. He bowed to Sonora and then clasped Gorman's hand.

'Welcome, friends,' he said, smiling, and then turned to Harl. His eye studied Harl's face and then the gaze lifted to Harl's hair.

The old man nodded and signalled that Harl should walk with him. 'My name is Naldor. Forgive the haste of this greeting, but word of your arrival has scared many. The council will see you right away. Speak the truth and things will go well.'

Naldor led them into a round chamber lined with rows of benches that faced a large semi-circular table. Seated around the table staring at them were six wise-looking figures wearing robes, five men and one woman. There was an empty seventh seat and Naldor walked up to it and took his place.

Harl's eye was drawn to the central figure. The man's deep red robe was even more embroidered than Naldor's had been, although his long white beard covered most of the artistry. His eyes flicked form Harl's hair to Gorman, before looking hard again at Harl. When he spoke, his voice was croaky and full of wisdom.

'Harl Eriksson, I am Kelvar, High Councilman, and I've requested you here to answer questions relating to how you came to be placed upon this land and what reasons you have for being here.'

Harl had been over this many times with Gorman and Sonora and they had a solid story, even if it was comprised mostly of amnesia in Harl's case.

He explained how he had woken to find himself in the bed at Sonora and Gorman's house and had been unable to recall any of his previous life other than his name.

Gorman stepped forward at this point. 'I have noted his affinity with wood and metal. It seems obvious that he was once a smith or carpenter from the skill he has shown since waking.'

His words obviously impressed the leaders, because several nodded and made notes on the parchments in front of them.

Harl took a tentative step forward. 'I have no memory from before, council members, but I wish to live a useful life. If Master Gorman is correct, then I would gladly use whatever skill I possess to aid this community. I will respect your judgement in this matter and thank you for the honour of this meeting.'

He bowed and took a step back next to Sonora. She reached out and squeezed his hand.

'And you, Sonora?' Kelvar asked. 'You found him just lying in the forest after the great hand was seen coming down?'

Sonora let go of Harl's hand and took a small step forward. 'That is correct, your honour. He was unconscious and unarmed. I thought it best to bring him to my home where my skills could revive him. He had no memory when he woke and, as you can imagine, was scared to wake in an unknown place.'

The lone female at the table stood to be heard. Her eyes were keen but friendly as she addressed Sonora. 'What is your professional opinion of his recovery and eventual integration to our ways?'

Sonora seemed surprised at being asked such a question, but she soon regained her confidence, obviously pleased to answer.

'Other than the memory loss, he has made a full recovery already. I do not know if he will eventually come to remember his past, but I have seen no ill will from him and, as Gorman has said, his skills will come in most useful.'

Kelvar stood as the woman retook her seat.

'We will retire to discuss these matters. You will wait here until our return.'

Everyone at the table stood and headed out through a single door into another room, leaving the three of them alone.

'How do you think it went?' Harl asked Gorman.

The old man shrugged and whispered. 'I see no way for them to sense the lie in your words, but who can tell? Our story rings true. Let us hope for the best.'

Sonora brushed a hair from her face. Her eyes were clouded with concern. 'What would they do if they ruled against him, grandfather?'

'Hush, let us not think on such things for the moment,' Gorman said as the side door opened.

The council returned to the chamber and took their seats. Kelvar stayed standing.

'Harl Eriksson,' Kelvar said. 'Although this council finds your explanation unsatisfactory, it is by no means your own doing. If the gods have placed you here then it is just. We declare you may stay and not be put to trial for the unusual manner of your arrival. Thus you will be a citizen of this realm and are granted an acre of forest land adjoining that of master Gorman and mistress Sonora. You will be in their care until you are able to support yourself financially.'

Harl sighed in relief and turned to smile at Sonora. He hadn't known what to expect but, deep down, he had hoped more than anything that he would be able to stay close to her.

It seemed to him that the proceedings were at an end, when, unexpectedly, one of the council men on the outermost side of the table leant over and whispered to Kelvar. Harl had noticed the slim younger man looking more suspiciously at him than the others throughout the proceedings, but he'd thought little of it.

Kelvar frowned and shook his head. The younger man pointed his finger at the leader's chest, obviously making a strong point as his face became an angry red. Kelvar's shoulders slumped and he finally nodded.

'You are also commanded never to produce children,' Kelvar announced. He had gone pale as he said it. 'The gods have deemed your life worth sparing, but your appearance shows a taint that does not flow through the blood of our people. We'll not risk the wrath of the gods by letting you bear children with our people. Any breach of this order will have dire repercussions for all involved. That is all I have to say on the matter.' He smiled in pity, as if the worst was over. 'Go forth, Harl Eriksson, and live a life of peace and contribution among us.'

The leaders stood up and headed for the door, but as they did, the female councilwoman made a bee line for Sonora.

'Sonora,' she said, a look of concern on her aged face. 'We've been hearing reports of an illness which has sprung up in the commons part of town. The reports we've had from the guards say that Mrs Gillman has passed away soon after catching it. Her son, Mendle, allegedly caught it before her. He's in a bad state and being cared for by the rest of the family. She was elderly and it might be because of that that she succumbed to the illness first.' She paused letting her words sink in. 'Things are not looking good for her son. Another report this morning told how a third family member is ill as well.'

'What are the symptoms?' Sonora asked, worry evident on her face.

'A blackening of the hands is the first reported evidence that both Mrs Gillman and Mendle spoke of. The darkness spread up their arms to the chest and Mrs Gillman began to struggle for breath soon afterwards. She passed away shortly after that.'

'I'll look in on them when I can,' Sonora said, 'but you must tell those caring for Mendle to keep their mouths covered in close proximity to anyone who shows this blackness. I'll have something sent down from the cottage as soon as possible.'

'Thank you,' the council woman said, looking a little more relieved than at the beginning of the conversation. 'I just pray it doesn't spread to any more of the people. Our priests have been praying each turn since the news.'

Gorman coughed at this, holding back a remark. The woman shot him a frown for his lack of piety as she turned and headed for the door that led from the chamber.

'What was that all about?' Harl asked. 'It sounded serious.'

141

'I don't know,' Sonora said. 'These things come and go, but when we get home I'll be busy for the rest of the turn mixing something to help. I must admit I'm not keen to go and visit the Gillman's house.'

Harl had to agree. It sounded like a nasty disease, even if it only killed the old and feeble.

He turned to Gorman.

'Well,' he said, hoping to change the subject away from the disease. 'The trial went better than I thought. No prison this time, and I get some land.'

'Land is the most important part,' Sonora said. 'Only a true citizen owns land.'

'They would consider it a dereliction of duty to leave him homeless,' Gorman said with a sarcastic grin. 'If they had done so it could be construed as an affront to the gods on their part. My own annoyance is the decree made by that whelp Jarlen. Pah! No offspring? An unfair sentence, to be sure, and all because of their own prejudices against change. It'll all end badly.'

'Why?' Harl asked, worried by the old man's sudden foreboding.

'Well it stems from my own knowledge of something called diversity. I doubt the populous have noticed, but in the last generation many births had been defective or miscarried. The leaders are aware of it, I'm sure, but whether they truly understand it is another matter. Without a diverse population the people will sicken and die. The same happens with plants. Sow from the same family of seed generation after generation and your crop will eventually wither away and die. I would have thought that the council could relate the two, but that Jarlen and his beliefs of a "pure people" will bring about our downfall before too long.'

Harl thought about Gorman's words. It was worrying, but he knew similar problems during birth were happening back in his homeland.

He followed Gorman from the room, but turned back when he reached the doorway. It seemed that each world had a room like this where judgements were meted out. He just prayed that Gorman's people were wiser than his own.

Harl was glad for the bright light outside after the dark council chamber. It seemed that the judgement had spread to the town quickly. Instead of the lingering gazes that followed him and Sonora when they arrived, there were now accepting nods from the people they passed.

An old woman stopped Harl soon after he left the hall.

'I have pity for you, son. They should not have taken the gift of children from you.'

He thanked her and moved on, but not everyone was so friendly. More than once, voices were raised just loud enough for him to hear, even though the speakers never showed themselves. But they all boiled down to the same argument.

'What right has he to land? Who knows what crimes he's guilty of? Better to give it to us and let us bury him under it.'

But it was a young girl who silenced them. She ran up to Harl and gave him a bouquet of bright red flowers he had no name for.

'The god has graced us with you, Mr Harl. He has marked you special amongst us and it is a blessing.'

143

The three of them stopped briefly at a tavern when Gorman declared a sudden thirst. A quiet spread through the busy room when they entered, but conversation was soon a dull roar again as they made for the bar.

The barman saw them approach and slid a mug of ale to Harl. Harl took a sip and his eyes widened in surprise. The taste was better than Harken's finest, rich and fruitful.

'This, good barkeep, is probably the finest ale I've ever tasted.'

The barman slammed his palm down on the bar and roared with triumph. 'A man of taste. Hear that? The best, he says! The best! A keg of ale to you, sir, with my thanks. I'll see it delivered to your holdings, and let no one say Olger does not reward a kind word. Is there anywhere on the land to store the keg?'

'There is nothing on the land so far except trees and squirrels,' Harl said, tipping the mug to his lips.

'What,' Olger asked 'is a squirrel?'

Harl was caught off guard and didn't know how to explain. He was about to say it was a common creature but he was saved by Sonora's quick wit.

'It is a rare herb and is used for ulcers of the intimate area, Mr Olger. You wouldn't be needing any now, would you?'

Olger's face flushed bright red and he mumbled something before turning away to clean some already spotless glasses. The room exploded with laughter.

Chapter 14

I did it! Thousands captured and not a single one left behind. There are

so many inside the rectangular container that I will have to build more

tanks to avoid them dying from disease caused by the cramped conditions.

The next few cycles passed with a quiet comfort that Harl had never before known. He woke early each cycle and helped Sonora look after Gorman and gather plants, many of which he was starting to learn a lot about due to her careful teachings. The three of them got on well together and even Gorman had said the house felt livelier than it had before.

Harl would take pleasure from the simplest mundane tasks. Chopping the firewood gave him time to remember the warmth of sitting with Sonora and Gorman late into the dark cycle. Even feeding the small clutch of chickens that roamed the lush garden between the back of the house and first fringes of the wild wood felt like spending time with friends. He would talk to them and gave them all names. Sometimes they would gather around him, as if listening to his words, and the weight of life eased in their presence. It was all absurd, of course, and he would find himself laughing as he shared his secrets with them, but it made him feel good. He was at peace.

Having Sonora around only increased his contentment for what he now saw as a new and happy life. He hadn't thought about his parents since being placed here, and that, more than anything, made him happy. He was part of a new family.

He would sometimes find time hanging motionless around him while he watched Sonora working. The way she was so in harmony with the woodland, picking only enough herbs for her needs and singing as she strolled under bright canopy was mesmerising. Birds would flutter around her and the sound of her laughter was more refreshing than the coldest spring water. Her movements thrilled him – so graceful and gentle – and then she would steal his breath away with only a single glance or smile.

Gorman became more than a friend. His trust in the old man grew with each cycle. Gorman would sit, whittling away at a piece of wood with a small knife, while he told Harl of the world. His senses seemed more alive than anything Harl could imagine. When Harl had been chopping wood for the fire, Gorman had laughed and then walked over, taken the axe from him and split a stubborn log that Harl had been battling with.

'Follow the grain of the wood, Harl. Work with nature, not against it.'

But it was on the thirteenth cycle after the hearing that Gorman sat him down and asked him what he was planning to do with his new land.

'I hadn't thought much about it,' Harl said, 'I should probably go and have a look at it. Will you join me?'

A grin spread across Gorman's face.

'I'm sorry,' Harl said. 'I always forget that you can't see. I see you doing things around the house and you seem so aware of everything that your blindness escapes me.'

'It is nothing to be sorry about,' Gorman said, 'and I wouldn't mind a stroll under the cool of the trees. Who knows what trouble you might need me to get you out of?'

They set out, Harl leading the old man sure-footedly through the trees as Gorman waved his stick left and right ahead of him. It didn't take long to reach Harl's plot of land. It was not far from the cottage and the swathe of land had a bountiful look to it, even if it did back on to the imposing black barrier.

He hated the constant feeling of confinement, even if it was only on one side. He knew that if the wall was suddenly removed then his old friends and house would be a short stroll away. Just how was Troy getting along? if only he could let Troy know that he was alright. Imagining the look on Troy's face as he introduced Sonora, the blonde-haired beauty, was something that made him smile.

Gorman insisted on being guided around the entire plot of land. He tapped everything with his stick and ran his hands over rocks and tree trunks. They discussed building a house and digging a well, and the techniques they could employ in doing so. Although Gorman could not directly help, his knowledge of construction far outweighed that of Harl's. It was the same in all things, and it seemed to Harl that there was no end to the man's knowledge.

'There is a mystery to you, Gorman,' Harl said as they sat before the fire. Darkness had fallen outside and he could hear the first patter of rain on the roof. 'You know so much and your skills far outweigh those of most men, despite your blindness. How is that possible?'

Gorman's sightless gaze bored into the flames for a moment before he spoke.

'Most men are blind, Harl. They go through life oblivious to the world around them. I only open myself to it and absorb it all. In my youth I studied everything, books, the skills of a hunter, the tenderness of a healer. Everything in life is important. And now-.' He raised his hand and brushed his fingers against his eyes. '-with these sightless eyes, my other senses reach out and take control. I can hear the tread of a footfall before any other man; I smell the individual spices in a meal as if they were arranged on the table before me. Never ignore what's around you, my lad. It's all important.'

Harl threw a new log on the fire and watched sparks flare up the chimney.

'It just seems so impossible to learn it all.'

Gorman nodded and patted Harl's arm.

'I will teach you what I can, lad, but I fear we may not have enough time.'

Gorman's words troubled Harl. He lay awake long into that dark cycle worrying what the old man had meant. What had he seen that others had not?

A few cycles later, Gorman returned Harl's bow and arrows.

'I can't say how glad I am to have it back,' said Harl. 'It's the only thing left to remind me of home.'

'It's a fine bow,' said Gorman, as he ran his fingers over the cool metal, 'I've rarely felt one of better quality.'

Gorman laid the bow on the floor and slid a knife out from behind his back. Harl stared at it and marvelled at the strange workmanship. It was the same knife that Gorman had used to challenge Felmar. The blade was the length of Harl's hand from wrist to fingertips and its metal shone a pale silver-blue in the firelight. He had no idea what metal it was forged from, but the skill with which it had been crafted was that of a master. Even his father could not have made something so perfect. He watched it gleam in Gorman's fingers as the old man rotated it in the firelight.

'Isn't that the knife you used against Felmar?' Harl said at last. 'Did you receive it from a gifting?'

Gorman shook his head slowly.

'No, not from a gifting, but it was, indeed, a gift. My father's father gave it to me. A family heirloom, you might say. It is made from a metal unlike any found in the world, or this world at least.'

Gorman handed it to him hilt first. The handle was bound not in leather, but a hard substance that sounded hollow when he tapped it, and was moulded to his fingers so that it fitted snugly in his grip. A small red button was set where the thumb could rest on it. Harl tested the knife's edge with his thumb and gasped as it instantly drew blood.

'Yes, it's sharp indeed,' laughed Gorman, 'and I've never needed to hone it. Not once. But there is more to it than seen at first glance. Pass me the knife and the ceramic bowl I used for my stew.'

Harl passed them over and Gorman clasped the knife so that his thumb touched the red button on the back of the handle. The knife emitted a slight droning noise that startled Harl.

'Fear it not,' Gorman said, 'but watch closely.'

He held the knife above the bowl and moved it downwards slowly. Before the knife made full contact, the bowl melted and split before Harl's eyes as Gorman moved the knife down. Soon it had cut right through the bowl and scorched the table underneath. Harl sat and stared in wonder at the man and the knife.

'It's unique,' said Gorman. 'Nowhere else have I seen such cutting power.'

An idea flooded Harl's mind.

'Will it cut the barrier?'

Gorman sat back.

'Yes and no,' he said. 'It will cut through the glass, sure enough, but it's not long enough to reach right through. I tried in my youth to my folly. The marks were found and an investigation held. No one except my family knew of the blade and so it was hushed up over time.' He put the knife in his pocket. 'Harl, I know why you are so keen to be free. I have been in the same situation myself. But let me tell you there is much more for you to learn. I will tell you all I know when I can, but first I want you to build the house for yourself before you continue this line of thought. It pays to keep up appearances.'

Gorman rose from his chair and walked towards his bedroom door.

'There are always eyes on us, Harl, remember that. Time is not with us, but we must be patient.'

Harl sat alone with his thoughts until the fire had dwindled to a few remaining embers of light. For the first time in many cycles he was afraid.

Chapter 15

I have built several more containers and have begun to divide the creatures into each. Now I must return to where I found them and continue to scour the area for the things they brought with them.

His bond with Sonora grew stronger each cycle. She was consumed by her work and spent all of her time brewing potions to take into town and help those close to the sick families. She never seemed to tire from it, but with all her work, and no matter how tired she was, she still found time for Gorman. And Harl seemed to be a part of that world now. They would sit together in the evenings laughing and telling tales, stealing glances at each other in the firelight. Gorman would sit there as well, a contented smile on his face as he listened to them, but Harl had no idea what the old man was thinking.

The cycles passed and they walked often among the trees and grasses discussing life in all the worlds around them. They would talk endlessly of the people inside each one, attempting to guess how many there were and what the differences would be. What would the people look like? How would the buildings differ? But what caught Harl's imagination was the worlds themselves. What strange landscapes would there be? Would they all be the same size, or would some be vast expanses where you could walk for cycle upon cycle without reaching the barriers? Sonora laughed at his wild imaginings, but he could see the excitement in her eyes at the thought of it.

Harl had started building his own house. He cleared trees and dug a well hole with the help of some local lads, rewarding them with a tankard of Olger's ale at the end of each cycle. The house took shape quickly with all the help and, within a few dozen cycles, it was almost complete. One cycle a cartload of stone came rumbling up from the town, pulled by four stout oxen led by a jolly man. The cart was soon offloaded and stored despite Harl's objecting and saying he hadn't ordered it. The man just laughed and then puffed up his chest and announced that the stone blocks were of the finest quality as specified in the order. Dozens of red roof tiles were carted up next, along with two skilled labourers who set about the task of fitting them immediately. Gorman had paid for all of it, of course, but when Harl had begged to pay him back Gorman just waved him away with a smile and said, 'You already have my lad. You already have.'

Harl spent most of his time building the spacious workshop attached to the side of the house where he would establish a new forge in the hopes of paying Gorman back for his generosity, despite what the old man said.

When that was finished, he spent his time recreating an exact replica of the bench he had made to honour his parents. This time he did not place it facing Sightwards but instead towards the opening of the valley far below the hills.

The next cycle after lunch he stepped from his home and found Sonora sitting on the bench waiting for him. At first he thought something was wrong, but the smile on her face told him otherwise. The cycle was as bright as ever and a cool breeze brought the sounds of animals deeper in the forest.

'It's wonderful, Harl,' she said running her fingers across the deep grooves in the wood.

'Thank you,' Harl said and meant it. He was immensely pleased that she liked it so much. He moved over and sat next to her as she turned on the seat to admire the faces carved on the back rest.

'Your parents?'

'Yes,' Harl said.

'Are they back in your own land?'

'No. They were lifted by god.'

'I'm so sorry, Harl,' she said, lowering her head onto his shoulder.

'It was a long time ago,' he said, 'and I was only a child. I argued with them over some trivial point and ran off. I obviously couldn't go far, but they came after me and as they were calling for me, the hand of God came and snatched them away.'

'It must have been dreadful,' she said.

'What about your own family?' Harl asked.

'There was just me and my parents,' she said. 'No brothers or sisters. My mother was taken when I was small and my father died soon after from an illness which had afflicted him throughout his life.'

Harl felt for her. At least he had memories of his parents, enough to remember their faces.

'Without my mother making her cures for him, he was unable to keep going,' she whispered.

'And how does Gorman come into it all?'

'He was close to my grandmother when she was the council's head healer for the town. My grandmother was still alive when my mother was taken and it was Gorman and she who looked after me when my father became too ill to do it. When she passed, Gorman took care of me.' She paused, clearly thinking of those she had lost. 'I owe him so much.'

Harl didn't want her to think too much on it, knowing how self-destructive it could be.

'Where does all his knowledge come from?' he asked.

'I really don't know,' Sonora said. 'He's always been knowledgeable, although it was only when his sight went that he fully revealed that side of himself. I am sure there is much he doesn't say.'

'He keeps things from you?'

'Maybe,' she said. 'Not in a malicious way, I am sure. But if he keeps things to himself then perhaps it is for the better. He is a good man.'

'I think we should ask him,' Harl said. 'I feel like there is something he is keeping back, but I am ready to accept his judgement on whether to reveal what he knows.'

They talked about how to ask the old man to tell them what he knew and only when the light went out signalling the end of the cycle did they realize how much time had passed.

'It's time we went back,' Harl said, wondering how they were to navigate through the deep darkness and wishing he had Gorman's talents.

Harl threaded his way through the dark woodland, Sonora's hand clutched in his own. But there seemed to be a storm brewing. He didn't know why. Perhaps it was that life seemed so perfect at the moment? Something like that couldn't last forever; everything withered and died in the end. But there was a growing uneasiness in the back of his mind over the last few cycles and he had to get to the bottom of it. He had a feeling that Gorman was as the heart of it.

If only he knew what the old man was hiding.

Harl knocked on Gorman's bedroom door to announce their return. The fire was crackling in the hearth to cast the only light across the room. A heaviness filled the air as though a thousand ears were straining to hear what came next.

When the old man opened the door and shuffled into the room, he looked tired, as if he had been waiting patiently all cycle for them to come home while dark thoughts weighed on his mind.

He looked at them knowingly once Harl had asked the question.

'I have wondered how long it would be before you came to me asking this,' he said. 'I will tell you what I know. Much of it I have been told by others, but a lot of what follows are the thoughts that have plagued me through the darkness of my life.'

He sat as usual in his chair by the fire and leaned back. His face darkened in the flickering light.

'Firstly, I know that life has not always been this way. How it was before I cannot say, but I do know there was a time when the people knew much more than they do now.'

He pulled the small knife from his tunic and toyed idly with it in one hand, rolling it expertly across his knuckles.

'The tools and weapons humans used in the past were more potent than any now in existence, maybe with the exception of my knife. I believe that the gods, as we think of them, are nothing but a different race, such as we are from the cows or the goats. They ensnared us using their greater strength and cunning and imprisoned us in these worlds. Also, as you now know for certain, the world is bigger than anyone realises. I remember Harl, that you spoke to me of a group of strangers placed in your own land who died within a short space of time from unknown respiratory problems.'

'The tale of the three men, yes,' Harl said, eager for more information.

'Since you have come,' Gorman continued, 'much has been revealed to me. I believe these strangers came from outside all the worlds you saw out in the vision. I think they may even have come from further than the vision.'

He took out a small flask from his robe, unscrewed the top and took a swig before continuing.

'For where do the gods go at the end of the cycle? To their own world is my guess, whether or not they themselves are trapped in a cube, I know not. I am not a philosopher or priest and cannot fathom as much as that.'

Harl was trying to take in what the old man was saying and leaned forward in his chair to focus on Gorman's words.

Gorman paused for a long time before continuing.

'There is a world beyond the vision, one that is as for the gods as our own world is to us. In that land there once dwelt an advanced tribe of people. They created works of intricate skill that none alive can now reproduce. My knife is an example of such work, although I am sure they made objects far more complex than a simple blade. They are not trapped by the constraints of barriers and walls as we are here and it is my guess that the strangers you spoke of came from those people. Why they died is another matter, but from what you told of your own experience within the vision, I would hazard a guess that the air is poisonous and deadly after a short time. I can deduce then that the wild folk have adapted to that air, just as we have adapted to ours within the barriers, and to force a person from one realm to breathe the air from the other would mean eventual death. Seeing as you suffered no ill effect coming into our land, I believe all the cube worlds contain the same air to a similar degree.'

Harl was so overwhelmed by this information and the guesses that the old man presented, that he wasn't able to respond right away. But he longed to test the theories. He felt even more trapped than before. Did people really exist beyond the Sight?

Gorman must have sensed his thoughts and frowned. 'It is only a guess, mind you, and I cannot confirm any of it. Venturing outside without precautions would be unwise, Harl.'

Sonora spoke up at this. 'I too feel the longing grandpa, at least to see further than the vision's end on the other side of the barrier.'

'Of course, my dear,' Gorman continued. 'You've been adventurous as long as I have known you and wandered the forests every turn, even as a child. But I ask both of you to delay such thoughts for the moment. I fear the time may soon come when no choice is left but to try.'

With that he broke off the talk and sat in his own thoughts for a time.

'Has it anything to do with the blacking illness that I have seen in the town?' Sonora asked eventually.

'It does,' Gorman said, shifting in his seat, 'but the first case was reported many cycles ago, so I think time is on our side. He took another swig from his bottle and sat back. 'I spoke with one of the roofers at your new place Harl, and at least two of the other men had not come into work that cycle. I did some investigating among the other workers and they all confirmed that the disease has spread among the farmers of the valley. Specifically those who worked the fields, pulling weeds and such, and that it started in their hands. The tips would blacken and the discolouration would spread up their arms, then their close family members would contract it.'

'I have heard the same,' Sonora said. 'Mendle passed away ten cycles ago and he was a healthy man to start with. Now his brother has come down with it.'

'How go things down in the town?' Gorman asked.

'People are starting to realize this illness might stick around unless serious action is taken,' she said, 'and I haven't seen the council doing anything to try and stop it.'

'And the guards?' Gorman asked. 'I heard from the workers that Felmar has been causing you trouble.'

'Yes,' Sonora admitted. 'He's approached me twice now, both times while drunk and boasting of his bedroom exploits.'

Harl didn't like where this could all lead.

'I don't think it is safe for you to go into town at the moment,' Gorman said, obviously sharing Harl's concern.

'What about my potions?' she asked. 'The people need them.'

'Have one of the letter boys take them,' he said. 'It may cost a bit more, but it will save a lot of trouble as things worsen in the town. Both of you must stay out of there as much as you can. We have everything we need for a few turns and with Felmar stumbling around tanked up on Olger's brew, things will be dangerous in town. Harl, will you go hunting next cycle? Sonora, you go with him. Afterwards you must both scout the town and farms to see what is happening. Have a look from a distance and keep away from anyone you might see. We need to know how fast the disease is spreading. Then we can better guess how much time we have left.'

Sonora shifted in her seat. 'What happens when we run out of time Grandpa?'

'Then the tank will turn on itself and we'll have to run to escape the chaos.'

Chapter 16

I have begun to categorize the lesser creatures I found living alongside them. It seems that like the jig weevil they have developed a crude form of husbandry.

Harl held the arrow fully drawn on the bow, the tension in his arms threatening to give way as he made tiny adjustments to the angle. The deer crept into sight again, its ears twitching for suspicious sounds. They had tracked it through the forest and it was only by Sonora's skill that they had not spooked it. She had suggested a path to cut through the trees that intersected perfectly with where the deer now cropped at the lush grass.

He released the arrow and watched as the deer toppled sideways, the arrow lodged deep in its head.

Sonora let out a cry of triumph, hunching low as she slipped past Harl into the clearing and knelt beside the crumpled animal, pulling a knife from her belt.

'A clean kill,' she said, tucking the knife away, obviously pleased she did not have to finish it off. She tugged the arrow free and inspected the head before handing it to Harl.

'I couldn't have done it without you,' Harl said, looping the bow over his shoulder as he bent to pick up the carcass. He slung the heavy load over his other shoulder and walked back through the woods.

Gorman had sent them out to hunt knowing that it would save Sonora a trip into town to buy food and supplies. Harl's own work had dried up due to the lack of farmers tending the fields. Whatever had happened, he did not want to go down to find out.

They headed for a spot just on the edge of the forest that overlooked the rolling fields around the town. Harl placed the deer on the ground and stood shoulder-to-shoulder with Sonora as she stared down across the calm river. Something was out of place, but he couldn't put his finger on it.

'There is no one in the fields,' Sonora said.

She was right. Usually the fields around the town were a bustle of workers and oxen, but he couldn't see anyone weeding, ploughing, or gathering in the over-ripe harvest.

'No guards at the gate either,' he said, shielding his eyes from the light as he peered towards the end of the bridge where it ended by the gates.

They could still see a scattering of people moving around below, but compared to forty cycles ago it was desolate. Tall weeds sprouted above the neat rows of plants and the water mills along the river bank stood still.

The fear of going down into town to find out the truth knotted his stomach. When he didn't think of the disease, life up in the forest was idyllic. But when he thought about town and the disease festering in the streets he just shivered all over. He wished the three of them could survive up here alone forever, but he knew in his heart that they would have to deal with town in the end.

They reached the cottage just as the light above the world cut out. Harl opened the door to let Sonora pass and light the candles. He squeezed through sideways to avoid knocking the deer on the door frame and used his foot to close the door.

'Any luck?' Gorman asked from his chair by the fireplace.

'Yes,' Harl said, slinging the deer on the stone floor. 'But it was difficult. The fields around town are completely deserted, but we did spot a few people in the streets.'

'I meant for dinner,' Gorman said, chuckling to himself. 'But I can smell something. What is that?'

'A deer, grandpa,' Sonora said as she finished the candles and sagged into a chair.

'Well done, both of you,' Gorman said, raising his flask in tribute and taking a long swig. 'Start a stew going, my child, and we'll talk about what you saw down in the valley.'

Sonora smiled, but it failed to cover up the tiredness in her blue eyes. She rose and headed for the kitchen counter as Harl grabbed a handful of vegetables from a bucket in the pantry and began chopping.

Gorman sat in silence after the meal. When their tale had finished, he had walked over to his fireside chair and slumped into it, his face clouded with worry. Sonora was clearing empty plates from the table and kept glancing at Harl in concern as Gorman's silence continued.

'Gorman?' Harl asked.

The old man sighed. 'I'm sorry, my lad. I didn't realise that the disease had grown as bad as that. It has shaken me.'

Without saying a word, Harl and Sonora moved over to sit down next to him.

'The time for action is nearing,' he said, 'but I must ask a favour of you both. It is essential that you make one final trip into town before the rule of law breaks down and looting begins, if it hasn't already. You must take the cart and bring back all the supplies you can. Don't let anyone know what you're doing. We will need food and equipment for what we must do. Purchase sturdy clothing and satchels to carry what you need if you must leave.'

'But,' interrupted Harl, 'we have no way to escape. We've talked for many cycles about it. There's no way to leave this damned prison.'

Harl slumped back in his chair and pulled his knees up under his chin. Just waiting to be struck ill by the blackness chilled him to the bone, but the thought of watching Sonora and Gorman blacken and die from the sickness... He had to clench his fists to stop them from trembling.

Gorman must have heard the strain in his voice.

'Don't worry, my lad,' he said. 'I have a plan, but first you must find the supplies.' He leant forward in the chair. 'This blacking disease will be the end of our world. There is no fighting it. But men's souls will blacken long before their bodies. In the final days people will turn to dark deeds.'

Sonora looked as worried as Harl felt. He moved his hand into hers and she gripped him back tightly.

'Take what you need from my valuables,' Gorman said. 'The trade prices will be excessive, I'm sure, but it will not matter any more.'

'We'll leave early,' Harl said.

Gorman leant back into his chair and closed his eyes. Harl had never seen him look so old and frail. The old man turned towards the window and opened his eyes to gaze sightlessly out into the dark.

'We are racing death, Harl, and I fear we have already lost.'

Chapter 17

I've collected the flora they seem to use and have started to create a compendium of the various species and sub species.

The gates to the town were sealed shut as Sonora and Harl crossed the long stone bridge that led up to them. Black smoke lingered above the houses from a recent fire. It felt like a grim shadow of the disease creeping over the streets. A single thin-looking guard eyed them suspiciously as they stopped the squeaking cart in front of him.

'Why are the gates closed?' Sonora asked.

'Orders,' the young soldier said. He opened his mouth as if ready to recite a mantra.

'Well open them up,' she said, cutting him off. 'People inside will need healing.'

'I'll 'ave to speak with the 'igh ups and get permission to—'

Sonora took a quick pace forward, startling the man. He stumbled backwards, rattling the wooden gates when he collided with them.

'Open these doors,' she said, standing over him and poking a gloved finger against his chest. 'Or you and those closest to you will be last on the list for medicine should they be struck down.'

Her words had an instant effect on the man and he clasped the iron ring set in the door and tugged it open.

'S-sorry, miss. It's just things 'ere 'ave been bad. I meant nothing by it.'

'Bad how?' Harl asked. He eased the hand cart down and rubbed his back.

The guard shook his head.

'Grim. I've not seen the like before. People are turning on each other or refusing to 'elp.'

'It can't be that bad, surely,' Sonora murmured. 'These people are friends and neighbours.'

The guard shook his head.

'Not acting like neighbours no more. Fear clouds the mind, miss. I've seen friends murder each other out of fear. I guess when a man's back is against the wall, there ain't no telling what 'e'll do.'

He turned to Harl and slashed a finger across his throat, then shrugged. 'But I've not seen it this bad. People is scared, miss. Scared. There's not much can fix that.'

'And the smoke?' Harl asked.

The guard shifted uneasily.

'Bodies,' he said. 'Too many to bury. Glad I got outside duty. The smell don't travel through the wall.'

When they passed the gate, Harl was shocked at the quiet that had been cast over the streets. A few stalls were open for trade, displaying a meagre mix of supplies, but of the people he could see, most were wrapped in layers of clothing as if to hide their features underneath. The stench was as bad as the man had said, a rancid, festering taint that assaulted the nostrils. He attempted to pull his coat collar up over his mouth and nose, but gave up, accepting the foul odour with a grimace. Carts stacked with bodies lay abandoned at the side of the road. Flies were crawling over them in a black shifting mass. Some people were slumped against the sides of buildings as though their strength had left them, while their neighbours hurried past ignoring their pleas for help. One of the figures rose on unsteady legs and staggered her way towards Harl and Sonora.

'Elaine?' Sonora asked as the ragged woman approached. The old lady's legs gave way and Sonora swept in to support her.

Harl almost pulled Sonora back when he saw the woman's headwrap slip. Dark, shadowed lines streaked her craggy skin as if slowly engulfing her face.

She saw Harl's look of shock and grabbed at the dirty shawl, drawing it tight about her face.

'Have you anything to help?' she asked, glancing hopefully at Sonora then at the satchel which usually carried Sonora's potions.

'I only have something to ease the pain,' Sonora said.

Elaine burst into a fit of phlegmy coughs. Her blackened fingers balled into a fist and a splatter of crimson flecked the dark skin.

'Can you wait until we come back?' Sonora said, once the hacking cough had passed. 'We won't be long. Meet us here on our way out.'

Elaine nodded and shuffled back towards the spot against the house wall, where she slumped down once more onto a jumble of ragged cloth scraps.

'This is dreadful,' Sonora said as they headed across to one of the remaining market stalls.

They passed two men arguing over a small sack of food. One of the men had drawn a knife, shielding it from view and keeping an eye out for the guards while he forced the other man to hand over the bag.

Harl touched a gloved finger to his belt, feeling for his own knife, glad that he had brought it with him. His bow was a visual deterrent on his shoulder, but at close range it would be useless against a determined attacker.

'I don't think we should stop for long,' he said. 'These people are afraid and hungry.'

She nodded her agreement as they walked along glancing left and right searching for potential trouble.

Two guards flanked the small stall midway along Market Road. Both men toyed with the pommels of their sword as a reminder to anyone passing by that the price of theft would be blood. They stilled as Harl and Sonora approached, wary of an armed man, but when the stall owner spotted Sonora he beamed at her and the soldiers' stares drifted back to passers-by.

'Sonora and Mr Eriksson,' the owner said, beckoning them over. 'Don't worry about the guards. It's just that people are a little unstable at the moment.'

The man hesitated on the last words. What had been happening in the town while they were safe up in the woods? The last time he'd seen the merchant, he'd been more than tubby, a bulky man richly appointed in the finest clothing, but now his fur coat was slack on thinning shoulders.

'What's been happening, Sanda?' Sonora asked.

The expression on Sanda's gaunt face dropped.

'Chaos. Things were fine ten turns ago, but now...' He gestured with his hand at the empty stalls on either side of his own. 'It got real bad when the food stopped coming after the farmers started tending their sick families rather than their crops. Prices have been rising ever since. The few who are still healthy are protesting outside the council chambers as we speak. I guess I'm lucky in that I've no family of my own.' He looked down and patted his flattened belly. 'But I've seen better. Now tell me, what do you need from my scarce goods?'

'We have quite a list,' Sonora said as she handed a small piece of parchment over to the man.

'Looks like you're preparing to hole up for a while,' Sanda said, running his gaze down the scribbled list.

'We know you probably can't get everything on there,' Harl said, 'but anything you do have would be a big help.'

'Forgive my asking,' Sanda said, reddening, 'but have you much for payment?'

'Here,' Sonora said, opening her satchel to reveal the gleaming contents inside.

Sanda peeked in and perked up, rubbing his hands together.

'I think I can get everything on the list,' he said. 'If you give me some time, I can speak to the other sellers for you and have everything ready for your return.'

'Thank you,' Sonora said. 'We'll head for the council tower and see if we can find out what the leaders plan to do about all of this. Then we'll return.'

'Be careful,' one of the heavies said. 'The guards have turned nasty since the protests started.'

Harl nodded his thanks and caught Sonora's look. Worry lines had appeared in her smooth complexion. What toll things were having on her? Could he watch her wither from worry as the world around her broke down? He had already been outside and he knew first hand that it was possible to leave a world behind. If they couldn't fix things soon it would break both of them.

Perhaps leaving was the only choice left?

Chapter 18

It is all about the correct air ratio. They respond best to a selective oxygen level far different from our own. It is similar to the higher mountain peaks, but I should be able to emulate it.

They visited houses en route to the council tower only to find homes packed with the sick and dying. Sonora handed out potions from her satchel to those who she knew best and any with children. She gathered as much information as she could. Scarcity was everywhere, food being the hardest to come by, mostly due to people hoarding; but no one knew what the cause of the disease was and everyone hoped the council would sort it out soon.

A dull roar grew in to angry shouts as they neared the tall marble tower where the council presided.

Clustered around the imposing white building were dozens of figures pleading for help. Some of the people shouted at the two guards who stood silent and stone-faced by the entrance, barring the door with crossed spears. Others were forced to disperse by the guards patrolling outside, but by the time the guards had come full circle around the tower, the groups had returned.

'I don't like the look of this,' Harl said. 'We should leave before things get out of contr-.'

'Sonora!'

Harl spun around at the voice to find Elaine, the sick woman they had met coming in to town, stumbling towards them. She tripped and collapsed to her knees, coughing blood onto the cobblestones as a fit of couching wracked her.

The crowd washed back from her like an outgoing tide, leaving a space around the helpless woman.

She stretched a frail, blackened hand up to Sonora.

'The medicine-' she croaked.

Sonora dug a hand into her bag and pulled out a vial. As she began to rush forward Harl seized her arm and she froze.

Dozens of faces had turned towards them and, like a gold coin in a street of beggars, their eyes locked on to the healer. The crowd surged forwards, stumbling over each other in their haste to reach Sonora. Elaine was trampled under the feet of the more energetic, who shoved their way towards them, scrambling past each other as they demanded the potions.

Harl tried to slide the bow off his shoulder, but it caught on his jacket, so he reached for the knife in his belt instead.

A coal-black hand raked Sonora's dress, clasping the thin material and spinning her around. Harl grabbed the fingers and yanked them away, glad he'd brought gloves.

'Please can you help?'

'My daughter...'

'My family...'

Sonora rummaged in her bag and pulled out potions as fast as possible. They were snatched before she could hand them over as hands pawed the bag's opening. She strained to pull the satchel back as the straps became taught, threatening to split and scatter Gorman's valuables into the crowd.

'It is not a cure!' Sonora cried above the pleading crowd as she and Harl were crushed in on all sides by desperate faces, some blackening with the disease under their ragged hoods.

When she had no more potions to give out the crowd still clawed at the bag. The stitches began to tear. Harl grabbed Sonora by the hand and pushed his way through the crowd, desperately shoving people aside as he made for the nearest guard.

A huge man, a head taller than Harl, blocked his path and glared down at him. The man's face was streaked with jagged black lines. There were thin streaks within the man's eyeball, as if the blood vessels inside pumped black instead of red.

'The bag,' the man growled.

Fear clutched Harl, but with Sonora in danger he reacted. He tensed and jabbed a fist into the man's stomach, doubling him over, before smashing an elbow into his face. The man crumpled to the cobblestones.

Harl stepped back, hoping, desperately, that the sickness wouldn't pass through his sleeve.

A sharp ringing of steel made the people closest to them stop pawing and grabbing at Sonora. The guard had spotted their predicament and had drawn his sword.

'Get back!' he shouted.

When only a few took notice and stopped, the guard strode forward and held his blade straight out at the crowd, giving Harl and Sonora a chance to break away. The big man had got to his feet and barged forward to the front. He scowled at Harl as if ready to rush him.

'Get back, Holden,' the guard said, wide-eyed as he swung his sword left and right.

A group of guards stormed out from between two nearby buildings and rushed over to aid the lone soldier.

Harl kept hold of Sonora's hand as they broke for freedom and ran back across town to the stall, leaving the guards behind trying to quell the mob.

'That was too close,' Harl said, seeing their cart loaded and waiting for them beside the merchant and his bodyguards up ahead.

'They're just desperate,' Sonora said. 'The council should be out there explaining the situation and fixing the issues. Instead they hide inside their tower behind armed guards.'

'They're more than desperate,' Harl said, angry that she had ignored the danger in her belief that everyone there was innocent.

'If it was me needing the medicine,' she said, 'then I hope you'd try to get some.'

'You know I would,' he said, 'but the only medicine for that back there was to get you as far away as possible before they tore you to shreds.'

She shook her head. 'I'm sorry, it's just hard to see people who once carried each others groceries home from market now trample each other to the dirt. These are not the same people.'

'It's all there,' Sanda said, as they came within earshot of his wooden stall. He tugged back a roll of thick cotton on top of the cart to reveal a jumble of supplies underneath. 'I'll throw in the cloth for free. But best keep it all covered until you're out of town.'

Sonora handed Sanda the satchel containing the payment and his smile widened as he poured the contents into a steel box beneath the stall.

'Take care,' the merchant said. 'Would you like one of my guards to see you to the gate?'

'You've done enough already, thank you.' Harl said as he gripped the cart's handles and heaved it towards the gate.

'Grandpa will be so pleased we got it all,' Sonora said when the stall was behind them.

Harl was glad they were on their way out. He grimaced against the weight and heaved the cart forward. If they survived the coming days it would be a long time before he came down from the forest again. The town sickened him.

A slur of raised voices came from between two houses on their left. Felmar and a group of guards stumbled out from an ally. Harl groaned at the sight. The men were staggering into each other, holding bottles and laughing among themselves as they tottered down the road oblivious to Harl and Sonora coming in the opposite direction. Harl kept his head down as they passed and pushed the cart ahead as he silently cursed the squeaking wheel.

'Should 'ave seen his face,' one said, waving a bottle at the others, 'when I told him his pretty wife deserved a real man.

Maybe I should go back an' make the point clearer.' He looked at Felmar, but the captain shook his head.

'Leave 'em be,' Felmar said. 'They'll all get what they deserve.' He lobbed his empty bottle over one shoulder and, as it smashed down on the cobblestones, he swiped a half-full one from a fat guard beside him.

'Hey,' the man said, but Felmar just glared at him.

The group paid them little attention and Harl thought they would slip past unnoticed, but then the fattest of the soldiers caught sight of Sonora.

'She's a pretty one,' he said, his neck craning round as they passed to keep Sonora fixed in his gaze.

'Hang on,' Felmar said. Their staggering footsteps faltered then stopped. 'Well, if it ain't pretty little miss Sonora!'

Harl's heart sank. He knew Sonora had been dreading any confrontation with Felmar and, worst of all, he was drunk and out to impress his cronies.

'Well, lads. Look at the dainty little lady. Would you-' He took a swig from his bottle, '-like us to handle your wares?'

His mates roared with laughter as they swung into a loose half-circle around Harl and Sonora.

Felmar staggered a bit and then drew himself up and saluted.

'And what,' he asked,' has brought the witch and her outlander down into town?'

The four men around them chuckled.

Harl bent and let go of the cart's handles. He stepped around the cart and placed himself between Felmar and Sonora. Felmar swayed backwards a little as Harl came closer, but his cronies

180

moved in a step, unwilling to see their leader cowed. Felmar took a pace forward and smiled.

'We're just here for supplies,' Harl said, indicating the cart with one hand, 'and to give out potions to help your people Felmar. The ones you're meant to be protecting.'

'We don't need your help,' Felmar snapped and then spat on the floor. 'Your potions don't work, witch. I've lost men to this plague. I've lost others to those rioting filth. They deserve to die. You only cause trouble. I wouldn't be surprised if you started the illness. What poisons do you peddle? Eh? You know what we do with witches, don't you? We burns them.'

Harl was surprised that he managed not to slur any of his words.

'We've no wish to stay, Felmar,' Sonora said. 'All we want is to be on our way.'

Felmar laughed. 'Not until you've handed over them supplies, witch. Me and the lads, well, we have ideas about getting out of here, and that little stash would come in handy.' He turned to his men and waved one hand towards Sonora. 'And I have a fancy to take you too. We could do with some... entertainment.'

The group roared with laughter.

The fat guard grinned and staggered forward to take the cart, but Harl shoved a palm into the man's pudgy belly and he teetered backwards.

The other men started forward.

Harl let the bow slide off his shoulder, grabbed it in his hand, and drew an arrow from his quiver with the other. He nocked the

181

arrow and drew the string back taught. The arrow's tip wobbled as Felmar's head swayed from side to side, taking in the threat.

'The supplies are ours, Felmar,' Harl said.

Felmar's gaze traced along the arrow as he snarled through gritted teeth. He waved his men aside and then took an unsteady step back.

Harl moved toward the gate, keeping the bow aimed at Felmar. 'Bring the cart, Sonora.'

She grabbed the handles and heaved it towards the open gates. Harl didn't turn his back on the group and kept the bow raised as they reached the gate and walked out onto the bridge. When he was out of range, he sighed and lowered the bow.

Felmar stood in the centre of the gateway. He took another swig from the bottle then threw it against the wall and spat on the floor.

As Harl turned away his heart sank.

Felmar was smiling.

Chapter 19

The squeaking roar from the container is constant as the creatures shout at me. I watched as they attempted to climb over each other to escape, some dying in the press. I will build a roof over the top and separate them into categories. More containers will be needed.

'The plan?' Harl asked as he dragged a coil of rope from the cart.

They had reached home without further incident and parked the cart just outside the front door. He had been constantly checking behind them on the way back from town, but neither Felmar nor his men had followed.

Harl could feel the cycle drawing near to the dark switch. Most of the supplies they had returned with were unloaded and stacked inside, but he wanted to get everything done before dark. He had no wish to be outside if anyone came creeping around. Better to shut the world - and Felmar - away and let the light bring fresh hope. He frowned. Hope seemed in short supply at the moment.

Gorman wiped a trickle of sweat from his brow and turned ready to take the next piece of equipment.

'And why so much rope?' Harl asked as he handed him a second and third coil.

'I'd hoped there would be more time to explain,' Gorman said, stacking the rope in a pile. 'But you need to make haste. There are some items I have kept safe that you will need. Come, I will show you.'

He walked inside and led them both into his room.

It was the first time Harl had seen inside Gorman's bedroom and he felt like an intruder in the old man's private quarters. Neatly stacked sets of identical clothing lay on top of an ornate dresser to one side of a four-poster bed. Pinned to the wall opposite the only window was a large piece of tattered parchment with a crude circular diagram in its centre. The majority was coloured blue, but there were green and brown splotches all over it, as if drawn with no apparent design in mind. They looked like nothing more than splatters of thick mud against the Sight.

A row of chest-high shelves supported a neat collection of rocks and small stones. Harl had seen most of them from his time in the quarry, but a single large piece caught his eye. It was the size of his fist and completely see-through, like glass or a diamond. Surely it couldn't be an actual diamond? There was nothing he could think of that could be that size and transparent except... Could it be a piece of the barrier, the one which Gorman had cut as a boy?

He looked out the window hoping to see the Sight, but saw only the thick woodland beyond. He lowered his eyes, disappointed, but then smiled in surprise. Perched on the windowsill was a tiny tree. Minute leaves clung to the gnarled branches and delicate white flowers shone like diamonds against the dark foliage. It was rooted in a shallow clay pot that was mottled and worn with age. A small selection of tiny garden implements stood in a rack next to it just waiting for Gorman's gentle hands to set to work. Harl reached out to pick up the micro-tree, but Gorman's insistent voice stayed his hand.

'Under there,' Gorman said, tapping his foot on a woven mat spread across the hardwood floor. 'We'll need to lift it up.'

Harl thought it was odd, but when they moved the mat it was obvious that Gorman had meant the wooden trapdoor that lay hidden beneath.

Gorman bent over and pulled up the flattened iron hoops set into the trapdoor. He took a firm grip on both and lifted. The trapdoor slid to one side on the floor.

'If you could move it back some more, Harl,' he asked, breathing hard.

Harl clasped the hoops and slid it further away from them. It was surprisingly heavy and it took his entire strength just to manoeuvre the thick door aside.

The opening revealed a small cavity about half a stride deep and twice as wide. A large metal container was crammed inside. It had been fashioned from the metal cases used to store liquid fire. About three of them had been cut apart and welded back together to form a larger container.

Gorman clasped two handles on either side of the container and hauled it out, placing it onto the bed with a thud. He flipped a small latch on the front and lifted the lid. A jumble of metallic items lay inside. Gorman reached in and pulled out a handful of small flat disks with what looked like whistle holes set in them.

'These,' Gorman said, handing one to Harl, 'once placed in the mouth, will allow you to breathe without trouble on the outside. They will also work underwater. I have kept them in as good a condition as possible, given their age.'

It sounded like magic to Harl.

'Where did you get them?' he asked, toying with the disk.

'They're from outside,' Gorman said, 'from beyond the vision, made by those who created my knife.'

'Though the archway?' Harl asked, amazed.

'Much further than that, my lad.'

'If we're to go into the vision,' Sonora said, 'then you must tell us more about the outside.'

'There will be time for that later,' Gorman said, deflecting the question, obviously impatient to continue. He pulled out a strange metal contraption that looked like a tiny crossbow without the bow. 'This is called a pistol. It's far more deadly than a bow. Press the red dot on the side to activate it and then squeeze the trigger to fire. It has an extremely long range, but, alas, has only a limited number of shots left. I'd guess about fifty or so. Use it only as a last resort in times of pressing danger.'

He rummaged inside the box again and produced a long thin object wrapped in metallic cloth.

'This holds the key to escape,' he said, unrolling the shimmering material to reveal a sword. It was made from the same metal as Gorman's knife and gleamed in the flickering light of the candle that trembled in Sonora's hand. He held the weapon up before Harl. 'It is long enough to cut through the barrier, although I have not dared to try it myself.'

Harl was elated. They finally had a plan, but before he could start thanking Gorman the old man pulled a final object out of the box. It was a small rectangle wrapped in soft leather. Gorman unfolded the leather cloth to reveal a fragile old book. It was worn and faded with age. The red leather binding was cracked and the edges tattered, but Harl sensed it was Gorman's greatest treasure. The old man ran his hand over the cover and Harl noticed that Gorman's fingers were trembling. The cover was as worn as the rest of the bindings and the writing on it was too faint to read. Gorman opened it to reveal pages covered with complex diagrams and text.

'The writing is much the same as our own,' the old man said, 'but with so many technical phrasings that understanding its meaning is almost impossible. But if I were to hazard a guess, then I would say it contains instruction for making something.'

Harl had enough time to read *"once the central component is fitted then replace the fuel linkage,"* just before Gorman flicked over to another page.

'The diagrams,' Gorman went on, 'depict machinery from the old times when man was much more advanced.'

'Like the sword, Grandpa?' Sonora asked.

'Yes dear, just like the sword and pistol,' he said, 'but on a larger scale.'

He gathered up the items.

'Here,' he said, passing the bundle over to Harl, 'you will need these with you when you go.'

Sonora frowned and laid her hand on Gorman's arm. 'You are coming with us, grandpa, aren't you?'

Gorman smiled and squeezed her hand.

'I'm old,' he said, 'and my time is mostly spent. The plan I have can accommodate only two people.' He turned to the direction of the window and murmured as though to himself, 'Although I would like to feel the sun on my face.'

Harl raised an eyebrow at Sonora, hoping for an explanation of the words, but she just shrugged her shoulders.

The sadness in Gorman's face disappeared. 'The plan is simple, but completely untested. You must head to the corner of the Vision and use the sword to cut a hole through, next to the black barrier. With a bit of luck and some fiddling, you can pull the cut section inwards. Then you should be able to lean out though the hole in the Vision and sink the sword into the black part of the barrier separating the worlds. You can then swing out and hold on to the sword. Sonora can climb out after you and hold on to your back. I suggest you secure yourselves together using a coil of rope.

'So,' Harl said, 'we'll both be hanging like fruits from a tree.'

'Exactly,' Gorman said and chuckled. 'By activating the sword you should be able to let your weight pull the sword down through the barrier which separates us from your old world until you slide all the way to the bottom.'

'As easy as that,' Harl said.

Gorman frowned. 'Probably not, but if you can think of another way then I'm all ears, even if I have no eyes.'

At the old man's tone, Harl immediately regretted what he had said.

'I'm sorry,' he said. 'I'm just worried. This is all so much to take in.'

'There is more yet,' Gorman said. 'When you reach the ground you will need to find an exit from the realm of the gods.'

'The archway,' Harl said.

'That is one way, yes,' Gorman said, 'but I cannot tell you exactly, as I do not know myself. Most likely there is an exit beyond the archway. Alternatively, you can head along the base of the wall of worlds and search for a way out at the end. I do not know how far you must travel, but the main problem is being seen. There's much more activity beyond the archway than if you follow the wall of worlds. It is a dangerous choice whichever route you take, but eventually there will be a way out.'

'Out into where?' Sonora asked.

'A place without the blacking disease,' Gorman said, 'where you can start a new life for yourselves without living in a cage. But if you make it there you may not see another human again.'

Harl felt the blood drain from his face. For some reason he had never considered the possibility that it would be just Sonora and himself when they eventually left. His soul focus had been on escape. What life would be like afterwards hadn't entered his mind. How would they survive? What would it be like to never see another person? He looked at Sonora and felt a fresh wave of love for her. If he had to face life out there at least he wouldn't be alone.

'That reminds me,' Gorman said, turning his blank eyes on Sonora. He reached out a frail hand to touch her. 'You must prepare the cloaks this turn, the way I told you, and stow your equipment behind the house. We must be ready to leave quickly.'

'What will you do afterwards?' Harl asked.

'When you have left,' Gorman said, 'I will re-seal the hole, but if I am unable, I will use the breathing device I have kept for myself.'

'And the people left behind?' Sonora asked.

'You have seen first-hand that there will be little stopping the disease without outside intervention,' Gorman said. 'If you can't find help from beyond the walls, then there will be no one left alive should you return.'

'But you said there is no one outside,' Harl said.

'I fear that will be the case. It may well be a one way trip and if so we will never see each other again. But there is no choice. It is the only chance for freedom and the only hope for a cure. So you must go. And soon. You leave on the next turn.'

Harl's stomach flipped. He had always wanted to live beyond the barriers. He'd dreamed of it every time he had stared out, but having been there once he had no desire to return to the impossible magnitude of those horrors. If only he could have a few more cycles inside. Only the fear of the blacking disease corrupting Sonora made him truly want to leave.

But it was a terrible choice and, as he turned to look out the window, the weight of it settled on his shoulders. He only hoped he was strong enough to bear it.

Chapter 20

They have made tools using some basic materials that I gave them, and used the tools to create crude holes to shelter in at the centre of the tank.

Harl barely slept. He kept tossing and turning or just lying on his back and staring up at the ceiling. The next cycle was going to change so many things. Just knowing that when he awoke he would be leaving this cherished life behind, left him cold and shivering. What were they going to face? How would they survive?

Things had been idyllic, like finding a second family to grow up with again. And then there was Sonora. He had fallen for many girls when he was growing up, but he had never truly fallen in love. Sonora was everything to him. She may have been a healer, but she'd bewitched him from the start and he hated the idea of taking her into danger.

Sleep overtook him in the end. Grim and dark, it dragged him down into nightmare after nightmare. In one, his hands slipped from the blade and he and Sonora tumbled down into the darkness of the Sight, only to be stepped on by the god as it walked past. Another nightmare showed Troy pressed against the

Sight, Rufus stabbing a dagger into his back time after time while Harl looked on helpless from the outside.

When Gorman woke him with a shake, he groaned and rolled over, horrified that the moment was finally here. He had slept part way through the next cycle, which only seemed to make matters worse. He looked around the plush room knowing it would probably be the last time he slept in a warm feather bed. The windows had been cracked open and the scent of the woodland outside blew in, ruffling the soft curtains. He had become used to the comfort and familiar feel of the room. It felt like home. It was home.

His stomach flipped again at the thought of leaving.

'It's time for you to get ready and go,' the old man said as Harl struggled from the covers to his feet.

'I know, I know,' he moaned to himself and then splashed cold water on his face from a bowl on the nightstand. He looked up into the mirror and saw the anxiety on Gorman's face. Only then did he realise that Sonora was missing. 'Is everything alright? Where's Sonora?'

'In the woods as usual, but no one has come to work at your house this turn, Harl,' Gorman said. 'I fear the worst. You must least leave as soon as it's dark. I heard shouts in the woods as I walked earlier. I do not know what is happening, but you must take care. Hurry, Harl. Hurry.'

Harl dashed outside and ran along the path that plunged into the woods, making for the spot where Sonora grew her plants. It was only a short distance and relief flooded him when her gentle singing reached him. He stepped out onto the tilled soil and worked his way carefully between the delicate plants. She turned at his footsteps and noticed his lack of breath.

'Harl?' she asked, concern in her voice. 'What is it?'

He rushed over to her and took her slender frame in his arms.

'I'm glad you're alright,' he said. 'Gorman was worried and sent me to find you.'

'I'm fine,' she said, accepting his embrace. 'Why was he worried?'

'No workers came,' he said, 'and he heard people up in the forest earlier.'

'I haven't heard anything unusual,' she said, 'but that's no surprise with my wailing drowning everything out.'

'I love your singing,' Harl said, knowing they weren't the exact words he wanted to say. 'We should head back.'

She touched his face.

'But you're alright?' she asked.

He nodded, but then lowered his head onto her shoulder.

'It's just that everything is changing,' he whispered, half-hoping that she wouldn't hear.

She kissed his cheek. It was just the briefest caress but it melted his fear and he held her tight against him.

'We should go,' he said at last.

She nodded and pulled away.

When they reached the edge of the forest they could see the whole valley and town spread below them. There were vast plumes of smoke rising from inside the walls and the faint flickering of flames could be seen between buildings. No guards patrolled near the gate and there was no sign of life within the walls except for the spreading flames consuming the last few buildings.

'Oh no,' Sonora said and slumped down. Harl reached out and caught her before she hit the ground and, crouching with her, he eased her down to the soft grass.

'This can't be happening,' she said. 'What is there left?'

Tears glazed her eyes. He reached his hand out to clasp hers.

'We have each other,' he said, wanting his words to reassure her. Although looking down at the burning town he felt they were woefully inadequate.

'What will happen if we manage to leave? What if we can't.-'

Her words were cut short as he leaned in to kiss her. The fragrance of her hair filled his senses as he felt a tender hand wrap around his neck, pulling him against her.

He moved his own hands beneath the fabric of her white dress, up her slender legs and shifted his weight to move above her, the troubles of the world forgotten.

'We should go,' Sonora said. She sat up from the long grass and slipped her blouse back on over her head.

Harl rolled onto his stomach and gazed over the valley edge down across the fields and winding river.

'Must we?' he asked. 'If we could just hold on to this moment a little longer...'

She smiled. 'You know we don't have time, Harl, and Grandpa will be waiting. We have to go.'

He sat up, drew her to him and sighed. 'I don't want this to end. So much has changed for me over the last few cycles, and now we face the unknown. I can't believe that I've found you despite everything that's going on.'

'I know,' Sonora said, kissing him softly on the lips. 'I feel the same, but we can't stay here.'

Harl lowered his head onto her shoulder.

'The truth is painful, my love.' he said.

A twig snapped behind them. Harl spun round to find Felmar stepping out from the shadow of the trees. He sneered down at them.

'So what are the outlander and his wicked witch up to?'

Four other men hacked their way through the shrubs with their swords and stopped beside Felmar.

Harl knew the predatory look in Felmar's eyes as they drank in the sight of Sonora's body before she covered herself and he clenched his fists ready to fight.

Felmar glanced at Harl's hands and shook his head.

'I wouldn't try anything if I were you,' he said.

Three of the men, including Felmar, had darkened fingertips. Blacking disease.

Harl stood, taking his time so as to not startle them. Felmar had his sword drawn and adrenaline coursed through Harl, but his mind was blank on what to do against so many men.

'So,' Felmar said, 'as the town burns, the two of you are rutting like animals, delighting in your heinous work as you hide up in the forest.'

The men around Felmar smirked and Harl felt Sonora's clothing brush him as she rose and stepped behind him.

Felmar spat on the ground. 'It makes me sick that you enjoy each other as people die below. But I didn't come here to enforce the laws placed upon you, outlander. No, I came here for a different reason.' He lifted his sword hand up and looked at the black streaks devouring his flesh, before pointing the sword towards them and pacing around them in a circle.

'The leaders have perished and I've assumed command.' He raised his other hand to inspect the dark cracks of disease spreading across the pale skin and flexed the digits as though to regain feeling. 'I was certain there was nothing I could do about this, but...' He smiled and tapped his chin with one dark finger, grinning. 'I heard a strange tale today. As the light came, the high leader was dying with me by his side. A harrowing sight, it was, watching him cough up blood on his bed clothes, and I would have left him to rot, but his words compelled me to stay.'

He paused and pointed his sword tip at Sonora.

'It involves your grandmother, witch.'

Sonora looked puzzled.

'No. I didn't know her,' Fergus said, seeing her look. 'I don't mix with witches and harlots. But as the old man choked on his last breath, he told me how she had once worked for him and the other council members, mixing potions and such like.'

He continued pacing around them and coughed, hacking into his balled up and blackened fist. Flecks of blood splattered the back of Felmar's hand.

'This disease affects the lungs eventually and the story the dying man told relates to a young boy placed within the world by the gods. He was found unconscious by a woman in the forest and carried in secret to the council chamber. His hair was the colour of fire and his strange clothes unlike any seen before. When the council members demanded to know where the boy came from, he told them he was picked up by the gods, although that is not the term he used. But before he could tell them any more, a fit of coughing overcame the boy.'

He continued pacing around them, sword held level.

'The witch eventually found a mixture that cured the child, but the cure was only temporary and he needed to drink it every cycle. I don't know what he told them after he was healed, and I don't much care, but I know who this man was and so do the two of you. That blind old fool.'

'Gorman?' Harl asked.

Felmar nodded.

'I don't believe you,' Sonora said.

Felmar laughed. 'His hair may be grey now, but it was not golden in his youth. It was more the colour of a dimming fire. He hid up here with the witch-' He stopped pacing and gestured at the forest. '- and stayed out of sight, wearing a hat on the rare times he ventured into town. I have come to the conclusion that the potion used on the boy might just work on this.' He held up his free hand and stared at the darkening vein-like marks again. They seemed to fascinate him. 'And you will make it for me, witch, as you make it for the old man now.'

'I can't,' Sonora said, 'I've no idea what you're talking about.'

'Lies!' Felmar said, spittle spraying from his mouth. 'The old man is alive and someone must be making his potion.' He pointed the sword at Harl, 'You won't be needed, but we'll keep the witch alive until me an' the boys have had our fun and she has delivered the potion.'

One man made a swipe for Sonora. She moved back and shoved the man away, but Felmar stepped forward and struck her squarely across the face with his hand, making her cry out and stumble to the ground.

Harl stepped forward and Felmar raised the sword to his chest. The point punctured his jerkin, forcing Harl to stillness. He cursed himself for rushing from the house without bringing his bow or even a dagger.

His attention was drawn by the faint patter of running men coming from behind him. He risked a glance. A large group of guards were running across the stone bridge in the valley far below them.

'Looks like the town is mine now,' Felmar said as Harl turned back to face him. 'That will be more of my lads coming to lend a hand.'

Felmar smiled at the men surrounding him. Lust was reflected in their eyes.

'Take the girl,' he said. 'And you,' – He looked at Harl – 'kneel.'

Harl dropped to the ground and his knees sunk into the damp grass.

The men stepped forward as Felmar held Harl in place, keeping pressure on the sword tip.

Rage seethed through Harl and he tensed, ready to rush Felmar. He knew he'd die soon after, but it was better than being made impotent by the sword. The first of the men grabbed

Sonora's hands and held them down over her head as she tried to shake him off. A second knelt in front of her and fumbled to unbutton his britches, a smile on his lips.

Harl took a deep breath, ready to spring.

'You don't want to do that,' a voice said from the shadows at the edge of the tree line, making them all turn.

Gorman stepped into view. He had Harl's bow held in one hand while the other gripped four arrows, one between each finger. His stick lay by his feet and the sword was strapped to his back.

'All this trouble for the potion?' he said. 'It won't work, Felmar. It isn't a cure for the blacking disease.'

'You!' Felmar sneered. He kicked Harl aside and strode forward towards Gorman, his sword held up ready to strike the blind man down.

Gorman didn't hesitate, flicking the hand with the arrows up to the bow in one swift movement. An arrow bolted from the string with a twang, striking Felmar through the face and forcing his head to snap backwards as he toppled over.

The man pinning Sonora sprang up towards Gorman at the same time as the one kneeling between her legs. They rushed towards the old man, but Gorman was too fast. He cocked his head to one side and, with barely a twitch, loosed two arrows in rapid succession. Both men were struck simultaneously, arrows jutting from their chests. The next arrow was already resting on the bow and pointed at the last man before his friends had hit the floor. He stood frozen with fear as his comrades moaned in pain beside him.

'I didn't want no trouble mister, honest,' the man said looking around at his dying companions.

'I don't believe a word of your lies,' Gorman said, his voice firm but calm. 'Now run and join your companions on the bridge before I cut your manhood off. If you are a man at all.'

The man took flight into the woods, racing towards the path that wound down into the valley. When he was out of bow range he began calling out to his comrades for help.

Sweat coated Harl's palms. He cursed himself for being a fool. The man would return with the guards and the three of them would be picked off as murderers.

They had failed already.

Chapter 21

Fascinating. Only once I have separated them can I see how much they vary as a species. I do not want to have them interbreed. I think twenty or so containers will suffice.

'Grandpa,' Sonora said, running towards Gorman and flinging her arms around him. Tears streaked down her face. 'I'm so glad you came.'

'Just in the nick of time I would say, my dear,' he said as he took her arm and started to walk away from the men. 'Will you bring my stick. Harl? Quick now, we must hurry. They're almost on us. We don't have much time left to cut through the barrier.'

'Is it true, Grandpa?' Sonora asked.

Gorman sighed as she gripped his arm and forced him to stop.

He cocked his head to listen.

'We've only a little time, Sonora,' he said, 'but yes, my dear, it is true. I'm sorry for not telling either of you. It shames me in more ways than one.' He tugged at her gently to get her moving.

Harl was speechless as he followed them. Had he really just witnessed Gorman kill those men? The old man had been so fast, almost inhuman. He remembered the confrontation on the bridge with Felmar which had left him feeling the same way.

After walking in silence for a short time along the moss-covered forest floor, Gorman spoke.

'When I was a boy I lived a life beyond these barriers, a life far from the realm of the gods that you can see through the vision.' He pointed through the forest towards the Sight and the vast space beyond it. 'I remember little of that life, for fear blocked much of my memory from those times. Children can adapt quickly where an adult would let their mind linger on the past. When I came here it was in the same way as you Harl, except I did not know of barriers or cages.'

He stopped as they brushed against a tree and ran one of his hands across the bark before moving on.

'My family lived in Delta, an underground city full of thousands of people, until death came for us and we were forced to leave. Winged creatures we called hivers attacked the city, killing hundreds. Of the people who fled Delta only a few survived. I left with my parents in a small convoy, but we were attacked en route by hivers. We had taken shelter in a small cave, when the hivers flew in and killed everyone I was with. My father, mother, my two sisters, I watched them all torn to shreds by the creatures. But by a horrible miracle I survived by hiding under the bodies of my family until the hivers had left.

'Eventually I stumbled out into the wild, not knowing where I was going. I walked for many turns, completely lost and utterly alone. I had my eyesight then, but my footsteps through that world might as well have belonged to a blind man. I had no idea

202

what path to take nor any clue to the way back home. In the end exhaustion took me and I collapsed. I don't know how much time had passed, but, when I awoke, one of the gods was towering over me.

'It scooped me up in its hand and I must have fainted from fear, as when I woke, I was lying on a bed and surrounded by councilmen arguing over my fate. I know now that your grandmother had brought me to the council tower in secrecy and when I started struggling for breath, it was she who managed to find a cure.'

'The same breathing problem as I had when I was in the god's realm?' Harl asked as Gorman stopped at another tree.

This time, as Gorman ran a wrinkled hand across it, Harl spotted a series of small carvings in the bark. They were old and healed over, but they must have been deep enough for Gorman to understand their meaning.

'The same,' Gorman said, changing direction, 'except reversed, if you will.' He gestured around them. 'Your lungs are used to air within this land, but mine were accustomed to the air in the realm of the gods. I was incredibly lucky to have her around to find a potion to correct my breathing. She must have mixed and poured dozens down me before one finally worked. She made me a large amount of the mixture and eventually taught me what ingredients to use to make my own before she passed.'

'And the things in the chest?' Sonora asked.

'I had them on me when the god picked me up. Your grandmother hid them in the forest before taking me to the council and mixing the potion.'

As they walked Harl noticed that not a single tree branch was below head height. All had been pruned over countless cycles. Had Gorman been slowly training the forest environment to his needs? Even where rocks lay there were always smaller ones scattered nearby as if to warn Gorman's feet before the larger hazards.

'Over time,' Gorman continued, 'my dependence on the liquid lessened. Now I only need a small amount and I think I could manage without it if I tried.' He rummaged a hand inside his jerkin and retrieved the small flask that Harl had seen him drink from.

'That is one of the reasons I took you in after your mother was lifted,' he said to Sonora. 'Your grandmother couldn't handle you all by herself and I owed her much. As for not telling you about all this, there are a few reasons. One is that I wanted to forget. I knew that I would never leave this place and to dwell on a better life would be my undoing. All of the councilmen who knew of my origin have died, except for the one Felmar spoke to. I guess they didn't know how to handle the situation without an uprising or change of religious ideals, so they kept silent. I also know...' He paused as if struggling to get the words out. 'I know that I am also the reason for the blacking illness.'

Sonora halted.

'Grandpa,' Sonora said, shaking her head. 'Why would you say such a thing?'

'Because it is true,' he said. 'I've seen the disease before, in Delta. Although it was not such a problem there. Our medical knowledge meant that it was easily cured.'

'That does not mean-' Sonora said, but Gorman cut her off.

'It must have lain dormant inside me. I'd been made immune as a child. All Deltan's were given injections to stop it. Although I don't know why it has taken such a long time to spread to the people here. There is no other way it could have come to be here and not exist in Harl's land.'

Shouts, muffled by the forest, drifted towards them from the far off cottage.

'It should be in sight,' Gorman said.

Harl looked around at the forest and spotted a pile of equipment tucked into one end of a fallen hollow tree. Sonora steered the old man towards it and grabbed a small backpack and shoulder pouch. She strapped them in place and then tied a belt around her waist. A long dagger hung in a sheath on the belt.

Gorman held the sword out to Harl and he took it with reverence, sure he could feel the power inside. He threw a bag over his own shoulder and looked at the old man. Gorman gave off such an air of protection that he wished the old man was coming with them.

'Come on,' Gorman said as if sensing the gaze. He cocked his head to listen. Harl strained his own ears but could hear nothing other than the sounds of the forest.

'There's no more time,' Gorman said, striding off through the trees. 'We must hurry.'

When they reached the corner of the world, the black barrier towered to their left and the Sight lay in front of them.

'Use the sword,' Gorman said. 'Let's test the theory.'

Harl pressed the button on the hilt and the weapon hummed. He placed the sword tip against the glass and leant forward, watching in amazement as it melted into the impenetrable material. He placed more weight against the blade and it slid deeper, melting through the glass until the pressure lessened and the hilt thumped against the wall. He was through.

'It works,' Sonora said, moving beside him to view the blade poking through to the other side.

Harl forced the blade around, slowly cutting a circle one stride in diameter until he finished at the corner where the ground met both barriers.

'And now for the tricky bit,' Harl said, taking one hand off the hilt to wipe the sweaty palm on his jerkin.

'If this cut section falls out,' Gorman said, 'it will be like a bell ringing the alarm for all to hear. You'll have to switch the blade off and drag it back inwards.'

Harl took a firmer grip on the sword. He cut a line into the centre of the block and depressed the button to switch the blade off.

'Has it worked?' Gorman asked.

Harl pulled the hilt and felt heavy resistance.

'Yes. It's stuck.'

'Good,' Gorman said. 'We'll all pull it inwards, but stand back after so it doesn't roll on top of you.'

Harl tugged, his feet tearing grass and slipping in the mud as Sonora joined him. The circle of glass moved inwards ever so slightly and when Gorman heard them heaving, he put a foot on the wall and yanked on the remainder of the hilt until the block slid backwards. It hit the ground with a wet thud as Harl and

Sonora fell on the ground panting for breath. Gorman stood to one side smiling.

Instantly, Harl could smell the difference in the air coming from outside. It was like a sour, tainted dust. He wanted to cough.

'Put the mouth pieces in,' Gorman said, slipping one behind his front teeth.

Harl pulled two out from his satchel on the ground and passed one to Sonora. The sensation was strange, but not uncomfortable, as he practised breathing with it in. The sour taste and tickling cough disappeared.

'Now remember,' Gorman said, 'when you get to the ground, stick close to the worlds to avoid being seen. Then you have two choices: straight ahead through the archway or follow the worlds to your right. If you make it outside, then be prepared because it is full of dangerous animals. Remember to keep an eye above you at all times; not all creatures live on the ground.'

'Glad you mentioned it eventually,' Harl said trying to make light of the situation, but Gorman just frowned.

'You have no choice, my lad,' he said. 'Keep your eyes open and weapons ready.'

Harl picked up his bow and arrows and slung them over one shoulder before snatching up the large satchel and looping it over the other.

Gorman stepped close to him so that they were face to face while Sonora double-checked her own bag.

'I cannot thank you enough for all you have done for me,' Harl said before Gorman could speak. 'You have taken my fears of the world and turned them into hope.' He held out his hand, then realising what he had done, he touched the old man's shoulder.

Gorman placed his own hand on Harl's.

'Look after her,' he said. 'She is most precious to me.'

'You have my word,' Harl reassured him.

They stepped back from each other and Gorman turned to where Sonora stood, tears streaming from her sapphire eyes.

'Will you not come with us, Grandpa?' she asked, attempting to hide her tears from the blind man.

'My time is almost over, my child, and I cannot make the journey you have ahead of you,' Gorman said.

She sobbed harder as she embraced him.

'I love you so much,' she said, struggling to speak through her tears. 'I'll never forget all you have done for me and all you have taught me.'

'And I you, my child,' he said.

Harl looked away as a tear streaked down the old man's face. It ran along the wrinkle lines until it dropped down Sonora's back.

Voices cried in the distance, presumably the other men had seen Felmar's body and were hunting the killers. The cries grew louder as the men closed in.

'Now you must go,' Gorman said, moving out of Sonora's arms and straightening. 'Good luck to both of you. Be cautious and be swift.'

'Will you be alright?' Harl asked.

'I'll be fine,' Gorman said. 'I will seal the opening when you've left, but now I must go and teach those fools a thing or two about manners.' A grin stretched his lips.

They stared at his back as he drew his knife and strolled off towards the sounds of pursuit, his stick in front. The last they heard was a faint hum emitting from the knife as he stalked away through the trees.

Sonora moved to the barrier and pressed herself against it.

'The god is pacing around as usual,' she said as Harl leant out the hole, 'not even looking this way. I never realised how out of proportion their legs are.'

Was she was trying to make herself forget Gorman's absence? Harl gripped the side and began to swing out.

'Wait,' Sonora hissed and Harl froze, hanging half out of the hole.

The god turned in their direction and walked straight past on the other side of the giant archway.

'It's safe,' she said and then tied a rope around his midriff to secure them together.

Holding the sword, he stuck his right arm out of the hole while gripping the edge with his left hand. He thrust the blade into the black barrier and felt it sink deep into the material. It went in easier than he'd imagined. Pressing the button on the hilt to fix the sword in place, he swung out and felt a nauseous sense of vertigo as the ground dropped away beneath them. He clung to the hilt as he dangled there clenching his eyes tight shut.

As he opened his eyes, Sonora slipped behind him and clasped her arms around his neck.

Harl squinted and peered down. He could just about see the grey floor thousands of strides below, but the glare from the wall of worlds spreading out to either side of them made it almost impossible. Light from the tanks poured out into the huge space, illuminating the archway opposite, but almost blinding in its intensity when you tried to look down. It was surprising how much lighter it seemed out here than when he'd been looking from inside the tank. The Sight had always seemed dark and vague with only the hint of features in the distance, like shadows haunting his nightmares. But it was different outside. The light threw everything into focus.

Through the archway he could see the giant table where he'd climbed out from the pile of bodies. The memory clawed at him and he turned back to the wall and faced the black line that separated the worlds. He looked right and thought he was dreaming. His bench sat there in the small grove of trees in his old world. He could see the carvings of his parents in the wood and the small flowers he'd planted around it. It sent a jolt of longing through him that was almost painful.

He drew a sharp breath. It was like looking into the world as a god. This was the exact spot where he had first seen Sonora's reflection. If only Troy had been standing there. He could have called out to him. He could have let Troy know that he was still alive. He imagined the shock on Troy's face at seeing him hanging from a sword hilt on the outside of the tank, his feet pressed against the wall and the blonde-haired beauty wrapped around him. He almost laughed, but suddenly flashes of his parents came to his mind. Had they looked back on the tank when they had been lifted? Had they seen him crying out to them as they were torn away?

It was all the god's fault, these prisons, the liftings, all of it just torture meted out by its callous hand. He wouldn't let the god take him. He would escape and live free. He would make his parents proud.

He tightened his grip and prepared for the decent.

'Ready,' he said, hoping he sounded confident enough to reassure Sonora. He pressed the button and felt a smooth jolt as the sword warmed up. The blade sunk a fraction deeper into the smooth black wall, then melted its way down in a straight line, cutting through the barrier and lowering them slowly towards the ground.

Chapter 22

I have to keep them a secret until I am ready to reveal them, but until they settle down I will pen another report on them and over time build up a collection of articles to place inside a book.

The descent was slow. At first the fear of loosing his grip on the sword hilt and falling had struck Harl in an almost paralysing wave of terror. The sheer height and scale of everything around them gave him waves of vertigo, but as the fear receded he began to admire the view on either side within the brightly lit rectangles. It was a glimpse into other worlds and it gave him a strange sense of disconnection. How was it possible to be out here looking in? He had lived trapped inside one of these cubes for so long that seeing everything spread out around him felt like a dream or a nightmare. How could it be real?

'Look!' Sonora said, tightening her arm around his neck and pointing her free hand at the landscape directly below their old world.

The entire world was full of thick, dense forest. It was even pressed up against the Sight. Huge, broad-leaved plants stretched out to steal as much light as possible in the tangled mass that grew beneath the forest. The trees themselves reached nearly to the top of the world. Some had put out thick horizontal trunks that were dotted with smaller plants along their length, like a second forest floor. A swathe of brown soil and decaying leaves formed a thick layer at the bottom of the world.

'I don't see anything,' he said, scanning the greenery for something out of place.

'It's gone now,' Sonora said. 'There was a person up in the canopy, or at least it looked like a person. I swear it was covered in thick black hair.'

'I think we'll see a lot of strange sights before we're done,' Harl said, focusing on controlling their descent.

The world on their right was bleak and barren. Shrivelled tufts of grass were scattered at random across its low-lying hills and a dry river bed snaked across the landscape, ending in a distant bowl-shaped pit. There were sheer grey cliffs in the distance. They backed up against the far side, as if the world was divided between the high ground on one side and low lands on the nearest. The whole place looked dead.

What it would be like to live in there? Sonora's world had seemed alien to him, but this just felt wrong. Dust swirled up against the glass as he peered in and he pictured walking around inside; no life, no trees, just the looming cliffs and desiccated grass. It looked tortured and lonely, as though the God had abandoned it lifetimes ago. He turned away, a shiver of apprehension running down his spine.

The next landscape to their right resembled both the worlds he had been inside. He could make out a town set squarely in the centre of the landscape. It was nestled between smooth, grass-covered hills, with a fast-flowing river running through the valleys to a large lake at one end of the world. Floating in the calm water were dozens of boats of various shapes and sizes. Small fishing boats trailed nets behind them and massive two-story vessels were tied up at the dock on one side of the shore.

He was about to ask Sonora what she thought of it all, but his curiosity got the better of him, so he turned to the world on their left.

It was brighter than any they had passed, casting a strong yellow light out into the god's realm. The landscape was the same golden colour and it took him a moment to realise it was formed entirely from sand. It looked like an endless riverbed. Mound after mound stretched to every side of the world and the light reflecting from the sand forced Harl to squint. Dotted across the rippling sand were scattered villages of crude, wooden shacks and canvas-covered huts. Dark, tiny figures moved between them, carrying baskets on their heads or leading scrawny cattle to the scant vegetation scattered around.

'Look,' Sonora said as they neared the ground level of the two worlds.

Harl turned back to the grass world and noticed a man staring dumbfounded at the two of them as they slid down the outside of his world. He was dressed in a material that Harl had never seen before. Large sections of the tan material were crudely woven together with thick thread.

The man took a step towards them and raised his hands as if to touch the clear barrier, but then turned and sprinted away towards a small village in the distance, waving his arms in the air.

'They won't believe him,' Harl said as the man disappeared over a rise in the land.

As they neared the floor, a flood of panic swept over him. They had miscalculated. The tanks were resting on a plinth above the ground so there was a cut in five paces above the floor. The gap was like a cut away section, leaving a drop twice the height of a man and, if they kept going, the sword would cut through and they would plunge down.

Harl looked to either side, trying to think of a plan as he pressed the button on the sword to stop them.

'Harl!' Sonora cried as they continued on towards the overhang.

The sword must have heated up more than before and was taking much longer to slow them. Panic washed over him as his feet kicked out into the empty space beneath the tanks. His arm muscles burnt in protest at having to hold their combined weight on the narrow sword hilt but eventually with just half a pace left before it cut right through, the sword stilled.

He looked left and right, seeing the god's realm spread out all around them, vast and open. He had seen it before, of course, from the top of the table, but being close to the floor made the space seem even more daunting.

He craned his neck around to glance through the archway and could make out god-sized desks and tables lining the area beyond. His arms twinged in protest, pulling him back to the predicament. He couldn't hold on any more.

'We'll have to drop,' he said, glancing down at the floor several strides them below.

Harl hit the button as Sonora muttered something about "leaving with a mad man" and the blade slid through the last part, coming free from the wall and plunging them downwards.

They hit the stone floor in a tangled heap, with Sonora somehow landing on top of him, knocking the air from his lungs.

'Sorry,' she said, grabbing his hand and hauling him up before rummaging inside her bag.

Harl stared at the tables through the archway. One of them had to be the table he had been on when he'd woken among the pile of dead. A shiver ran through him at the memory and he looked away.

It was all so big.

Along the base of the worlds he could make out the only object within walking distance. Half-hidden under the tank wall overhang was an oblong silhouette. Harl guessed it must be as big as a hay barn and protruding from the top was what looked like a giant handle held up horizontally by two struts.

She pulled out two cloaks and handed one to him. The colour of the material matched the grey floor exactly.

'So that's why Gorman had you dye them,' he said, wrapping the light cloth around him.

When they both had the cloaks on and hoods up, Harl looked around the impossibly open space. It was like being a beetle or a rat inside someone's house, and it was terrifying. It was dark compared to the land they had left behind, as if the space swallowed the light. Only a faint shine filtered down from above.

Harl looked up, the dizzying sense of scale magnified as he lifted his gaze from the ground, up past level upon level of worlds to where a light stared bleakly down from above. It was the same kind of illuminating strip that shone light down inside the tanks, but this one had to be massive considering the scales involved. And yet it cast hardly any light over the scene. Only the tank light gave a real glimpse into the gloom around them. The glow highlighted the wall opposite into a lighter shade of grey than the floor, but it was still just a dismal expanse stretching away from them. It all felt so empty and lifeless. Only the giant archway gave a hint of life, but even then it was just Harl's tortured memories. He could still feel the god's hand clasped around him as it carried him back to the tanks. It was difficult to breathe, the very air toxic around him. The coarse skin on the god's hand felt like rock against his body and he gasped for air as it reached up and up, finally coming to a stop above Sonora's tank.

It had been a torture more suited to a nightmare, but there was a nugget of hope in it. Those few agonising moments had paved his way towards Sonora. And that was a price worth paying.

His gaze was drawn up to the wall of worlds beside them. The plinth the worlds stood on left a five pace overhang. The space underneath was littered with small rocks and debris, as if swept out of sight by a giant broom.

Edging out onto the open floor from the overhang was the handled box. It was the only object of any interest even remotely close to them and seemed the best place to head for.

'Harl,' Sonora hissed, pointing towards the archway.

The god was stomping towards it.

'Get under,' Harl said, tugging her cloak as he pulled her beneath the worlds.

They hunched under the overhang, peering out, and breathed a sigh of relief when the god passed the archway and didn't come through.

'Better get moving,' Harl said, knowing that if Gorman failed to seal the hole and the god noticed, then it would look in their area for any escapees.

They headed for the box. It was massive, more the size of a house than anything he could call a box. But then he tried to picture it from the god's point of view and it seemed about the right size. And yet it was still huge.

They scurried along under the overhang, following the line of worlds toward the strange structure. They both kept glancing up at the archway, expecting a god to step through at any moment and scoop them up.

As they neared the box, Harl was stunned by the size of it. It towered above them at almost three times the height of a man, its sides dented and scratched by a life of heavy use.

'What is it?' Sonora asked.

He reached out to touch it. It was rougher than he had expected and made from cold metal, the impurities of its casting obvious. A plethora of grooves and hollows scarred its surface. He ran a finger inside one and tried to picture what could gouge such a deep cut into metal. But then it was all on such a giant scale.

The god's hands were large enough to scoop an entire house up in one fist. This scratch would barely register.

It was unnerving.

'Some kind of carrying tray?' he guessed, thinking of the basket Sonora carried her herbs in.

He slid his whole hand into one of the small cracks on the side. It seemed solid enough when he pulled at the metal. Without waiting, he placed his foot in one of the lower grooves and then climbed up off the ground. His foot slipped and he dangled from one hand as he scrambled to get purchase with his other limbs.

He cursed his haste. If he was injured, it would be only Sonora to tend him. Staying in one place while he healed would mean running out of food rapidly as well. There was no way she could carry him to safety and that meant the only end would be discovery by the giant gods. They would be thrown back into a tank and have to escape all over again. Assuming they survived.

He sighed and took a moment before he began to climb. Hand over hand, he gradually neared the top, breathing a sigh of relief as his fingers caught the top ledge and he heaved himself up. He leant over the edge and looked down inside.

The interior of the tray was split into two sections by a chest high barrier that formed long shallow compartments on either side. A group of transparent cubes at the far end drew his eye. Each cube was a closed box about five strides wide and the height of a tall man. A metallic square in the top corner connected to the outside via a pipe.

It took him a moment to realize he had seen the boxes before. They were the vessels used by the gods, the place that a person was put into after being lifted. He'd only seen them from a distance, but it was something he couldn't forget. They were the same cubes he'd seen his parents placed in as a child.

Stacked in the closest compartment were what looked like giant gardeners' tools. They were similar in design to what he'd seen on Gorman's window sill – the ones used to cultivate the miniature tree – but scaled up for the hands of a god. There were pots filled with water and an unstable looking pile of large boulders, similar to those in the quarry. Seeds lay scattered all over the floor, clearly spilt from the bulky woven metal sacks that had been stuffed into one corner.

'What's in there?' Sonora called from the outside once he'd jumped down into the box.

'Tools,' he said.

He could hear Sonora's feet and hands scrabbling against the side as she climbed up. He hopped up onto a huge trowel and, with a little effort, managed to get himself back up to the rim of the box where he could look down on her. She threw the bags up for him to catch.

'Here,' he said, extending a hand.

'I've got it,' she said and then climbed the rest of the way to the top more quickly than he'd managed. She forced him to one side as she pulled herself up and over the edge.

'Where did you learn to climb like that?' he asked, impressed.

'Harl Eriksson,' she said, smiling, 'for all it might seem, I do have my own talents.'

'So I see,' he said, looking her up and down. 'You're made of stern stuff.'

Her smile widened then vanished as a deep thudding noise drew their attention. The noise became physical, rattling the tray. Harl ran higher up the trowel to get a better view and was horrified to see the One True God striding directly towards them.

Chapter 23

Karvac has seen them. He stormed round after I refused to pay the debt and broke the door down. I was setting up one of the tanks when he barged in. It was no use, I had to answer all his questions before he agreed to secrecy and belated payment.

'Quick,' Harl said, ducking down, 'get behind something.' They had just enough time to crouch between one of the small cubes and a giant crumpled rag before the god loomed over them. It swallowed the space around it, turning Harl's field of vision into a moving mass of silvery clothing. It's yellow eyes gleamed down at them, scanning the inside of the tray.

After a brief look, the god leant over the giant tray and grabbed the handle.

They were forced to the floor as the god lifted the tray up. Harl staggered as the tray swung and he grabbed hold of Sonora as they were pushed up against the side of the cube. On the return swing they were flung against the bundle of soft cloth.

'Watch out!' Harl shouted as one of the large boulders rolled towards them. He wrapped both arms around her and leapt out of the way as the boulder tumbled past and lodged into the bundle of cloth. They dived under the trowel as several smaller rocks followed it.

Harl peeked out.

'I think we're going through the archway,' he said.

The trowel scraped and shifted above them.

'We need to get out,' Sonora cried as the trowel rocked lower, forcing them to their hands and knees.

They scrambled out and stood up only for the motion of the tray to slam them against the side wall. The tray dropped away beneath Harl's feet and he felt weightless for a moment before realising that he was falling. Sonora was clinging to the tray wall, terrified, as she looked up. The tray hit the ground with a deafening impact that sent tools shying across its inside. Harl crashed to the ground and screamed as his knee hit one of the boulders. He grabbed his knee and struggled away to safety, then ran his hands over the injury, but it was just a bang, nothing broken.

The god turned away from them and, for the first time, Harl heard it speak. The harsh language was full of inflection and meaning. It was like a rockfall, a deep rumbling of sounds that rose and fell with a hypnotic cadence vibrating with such a low bass note that it felt like it was passing right through his body.

A rough choking sound came from another god as it entered the room. It sounded like a dog hacking up a bone, only magnified until the very air seemed to shake with it. Was the sound was a greeting? The One True God repeated it in return.

He couldn't see the god above them any more so he assumed it must have moved off. Wondering if he should look over the side, he turned to tell Sonora to stay low and stumbled over his words as he saw that she was already standing on the trowel and peering over the edge.

'He's gone over to another one,' she said.

Harl clambered over the smaller tools and on to the upturned trowel. It was an easy climb up the trowel to the top of the tray wall. He scrambled up and peered over. The god that had picked them up was a long way off now, speaking to a bulky, rotund creature that was obviously one of the lesser gods.

Harl noticed that the tray had been placed on a table in the centre of the realm. They were roughly in the middle of the table and the surface dropped away to nothing about a hundred paces away. Harl was used to seeing an edge to the world, but there was something chilling about being stuck up on the table. He felt exposed. The lack of walls was unnerving. It felt like all of that emptiness was pressing against him. Ridiculous, of course. How could it press against him?

He turned to look back at the archway and saw the cubes of light containing all the worlds. A shiver ran down his spine.

'Do you think the gods...' Sonora's voice trailed off as she turned to face the wall of worlds. 'Is that?'

'Yes,' Harl said. 'It's our home. Or one of them is, anyway. The archway hides most of them. If you stepped beyond it you'd see the worlds spreading out across the wall in that part of the god's realm.'

'It's beautiful,' she said.

'It's a prison,' he said, turning away from the view.

'Has your life in them been so bad?' she asked, pulling her gaze away to look at him, her hands planted on her hips.

Harl understood her point.

'No,' he said. 'I wouldn't have met you.'

She smiled, but her face changed from happiness to fear in a heartbeat as her eyes flicked up over his shoulder. 'Harl! It's coming.'

They ducked their heads below the rim of the tray and a distant booming rattled the objects around them. The noise grew louder and vibrations tremored through Harl's shoes. The god was heading for their table. Harl ducked lower as its yellow eyes swept across the tray. Another god was following along behind and Harl watched as they strode around the table and headed for the archway.

The One True God came to an abrupt stop, almost forcing the other to crash into its back. It's face whipped around to look straight at them. It paused, staring at the tray for a moment, and then it turned and marched towards them.

'Down,' Harl said, slipping off the trowel and rolling underneath to hide.

Sonora slid down next to him and he wrapped an arm around her, drawing her deeper under the curved metal. The god's hand reached in and grabbed two of the clear square containers. The god then turned and walked through the archway to join the lesser god, who was staring into a tank.

'Do we run?' Sonora asked as Harl rolled out and climbed up the trowel, his feet skidding on the smooth metal.

He stayed silent, his focus on the archway. He could see a few of the tanks beyond the two gods. The lesser god had its back to him and was still looking inside. The One True God had disappeared further through the archway, but after a moment its arm reached inside one of the tanks through the opening in the back of the world. Shortly after it retracted and the opening closed.

'What is it?' Sonora asked from below.

'I think someone has just been lifted,' he said and ducked down below the lip as the archway filled with the titanic mass of the returning gods.

It seemed so horrifically easy standing on this side of the Sight. The hand had casually reached in and plucked a tiny creature from inside the world. But the harsh reality was that the person lifted would have their life snatched away and those living on the inside would grieve for cycles over the loss of their loved one. The casual nature of the god's act was chilling. It had no empathy for the humans trapped inside the worlds. Just what did it think they were? Cattle? Insects?

Harl slid off the tools and crouched in a small gap next to Sonora.

The table shook as the gods returned, their voices booming like an endless series of rockfalls. The table shuddered and Harl risked a glance through a hole he'd found in the side of the tray. The One True God had just placed the two clear cases next to each other about fifty paces away on the tabletop. Each one now contained a terrified human. They were dashing around frantically

227

within the confines of the containers, their hands clawing at the clear walls as they searched for an opening.

One case held a middle-aged man and the other a young boy. They were both dressed in leather jerkins and simple trousers, but it was the bright orange hair and pale skin that marked them as different from himself and Sonora.

Harl and Sonora rushed up the trowel and peered over at the two humans. The older man was beating his fists against the inside of the glass. Fresh bruises scoured his face and arms as if he had attempted to fight back against the god. A flicker of pride stirred in Harl at the thought of such bravery.

'The boy,' Sonora said, drawing Harl's gaze to the other cube.

The young lad was standing stock-still, both palms resting on the glass as he stared at them in shock.

The older man stopped to see what had made the boy so fixated. As soon as he spotted them, the same look of disbelief crossed his own freckled features. His lips moved as if begging rescue, but the container's glass walls blocked the sound.

Harl couldn't stand it. He hooked a leg over the tray wall and started to scramble over. Sonora grabbed him and pulled him back.

'We can't help them,' she said, shaking her head.

Harl was torn between attempting to rescue them and the knowledge that it was futile to try. It would risk all their lives and he couldn't chance Sonora's freedom over that of a stranger.

The man glared at Harl as though he was a coward. He punched his fists against the container as if hitting Harl for his inaction and roared a string of silent curses.

The boy was still motionless. The blood had drained from his face but, unlike the man, it was obvious that the boy understood.

A god's shadow fell across them all and it reached its weathered hands down to clasp both containers.

Harl crouched lower. The boy stared down at him, tears flowing from his eyes as the boxes were wrenched up into the air.

Harl's gut twisted in anger at himself. How could he just sit there and watch it happen? What kind of monster was he to let the beast snatch them away? He locked stares with the boy until the hand had lifted them far above the table top. All he could see now was the soles of their feet through the transparent base of the containers.

The One True God stacked both boxes on top of each other in one hand and extended it towards the lesser god. The other tugged open a bag attached to his belt and plunged a hand inside, withdrawing two shining orbs clasped between his four fingers. Each sphere was the size of a person and glowed with an internal light that hurt Harl's eyes to focus on. A tangle of pulsating lines coiled inside, reds, golds and sapphire tendrils swirling around like fire reflected in water. The lesser god placed the orbs in the outstretched hand of the One True God and with the other hand snatched up the two boxes.

'It's a transaction,' Harl said, keeping his voice to a whisper but unable to hide his disgust at what was happening. He had made enough similar deals in the tool shop to know this was a sale. Not just any sale, but the sale of people.

He stormed up and down the trowel once the gods had left, his fists bunched up in anger.

'Damn it!' he yelled. 'We have to stop this. Put an end to this...this sick trade.'.

'I know,' Sonora said, 'but what can we do about it? It's just the two of us, Harl. Perhaps we should think of ourselves first?'

He knew she was right, but the selfishness of it horrified him. How could such a terrible trade be happening with no one aware of it? Worst of all was the thought that those back home even worshipped such creatures. They had no idea of the gods' true nature or the horrific fate of those who were lifted. And it was all for some kind of profit. The creatures disgusted him.

'We have to do something,' he said and pointed to where the gods had left. 'They're raising us like cattle bound for market. That's why we're kept in the boxes. We're just some type of living commodity. We should be free.'

'Free where?' Sonora asked. 'Inside the worlds isn't so bad.'

'They're not worlds,' he said, slumping down inside the tray. 'They're holding tanks, and this-' He gestured at the roof to emphasize his point. '-is a shop. We're being bred for money, Sonora. They're no more gods than you or I.'

'What do they want from us?' she asked.

'I don't know,' he said, shrugging. 'Whatever the answer, it's not right.'

Sonora put her hand on his shoulder. 'We need to get moving.'

Harl sighed and clambered up the trowel to the top of the tray wall. Cupboards and shelves lined the distant walls. The more he thought about it the more the place began to resemble his own shop. Boxes of packaged products were stacked neatly on the shelves. Each one had a clear front and he could see faint green blobs inside. He squinted to see them more clearly. Trees. The boxes held trees.

A stand next to them contained stacks of empty tanks that varied in size. Harl didn't realise what he was looking at to begin with, but then he recognised them for what they were. Worlds. They were empty worlds. He could see some of them perched next to empty packing crates ready to be shipped out. The sickening reality of it made him clutch the edge of the tray with shaking hands. It meant that worlds and humans were shipped goodness knew where. How many were there? How far away? Images of those glass prisons flashed through his mind with gods staring in at them. How many humans were imprisoned like that?

Would the torture never end?

He knew they needed to get somewhere with more cover, even the ground would be preferable, but he had no idea how far it was to the floor, so there was no telling if their ropes would be long enough. Going to the edge of the table was a gamble. It would leave them exposed. If the god came back they would be seen instantly.

He was about to suggest they got away from the tray when everything began to shake and the god strode into view.

Harl ducked down, but he was too late. The god stopped by the table, a questioning look in its piercing yellow eyes.

'Get underneath,' Harl hissed, staying hunched over as he slid off the trowel and scrambled back underneath it. The gap was only just big enough for the two of them.

A shadow fell over the tray and Harl imagined the god's eyes searching for the cause of the movement. All he could hear was his own breathing and the deafening pounding of his heart. If the god lifted any of the tools aside it would find them, but if it rummaged through the tools it would crush them in the jumble. They were powerless to stop any of it and there was nowhere else to hide.

Nothing happened for a moment, but then the tray lurched up and swung to the side as the god lifted it from the table. The trowel shifted above them and they huddled together underneath it as it rocked from side to side. Harl grasped Sonora's hand, hoping to reassure her, but her breathing was heavy and her eyes wide with fear.

The tray jolted beneath them. They were flung sideways by the impact and the trowel crashed down next to them. Harl looked up. They had stopped. He couldn't see much from his position against the wall, but the roof looked different and there was far more light.

A series of low grunts came from the god as though it was talking to itself. It was stood next to the tray, one of its massive legs only a stride away. Harl could easily reach it with Gorman's sword if he tried. He had a brief vision of leaping from the top of the tray and screaming a battlecry as he plunged the blade into the god's ankle. But what would be the point? Would it even damage the creature? It would be Harl's last act as the god would surely turn around and stamp its massive foot down on him as though squashing a bug. But it was tempting. Inflicting just a moment of pain would be a tiny measure of payback for all the torment it had caused.

The god stepped away and the guttural sound of its voice faded as its footsteps became a distant scuffing.

'We need to get out,' Sonora said as she shook Harl to break his trance.

He scrambled back up the trowel. It had dropped down from the rim of the tray, but it was still close enough to the top for him to see over the edge. They were on the floor next to the wall of worlds. The god stood a few hundred paces away peering into one of the tanks. The light from the wall of worlds bathed the god in an eerie glow that made it look even more sinister.

'It's still close, but let's get out,' he said, turning to look in the opposite direction.

There was a gap between the end of the worlds and the wall.

'The wall of worlds ends a short distance away. I can see gap beyond it. If we can get around that corner we'll be out of sight. But we need to move fast and stay under the overhang.'

He looked over the edge of the trowel. What would happen if either of them slipped on the climb down? Sonora tapped him on the shoulder and he turned to find her holding the rope out to him. He smiled at her quick thinking.

'It might notice the rope afterwards,' he said, then saw her scowl. 'But we'll take the chance.'

He tied one end of the rope around the handle of the trowel and slung the rest of the coil over the side.

'Ladies first,' he said.

233

Sonora did not reply, she just swung a leg over the side of the tray, gripped the rope, and then slid from view.

Harl hoisted himself up and scrambled over the side. He let go of the rope as the god stomped back towards them, the floor vibrating in rhythm. Small mounds of dirt and debris scattered across the barren grey floor bounced around them as the steps grew louder and the vibrations intensified.

'Underneath the edge,' Sonora said, pulling him into the shadowed overhang below the worlds and then throwing her cloak over herself as a canopy. The material's colour matched the floor perfectly. It was exceptional camouflage even at close range.

Harl did the same as the god stomped back towards them, but pulled his head into the hood so that he could still see what was going on.

The god's hand came down, clasped the tray's handle, and lifted. The tray rose up as the god walked back through the archway. Lights from the worlds flickered off, one by one, dimming sections of the floor until it left them in complete darkness.

They were free.

Chapter 24

My illness worsens. Maybe all the excitement has taken its toll. I will push on with the plan no matter how much Karvac demands I rest.

They got little rest during the course of the blackness. As they got ready to settle down, Sonora sat up and stared out into the darkness.

'What is it?' Harl asked.

'Did you hear that?' she said. 'Something is out there scuffing the floor or moving across it.'

He grabbed the sword and stood, letting his cloak fall to the floor as he walked out from under the overhang.

'Out there,' she said, pointing into the halflight where the black shadows from beyond the archway merged with the wall.

He stopped and strained to see into the gloom, but couldn't make out anything, so he closed his eyes and concentrated on the sounds. Sonora's frightened breaths came from beside him. He focused beyond them and let them fall into the background as he reached out into the darkness for any sound.

A faint scrabbling came from somewhere far in the distance. It was barely audible to his ears, but Sonora was right, they were not alone.

After what seemed an age the sounds faded.

'I'll keep watch,' he said, hoping that he sounded more confident than he felt.

Sonora crawled back under her cloak and settled down. He could hear her tossing and turning as the dark cycle crept by.

Perhaps her thoughts, like his own, were fixated on the practise of selling people? It was barbaric. The thought of any human being sold made him sick. It stripped away any sense of freedom and the shuddering implication that there might be thousands of tank worlds out there chilled him to the bone and made the darkness pressing down around him all the heavier.

Or maybe Sonora was still worried about whatever creature was lurking out there in the darkness? Harl had no way of telling what the darkness was hiding. It could be anything, one of the gods walking around, humans trapped in jars, or just the wind playing with their senses.

But he just couldn't shake the images of that man and the boy trapped inside those transport cubes. Even the thought of a creature lurking out in the darkness seemed like a shallow fear compared to the churning nightmare that all those people were enduring.

How could the gods be selling people?

Seeing his parents lifted had severed his link to religion long ago, but his core ideas still clung to those beliefs. He had always been taught that the gods cared for humanity. The gifting was a blessing from the One True God which demonstrated its benevolent nature. Yes, people were taken, but it was just a punishment meted out by the gods. The Eldermen had always put it down to people straying from their beliefs or committing crimes. The liftings were just the One True God's way and, whether you believed in the teachings or not, it was a fact you had to live with.

But all of that had been on the inside. Leaving the tanks had revealed too many truths. People weren't lifted for punishment or to be taken to paradise; they were lifted to be sold.

How long had the barbaric market been running? What kind of profit was there in a human? The giftings, the other worlds, the variety of people segregated within them, it was all artificial. The tanks had been set up for them by the gods and, like fish bred in a barrel, humans swam endlessly around waiting to be picked. They had no way of knowing that they were being bartered and sold. They were just playthings used for the amusement of the creatures they worshipped.

His mind reeled under the onslaught of it all. In the end exhaustion won out. He slipped into a deep sleep and dreamt of joining the flame-haired boy and man in his own container. The sides would shrink every time he moved until it crushed him and he reappeared in a new container for the process to repeat itself.

It was still dark when Sonora's movements woke him. A flicker of light shone out across a space at the far end of the realm. They had come from that direction and, as Harl stepped out from the overhang to take a look, another section lit up, followed by a third and a fourth. The lights inside the tanks were switching on one at a time and he watched, amazed, as the whole wall of worlds flickered into life. The long realm was bathed in light from the worlds, revealing the rough textures of the walls and the smooth, polished floor. They stood in what could only be described as a hallway for giants. The floor, the roof and the walls were washed in shades of ashen grey.

They ate a brief meal while casting constant glances up at the archway as if expecting one of the creatures to enter at any moment. A soft wind blew through it and stirred small bits of debris on the floor. It brought with it a faint smell of something foul, an odour of corruption that seemed to match the sickening trade that occurred on the far side.

'Along the base of the tanks or through the archway?' Harl asked, standing, finally, and slinging a bag over one shoulder. He knew they had been avoiding the question.

They could leave the safety of the overhang and head directly for the archway. There might be shelter under one of the tables out there, but it was a gamble. Without the safety of the overhang they would be easy to spot by the gods as they tried to cross the floor, and there was still the risk of being snatched up by whatever they'd heard during the night. Moving was a risk, but so was staying put.

'Too much activity out there,' Sonora said, nodding at the archway. 'Grandpa did say to head along the side if we didn't want to risk being spotted, and after seeing those poor people...'

'Along the base then,' he said.

He turned his right shoulder to the worlds above and, staying beneath their overhang, they trudged along the line of worlds as they headed for the wall at the end of the hallway of the gods.

There was a sense of weight bearing down on Harl from the worlds above. He knew it wouldn't collapse, but every now and then he considered leading Sonora more out into the open just to lessen the feeling. And yet each time he was about to step out he'd catch a glimpse of the god through the archway and it would force him to bear the weight a little longer. It wasn't even the weight of glass, metal, and earth that stood above him that was the problem, it was the knowledge of all those lives, all those people. So many men, women, and children trapped in their cages, oblivious and innocent of the true nature of their slavery.

When they were most of the way to the wall, Sonora stopped.

'What was that?' she asked and stepped out from under the ledge.

Harl took a moment to adjust the pack on his shoulders. Something inside was poking a sharp edge into the small of his back.

'I didn't hear anything,' he said, rubbing at the sore spot.

Sonora looked up into the world directly above them and burst out laughing.

'What is it?' he asked, wondering what could be so funny at such a time. A lowing noise reached his ears as he moved out to join her.

'Cows,' she said, pointing to dozens of cows squashed up against the glass front of the world.

'It makes sense, I suppose,' he said. 'The gifted animals must have come from somewhere.'

239

'It looks like there are hundreds of them, possibly thousands if their world is as big as ours was,' she said and then laughed again.

'What's so funny?'

'Can you imagine the smell in a world full of cows?' she said. 'I wonder if they have a hierarchy.'

'Probably,' he jested, 'with stubborn elders who demand the finest grass from the land.'

She laughed and kissed him.

The end of the hallway was a dull wall, a featureless vertical expanse, but from their position Harl could tell there was a space beyond the worlds that hinted at a turn at the end. He didn't know what to expect when they reached it. His entire life had been spent inside the walls of his own world and now he was walking past world after world. How did you even picture what might exist beyond them?

'Do you think Gorman knew?' Sonora asked, interrupting his thoughts.

Harl said nothing for a while, remembering all that the old man had told them. 'I think that he knew we were imprisoned. I don't know if he knew why, but I'm sure he had his suspicions.'

They walked in silence until Sonora asked the question that had been burning in his own mind since their descent.

'Are we just going to leave all those people behind?'

'What can we do?' he said. 'We can't cut our way into each tank to rescue everyone. For starters, there's no way back up. But even if we did manage to get back inside, I doubt anyone would believe us. Too many cycles behind barriers has left us without the ability to comprehend what lies outside.'

Sonora stayed quiet.

'What's wrong?' he asked.

'All those people trapped inside. There must be thousands...'

'Maybe tens of thousands,' he said. He looked around at the grey walls and featureless floor.

'Not much out here, though. I'm beginning to think that things have changed since Gorman was a child.'

She took it all in silently as if weighing his words.

'What's that?' she asked, pointing into the distance.

A brilliant glare of illumination broadened across the smooth floor ahead of them. It shone out from near the end of the towering stack of tanks as if a fire lay around the bend ahead. He might have been afraid, but he lengthened his stride instead and reached out for Sonora's hand. She was with him and that was all that mattered.

The wall of worlds stopped ahead of them like the corner of a towering cliff. The edge was a perfect square angle and, when he looked up at the worlds stacked one on top of another, Harl was reminded of a kitchen cabinet stacked full of boxes, only this one was massive beyond his wildest imaginings and each box was a self-contained world. Harl looked around the corner and instead of another corridor he found himself staring at a line of dazzling light spreading from underneath a giant door. It was a gap about shin high and was too small for them to crawl under.

He drew a deep, slow breath as he craned his head back to take in the immensity of the door. Gorman had warned him not to judge anything based on his own life, but the titanic scale of what faced him was overwhelming. The metal door climbed five hundred paces into the air. The glass worlds were tiny compared to it. A god could have stacked three on top of each other and still had space to push them through the doorway. A handle jutted from the smooth metal halfway up, but it was the length of a row of houses, and almost as wide.

Sonora touched his arm and he just shook his head.

'How are we supposed to open it?' he said.

She took a step back and studied the door, then turned to him.

'We'll find a way,' she said, smiling as she laced her fingers through his. But then all colour drained from her face as she noticed something over his shoulder.

He spun round fearing that the giant was glaring down at them. Instead, the huge creature was striding through the archway, holding a pair of giant buckets and its tool tray. It turned away from them and headed further down the hallway, then peered into one of the tanks. It lined the buckets up along the floor at its feet and then put the tray down next to them and drew out the trowel. Reaching up, it popped a large section of the lid off a tank and reached inside, scraping soil, buildings, and trees away with the trowel, only to dump the mixture into a bucket and reach in for more.

'That's...' Harl didn't know how to finish the sentence. Sonora was quivering at his side. He didn't need to say anything else.

The god was emptying Sonora's home.

'I'm sorry-' Harl said, thinking of Gorman as buildings and great mounds of soil tumbled down into the buckets at the god's feet.

'There's nothing we can do,' she said, tears rolling down her face as she turned away.

The god stooped down to retrieve the buckets, whirled in place, and then stomped towards them. Harl's legs felt wobbly. He tried to get them to move, but nothing seemed to be working. The god just kept getting larger and larger, closer and closer, a horror so immense that he just waited for the footfalls to crush him. And then he blinked and whatever hypnotic hold the giant had cast over him crumbled.

'Run!' he yelled, and dragged Sonora after him as he raced for the door.

He glanced back and found that the god was almost on them. Its terrifying stride devoured the distance between them and Harl had to force his gaze away from it to concentrate on where they were going. The door was still a hundred paces away. They'd never make it. He searched for somewhere to hide, but they were out in the open and the overhang was too far away.

He stumbled as the god's foot slammed down close behind. Sonora fell over, crying out as her hands scuffed the floor, but Harl dragged her back up and they ran on.

A shadow enveloped them. Harl looked up. The god was on them, its great foot plunging down. He grabbed Sonora around the waist and skidded to a halt. With one last look up at the foot he braced for the impact. It would be the end of them. They would be squashed into a puddle of blood and brittle bone on the floor. He closed his eyes, but then roared in anger and threw them both backwards.

They crashed to the ground and his head smacked against the floor. Stars burst across his vision. He held tight to Sonora and fought against the pain as he opened his eyes. The god's heel was a hand span above them, swinging past like a pendulum. The ground shook with the impact as the foot landed ahead of them.

Harl only had moments to think, but a cord jutting from the back of the god's shoe swept past and he wrapped an arm around it and held tight. Somewhere in his mind he was shocked by the fact that the god wore shoes. It just felt so insane. Why would the god need them? But then the thought was gone, lurched out of his mind as the god moved forward and they were swept away with him.

The movement almost tore Harl's arm from the socket, but he held on, aware that Sonora was still clinging to him. They crashed to the ground again and the pain was too much for him. The world blacked out for a moment and then he found himself being dragged along again, but this time it was Sonora.

'Quick!' she whispered. 'The door! He's opening the door.'

Harl watched as the giant figure swung the door open in front of them. Dazzling light flooded the hallway. It blinded him to everything.

'Get up,' Sonora pleaded. She half-dragged, half-lifted him to his feet, and they staggered forward.

The god stepped into the open doorway, a towering darkness against the alien glare. Harl raised his hand to shade his eyes, but it didn't help. It was like walking into a wall of blazing white fire.

They just limped after the god, hoping that they had enough time to get out.

The god headed out into the brightness and there was a loud crash, then it turned back and strode towards them. Harl pushed Sonora to the right as the god's foot appeared overhead again, but it just swept over them. They staggered another few steps, but Harl slipped on the floor and knocked Sonora down with him.

He twisted round and watched as the god reached out for the door and swung it shut towards them. In the moment before it closed Harl caught a glimpse of sadness in the yellow eyes. The purity of the light beyond let him see the detail on its face where he'd never seen it before. Sadness? It was the first tender emotion he'd ever seen on one of the gods. He blinked his eyes several times and then the thought washed away from him.

'We're out!' he cried.

'No, the frame, Harl. The frame! We aren't clear of it.'

He saw it at once. They were still inside the hallway by a good ten paces. The door was going to swat them like flies. He wrapped his arms around Sonora and looked into her eyes. He hoped she knew that he was sorry he'd failed her, but it didn't matter in the end.

The door slammed into them and the world tumbled away into blackness.

Chapter 25

They are subsisting on our foodstuffs, but as with any creature taken
from its natural environment, its nutritional needs will be at an
imbalance. There have been loses.

Harl opened his eyes, but was blinded by a blaze of white, forcing him to squeeze them shut again. He scrabbled in a circle on his knees as he waved his arms around in panic trying to find Sonora.

'Harl?' Sonora cried, 'I can't see! Harl?'

'Me neither,' Harl replied as calmly as he could.

He shuffled forward, groping air until he touched her, then wrapped his arms around her and they clutched each other tightly.

'It's okay,' he said. 'I'm not going anywhere, but I think we need time to allow our eyes to adapt to the change in light. Just sit still and don't move for now.'

He found her hand, squeezed gently and the pressure was returned. They sat on the dusty ground, holding one another as their other senses expanded to fill the void left by their sight.

Harl noticed a warm heat being cast all over his body. It did not feel like flames but like standing far off from the gifting bonfire. He raised one hand and could feel the heat against his skin. It was a pleasant feeling, even if it was strange. He smiled at the feel of it touching his face and drew a deep breath.

It was so peaceful.

A gentle breeze brought strange sounds and smells, as though they were sitting in the middle of a forest enjoying a picnic. The rustling of leaves combined with the heady smell of grass and a hint of flowers to give him a sense of home. He could picture Troy at his side as they laughed at some shared joke. The feeling of home was so strong that he could feel tears welling at the corners of his eyes. He scrubbed a hand across them. It was just ridiculous and yet he breathed in the sense of peace as though it was part of the air.

He gathered his courage. 'I'm going to open my eyes now,' he said. He didn't know why he said it, maybe just to reassure himself. He thought of Gorman and how the blind man had coped so well with the world and some hope returned to him. Even if he couldn't see again he would make it work.

As he opened his eyes, the whiteness faded until his sight returned to normal. He gasped and brought his hand up to shield his eyes. A ball of yellow and white light blazed in the air, far ahead in the distance. The span to it was unimaginable and everything else around it was a startling blue, like Sonora's eyes. The fiery ball hurt his eyes when he looked at it and he kept blocking it with his hand and then daring another glance in fascination. He'd never seen anything so enchanting. It felt like he was looking on into the distance forever, no walls or barriers, no sign of a limit to the world. There was just the endless blue and the burning orb.

He lowered his gaze, blinking as the after image of the yellow-white ball stayed imprinted on his vision. They were sitting in the centre of a huge clearing. Orange, dust-covered ground stretched ahead of them to a wall of thick grass blades that were as wide as a man at their base and peaked to a point five strides above. Each one flopped over at the top and weaved in with the others to form a canopy over the grass forest.

But that wasn't the end of it. A gigantic tree stood above it all in the distance. It was like nothing he had ever seen. Its impossibly high limbs stretched out over the forest of grass stalks, splitting into hundreds of branches, peppered with leaves that shifted in the breeze. It dwarfed the gods and, even at this distance, he could see the deep grooves and crevasses in its bark. It had to be at least half a cycle's journey to it, perhaps more. There was no way of telling. Distance was something he just couldn't understand out here. There was so much of everything. It was overwhelming.

He looked back up overhead and the blue climbed up and up and up. There was no sign of a roof or light directly above them; there was only the endless blue and the ball of light. He shivered. He didn't know whether it was from excitement or fear.

Sonora gasped as she opened her eyes. After a moment she looked around then up at the ball and chuckled to herself.

'What is it?' he asked.

'The sun,' she said, pointing up at it. 'Grandpa used to tell me tales of his home when I was a child. I thought they were just stories, but now I see they were true.'

Harl stared around, trying to take it all in.

'I can't believe it,' he said. 'It feels so warm. Do you think that's what Gorman meant when he said he wanted to feel the sun on his face?'

She shrugged.

The openness of so much space dwarfed them to insignificance. He turned to take it all in and found himself facing the structure they had come from.

An immense silver wall stretched away left and right and shot off so high into the air that he couldn't tell where it stopped. Could it really be a building? He could see the huge door that they had just come out of, but even that knowledge seemed an impossibility. The place was just too big. The sun reflected off the building so brightly that Harl was forced to look away.

'Which way should we go?' Sonora asked.

He didn't know what to say. He hadn't really considered their next move beyond getting away from the dimly lit interior of the god's realm. And now his mind was reeling from everything he'd seen.

'I don't know, Sonora. I hadn't-'

A terrifying croaking shriek cut his words off. The giant grasses on the left side of the clearing thrashed around as if something was carving a path towards them. The stalks rustled and crumpled over as a second cry split the air. The horrid sound rolled over and over, like a tortured animal squealing its last few breaths, but it was deeper, harsher, and sent a shudder of fear through him.

The grass stalks buckled apart and a creature scuttled out into the open. Its bright yellow body was segmented into two parts that were striped with black lines and supported by six, clawed legs. Large arm-sized pincers protruded from its jaw, making the creature a full three strides in length.

It froze, its bulbous eyes staring at them, then snapped its pincers, twitched its abdomen and charged. Dust rose in a cloud behind it as it scurried towards them.

Dropping the bow from his shoulder, Harl had an arrow ready as the beast raced in for the kill. He tracked its path and released, but the creature flicked its jagged pincers and the arrow bounced off the hard bone. Harl cursed and loosed another. This time it struck its mark, embedding itself in a front leg joint. The creature stumbled and let out a hideous screech, but it didn't even slow.

'The sword!' he shouted to Sonora, but it was too late.

The monster barrelled into him, pushing him backwards so that his feet scraped lines in the dry soil. He shifted his grip and held the bow like a horizontal staff to fend off the pincers as they snapped and clawed at him, trying to tear his belly open. The creature spread its legs and shoved hard, knocking Harl over. They rolled backwards in a heap and the bow flew from his grip. He grabbed the monster's bug-like head and dug his fingernails into its bulbous eyes to keep the razor-like pincers from slicing into his face. The creature clacked and lunged at him until his arms shook with the effort. Possibly sensing the weakness it pressed its advantage, jutting its head forward to tear at his jerkin.

The beast shrieked in pain and jolted forward. Its legs splayed out into the dust as it sagged on top of him, convulsing, before falling still.

Harl gasped. He was still gripping the thing's head in his hands, his fingers sunk into its black, faceted eyes. But there was no movement in it any more, no sign of life. Holding his breath, he rolled the head aside and used one foot to kick the creature over. He stared at it, numb from shock as the legs crumpled up like a dead fly, and then rolled his eyes up to where Sonora towered over him, sword humming in a two-handed grip. Her eyes were on fire, her face twisted into a feral snarl.

She drew a deep breath and lowered the blade.

'You've saved my life twice now,' he said, standing. He kicked the creature and its abdomen tore away, spewing yellow blood as it rolled across the dirt.

Sonora looked down at the sword, wide-eyed as if horrified by her own actions. She shuddered and then grimaced as she tried to wipe the creature's blood from her face with the back of one hand, but only succeeded in smearing the gore. She looked daemonic with the blood coating her. Her eyes had a feral look to them, like a cornered predator, but she seemed calmer than she ever had. A feeling of power radiated from her, and yet the pity and regret of what she'd done was etched across her face. In a strange way it made him love her even more.

'I'm sure you'll have a chance to repay me,' she said.

She offered her hand to help pull him up, but then her head snapped up and she spun on the spot, slicing the sword down in an arc as another one of the creatures pounced. She severed it in two as more of the croaking shrieks erupted from the giant stalks where the creature had first emerged.

'Quick!' she yelled, 'I don't think we can kill a group of them.'

Harl snatched the bags and bow off the ground, then sprinted for the thick stalks on the opposite side of the clearing. Bursting into the first wave of grasses, he ducked low as the canopy above them shifted with the bodies of half a dozen more monsters as they scuttled across the tops of the grasses to reach them. Moments later they broke through and crashed to the ground, hissing as they scurried after him and Sonora.

Sonora stumbled and let go of the sword as the closest monster spread its stubby wings, lurched into the air, and then flew on to her back.

Harl roared and kicked the beast off her, but Sonora overbalanced and landed flat on her front, sprawled in the dirt. He grabbed her hand and tugged her up, then snatched the sword up off the ground with his free hand, and threw the scabbard aside as he swung the blade around towards the beast as it pounced. The ancient steel sliced clean through its head, jarring his arm as the body rolled in mid-air and crumpled to the ground.

The stalks wobbled and another monster lurched towards them, launching itself off the stalks one by one, as it closed the gap.

'Go!' Harl shouted, turning to face the creature in the hope that he could buy Sonora time to get away.

But there was not enough time. The monster launched itself into the air from halfway up a stalk and then plummeted down towards him.

Harl rolled onto his back and then kicked out at the last moment to send the creature tumbling away. It crashed to the ground and hissed as it twisted around, trying to get its feet under it, but Harl jumped up and plunged his sword down into the writhing tangle of limbs and wings before it could react. He looked around frantic, expecting the rest of the creatures to rush him, but they were still far behind them. He waited a moment to be sure, then spun and raced after Sonora.

He just prayed that she was still alive.

Chapter 26

The micro tools, vehicles and plant species that I recovered in and around their nest will open entire new areas of research in nano-machines and microbiology.

Harl found Sonora in a small clearing next to a giant log. She was bent over double, catching her breath, and relief flooded her face when he came crashing through the grasses. The clearing was bare other than the log. To a god it must have been a mere stick, but to Harl it was as thick as a felled pine tree.

'There might be more,' he said. 'We should get as far from here as we can.'

Cautious to make as little noise as possible, they crept between the stalks and smaller clumps of foliage in the hope that they could avoid any more of the giant insects.

Unfamiliar noises peppered the alien forest. Small clicks, chirps and rustlings filled the air around them and seemed to echo up out of dark holes bored in the ground. Some of the holes were big enough for a man to climb down and Harl dreaded the thought of what might be down there. Each time they came close to one he would steer their path away from it just in case.

The grass stalks became more and more oppressive as they threaded their way through the forest. Dozens of stems curled overhead to form a canopy ten paces above them. Sometimes the stalks grew so close together that they had to cut through them with the sword. It was dangerous and tiring work

'It feels like there could be anything hidden in here,' Sonora said. 'It's so close it makes me feel trapped.'

'Reminds me of the mines,' Harl said, remembering the tightness of the enclosed tunnels. He pulled an arrow on to the string and held it ready by his side. 'I want to be far away from those critters before we rest up.'

They glimpsed the sun rarely as they walked along. The grass stalks cut out most of the light to leave everything coated by a deep layer of shadows. The wind would rustle the grass forest around them and slanting beams of sunlight would break through. They would give life to the shadowed world around them in ways that Harl had never imagined. Dewdrops sparkled on the ground and tiny rocks gleamed with vibrant colour where they peeked up above the soil. There was a richness to the scent around them that filled Harl with a sense of wonder. It was as though this endless sunlit world was revealing a fresh magnitude of sight and sounds that he had never experienced.

They kept walking deeper into the grass, constantly checking behind them. Eventually the odd little rustles and distant calls became normal and the dense grass thinned until they were standing in a small clearing. The light was warming, making everything feel alive. Bird and animal calls filled the air, but even the wind had fresh vigour out here. It had only ever been a muted whisper in the tanks.

He glimpsed a dark crevice between a mass of large boulders and soil. The entire mound was ten strides high and coated in a thick tangle of maroon moss. The vibrant moss was held together by a framework of thick roots coiling down between the rocks from the giant grasses above.

A small puddle of water lay nearby and Harl knelt next to it, checking for tracks.

'Nothing's been here recently,' he said. He stood and tried to peer into the dark opening where roots curved into the hole from outside. It looked as if it opened out into a wider space further in. 'We can stay here if it's safe inside.'

'Check now while it's still light,' Sonora said, plucking some of the moss from the mound and inspecting it.

'Who's to say if the light goes out here?' Harl asked.

He thought of the sun's warmth never leaving. Even though it was pleasant, at times it could be too much. He had spent most of the time trekking through the grasses in a heavy sweat and longed for the cooler climate he'd known inside the tank.

He drew his sword and approached the dark opening. Now that he was closer, he could see that it led to a cave. The walls were rocky, rather than just packed earth, and covered in thick roots that ran back inside. The weapon hummed loudly as he activated it and held its point out to as if to threaten the darkness ahead.

Every muscle in his body was tensed for action.

'Hello?' he said.

Animal sounds and the rustle of wind still came from around them in the dense forest, but only silence left the hole. He took a deep breath as he started to step into the darkness, but then stopped.

Reaching into the satchel, he pulled out a small bottle of the fire liquid that Gorman had insisted they take and poured it onto the end of a stick. He stowed the empty bottle and used his flint and steel to shower sparks down over the stick. The tip blossomed into a bright yellow flame and the darkness retreated as he held it out in front of him. Sword ready in his other hand, he ducked under the overhanging roots that ran along the roof and stepped inside.

The roots stretched twenty paces to the back of the cave where they ended in a gnarled twist of knots. Dry leaves coated the dirt floor.

'It's safe!' he called back to Sonora. His voice echoed inside the cave.

He turned to leave and the old twigs and dried leaves crunched under his feet. The place was damp and empty. His torch flickered as a gust of wind blew in from outside and, in the shifting light, he noticed something on one of the walls.

'Sonora?'

'Are you alright?' she asked from the entrance.

'You have to see this,' he said, holding the torch up against the wall to get a better look.

She came to stand beside him, her mouth hanging open as she stared at the stone.

'It's amazing,' she said.

A collection of drawings were etched into the soft rock on one wall of the cave. Strange symbols and pictures of men and women were drawn all over it, as though someone had returned, time and again, to flesh out whatever story was being told. There were humans running from creatures flying high in the air and, in other places, groups of people had surrounded monstrous things on the ground and were killing them. Axes, knives, spears, and arrows peppered the scenes in the hands of the humans, but it was the maroon paint that both horrified and fascinated Harl. It looked like blood.

'Amazing,' Sonora said as she reached out a hand to feel the grooves. 'So there were people here once.'

She picked at a symbol and pulled out a pinch of lichen. She sniffed it and then rolled it between her fingers.

'These are old,' she said, looking up at one of the largest murals. 'This lichen takes a whole childhood to grow.'

The mural showed three men holding up what Harl assumed to be open books. The book in the third man's hand had been deliberately scratched out.

'What do you think of this?' Harl said, pointing to the defaced image.

Sonora moved his arm so that the torch shone on it more clearly.

'The scratches are recent,' she said. 'There's no lichen growth covering them so it means someone's been here within our lifetime.'

Thinking of books made something connect in Harl's memory.

'I've seen these symbols before,' he said. 'They're the same as some of the symbols in Gorman's book.'

'Does the book say what the symbols mean?' Sonora asked.

Harl shook his head. 'No. At least not that I can find. I don't even know what some of the words mean.' He handed Sonora the torch and then slid his pack off. It took him a moment to find Gorman's book, but then he flicked through the pages until he found the right one. 'See just here? Those are the same symbols, right next to where it says "printed circuit board". But what is that supposed to mean?'

'I don't know,' Sonora said, looking at the symbols neatly stamped on the paper.

'Perhaps the people who drew these on the wall are connected to the book somehow?' Harl said. 'It would make sense after what Gorman told us. It means there might be people living in this region.'

'I doubt there are any left,' Sonora said. 'The pictures are far too old.'

'But some of them could be more recent,' he said. 'So there's a chance.'

Sonora shrugged and handed him the torch.

Harl's stomach gave an audible groan.

Sonora chuckled.

'Maybe there's a vendor nearby that sells food,' she said.

Harl laughed. 'I'll rustle a fire up.'

He gathered some dry, shredded grass from the ground and piled it into a small fire just outside the cave entrance. Water was soon boiling away and Sonora began to prepare a small stew.

After a time, it began to grow cold. Harl looked up, wondering why the temperature had dropped and noticed that the sun had shifted from its place in the sky to fall behind the tips of the tall grass.

'It moves,' he said to Sonora.

She looked up from the stew.

'The blue is changing as well,' she said. 'It's a different hue than earlier.'

'This place is strange,' he said.

Once the stew had been cooked, Sonora handed him a bowlful and they both leant back against the soft mossy boulders and stared up.

Fear grew in Harl as the colours above shifted. The endless blue grew darker until it disappeared altogether in a fiery wash of yellow and orange hues. The colours streaked high above their heads as though the roof of this world had been set aflame. And yet with each passing moment the light faded away.

'I don't understand this world,' Harl said. 'Why does it get colder when the sky turns the colour of fire? Surely it should get hotter.'

'Gorman would've known,' Sonora said.

It hurt Harl to hear the hollow loss in her words.

'I miss him too,' he said. 'He knew more than anyone I ever met. Not that Troy was a bastion of knowledge.'

'You miss Troy in the same way?' she asked.

He nodded. 'Growing up with him was an adventure.'

He pulled her closer to him and they snuggled down together by the fire, keeping each other warm as darkness crept between the stalks. The shadows spread into the clearing like the blacking disease, enclosing them in a sphere of firelight.

Sonora shifted and looked up from the fire.

'Harl!' she said, shaking him and pointing to the sky.

He almost jumped up ready to fight, but she clutched him tight as she continued to stare upwards.

'It's so beautiful,' she said. 'What is it?'

Harl looked up. The darkness was lit by thousands of tiny lights shimmering down at them from far away in the distance. They were everywhere, tiny and mesmerising, twinkling points in the endless dark. His breath caught in his throat at the sight and he relaxed. It was beautiful, enchanting, like a tale spun by a toothless elder, but this was real. All of his fears melted away and they gazed up at the display as the fire crackled and danced next to them, happy to wonder in silence at the surreal sight.

Eventually he spoke.

'Do you think they're placed there so we can know there is a roof to this world?'

'Maybe,' Sonora said, doubtful. 'Perhaps the sun divides and becomes whole again after it has rested? Even a fire must go out eventually and so maybe it must rest before it comes back again.'

'Don't know of any fire that springs to life again,' he said. 'Maybe it's both.'

They chatted long into the dark cycle about what the lights might be until, eventually, they snuggled into the dry moss just inside the cave and let sleep take them. It didn't matter about the where they were or what they might face on the next cycle. They were safe.

They had each other.

Chapter 27

*I have succumbed to illness and write this from a hospital bed. I will
be discharged this evening and book an operation for a return visit.*

Harl awoke perplexed to see that light was slanting in from one
side of the world. He didn't wake Sonora; she was in a deep,
restful sleep beside what remained of the fire, its embers buried in
ash. Instead, he stood up and glanced at where the light was
creeping across the roof of the world.

It was strange to watch light growing across the world. He
couldn't shake the feeling that it was like watching a dying fire in
reverse. Instead of the light falling away as it had on the previous
cycle, the soft glow spread across the sky and intensified. After a
short while he saw that it was coming from the sun, which
climbed above the horizon of grass stalks and swept up into the
sky like some fiery chariot. The light became brighter as the
darkness transformed into the same dome of scintillating blue that
it had been on the previous cycle. But there was no roof and no
strip of light above him, just that ball of fire and the infinite sense
of blue.

Noises perked up from the stalks around them, chirruping
sounds he associated with strange animals laying claim to territory

at the start of a new cycle. He had expected the ground to be wet from the dark cycle's rain, but there was no water except a thin sheen of mist that coiled over the carpet of fallen leaves. He swept his foot through it, not sure what to expect, but soon gave up and stopped to check their equipment and supplies.

It was all there, the ranged weapon Gorman had given them, the book, fire liquid, and enough food for about two more cycles. He fingered the pouch of salt for preserving food and began to worry about how they would find any out here. Did he have to dig for salt and metal? The god had always provided things like that in his world. How would they cope in this strange land? Perhaps there would be boulders like the one in the quarry and he'd be forced to dig his own tunnels through them.

'Is there enough?' Sonora asked from where she lay propped up on an elbow next to the fire, his grey cloak still wrapped around her.

'We'll need to gather more,' he said, wondering how long they could last without a proper source of food. 'I'll see what game there is to hunt nearby. Can you get our packs ready?'

She nodded as he grabbed his bow and then eyed the thicker part of the grass forest where the most noise had come from earlier.

'How will you find your way back?' she asked.

'I won't go far. Call out loud if you need me,' he said as he ducked out from the overhanging rock.

'Perhaps you should call out if *you* need me.'

He laughed and began weaving between the thick stalks, scanning the dense forest.

The sounds of Sonora gathering their supplies together faded as he walked a small circle about forty paces into the forest, making sure to keep the camp to his left.

He stopped when a faint scrabbling came from behind a tight clump of stalks. He hunched over and crept towards it. The noise grew louder until, as he slipped between two trunks, he spotted the source just a few strides away. It was a cow, but no ordinary cow as he knew them. It was covered from head to hoof in a long coat of thick, green-tinged hair. Two straight horns jutted from its head, tilting left and right as it cropped at a patch of damp moss. It was more the size of a calf than one of the milking heifers he was used to and its shaggy coat and small stature made it nearly invisible against the giant grass. If it hadn't been for the sound of chomping he could have looked straight at it and not seen the animal.

Harl pulled his bow from his shoulder, nocked an arrow, and then used all his strength to draw it back before releasing. The arrow hit the cow directly in the head and it toppled over, landing with a thud in the ankle-high moss it had been devouring. He pulled out a small knife and finished the beast, skinned it, and then cut thick slices of warm meat from the body. Wrapping them up in the hide, he slung it over one shoulder and headed back to the cave.

When he returned, Sonora was nowhere to be seen. Worry filled him. Anything could have happened to her. Had the beasts found them? He hadn't heard anything so he clung to the idea that she was safe.

'Sonora?' he hissed, panic rising. 'Sonora!'

'Harl?' Her voice came from behind a clump of dense moss that had trailed its way up to the top of the stalks.

'Where did you go?' he asked. The rapid tattoo of his heart slowed to its regular beat as she stepped back into the clearing.

'I just wanted to have a look at some of the plants around here,' she said, waving a bunch of bright green leaves at him. 'I found banewart growing at the base of these grasses. It's the same as it was at home.'

She paused and her eyes dropped to the dirt and grime that had spattered her clothes.

Her face hardened as she clenched her jaw, fighting something.

'I guess I can't call it that any more, now it's gone,' she said.

He stepped closer to her.

'Do you think we can survive this?' she asked.

'We've been given a chance to live, unlike the others back home. So yes, I think that together we can do it. I wish I knew where we go from here, but maybe if we get through this forest we can find a place to call a home.'

He thought about all the dangers out here compared to the safety they had known in the tank. Freedom had risks attached, but he knew there had been no real choice in the matter. Staying in the tanks would've been a death sentence.

'It's time we moved on,' he said, stuffing the meat into his bag and slinging the satchel over his shoulder.

They struck a good pace as they wound their way through the grass trunks towards where the tree reached over the forest. It jutted out high above the grasses into the blue beyond, magnificent in the way it swept up and out to tower above them. Harl had never seen anything so immense. It dwarfed even the gods. He could picture one standing underneath it and trying to reach up to touch the branches, but they were beyond even its gargantuan reach. How far down would the tree's roots reach? He had dug down into the soil so many times to shift the roots of small bushes in the fields and yet their depth always surprised him. But this? How deep would it go? How deep could it go? He shivered at the thought. Too much soil. Too much rock. It was pressing down on him even as he imagined the roots stealing their way down into the lightless depths.

He shook himself and lowered his gaze. He didn't want to think about it. It was too much like the mines.

A shadow swept over them. It blotted out the sun for a moment and they froze. It passed quickly but left a worry in Harl's mind. How could something block the sun like that? Things were too big for him in this world.

He walked on and took Sonora's hand. It felt good to have her close. Everything else was too strange and unreal. Even the air had grown humid and muggy, muffling sounds of danger that lurked on all sides.

He didn't know whether he liked this alien world.

After a time, the sun was directly above them, as it had been on the previous cycle. He could see a pattern emerging. It seemed to move from one side of the blue abyss above them to the other. But its strength waxed and waned. It was hottest and brightest when high above them, but when it dropped to the sides its heat and light would diminish. And it had a strange effect on the landscape. Shadows seemed to move with the sun's path. In his world a shadow had always been a static thing, unless an object was moved, but out here in the open space the shadows shifted across the landscape even as the sun rode along far above them. They would even fade away from sight only to creep back into existence once the sun had moved on.

Looking up he saw dark grey, cotton-like objects moving in front of the sun, dimming its potent light. Sonora flinched and let out a small startled noise.

'What is it?' he asked, pulling the bow from his shoulder.

'Water,' she said. 'I'm sure some water just landed on my head.'

It was strange as there was no roof above them for it to fall from. He looked up again towards the cotton-like mass and, as he did, a droplet of water hit his own face, then another, and in a few moments water was streaming down on them.

They both laughed at the refreshment as it coursed down their faces and danced around in a moment of odd joy.

Their old land did have rain, but to actually see it was a new experience. Rain would only fall during the dark cycle in the tanks. But out here it felt like life was both giving and oppressive at the same time. Was everything out here so contradictory?

A blinding flash of light forked down on the horizon above the stalks. Harl yelled out in surprise and Sonora's laughter turned to a piercing scream.

'What was that?' she cried.

He wrapped an arm around her and could feel her trembling beneath the cloak.

'I don't know,' he said, 'but we should find cover in case it comes closer.'

Rain lashed the stalks that rose around them and streamed down to soak the thick coating of moss on the floor. There was little shelter to be had among the grass and he felt suddenly exposed.

'Which way?' he asked, drawing his hood up to fight the bitter rain.

A noise louder than the shout of the gods cracked across the world. They both fell to their knees, hands clamped tight over their ears. It was the loudest noise Harl had ever heard and he could feel the vibrations of it pass right through his bones. It was invasive, trembling through his flesh and making his stomach quiver until all he could do was hunch over and hope it passed quickly.

Once it had stopped, he stood up and looked over Sonora. Neither of them was hurt, but for some reason Harl had expected to be. Such a loud noise could only come from a god. He glanced at the horizon, but the grey, smoky sky showed nothing of the giants. He scanned the terrain through the pelting drops.

'There,' he said, pointing to cliff face visible through the grass. He could see a dark shadow against the rock that looked like a cave entrance. 'Could be a place to shelter.'

They ran between the stalks and under the looming edge of the cliff. Harl had been right, the shadow was the edge of a cave entrance and they dashed inside. The entrance narrowed and dropped lower until they were forced to scramble along on their hands and knees. Harl was in the lead and flailed one arm around blindly to feel his way in the darkness.

He sensed the cave opening out, before he felt the rock walls sweep away beside him and stood, reaching up in the darkness to guard against knocking his head on the rock above. Something was crunching under his feet, but he paid it little mind as he guided Sonora further in.

He needed to get a fire going. Sonora was already shaking from the cold; if she became sick he'd struggle to help her. She was the healer, not him.

He dropped to his knees and fumbled through his bags until he found a flask of fire liquid. He poured a small amount onto the ground and used his flint and knife to shower sparks down on it. The cave lit up instantly when it caught.

He whipped his sword out as the light flared and took a quick look around. Nothing leapt out at him, so he laid the sword on the ground and then fed some of the kindling Sonora passed him onto the fire. It hissed and crackled, but the fire was relentless and he soon had a steady blaze going.

Sonora made a noise of disgust and when he looked up he could see that she was studying the cave. He took a better look around himself when she started to frown.

The floor was covered with crumbling white bones. Clearly human, they had been cracked open for their marrow. Harl did a quick count of the skulls. At least ten people had died inside the cave.

Other items were scattered across the floor as well. Cooking pots, rotten bits of clothing and other items that were just too rusted away to make out.

Unlike the other cave, there were no markings on the walls other than deep grooves and something like weapon strikes. He found several shallow lines close together that looked like they had been clawed out by some creature.

'It's a tomb,' Sonora said.

Trying to keep clear of the bones, Harl kicked some of the rotten rags onto the dimming fire. When they had caught, the extra light gave him a better view of the rusted items. He recognised a few of them as arrow heads and one was a saw blade, but one of the half-buried skeletons was clutching a rusted knife, much like Gorman's. He pried the knife loose and turned it over in his fingers.

'It's the same blade as Grandpa's,' Sonora said.

'Perhaps they came from the same place?' Harl said. 'Or maybe they traded with Gorman's people? Who knows?'

'I wonder what happened to them?' Sonora asked, stooping to pick up one of the skulls.

'Looks like they were defending themselves,' Harl said, skimming his foot over a bone that resembled a claw.

'From something vicious,' she said as she turned the skull over in her hands to inspect the gruesome find.

One side of the skull had a distinct groove along it, clearly from where something sharp had sliced down to the yellowing bone.

'Why are there no skulls from the attackers?' Harl asked.

'Maybe they were removed by the victors?' she said. 'Whatever happened, those inside came off worse.'

They huddled by the fire to wait out the rain. Every so often the entrance would light up and the now familiar deep rumbling sounds would echo into the cave.

'Will it stop?' Sonora asked, cringing every time the booming sound rumbled into the cave.

'If not, we'd better get used to it.' Harl said.

She laughed, and, for the first time since the illness had struck her homeland, she became her old self.

'You've been touching the scorch marks by the entrance,' she said.

'Yes,' he said, not understanding.

'And then you had an itchy nose,' she said, her grin widening.

'Probably,' he said. 'Why are you laughing?'

'You would look handsome with a moustache.' She reached out and rubbed the edge of her cloak just below his nose. When she pulled it away and showed him, he could see a black smear across the fabric.

'Soot!' she giggled.

A rustle sounded from outside. Harl snatched his bow off the floor and leapt up, nocking an arrow as Sonora scrambled to her feet and drew the sword. He pointed the arrow at the cave mouth. A shadow flashed past, darting from one side of the opening to the other. It was only a silhouette in the gloom, but was it the same creature that had slaughtered the cave's last inhabitants?

Harl bent to the fire, grabbed one of the bones from beside it, and then used the bone to flick some of the burning rags closer to the entrance.

He tensed, ready to lash out and fight another vicious monster.

Chapter 28

A thousand charges! An outrageous price for medical care. It's time
I let the world know about what I have found.

Sonora burst into laughter. 'It's a cow!' Harl relaxed and stepped back inside. 'Good, he said, 'I'm too tired to keep fighting.' He glanced up. Darkness was coming again.

Even though the creature had been harmless, Harl was unable to sleep. He kept casting glances at the opening and then turning over to find a position where no stones were digging into him.

When sleep finally took him, he dreamt of the terrified people barricading the entrance with bags of equipment as they held pointed spears to it. High-pitched screeches announced the arrival of the same creatures he and Sonora had fought when they had first stepped outside, but this time there were dozens of them. They swarmed towards the entrance and clawed at the men defending the opening, mandibles clacking as they hissed and writhed their way inside. Men fired pistols at the nearest creatures as they scuttled along floor, walls, and ceiling, before pouncing on the terrified people inside.

The screams of the dying threatened to deafen Harl. He was rooted to the blood-soaked ground and could only watch as the monsters slaughtered everyone and tore their flesh away in a feeding frenzy that almost choked the life from him.

But then the creatures screamed and began swarming towards the cave mouth as a dark shadow fell across it. The cave shook and rocks tumbled from the ceiling as one of the god's hands smashed its way through. It thrashed around, snatching at anything that moved, knocking creatures aside as it clawed its way further and further inside. It grabbed Harl and dragged him along the ground towards the exit, his fingers scrabbling at the earth and rocks as he tried to escape. His screams tore through the darkness around him, but it was too strong. Too deadly.

He was yanked out of the cave and blissfully out of the nightmare.

Sweat ran down his face as he woke from the horror. Sonora was crushing a handful of leaves and carefully inspecting the result. She stopped when she noticed he was awake.

'Didn't mean to wake you,' she said.

Harl smiled at her. The rain had washed the mud and gore from her face and she looked incredibly pretty, even in the gloom. The constant deluge of rain outside had stopped and a faint light streamed in through the mouth of the cave.

'We slept through the dark cycle,' Sonora said.

She'd topped up the fire and prepared some steak from the previous cycle's kill by cooking it over the flame on sticks sharpened into skewers. Stepping around the fire she handed him one of the succulent smelling skewers.

'What's our next move?' she asked, taking a bite of one.

He rubbed a hand across his face to dislodge the last touch of the nightmare and then chewed on the piece of steak while thinking. His mind had been so full of questions last cycle that he didn't really know what to do now. He didn't like the thought of staying in the cave any longer after the nightmare. But what else was there?

'We should make it to the base of the tree this cycle,' he said, pulling at the juicy meat.

'Is that where we're heading then?' she asked, seemingly unconcerned that they had no final destination.

'It's the best I have,' he said. 'It's the largest visible object out there, so perhaps we could look around?'

'It's a thousand strides high, Harl. We can't climb it.'

'Then I can carve a way inside the base with the sword and hollow out a house,' he said, suddenly confident that they had a destination.

As the light grew brighter, they picked up their gear and began the winding journey towards the trunk.

The walk was not difficult. There were less giant grasses under the tree canopy, making passage easier. Sonora explained that the grass stalks needed more light to grow than the canopy provided, so they just withered and died. It was the same as the forest at home, just on a much bigger scale. Small plants didn't stand a chance in the shade.

Dense clumps of moss seemed to thrive in the shadows, though. They peppered the ground and, just like everything else in this world, they were massive compared to what they knew from the tanks. They formed great bushes and mounds, but rather than the vibrant greens they were used to, these mosses were a tapestry of russet hues.

Giant, decaying leaves blanketed the ground between the moss clumps. Harl picked one up at one point; the size was staggering. He wrapped it round his shoulders like a cloak, much to Sonora's amusement, and then swept it down onto the ground again so they could sit on it while they ate.

But as the cycle wore on, the breeze brought a chill. The dense canopy blotted out the sun and, without its heat, they were soon shivering. Harl began to feel uneasy. Each step seemed to heighten the feeling until, eventually, he stopped and strained to hear any sign of what was troubling him. Then he spotted a tinge of movement beside a thick clump of stalks. Nothing definitive, but he was sure something on two legs had popped out then slipped back again. He peered between the stalks and cursed, as shadows from the canopy tricked him as he tried to see what lay ahead. Leaves swayed and branches reached out across the path, all of it dark and threatening. Half of what he saw was unreal, shadowed figments that danced and teased at the edge of his vision. Whatever it was, it was a natural at remaining undetected among the straight, leafless stalks.

He kept his bow in hand as they pushed on through the cycle, not speaking much for fear of attracting unwanted attention. Eventually, the forest thinned and the stalks came to an abrupt halt. A vast plain stretched away before them. They were much closer to the trunk and it dominated the view now that the forest had fallen away. Thin red lines were visible deep between the crevices of bark. It looked like a second layer underneath, almost like a poisonous creature's skin, warning that any attempt to harm it would prove fatal. Perhaps cutting into it had been a hasty idea.

He looked left and right at the edge of the vast plain. The ground was bare, sandy soil that stretched around the base of the tree. Small rocks and bones littered the ground between a few weather-beaten boulders.

A shrill piercing noise rang out overhead. With a sinking feeling Harl looked up into the branches of the tree.

They were not alone.

Chapter 29

An open day. That is how I will reveal them to the world. I will
terraform each tank to better show off the fauna and flora I discovered
with them and invite the highest in society to attend.

Harl ran his gaze across the branches high up in the tree. A dozen of the segmented, yellow and black striped creatures were perched on a single branch high over the clearing. They fluttered on and off the branch as they squabbled over positions and, every now and then, one would swoop down to gain speed before stealing a new place on the perch. He couldn't be sure from such a distance, but they seemed larger than before, perhaps as big as a cow, as if the previous monsters were mere adolescents.

'Just our luck,' Harl whispered, stepping back deeper into the grass line. He pointed to the base of the tree. 'I'd thought to cut into the tree using the sword and make some kind of cave for us, but can you see the gap between those gnarly roots?'

Sonora nodded, her eyes flicking from the hole to the creatures.

'We could hide in there,' Harl said. 'It probably goes quite far in. There's no way those creatures can overwhelm us if we're in there. It would be easy to hold them off with the sword.'

'I don't like it,' Sonora said, looking over the bare expanse of dirt and rock then up again at the creatures. 'It's a perfect place to be caught by them.'

Harl thought about it. Maybe they could keep searching, but he didn't like the idea of wandering around trying to find somewhere safe. There was too much risk. He'd never really faced danger before. All these monsters just attacked mindlessly. He and Sonora were just another food source and the idea of constantly fending of hungry beasts was horrifying.

He nodded up to the canopy where a cluster of red had caught his eye.

'Food,' he said.

She turned, eyes wide, 'I'm not eating one of those creatures.'

'Shh,' he said, shaking his head. 'Up there.' He pointed up into the branches to where a huge red fruit was weighing down an offshoot. Greener fruits were ripening to the same rosy red higher up beyond it.

'We need to eat,' he said, making up his mind. 'We'll be out of food in five cycles and there's no telling when we might stumble across another cow.'

'I don't care,' Sonora whispered. 'We're not crossing that death trap.'

Making it all the way across to the trunk was almost impossible without being seen. He looked for a way around the problem, but there was too much bare ground between the end of the grass stalks and the base of the tree. No matter which way they went, they'd still be exposed once they left the grass line. The creatures would see them and swoop down.

He spun around at a rustling sound coming from behind them in the stalks and caught a glimpse of something long and black sliding along the ground. Two red eyes locked on to him before the creature disappeared into a patch of thick, knee-high moss. A shiver ran up his spine and he tightened his grip on the bow. The creature was as long as two men lying head to toe and as thick as a small tree trunk. It was as if one of the giant grasses had uprooted itself and learnt to snake across the ground, moving from shadow to shadow.

'Harl,' Sonora whispered. 'Did you see that?'

'Yes' he said, bringing the bow up. 'Whatever it is, it knows we're here. The flying creature's don't. We have to risk it and cross.'

He reached for the arrows in the quiver, wondering if he had enough, then cursed. He still had Gorman's pistol; he'd forgotten all about it. Why hadn't he remembered last cycle during the attack? He thrust a hand inside his bag and grabbed the pistol.

The creature slipped from the moss into a clump of dead leaves, attempting to hide itself, but it's slick body was too long to conceal and the tail end twitched beside the pile. The red eyes fixed on them, glaring from under the leaves. Harl couldn't take his own eyes off the thing, terrified that if he moved the spell would be broken and the creature would attack. The ruby eyes sunk down into the shadows as if it was coiling its body and then the creature burst from the leaves. It snaked across the floor towards them and lunged.

Harl raised the pistol, but Sonora grabbed his other hand and yanked him out into the clearing as the monster's tooth-ridden mouth snapped where he'd been standing. They stumbled out into the open and the slithering beast twisted away, shying back from the clearing as if afraid to reveal itself. They watched the bony tail slip from sight as it sped back into the leaves.

Sonora swung her sword up ready and scanned the grass stalks, waiting for any sign of the creature as it re-emerged. The sword emitted it's eerie hum as she planted her feet wide, breathing hard. Nothing moved. She looked up and around to the treetops where the flying creatures still bickered among themselves before squaring up to the line of grass.

Harl was mesmerised by her. She looked so alive, so ready to face the danger. He had to force himself to do it, but it seemed second nature to her. He hadn't noticed it inside her old world, but since the previous attack he had realised just how strong she was. Perhaps facing death had unlocked some hidden reserve inside her? Or was he just truly seeing her for the first time?

He didn't know, but he loved it.

He crouched low, unsure which direction to risk. The tree or back in to the grass? They had proved themselves once against the flying creatures. At least he knew they stood a chance that way.

'The tree,' Harl whispered and started for the trunk's base, trying to seem as small as possible to the creatures above. Perhaps they could slip past and make it to the gnarly roots without being seen? It was over two hundred paces away, but the sight of the roots curling into the ground around the gap was tantalising.

The clearing itself was carpeted with bones. They were scattered across it and many of them looked like small rib cages, about the size of a pig, but the colour was more silver than white. The broken segments reminded him of the long legless thing in the stalks and he guessed that death had been the fate of many to slither too far into the clearing. But it was a sobering sight. If the creatures above him could do that to something so large, then Sonora and he stood little chance if spotted. Had he made the wrong choice?

His gaze flicked up to the branches overhead. Still no movement. He then glanced back to the pillared grass stalks behind them, before swinging his head around to look at the hole between the colossal trunk's roots. They had covered a third of the distance to the base when a single screech of alarm came from the creatures above.

Harl and Sonora froze, staring up as the insects burst in to a chorus of horrid shrieks and calls. They launched from the branch and swooped down in a buzz of wings.

Harl raised the pistol. The weapon felt inadequate and puny in his grip compared to the bow, but he aimed at the creature leading the dive. Its companions fell in behind it, then darted to the side as they tried to flutter past and hit their prey first.

Harl squeezed the trigger. A crackling bolt of blue light erupted from the end of the pistol and shot up at the group. It missed the leading creature but hit a slower one behind. The beast exploded in a shimmering puff of bright blue light, and gory black pieces of it rained down on the parched soil below.

Harl stared at the thing in his hands, marvelling at the power contained within the device. It took his mind a moment to grasp what he had done. So much power locked away in such a small object. An arrow was deadly in the right hands, but it could be used to wound or disable. This weapon, this pistol, it was something that would utterly destroy it's target.

'Harl!' Sonora called.

He shook his head to clear it and focused on the creatures above.

The group had split apart in the aftermath of his shot, but they'd re-grouped. He grimaced and tried to force the fleeting thoughts of the pistol's implications from his mind so that he could fire again, but his hands were shaking too much. He tried to calm himself as he would with a bow: breathe in, breathe out, aim, shoot. Six rapid shots and four more creatures exploded in waves of blue light and blackened chunks of meat.

The remaining five screeched in fury and buzzed to the ground half way between them and the trunk. Harl smiled, knowing that there was no way the creatures could reach them before he could squeeze the trigger.

One creature hissed and then started to rub its wings together. The translucent flesh screeched with each movement like a thousand reed blowers going off at once. Harl clamped his hands over his ears as the sound intensified. The other four creatures joined in, chorusing the harsh sound across the clearing and out into the giant stalks of grass all around. And then it was gone. The insects fell still and the whole forest became deathly silent. Harl drew his hands away from his ears and turned to Sonora. She was opening and closing her mouth as she shook her head to try and clear it.

Then the call was returned from somewhere distant and high above them. He glanced up to see dozens of the giant insects swarming down from between the leaves, screeching and clacking their mandibles.

'The gap,' he yelled above the agonising sound. 'Run!'

Firing at those in front, he dashed towards the crevice between the roots. The creatures split apart, one by one, in a shower of blue light and bloody yellow gore.

Despair pounded into him as a dozen more of the flyers touched down directly in front of them. The creatures folded their wings back and then waited there with their pincers snapping.

More insects circled around overhead and landed behind Harl and Sonora. The clicking and screeching calls increased as each one added its wings to the chorus.

The closest one leapt at Harl, wings spread, pincers snapping. Adrenaline flooded him. He lifted his pistol and kept firing until he'd severed the creature's head from its body. The head and mandibles crashed to the ground but kept twitching and snapping as if they didn't realise they were dead.

Sonora tripped on a carcass and fell to the ground. As she rolled, one monster launched itself high into the air and dived at her. She kept rolling out of its path, but it banked mid-air and grabbed her pack in its claws. It beat its wings as it dragged her across the dusty ground to its family. Harl stopped and fired the pistol as she was dragged away. The shot hit true and the creature was blasted off her.

The flyers pressed in on all sides and he fired again at the closest to give Sonora enough time to stand. He fought to gain ground, but they were barely past the halfway point to the tree. Stepping forward, he shot insect after insect in turn while Sonora kept her back to him and carved anything that came too close in two. They were in a sea of yellow blood, pressed in on all sides by snapping pincers. Two flyers raced at him and he took the first down in a flash of molten blue. The second rushed in. Its pincers snagged his foot and he toppled over. He pressed the barrel against its head and pulled the trigger. A plaintive beep came from the pistol and he pressed the trigger again and again, but the weapon refused to fire.

'Damn you!' he screamed and then kicked the creature in the face to dislodge it.

He glanced around at Sonora. Her movements had become sluggish. She could barely raise the sword and sweat coated her brow. He could see the exhaustion in her eyes as she spun in place and sliced through one of the creatures. She stumbled, but then braced herself and forced her trembling arms to raise the sword once more.

The creatures clicked their pincers and hissed as if sensing their prey tiring.

Time slowed and Harl let the pistol slip from his hand as he looked at the woman he loved. She was panting, caked in yellow viscera, and held the blade out ready for the next attack. He could see her strength ebbing away as the weapon slowly drooped down.

She seemed to sense his gaze and turned her back on their attackers to face him. She let the sword fall from her hand and reached out to him, burying her face against his chest as he pulled her close. The hissing grew as the monsters closed in. He held her tight and closed his eyes.

Let it end quickly. Let it all be over.

Chapter 30

Word has spread and several prestigious scientists from from various manufacturing factions have shown interest in coming to the open day.

The embrace lasted for what seemed an eternity. Time stretched with the expectation of pain, but it never came. Instead, a long, drawn out note of a horn sounded. Voices shouted, human voices. Harl snapped his eyes open and turned to face the creatures again. They had turned towards the new threat coming from somewhere beyond the grass line. One of the creatures hovering above them shuddered and then crashed to the ground, a feathered arrow protruding from its bulbous abdomen. Arrows suddenly rained down among the creatures, transforming their hissing cries into squeals of anguish and pain. In a matter of moments the creatures knew they were overwhelmed and scattered into the air with a buzz of wings as they vanished up among the leaves.

Harl looked around for the source of aid and spied faces darting in and out of view behind the grasses where they had entered the clearing. It was hard to distinguish them from the grass at first glance: their skin was a green-brown colour that blended with the plants around them. But the more he looked, the more faces popped out from behind the stalks or could be seen crouching in pockets of moss. Sonora was holding his hand, but let go so she could pick up the fallen sword.

'Who are they?' she asked as more than a dozen men and women stalked out onto the dusty clearing.

They were clearly a well organised group and were dressed in an odd mixture of tanned skins and woven brown material fashioned into cloaks and waistcoats. The majority of them were men, but both men and women had long hair that had been braided and tied back into ponytails. It revealed runic tattoos around the neck, barely visible on their strange green and brown patterned skin. All of them had a bow in their hands and a quiver strapped to their backs.

'I have no idea,' he said, trying to casually pick up his own bow, 'but I think we're about to find out.'

The group approached. They seemed wary of their surroundings and kept casting furtive glances above them as though expecting more of the creatures at any moment. They stopped about twenty paces from Harl and Sonora, clearly cautious about coming any closer. Harl counted fifteen.

One of the men, his chest covered in a supple leather chest plate that left his arms bare, stepped forward. A thick black beard covered the majority of his face, but Harl could still see the pale streak of a jagged scar running down one of his cheeks. His beard was tied into a single plait, similar to his hair, which was braided back over his skull and then tied behind his head like the others. He looked grim as he studied them, but there was intelligence in his eyes and it gave Harl hope.

The man was still a good ten paces away when he spoke.

'What tribe are you from?' he asked. His voice was deep and powerful. He cocked his head to look them up and down with dark, curious eyes. Maybe he did not expect an answer, but he looked to those either side of him, as if gathering his confidence to approach Harl and Sonora, then walked towards them leaving his men behind. He clasped a bone bow lightly in one hand, his other hovering just above a knife strapped to his thigh.

The bearded man strode closer and what Harl had first thought was a green and brown skin colour, was actually some form of camouflage painted expertly on the man's face. Underneath, his skin was weathered, but Harl guessed them to be of a similar age. There was a vitality in his eyes that gave a hunter-like impression.

The leader stopped three strides away and Harl resisted the impulse to step back. The man towered over him and he clenched his fist around the bow, ready to defend Sonora.

'What tribe are you from?' the leader asked again, his dark eyes roaming over both of them and stopping on Harl's hands.

'We have no tribe,' Harl said, his voice coming out ragged and croaky as he tried to quell his fear. 'But,' he went on, unclenching his hands and not wanting to seem ungrateful, 'we thank you for your aid.'

By this time the leader's men had closed in behind him. They all had the same worn but keen look to them, like an old knife blade sharpened until it was wafer thin. Strong muscles flexed beneath the crude paint covering their arms. Their equipment was worn as if it had been passed down for generations.

'No tribe?' the man asked. 'Where are you from?'

'We came from there,' Harl said, pointing to where the top of the grey building could be seen over the grass forest.

'That cannot be,' the man said, shaking his head. 'None come from there, only Aylen. As for helping you, we considered letting you die. We've tracked you since you defiled the cave of skulls. You must be held to account for going to a forbidden and sacred place.'

Harl felt sure he had done nothing wrong, but there was an undercurrent of tension rippling through the group and they shifted uneasily at the bearded man's words.

'We didn't know it was sacred,' Sonora said. 'We just needed shelter from the sun shouting.'

'The sun shouting?' the man asked, raising an eyebrow.

'The sun,' Sonora said, peering up through the canopy. 'I figured that if something moves over it, it would call for help for it to be moved.' She finished this dubiously, perhaps realising she did not really know enough about it.

'Ah, you mean the thunderstorm,' the man said. He looked at them again as if seeing them in a new light. 'You've not seen this before?'

Sonora shook her head.

'This is strange indeed,' he said, absorbed in thought for a moment. 'Hmm... Well I am Damen, son of Terman. I am leader of this hunting party. You fight bravely. But your weapons, where did you find them?'

'I am Harl Eriksson and this is Sonora,' Harl said. As for the weapons, they were gifts.'

Damen looked interested at the news. 'We've only seen such weaponry in the hands of the Enlightened ones. Where are you going to?'

'We were hoping to make shelter near the base of this tree,' Sonora said, gesturing to the enormous trunk.

'There is no good hunting here,' Damen said. 'Come, Sonora and Harl of no tribe, you'll camp with us tonight, eat our trophies and then we go to the Enlightened ones.'

'Where,' Harl asked, 'is tonight?'

Damen looked at him as though he was speaking a different language. 'It is not a where, it is a when.'

He must have noticed Harl and Sonora's look of utter confusion.

'When the darkness comes it is night, and it will soon be tonight. You will stay with us and eat. You may add your meat from the cow you slew. Assuming it was you,' he said, looking at Harl's bow with admiration.

'It was. You may take what you want of the meat,' Harl said, hoping it was a good gesture.

'I am not a thief,' Damen said, 'but if you were to give your meat to the fire, we'll share among the group.'

'Of course,' Harl said.

'First, we must return to our camp fire. It is not far,' Damen said, pointing across the open ground into the dense grass stalks further around the tree. 'Can the two of you walk or are you injured?'

'We're not hurt,' Harl said, thinking how lucky they'd been. What if the creatures had been venomous and injured them? The thought of lying there as the poison coursed through their veins made him shudder.

Damen led them back into the forest. They skimmed the edge as they worked their way through the grass on the outskirts of the clearing. A few of the hunters laughed and boasted of their exploits during the fight as they walked. It was all good-natured and Harl found himself smiling at the camaraderie. Some of the men carried the remainders of the creatures, either as trophies or food.

'What were those things?' Harl asked Damen.

'Hivers,' Damen said.

Harl remembered Gorman using the term, but kept the thought to himself. Just how much more had the old man known about the world outside the tanks than he had told them? Had he lived among these people at one time? There was no way to answer any of the questions. He was just glad that Gorman had been a part of his life. He missed the old man, but he was stronger because of knowing him, even for so brief a time.

'They live among the tallest trees and come down to hunt in certain areas,' Damen continued. 'Like the one you tried to cross. They are vicious in a group and hunt for both for meat and trophies. Their armour is useful for cooking pots and the shards on their mandibles make good arrowheads.' He shrugged. 'But alone, they are not so formidable.'

Harl recalled the terrifying moment when he was pinned by one and Sonora had saved him. The creature had been almost enough to kill them by itself. These men and women were clearly a tough people.

A harsh cry made them all whirl around. One of the men was clutching his forearm. Blood was seeping through his fingers and dripping to the ground. He was glaring at a metallic tinged shrub next to him.

'Be more careful when close to ripshrub, Uman,' Damen scolded the man as he inspected the wound.

'I was trying,' Uman said, 'but I had to check the flower. It is a rare sight this season and the wives pay well for it.'

'Not if it is covered in your mucky blood,' Damen said, eyeing the flowerhead on the ground.

Uman was more slender than Damen. His legs looked suited to running and the soles of his sandals were worn thin from extended use. His hair was shaven to the skin, as if someone had run a blade over his skull or burnt it off entirely.

Sonora moved over to have a look at his forearm.

'Here,' she said, reaching into her bag and pulling out some of the banewart leaves she had picked by the cave. She took a large leaf and placed it on the man's arm.

'Stinkweed?' Uman said, flinching back from her touch, but she held his arm firmly and, taking a small cloth from her bag she tied it around the wound.

Uman looked around at the others.

'But it's just a weed,' he said, 'useful only if you're wanting to dye cloth.'

'Nonsense,' Sonora said. 'Apply it to a wound and you'll escape any greening sickness. Leave this on for at least half a turn. It will dull the pain and help it to heal.'

Uman looked down.

'It pains me less already,' he said, turning the arm to inspect the bandage. 'But how long is a turn?'

Sonora looked uneasy, as if she was unsure how to explain such simple principles.

Harl spoke up at this. 'A cycle,' he said.

'Cycle?' Uman asked, still perplexed.

Harl sighed inwards at the difficulty of language. 'It's the time for light to come and go before darkness.'

Uman looked up at him.

'A day?' he asked, watching as Sonora finished wrapping the wound.

'It is difficult for us.' Harl said. 'The worlds that Sonora and I came from had different terms for these things. For me, Sonora's turn was a cycle. The light cycle was when the lights came on above our world and then in the dark cycle the rains would come and the light would die. And now your world has different names for things as well. It seems that you call the dark cycle, night.' He struggled to pronounce the new word, but Uman obviously understood him and nodded.

The group began to murmur to each other. Harl heard the words 'Enlightened' and 'healing skills.' What had made them so restless? Was it taboo for a woman to do such things in their culture?

'Quieten down,' Damen said to the others. 'We must be moving again, and quietly this time. We don't want a swarm of hivers on our backs, so go quiet. We're close to camp.'

'Not afraid of a hiver,' one of the women said, toying with her bow string.

She had scruffy blonde hair that was tied in a ponytail and curled down over her broad shoulder. Her armour looked scratched and stained as she took a moment to stretch her legs.

'Of course not,' another man said, 'but we don't want them hovering over camp tonight. I could do with a good bit of sleep. Been tracking those two for too long. Unless you want to stay behind, Elo, and guard our rear?'

Some of the group chuckled at the joke, but Elo stopped stretching and stared hard at the man. Bunching her hands into fists, she took a quick pace towards him and he stumbled backwards instinctively. She laughed and the rest of the group joined in at the man's expense before she turned to scan the surroundings again.

'Enough!' Damen ordered, although there was a twinkle in his eye. 'There is still danger around. Elo, scout our path ahead. Uman, cover the rear.'

Harl ran forward a few steps to catch up with Sonora. He had no idea where he was going, but as he looked at Damen marching along ahead, he had a feeling it was going to be interesting.

Chapter 31

While awaiting the duplicate seeds, I have scoured the local hills. I returned with at least fifty small tree types and will begin cultivating them immediately.

Damen led them on a route that skirted around the base of the tree, and only moved out from under the grass canopy when they reached a dense part of the forest, ducking back in as soon as it was possible. It was difficult to judge what he was thinking, but Harl kept pace with the man and found it strange that he had already come to trust that Damen and his group of hunters would keep them safe.

Harl gave the tree branches an uneasy glance, but there was still no sign of the hivers returning, so he looked back down. Damen had vanished through a narrow gap between two stalks. Harl looked at Sonora and shrugged, before following. A short walk brought him to the hunters' camp.

The camp was completely enclosed by the grasses. They formed a solid wall around it and soared up overhead to where rope had been weaved from grass tip to grass tip to make a crude net. Harl assumed it was because of the chance of hiver attacks during the dark cycle, or night as Damen called it.

A makeshift canvas tent, supported by rough-hewn branches, took up nearly a third of the circle. Just outside it stood a ring of stones in which dry wood had been piled. A cooking spit completed the picture and two of Damen's men began work on lighting a fire beneath it. The wood was still damp and the pair struggled to get it to light.

'Here,' Harl said, moving to the men and pouring the last drops of the fire-liquid onto the heap. 'Stand back.'

He showered sparks down and the bundle of wood and twigs burst into flames. The two men stumbled backwards.

'What was that?' one asked, waving his hands through the flames as if to check they were real.

'The last of our fire supplies,' Harl said.

The two men watched him suspiciously for a while before jamming a few logs on to the roaring fire.

He turned his attention to the small campsite hemmed in by the tight wall of grass stalks. There were a dozen or so beds dotted around it. Each one seemed to be made from large, dried leaves propped up off the floor with sticks or logs. They looked comfy enough, but Harl didn't like to think about what might be crawling around inside the leaves.

'Place all gathered food in the store, people,' Damen said to the group and then watched as those carrying the hiver meat placed their grizzly haul inside the tent.

'Harl, Sonora,' he said, gesturing to the tent. 'Come, place what you can spare inside.'

They went to the covered entrance and Damen held the flap open. A wealth of food and equipment were heaped on opposite sides of the square space inside. Bows and spears with crude metal tips were propped against huge bundles of arrows. Most of the arrows had wooden shafts and flights made from cured plant leaves, but the tips varied from metal to bone, or just plain wooden points.

'We keep everything we make and find on our gathering in here for when we return to Delta,' Damen said, noticing their interest.

'Delta?' Harl asked.

'Isn't that where Grandpa came from?' Sonora said to Harl, before turning back to Damen.

Damen looked interested at the mention of someone coming from Delta.

'Have you a cure for a blacking disease?' Harl asked before the hunter could ask more. 'We left to find a cure-'

'There is no true cure,' Damen said, 'not for those already infected. We are protected from birth by an injection.'

'Injection?' Sonora said. She paled as she glanced at Harl, but then frowned and turned back to Damen. 'Does it work after the disease has been contracted?'

Damen shook his head. 'I am sorry, Sonora of no tribe.'

She looked crestfallen and Harl knew there was no way to bring her out of the darkness of her mood. She would find a way out by herself.

'Tell us about Delta,' he said.

'Our home,' Damen said, a hint of longing in his voice. 'It is all that is now left of our accomplishments. Too many times have we been driven out, only to return and rebuild with what we can find. Or so the stories tell.'

'What is it like?' Harl asked, taking a seat beside Sonora on one of the logs by the fire.

Damen thought about it for a moment. 'It's a collection of wood, brick and stone buildings that surround a large cave system where the Enlightened live.'

'The Enlightened?' Harl asked wondering if they thought the same about these Enlightened as his own people did about the gods. 'You've mentioned them before. Are they human?'

Damen chuckled and slumped down with his back against a log. 'Yes, I believe they are, but they have much that the common folk do not.'

'What do you mean?' Harl asked. 'Are they bad?'

'Like a wet plank of wood,' Damen said, 'they support the community, but inside they're slowly rotting.'

'How many people are there in Delta?' Sonora asked.

'Around a thousand of us,' Damen said. 'The Enlightened ones tell us there used to be many more, but over time we have become a fading people.'

With the sun going over and the night coming, the group gathered around the warm fire and basked in the glow it cast within the campsite. Two men fetched food from the storage and began skewering it on sticks that hung out over the freshly lit fire. The smell of cooking filled the air and Harl licked his lips in anticipation.

When it was cooked, Sonora questioned Damen and the group about life in Delta while Harl cleared several skewers of succulent steak cubes. It had come from the cow he had killed and he thanked his luck that they had stumbled across it.

'The Enlightened are the keepers of technology,' Damen said, plucking a skewer for himself and stripping it clean in one mouthful. 'They claim that the weapons and items they are custodians of are beyond us. In return for bringing any technology we find to them, they provide the people with shelter, food and education.'

'And they live in a cave?' Harl asked, wondering why people such as Damen would need others to provide them with shelter.

Damen nodded. 'It is lined with metal panels that were brought into the caves when Delta was founded. The deepest chamber is where the Enlightened live. It's where they decide the fate of the people living outside. Most people have not seen inside and only those who are willing to train can go there feely.'

'How many of these Enlightened are there?' Sonora asked. She began picking at something akin to a potato but seemed to have little appetite.

'Who knows?' Damen said, shrugging. 'Maybe fifty, possibly more. It's hard to know for certain.'

'Can you not go inside and find out?' Sonora asked.

'No,' he said, 'not all the way inside. Most wouldn't dare. It's guarded by a select few soldiers who carry the most potent weapons, but I doubt there's a proper warrior among them. They're all spineless lackeys who'll do anything to curry favour with the Enlightened.'

'What sort of weapons?' Harl asked, wanting to delve deeper into this strange culture.

'Much like your sword,' Damen said, looking at the weapon lying on the ground next to Sonora.

'One more question?' Sonora begged, as if the desire to learn burned inside her. 'How did the first people find Delta?'

Damen rolled his eyes as though reluctant to tell the tale, then leant back and stared up at the stars.

'The stories tell,' he said, 'that seeking shelter from the harsh elements and the wrath of the Aylen, our people stumbled across the Delta rock. What they thought as they approached it, I do not know. The rock juts up from the forest, sheer and defiant, with a vast outcrop reaching out over the land on one side. Its shadow would have engulfed them as they approached the cliff underneath, dark and forbidding. It must have seemed so strange to them, that gigantic cliff hidden beneath the outcrop, like the brim of a hat covering the stony face before them. We call it a rock simply because that is what it must seem like to the Aylen, but to us it's more mountain than rock. What did those first settlers see it as? A place of sanctuary? A home? I've no idea. Perhaps they didn't even think along those lines? Perhaps they just stumbled into the cave in exhaustion. And yet they found no safety there, only horror.'

'The hivers?' Sonora asked.

Damen sat up and stirred the embers of the fire with a stick.

'Possibly,' he said. 'No one really knows. It'd explain their relentless attacks on us. But whatever the creatures were, they infested the place. The battles and bloodshed that our people suffered in those times still plague our nightmares. But in the end those first settlers pushed so deep into the tunnels that the creatures were driven out. They found the queen and destroyed her. There was no mercy, no thought of sparing anything, even if it had been possible. They just slaughtered everything.'

A cold gleam reflected in his eyes as he stared into the flames. 'Must have been a glorious hunt.'

'But they're hivers,' Harl said. Even the word made his skin crawl. 'They're vicious.'

Damen frowned.

'True. But how much of that is our fault? It's a stupid thought, I expect, but maybe the hivers remember what we did. What kind of crime must it have seemed to them? Their Queen, the centre of their existence and community – if you can call it that – was killed by us. Murdered in front of them. If they can feel hate, then I'm sure they'd hate us. In a way, we deserve it, but what were our people to do? The strongest will rule.'

Silence fell and Damen returned to stirring the last glowing embers of the fire with his stick.

'So they're intelligent?' Harl asked.

Damen shrugged.

'Perhaps. The Enlightened ones don't think so. But they hunt us over and over. It never ends. Is that intelligence? Is it only instinct or are they out for revenge? To them we're the prey and they hunt us, simple as that. There are too many questions for me. I don't have the answers.'

'We kill them easy,' the scruffy blonde-haired women in the group said to the nods of the others.

'They're a dangerous foe in groups, Elo. Never forget that,' he warned. 'Too many have died fighting them for you to say such words.'

Elo nodded, her eyes blazing. 'Yes, I remember many not now with us. But they fight good. Win much glory. Hivers come so we kill them. It's no intelligence, just claw and pincer and blood. They come; we kill. You kill more than most.'

Damen sighed and then threw his stick into the fire.

'It's not a proper hunt,' he said and then grimaced. 'But I've spoken too much of our lives already, Harl of no tribe. We'd like to hear your story.'

The men and women around the fire nodded and huddled closer to the flames, some getting up off beds to listen.

'It's a long one,' Harl said, wondering where to start.

'We've the whole night,' Damen said. He reached for a waterskin and took a long swallow before waving Harl on. 'And I have a feeling it's going to be a strange tale, so tell on.'

Harl told them of their previous life inside the cubes. He described the world he grew up in, of the giftings and religious beliefs that the people trapped inside the cubes held for the gods. When Harl first mentioned the gods, Damen's people started saying the name Aylen aloud and nodded to each other across the shrinking flames of the fire. Harl guessed it was the name they had given to the gods as a collective. But there was little reverence in the way they spoke of them. It intrigued him.

He spoke of Gorman, telling how the old man had planned their escape from the tank, and then sealed himself inside to face the horror of the blacking disease alone. Damen nodded in admiration. It was almost too much for Sonora. She curled her arms around her knees, tears glistening at the corner of her eyes, but her sad smile told him to continue.

And then, finally, he recounted how they had traversed the floor of the shop, their experiences inside the tray, escape, and the dawning truth of their existence as slaves to be sold.

Murmurs ran around the camp, but they were hushed and everyone seemed to be clinging to his words. Shock was evident on their faces in the amber light. It was clear that they had never known about the existence of humans beyond the fringes of Delta.

Damen spoke after a long deep silence.

'This is troubling news,' he said. 'The Enlightened must hear of it.' He stood up and addressed the group. 'We must pack tonight and be ready to leave for Delta in the morning. The city awaits our return.'

Chapter 32

It is complete! The first completed tank of many and I have managed to install a much more efficient air filter and water system. The seeds have germinated, as far as I can see, and the micro-trees thrive under the lighting.

When Harl woke the next day, it was to see Damen's braided beard and beady eyes hovering just a handspan above his face.

Harl scrambled back in surprise, but Damen only grinned.

'Come, eat,' he said. 'We must be going soon.'

Everyone was awake and scurrying around the campsite. Bedding was scattered across the floor and the canvas covering the tent of supplies had been dragged aside, leaving only its skeleton behind. It looked like an Aylen had torn the place down.

Harl sat up and accepted a chunk of meat that Damen passed him.

'Thanks,' he said, tearing a bite off a bit of the cold meat and wondering what the cycle would bring.

Travelling with these hunters would be a much safer option than himself and Sonora wandering alone, but could he really trust them? He was confused by their motives. They seemed friendly enough and it was obvious that Damen cared for his men, but they could just as easily have cut Harl and Sonora's throats during the dark cycle or not risked saving them at all in the first place. What did they want?

He watched Sonora talking to Uman as she patched up the ripshrub wound from the cycle before. He would trust them for now at least. It would be easy enough to slip away into the grasses later on and, even if things turned nasty, they still had the sword and bow. Not that it would help them much. These men and women were seasoned warriors. If they wanted to overwhelm Harl and Sonora, it wouldn't take much effort. But he had to trust someone. To make a life for themselves in this strange new world they would need all the help they could get.

They broke camp soon after and walked with their backs to the Aylen's shop as they pushed deeper into the grasses beyond the tree. The further they got from the building, the better Harl felt. They all carried an extra pack of food and a bundle of arrows, while everything else was piled onto a pair of canvas stretchers that creaked with the weight as Damen's hunters struggled along.

Uman slipped in next to Harl as he left the clearing behind Damen.

'I'm curious, Harl,' he said, rubbing his shaven head. 'May I look at your bow? I've never seen one like it before. Damen has told me of the ones hoarded by the Enlightened, but this is the first one I've seen.'

'Sure,' Harl said, unslinging the bow from his shoulder and passing it to Uman.

Uman peered along the string and nodded to himself as he touched it.

'It is beautiful,' Uman said, 'much like your woman.'

Harl frowned at the man.

Uman bowed his head and placed a hand on his heart. 'I meant nothing bad by it, Harl of no tribe. I myself have a woman and will not look elsewhere. When her temper is roused it is like the sky thunder. I mean only that you are lucky.'

Harl laughed at this description.

'Where did you get such fine clothing from?' Uman asked, seeming to gather courage from Harl's laugh. He was looking at the shirt beneath Harl's leather jerkin and the red leather boots Harl wore. Harl's shirt was made from a fine cotton and, even though his boots were worn, they were far better than Uman's hide sandals, which were almost falling apart.

'I'd like to be able to make such things for my woman, especially the robe Sonora wears.'

Harl looked at Sonora's fine spun dress flashing under her cloak. Maybe Uman had not seen that type of material before.

'It is called cotton' he said. 'It's made from a plant that grows in our homelands.'

'A shame,' Uman said, 'but I hope we can learn much from each other.' He smiled and handed the bow back to Harl, then jogged a few paces to catch up with Damen, who had stopped on the edge of a clearing and was gesturing for silence while he scanned above the stalks.

Damen crouched and thrust an arm out to indicate that they should to do the same. His men lowered the stretchers to the floor and then slipped bows and weapons out, ready to hand. A faint buzzing noise sounded beyond the grass stalks. Damen glanced up, but shook his head and raised a finger to his lips for silence.

Harl looked up. He couldn't make anything out beyond the grass stalks – it was all too much of a tangle – so he lowered his gaze to the waiting hunters as Damen listened patiently.

One of the younger men in the party was clenching his bow so tight his hand shook. He saw Harl staring at him, frowned and made a visible effort to stop the shaking.

The buzzing grew louder until Harl saw a mass of shadows pass in front of the sun, the buzzing sounds whipping over their heads one at a time. It was a swarm of hivers flying fast overhead, dozens of them. When the last one had passed and the noise became distant, Damen made a hand-signal to continue.

They walked for an age, weary as they trudged between the thick stalks. The ground was littered with animal marks and Harl shuddered when he saw several deep claw marks gouged into stalks around them. A line of yellow blood trailed away into a crevice under a nearby boulder. He pressed on, glancing back at the dark hole until it passed from sight as they skirted around a huge heap of fallen branches.

They stopped that night beside a cluster of large rocks carved with symbols. Harl guessed that they were markers of some sort, the same kind of thing that Gorman had used the trees for as he navigated from place to place.

Damen deemed it unsafe to light a fire.

'The hivers seem to be hunting us, but that's not what's got me worried,' he told Harl. 'There has been Aylen activity along this trail, so we need to take an indirect route home.'

Their meal that night was cold and dismal. Damen handed out what remained of the cold meat and Uman gathered some soft fruits from bushes growing midway up the grass stalks. They were bitter and dry, but at least it was something.

Damen questioned them some more about their old home, asking how many lived in the tanks, how they mined the ores, and a myriad of other questions.

'Why have the Aylen separated your people?' he asked at one point. 'In Delta all types of people mix. Light skinned, dark skinned and all in between.'

The concept of so many variations staggered Harl. He had marvelled at Sonora's golden hair and sapphire eyes. What caused such oddities in a person?

'They breed us like cattle,' Harl said after a moment. 'They seek pure bloodlines, so they isolate stock and refine the traits they desire. My own people were all dark of hair, but the people of Sonora's world were all golden. It is a horror I cannot see a way to justify. They seek profit at the expense of our lives and it only makes me loath them all the more.'

Damen fell silent, clearly lost in thought. Finally, he looked back at the building and his face darkened.

'Then it's time they tasted death,' he said. 'It will be a worthy hunt.'

Chapter 33

I have emulated a complete landscape inside the first tank. It's like a whole little world that exists inside the glass space. It's only soil and rock for now, but the seeds I picked up from where the creatures were found have been sent to my old research lab for growing.

It rained as they left the camp the next day, drenching the hunters so that they were cold and shivering as they walked along under the grey, clouded sky.

Harl was amazed at the difference the influx of water made to this world. Small creatures scurried about in a rush to get the water, and insect activity intensified around them. Water pooled on leafy plants and dripped down from the canopy. He couldn't get over being able to see the rain. It had only ever come during the dark cycle in his world, but out under this open sky he could see each droplet falling through the air and bouncing off the plants around him. When the other men complained at the soaking, he and Sonora just laughed and lifted their faces to the torrent and let it wash over them.

Damen was constantly scanning the surroundings for dangers as they trudged along. His gaze would switch from stalk to stalk, from the ground to the air. Harl sensed something of the predator about him, that constant alertness, the ease with which he moved. It was frightening in a way, but also reassuring... Provided he was on their side. Every now and then he would send Uman out to gather reports from the scouts.

It was halfway through the day when Uman and one of the women returned with news. Damen had ordered a rest for a few brief moments and a quick camp had been set up, but as the group sat eating, Uman and the other hunter moved quickly up to Damen and talked animatedly about something they had seen.

Harl edged closer, keen to know what dangers lay ahead, but their words were too quiet.

'What is it?' he asked Damen once the discussion was over. The hunter was frowning as he paced back and forwards in thought.

'A change in the land,' Damen said. 'One that was not there on our journey out. Uman spotted it after we heard an Aylen pass. I have tried to take the longer route to avoid where the Aylen had been, but with the hivers hunting us I believe we must risk being exposed so that we can reach home sooner. But this change disturbs me. It can only be the work of the Aylen. They seldom stray this close to Delta, so why they have chosen to do it now is worrying.' He looked at Harl and Sonora as if it was their fault, but then seemed to dismiss the idea.

Damen pushed them from the makeshift campsite and, as they wound between the stalks, Harl looked up from navigating the treacherous ground and froze.

The forest had come to an end and an open expanse of dark, fresh-tilled soil climbed a gentle slope ahead of them. The churned earth ran all the way to a series of vast, distant hills, all of it barren and strewn with shards of rock and mounds of boulders. It looked like an Aylen had dug the land over with a shovel before planting what passed for giant potatoes. It was an empty wasteland that smelled of damp, dirt and faint mildew.

'We have to cut across,' Damen said, waving between two of the largest hills to where the grass forest started again. 'Stay close,' he said, nocking an arrow. 'The Aylen might return.'

They trudged across the loose, slippery surface. Even the hunters were unsteady. They kept glancing at their feet to check their footing, before sweeping their gaze back up to the sky to check for potential enemies. The surface seemed strange to Harl. It was far too soft and loose for natural terrain. They almost had to wade through the soil, their feet constantly sinking deep into it.

It was only when they had covered most of the treacherous ground that Uman broke from the line and crouched beside what looked like a pile of round stones. A small hand poked out between them. It was streaked with dark lines that threaded along the vein tracks.

It took Harl a moment to realise that the stones were cobbles.

'Don't touch it,' he said as Uman reached for the open palm.

Uman froze and then looked back at him.

'It's just a hand,' he said.

Harl shook his head.

'We must get away from here,' he said. His gaze traced the dark lines covering the child's hand and a shiver ran down his spine. He'd seen those lines before.

Uman frowned at him as if leaving a dead body to the wild creatures went against their duty.

Damen and the others had halted and then marched back to see what had their attention.

'What is the problem?' Damen asked.

Sonora crouched beside the hand. Her gaze travelled from the blackened hand to the landscape around them. She stopped, staring at a heap of wooden wreckage a hundred paces away that had looked like a clump of dead grass stalks when Harl had first noticed it from a distance. Instead it was the frame of a wooden house that had crumpled in on itself and become half buried.

Harl watched as she glanced from the wooden structure down to the small hand again. She knelt down next to it, suddenly, and pulled at the cobblestones.

'Sonora wait,' he said, but it was pointless. She tugged at the stones and, as they tumbled back around her feet, a blackened face was revealed. It was a little girl, partially covered by long strands of wet blonde hair. Her face was frozen in a look of horror.

Sonora resisted the urge to drag the body from the rubble. Instead, she staggered to her feet and back-pedalled away. Harl caught her as she collapsed.

'Daisy,' she said, chest heaving as she sobbed.

'You know the child?' Damen asked.

Sonora did not answer.

'It must have brought it all out here,' Harl said, easing Sonora down, 'and just tipped it.'

'I do not understand,' Damen said.

'This was our home,' Harl said. 'After the disease spread and we had left, we saw one of the giants carrying the tank's contents away.'

Sonora's sob made him turn back to her. Tears streaked her face, carving rivulets in the dirt that coated her pale skin. He knelt in the fresh soil and wrapped his arms around her, pulling her close. Rage coursed through his veins as he held her trembling body to his, her tears warm against his skin.

How could the Aylen do this? Did it have any feelings? He had lived his entire life believing it a god, but now here, in this barren space, where the dead lay in the tormented mounds of rubble, he saw the Aylen for what it was. A monster.

'Will it be safe for you to cross?' Damen asked.

Harl looked at the child's face and shook his head.

'I don't know,' he said.

'We should not linger,' Sonora said, wiping her eyes and standing.

'I agree,' Damen said. 'We'll send word to the Enlightened when we get to Delta.'

They pushed on through the landscape. Every now and then something would remind Harl of the life he'd shared with Sonora and Gorman at the house, the spire of a building or a blackened face that he'd once spoke to. Sonora looked away every time a body came into view, focusing on the grass stalks ahead, the sky, or rocks, anything but the bodies and the decimation around them. Harl had expected her to run to the nearest body and check for vital signs in her caring way, but, like him, he guessed she had no desire to touch anything that might infect them.

Harl froze, causing Uman to unsling his bow and crouch down ready to fire at the first sign of danger. Harl waved a hand to let him know it was not needed and walked over to what had caught his eye. Lying on it's side, still partially encased in its broken pot, was a tiny tree. It was neatly trimmed and lay there, bare-rooted, as if waiting to be re-planted by a kind-hearted owner. It was like a miniature piece of art and it was obvious that someone had once cared for it deeply, but now it was just another piece of debris.

Anger flared up inside him. He snatched up the tree in one hand and lobbed it as far as he could, hating what it represented.

The others had continued ahead and only Uman watched his action. He just nodded, as though he understood, and then trudged on after the others.

Once in the forest, the horror behind faded to an uncomfortable memory. A mountain formed on the horizon. It stood out beige above the thick green stalks, its tip glinting momentarily in the bright sunlight.

Damen slowed at a rise in the land and shielded his eyes against the light as he peered at the oddity.

'That's where Delta lies,' he said, thrusting a hand out. 'Most of it is hidden in tunnels under the mountain, but many of us live outside in an area under the overhang. A wall shields us from the wild lands.'

'Wall?' Harl asked.

'The Enlightened built a circular wall around the rock to hold off the beasts that plague this land.'

Sonora came over to Harl's side and clasped his hand in her own. He knew what she was thinking. Was this somewhere they would be safe? It was such a fragile hope, but when he looked at the faces of the people around him it seemed to strengthen. There was joy in their eyes when they looked at the mountain looming over their home.

'The rock,' Damen continued, 'hides us from Aylen when they pass.'

'And the flash of light on top?' Sonora said. 'It's a bit easy to spot something so bright like that,'

'That's the energy making panels,' Damen said. 'We hide them when an Aylen comes past. But they rarely do. Maybe once or twice a year.'

'Is that often then?' she asked, obviously lost at the strange word.

'Twice every four hundred days,' Damen clarified.

'And you've managed to go unnoticed?' Harl asked.

'Yes,' Damen said. 'Luckily we have remained undiscovered, at least the Enlightened tell us as much.'

'The Enlightened?' Sonora asked. 'What's their responsibility in Delta?'

'Each of them has a role,' Damen said, 'either in running the city or constantly repairing the artefacts they keep in Delta.'

'So what makes someone a member of the Enlightened?'

'It's down to knowledge,' Damen said. 'Enlightened children are taught about technology by their parents so that they are ready to take over the duties when they grow up.'

'What type of technology?' Harl asked, thinking of the weapons Gorman had given him.

'I don't know all of it,' Damen said, 'but we do see some. Many are weapons, much like the sword you carry. Others you also have, such as the air cleaners, although none now need to use the mouthpieces. The Enlightened say that at one time every person needed one, but each generation seemed to need them less and less, until the need died out.'

'Fascinating,' Sonora said. 'Gorman had managed a similar feat but within his own lifetime, thanks in part to a healer's skill.'

She paused and Harl thought she was remembering Gorman. Instead, she spun around and tore the sword from its sheath as the others in the group ditched packs, dropped stretchers, and pulled out their spears and bows.

A buzzing sounded overhead and Harl turned as a pair of hivers dropped from above to land on the back of two hunters. Instinctively, both hunters bent double and flung the creatures to the ground. Sonora stamped a foot down on the nearest, holding the writhing body down as a bulky woman drew a dagger and plunged it into the abdomen. Sonora swept her blade down in an arc to sever the insect's head.

Harl strung an arrow and turned to the second hiver. It was already a pin cushion of feathered shafts and twitched feebly as Damen strode over to it and plunged his spear down, skewering its yellow and black body. It shuddered once more and then fell still.

326

'A scouting party,' he said. 'Keep your eyes peeled for the rest.'

When no other hivers appeared he shrugged and trudged on through the mud.

Uman jogged over to him.

'Perhaps we should inform the Enlightened, Damen?' Uman whispered.

'It was only a couple of hivers, Uman,' Damen said, his words were boastful, as if reassuring the entire group. 'We can deal with the rest, if they dare come at all.'

'It's not the hivers I mean,' Uman said, his voice dropping even more. He inclined his head meaningfully at Harl and Sonora.

'Of course,' Damen said, realising what he meant, but his deep voice still carried to Harl. 'Take Yorol and Ingor and tell the Enlightened of the newcomers.'

Harl felt unease as he shouldered his equipment again. Just what were they walking into?

Chapter 34

The original seeds have returned with the assurance that Gilvark and his team can duplicate the ones he kept. The price is high but worth it. The open day is drawing near.

The ground under foot became softer as it levelled out ahead of them. Water pooled along the worn trail and small streams threaded their way across the path. Every now and then Harl would misplace a foot and it would slide out from under him, almost forcing him to do the splits. Each time laughs and jokes about tearing his manhood apart would erupt from the group and even Sonora was smiling when he caught her eye.

When Uman returned, there was a worried look on his face. He jogged right up to Damen, panting from effort.

'The Enlightened ones do not believe the tale,' he said, bending over double to rest his hands on his knees. 'They even suggested that the technology was stolen from them and are planning something for our arrival.'

Damen turned to Harl and Sonora.

'Is this true?' he asked.

'Of course not,' Harl said, indignant at the accusation. 'Do you honestly think we would create such a story?'

'No,' said Damen, 'I do not. I saw your face when you told the tales and I witnessed the remains of your old land. It is unjust that you have been judged so. My orders will most likely be to hold you as prisoners until we reach Delta.'

Harl's face darkened at the treachery.

He was about to protest when Damen froze and stared up into the canopy of grass behind Harl. The hunter's face contorted into a vicious scowl as he tore his short sword from its scabbard.

'Above us!' he roared.

Harl turned to find four hivers balancing on the tops of the stalks above them. They must have tracked the group, silently skittering over the tops of the stalks as they kept pace.

They swept down towards the nearest men. One hiver veered off at the last moment and then dive-bombed Harl. He threw himself to the muddy ground as pincers raked the air above him. The hiver spread its wings, flapped them to change direction, and landed on Damen's back. Its spindly legs scrabbled to gain purchase as the big man flailed around trying to dislodge it.

Harl sprang to his feet and leapt forward. He grabbed the creature's squirming abdomen and yanked hard. The hiver tightened its grip on Damen and tried to bite down into his neck. Harl roared and slipped one arm right around the creature and yanked it loose. Its claws shredded Damen's jerkin as the creature was torn free.

The hiver hissed and screeched as it writhed in Harl's arms. It was the size of a calf and he let go to throw it aside, but it twisted around to bite his face. A rock cracked his heel and he fell backwards, holding the creature at arms length as he landed on his back. He tried to get his feet under it to kick it off but its squirms made it impossible. The claws cut his arms, tearing the skin like a knife. His arms buckled under the onslaught. It was winning, inching closer and closer, hissing, snarling, screeching.

A jolt shot through Harl's arms and the creature spasmed. Its head rolled clean off, leaving Harl holding the abdomen in both hands as it spewed blood all over him. The legs continued to thrash and scrape at his chest for a few heartbeats more, before death reached them, and they curled inwards in defeat.

Yellow blood gushed out over Harl from the severed portion and he continued to hold it as he looked up at his saviour, Sonora, standing over him. Gore dripped from the melting-blade she held casually in one hand.

'You can let go,' she said.

Harl tossed the hiver body aside and rolled away from it. He took a few deep breaths and then stood and wiped the gore from his face as he looked around at the carnage.

Damen had been cut across his back but seemed not to care as he scanned the stalk tops for more threats. Elo was sitting nursing a nasty gash on her arm as the others finished the creatures off. Sonora rushed to her, grabbed her arm and plucked the water skin from the woman's belt before washing the wound clean. Elo looked at her, astonished. Sonora had dispatched the hiver attacking Harl with ease, and was now coated in its slick yellow blood and acting as if nothing had happened.

331

None of the others had been seriously hurt. They looked defiant and calm as they cleaned weapons or casually boasted of the fight. Harl's eye was drawn again to Sonora as she bandaged Elo's arm with some cloth, but he found Damen staring hard at him.

Had he done something wrong? He tensed, ready for action, remembering the talk of taking them prisoners.

'You saved my life,' Damen said, stepping around a carcass as he came towards Harl. He was nearly a full head taller than Harl and tilted his head to look down at him. 'I would not have made it if you had not pulled it off me. I should have been more alert after the last two.'

'I did what I had to do,' Harl said, stooping to retrieve his fallen bow. 'Even as a prisoner.'

'I owe you a blood debt,' Damen said, snatching the bow from the floor before Harl could reach it and then holding it out to him. 'And it is one I hope to repay. Do not worry about being a prisoner either. I'll do no such thing. You may leave now if you wish.' He gestured to the surrounding land and glanced at Sonora. 'We'll not hold you when you have shown only friendship and bravery.'

'Where would we go?' Sonora asked, looking around them at the alien landscape.

'That I cannot say, but you are welcome to stay with us until we reach Delta if you want to,' Damen said, scratching at his beard. 'But I cannot guarantee your safety. The crimes they accuse you of are bad, but as much as I can, I will stand by you.'

'And I,' Uman said, giving them a confident smile and an unpractised wink.

'We'll go to Delta,' Harl said, glad to have allies in whatever came. 'We've no choice, and I do not think we can survive out here indefinitely. These Enlightened will have to see reason, at least with the news we bring about the others still trapped inside. They must help us.'

'It will be a struggle, Harl,' Damen said. 'There is no definite proof other than seeing the bodies and soil, and I do not believe they will accept your explanation.'

'Would they not consider that proof?' Harl asked

'We are not Enlightened, Harl. If they do not want to accept it, they won't. There is little we can do to sway them.'

'We have to try,' Harl said.

He was not sure how he would do it, but he knew these people had to be shown the cruelty behind the Aylen.

As they pushed through the stalks, the mass of sandy-coloured rock that was Delta rose above them. Signs of habitation were scattered along the worn path which Damen led them down. Bones, broken arrows and trampled vegetation lay to the side of the path and, at times, Harl saw patches of cleared land, possibly used for crops, now fallow and empty except for the weeds that had invaded in the absence of a farmer.

A dense wall of felled grass stalks appeared ahead of them. They had been tied together and balanced upright in a ring to form a barrier. A boarded wooden gate blocked the road and two men lounged to either side, spears in hand as they chatted away. One spotted them and jumped up off the wall.

'Hold!' he ordered, stepping forward. He was dressed in leather armour fashioned from some outlandishly furry creature. 'You have them, Damen?' he asked when they got close enough for him to recognize the group.

Damen strode up to the man, leaving Harl a few steps behind.

'They came freely with us, Inam,' he said. 'I have given my word to their safety.'

'That is not for you to decide,' Inam said.

'Nonetheless,' Damen went on, 'I will escort them to the Enlightened ones and save you a journey into the caves.'

Inam paled and nodded, calling for the gate to be opened. It swung out after a moment and they entered Delta.

Beyond the gate, the ground was formed from large, dusty tiles of smooth rock. Harl took them to be man-made and judged that once, long ago, they had been meticulously placed. But many were now split and broken and the cracks had become a home for shooting weeds.

Two-story houses made from the same brick material were scattered to either side of the roadway. The buildings were sandy coloured to match the rock around them and their roofs brimmed over with trees and plants that hung over their sides.

The path led directly to the base of an overhanging cliff. The cliff was staggering in size. It rose so far overhead that it dwarfed even the height of Harl's home-world. The overhanging rock jutted out across the land into the forest around, casting a deep, ominous shadow over a set of carved steps that seemed to lurk in the gloom. They led to a cave opening in the face of the sandy rock, but it was too dark to see much of what was inside, just a bricked-lined entrance that was supported by pillars, as though holding the whole of the rock up by themselves.

They walked through the main part of Delta's central street towards the steps. People were bustling around them, paying little attention to another group of hunters returning. Harl was amazed at how similar and yet how different the people and things around them were. Some things he recognised right away, metal forges, tanners and fletchers, but others he had little idea of. The sound of repetitive roaring came from a few buildings lining the road. Each one was fashioned from crude bricks with chimneys pouring out white smoke. It curled in a mass beneath the overhang before billowing its way out into the open air and rising into the sky.

'What are they burning inside?' Harl asked Damen as they passed the first of the closed up buildings. 'Doesn't the smoke attract the Aylen?'

'They are machines that use steam from boiling water to move things.' Damen said as though reciting the words from a book. 'The water is heated using coal and the rising steam is squeezed into a metal container, which in turn pushes or pulls something. I don't fully understand, but the result is the ability to move objects, mostly metal, to perform a task. In this case the machine inside is making clothes. As for the Aylen, it is only done for short amounts of time and our lookouts give us enough warning.'

'It's a loom?' Sonora asked.

'Yes,' Damen replied, 'but it is many looms together, that way we do not need a lot weavers to make clothing for ourselves. Just one or two people can produce as much as fifty individual hand weavers make in a day.'

Harl was amazed at the revelation. It seemed impossible that a machine could replicate the work of a skilled pair of hands. And how could that one machine replace so many?

'How does it work then?' he asked, unable to remain ignorant.

'I know a little, mostly from my father,' Damen said 'and it would take a long time to learn, but if you like I would be able to teach you. But it would be easier to learn from those who work the machines. Few Enlightened take an interest in steam power, but we have used it since before the split. In many cases, our knowledge even exceeds that of the Enlightened. It's the weaving machines that are their purview, though. We had only ever used steam power for pumping water and milling our corn into flour, but then the Enlightened adapted their weaving machines to work with our power source and the results were incredible. I don't know how half of it works, though, even the steam engines. I know the theory behind it all, but I would not be able to craft one of the machines or operate it without supervision. The same steam principles allows us to heat our cave system and pump water up from the depths below.'

He pointed to another of the smoke-belching buildings. Its sides were riddled with pipes running in and out of holes bored through the brickwork. 'That is where we draw up water from the deep well.'

This made Harl think of one aspect of this new world he hadn't considered.

'How deep until the bottom?' he asked. It had to be a long way compared to inside the containers, but he just couldn't picture it in his mind..

'The well goes down over two hundred meters, as the Enlightened teach it,' Damen said. 'That's nearly two hundred and fifty of your paces, I would guess, but there is no bottom, not that we've found yet.'

'What is down there at such a depth?' Sonora asked.

'Rock and water,' Damen said. 'Those two mostly, but seams of iron or coal can be found down there as well. We use the coal as fuel for the steam engines to power machines that dig the hole deeper and return finds from below.'

'A perfect cycle,' Sonora said, obviously impressed.

'It's not perfect,' Damen said, 'but it works.'

Chapter 35

The duplicated seeds have arrived. I now have hundreds of varieties to test inside the tanks.

The smoke cleared as they moved away from the buildings. People still bustled around, some pushing carts, others busy at their stores shouting out offers to those passing by. Harl found it fascinating. He had never seen so many people in one place and it felt more alive than anything he had ever seen. But at the same time he found it unnerving. The crowded nature of the place pressed against him. He found it bizarre that a sense of claustrophobia began to threaten him. How could it when this world was so big compared to his own? It was just ridiculous. But it was the people, so many of them, all crowded around, rubbing shoulders, shouting, working, there was just too much going on.

As they passed the last of the engine buildings, most of Damen's hunters bid them farewell and slipped away to the scattering of smaller grass-topped huts behind the main street, leaving only Damen and Uman to escort them deep under the overhang.

Harl climbed the steps towards the main entrance and marvelled at the brick archways supporting the pillars either side of it. They must have taken a great deal of skilled labour to round off so well, unless some of their strange technology could produce such precision.

Damen halted at the entrance. A solid metal gate stood in a recess below the archway. It blocked entry and was dented and scratched all over, as if hacked at by the claws of savage creatures or a dozen men wielding swords.

Damen noticed Harl running his fingers down the rusted scratches.

'We shelter inside when the hivers come in great swarms,' Damen said, moving to a small metal box mounted at head height next to the gate.

To Harl's bewilderment, he pressed a button and spoke to it.

'Gathering party, number fourteen. Damen,' he said and stood waiting as if it was completely natural.

To Harl and Sonora's utter astonishment, a vibrating metallic voice blared back directly from the box.

'You are welcome, Damen son of Terman,' it replied. 'You may enter and proceed directly to the Enlightened meeting chamber.'

Before Harl could speak, a hissing noise issued from the gates and they swung open of their own accord. A gust of steam billowed out from behind the door.

Damen saw Harl and Sonora staring in shock at the box.

'It's called a speaker,' he said. 'It links to other distant ones using a power called electricity and allows us to communicate. You'll learn more in time, or we'll be here until tomorrow with me trying to explain it.'

Two guards ushered them into a rock-walled corridor. It was very rough near the entrance but became smoother the further in they went, eventually changing altogether. Metal panels took over, studs and rivets holding the panels in places. There were patches of rust in places, but it was obvious that they were well-maintained and only the years of use had tarnished them.

Damen and Uman stayed in tow as the guards fell into step behind them. The corridor led straight ahead. There were no fire holders on the wall to light the way, so when the gates hissed and swung closed, Harl was surprised not to be engulfed by darkness. Instead, light beamed down from the ceiling at intervals where bright tubes as long as a man had been attached. They lined the way towards a junction at the far end of the metal sided corridor, and it took him some time to realise they reminded him of the light from the roof of the world back home, only in miniature. Had the humans made the same form of light as the Aylens who kept them in the tanks? If so, it proved once again that the gods were false.

He stopped to stare at the tubes and Damen halted after a few steps, realising that Harl and Sonora had fallen behind.

'What is it?' he asked. 'We really should be moving. The Enlightened do not like to be kept waiting.'

'Did the gods give you the lights?' Harl asked, staring until his eyes burned. He wanted to believe that man had created them, but it seemed too much to hope.

'The gods?' Damen said, confused, but then he laughed. 'No, it was the Enlightened. They work on the same principle as the speaker box in the door by using electricity.'

Harl was about to ask more when another, more refined voice, spoke from ahead of them in the corridor.

'Electricity is the same power used within the ranged weapon you have on you,' the voice said. 'We call that a gun and I'm afraid you will need to hand it over for safe-keeping before we can proceed. The same with your sword, mistress.'

Tearing his gaze from the lights, Harl saw that the voice belonged to a thin, middle-aged man dressed in a long, dirty white coat, its edges ragged and frayed. He had a cropped fuzz of shocking white hair on his head, similar to Gorman's, and his small, intelligent eyes squinted out from behind wire-frame glasses.

He stepped forward and waited patiently as Sonora unslung the blade and then handed it over. Harl reached into his satchel and pulled the pistol out. He was reluctant to hand it over, but then he remembered that it was empty, so he passed it across. The man nodded his thanks and tucked the pistol into one of his coat pockets.

Harl slipped the bow off his shoulder and looked at it in his hands. He didn't want to part with it. It was a different feeling compared with the pistol. The bow seemed much more a part of him, somehow. Perhaps it was a more direct link to his home? He pictured his days with Troy again and their adventures using the bow Troy's pa had once owned. He just didn't want to lose any of that.

Damen obviously sensed some of Harl's dilemma. He stepped forward and laid a hand on Harl's shoulder. 'I will take the bow, Harl. It will be safe in my keeping. Have no fear that it will be

342

returned to you. I sense that we will hunt together many times, my friend, and a hunter always needs his bow.'

Harl nodded and handed it across, grateful for the other man's words, but he still felt a wrench as he passed it over.

The man in the white coat had frowned when Damen stepped in, but he seemed to dismiss it and moved on.

'Thank you,' he said. He kept shifting Gorman's sword between his scrawny hands as though he was uneasy and didn't know what to do with it. 'My name is Kane. I am one of the Enlightened ones here at Delta. I am in charge of teaching the ways of electricity to those who are keen to know about it.'

The slow and deliberate way the man spoke reminded Harl of the how Gorman used to lecture children. He glanced up at the light tube again and Kane raised an eyebrow as if Harl might be a potential student.

'It is our most fundamental power,' Kane said, 'and we utilize it in many aspects of our life, such as creating light and speaking over distances. It also keeps our crops growing in the cave farms and even heats up and cooks our food. But come, you both should have a look around. Damen, you may stay if it pleases you.'

Damen glanced at Uman, who shook his head and then turned to say goodbye to Harl and Sonora, before walking back the way they had come.

Sonora spoke up, 'I thought you said we would be prisoners here.' She looked at Damen before turning back to Kane.

'Unfortunately,' Kane said, 'we cannot let you leave until we have established the truth of your tale about our brethren within the Aylen's lair. There is also the delicate matter of desecrating one of the sacred cave tombs, which many will not look kindly upon.'

'So what happens now?' Harl asked, wondering at the importance of the tombs. The thought made him think of the book and he touched his satchel, glad to still have it.

'A trial will be held in a day or two,' Kane said. 'Until that time you will remain with someone, and I suspect that person will be me.'

He didn't look too bothered by the conclusion and Harl guessed he was keen to start teaching them. But Harl didn't really like the idea. He was fascinated by all the marvels he was seeing, he just didn't like the way Kane presented the information. The man's condescending tone made him feel like a stupid child.

'Come,' Kane said, indicating one of the passageways with a bony hand and then patting Harl on one shoulder, 'you must be hungry and full of questions. We'll fill your stomachs before we fill your minds.'

He led the three of them down the metal-lined corridor, their feet reverberating on the steel grating that covered the floor. They passed several rooms with their doors open and Kane stopped at each one to briefly explain the room's function.

'This is the spares workshop,' he said, stepping through the mechanical doorway.

The room had six or seven similarly dressed Enlightened all taking apart what looked like old metal salvage, only to put it back together into various tools and items. Harl had no idea what they were, despite the drawings of weapons and all manner of devices lining the walls, complete with measurements and complex labels.

'All of our equipment is constantly in need of repair,' Kane said, picking up a small metal box from the nearest table and turning it over in his hand. 'And it is here that the gathering teams bring any items they find. You both have some equipment in remarkable condition.' He looked at the sword in his hand before touching his coat where the pistol was stowed.

'The gun you gave me, for example, is one of the cleanest I have seen.'

Harl spoke up at this, thinking it had not been a permanent gift. 'We didn't see any of your people wearing or using similar weapons when Damen discovered us.'

'That is true,' Kane said. 'We do not issue most of this to our gathering parties. The vast majority is stored for when trouble comes, usually in the form of hiver swarms and other unknowns. When that happens it will be given out at the proper time.'

It seemed odd to Harl that the gathering teams weren't issued the weapons. They risked their lives every day for the community and yet they were forced to use simple weapons that were of little threat against the monsters existing beyond Delta's walls. Perhaps Damen had been right and the Enlightened ones hoarded them for their own needs? He looked briefly at Damen, but the man was still standing in the corridor and just scowled. Either way, it had to be a source of contention.

'They don't mind?' Sonora asked.

Kane shrugged as he headed back out the door to lead them down the corridor again. 'That is the way it is.'

Damen growled just loud enough for Harl to hear.

They passed a room that contained hundreds of cords hanging from the ceiling. Each cord led to a metal box against the wall. Kane explained that it was the way electricity was moved around the city. Sunlight was captured using special glass and metal panels sat on the top of the mountain. It was then fed through the city by the cables. It seemed a ridiculous notion to Harl. How could you capture light?

'The sun panels are a top priority for the functioning of Delta,' Kane said. 'With no electricity from the panels, the farm lights would shut off, and little would work in and around the city. We could still function, but it would be at less than half the rate and people would soon begin to starve.'

They arrived at what Kane said was to be Harl and Sonora's living chambers.

'My old home,' Kane said as they entered a cramped but luxurious metallic square room. 'It was where I lived before I joined the council last year.'

There was a level of comfort in the furnishing that must have made Damen uneasy, because he seemed not to look at anything for too long. Harl guessed the hunter was not used to living in such a place.

The bed was a metal construction with a soft grey cover placed on top of a stuffed mattress and there were strange appliances set in the walls. A warm breeze wafted out from a vent in the base of one wall and flowed through the space to an open door which led off to what Harl assumed to be a toilet.

346

The three of them sat down at a polished table on one side of the room while Kane moved around pointing out the different features.

'This,' he said, standing next to a square panel in the wall, 'is an electric cooker. We cannot use it for long periods at a time as it uses valuable electricity, but it does a wonderful job and cooks food in moments.'

Kane moved to the cooker after taking some meat from a cupboard and placed it inside. He then closed the door and turned a dial on the machine. The cooker made a light humming noise which reminded Harl of the sword he had received from Gorman, then the machine cut off.

'Go and take it out' Kane said. 'Careful though, it might be hot.'

Harl opened the door and a wave of heat and steam rose from the slab of meat as he picked it out and took a cautious bite. It was hot and tasty. He pulled it away, staring at the instant meal in his hand as he marvelled at the power of the machine. It had cooked the piece of meat in moments and yet Kane seemed to take it for granted. It could revolutionize life for those inside the Aylen's slave shop. He handed the meat to Sonora and her eyes opened wide in wonder as she devoured the succulent slab.

Kane went back over to the cupboard and drew their attention to it with a flourish of his hand. He tugged open the door and Harl felt a slight drop in temperature billow out from inside.

'This is a cooler,' Kane said, 'It keeps meat and fruit at a low temperature to better preserve them. It is the opposite of the cooker. Meat can last much longer inside the cooler than in the open before spoiling. It is completely sealed when shut, except for a tube that pumps cold air inside, and another one that takes it out again. Most of our electricity goes into a large collection of coolers, so that we can keep food fresh for the people, as winters can be hard.'

'What are winters?' Harl asked, one of a hundred questions flying around in his head as he sat at the table.

Kane looked at him, astonished, then up to Damen.

'They do not know the seasons?' he asked.

'I think not, Enlightened one,' Damen said.

'Then their tale rings more true,' Kane said. 'Could there really be more of them?'

Harl was indignant at this blatant disregard for their words.

'We did not lie,' he said, standing up as frustration seethed inside him. 'And we did not make up stories about losing our families and friends.'

'No,' Kane said putting his hands up as a guard peered into the room, 'of course not. It is just difficult for us to hear about all this when we thought we knew better.'

'No harder than me finding out about this electricity you use for miracles,' Harl said.

'I understand how you feel, Harl.' Kane said 'but-'

'But nothing!' Harl said, slamming a fist on the table to make Kane jump.

Damen's hand hovered above his dagger, but he shook his head at the guard who had stepped through the door.

'All of this-' Harl went on, gesturing wildly around the room. 'All of this and you never once thought to help us when we were trapped inside that... that place.'

'They didn't know, Harl.' It was Sonora's voice, soft and calming beside him. Her hand lowered to rest on his. 'They still don't know.'

'It's true, Harl,' Kane said, 'None of us have ever been inside, let alone come out as you have.'

Harl took a deep breath. He couldn't say why he was so mad, but seeing Kane with his cooker and comparing it with life inside the box...it felt unfair.

'Do you need me to stay?' Damen asked Kane, his face a hard mask as he looked at the meat still in Sonora's hand.

'No,' Kane said, 'you may head back outside, Damen, but return early tomorrow, as you are able.'

Damen said his goodbyes and left the room.

'I am sure you two have much to think on,' Kane said. 'I will return in the morning, but should you need me before then you can press the button on the speaker machine, talk into it, and I will return. For everyone's safety there will be a guard outside, but they will not act unless you attempt to leave without strong cause. I hope you understand.' He smiled and left them both with their thoughts and to wonder at all they had seen in such a short time.

After they had both used the cooker to magically heat more meat, they washed using a water basin. It was another bizarre contraption that took them them a while to figure out. Harl couldn't get over the wonder of turning a small handle on top of it and then watching as the water shot out into the basin. He kept turning it on and off to Sonora's laughter. What was even more astonishing was that there was a second handle that let out a flow of hot water when turned. They couldn't understand it, but the magic of it made them feel like children.

Exhausted, they collapsed together on the soft bed.

'It's like a dream. Both good and bad,' Sonora said. She gestured around the room with her hand. 'Do you think we can adapt to all this?'

'We've no choice,' Harl said, snuggling down into the warm blanket as she pulled it over them, 'but I admit it's better than sleeping in a cave wondering when the next hiver might find us.'

'Why do you think Damen was so eager to leave?' she asked.

'I'm sure he has family awaiting his return,' he said.

'He seemed angry when we ate the meat.' she said. 'It could be he doesn't have these luxuries in his own home. He said that the Enlightened ones keep many marvels for themselves.'

'I'll ask him when we next meet.' he said and thought it strange that Damen had left so suddenly, but like Sonora's questions, his thoughts were all over the place.

The technology, as Kane had called it, was something that fascinated him. Even with all that Gorman had shown him, it had nearly been too much. He knew his own people were living a backwards life compared to those in Delta. But it was a life without real fear; only the gods were a threat.

How much had mankind missed out on because of the Aylen? He no longer believed the words of the priests. They were not gods or entities to be revered; the Aylen were a horror beyond imagining. Everyone trapped inside the tanks believed it was the only way of life and yet there was a whole world beyond the barriers. They were prisoners and slaves held by the whim of monsters. It had been their way of life for generation after generation, and it would be the way of life for as long as children were born. Why had the Aylen done it in the first place? And what did the future hold for his people?

The questions bombarded his mind as he lay there in bed, Sonora sleeping softly at his side. He didn't know what he was going to do and he didn't know how he was going to find out, but he did know one thing.

The answers lay in Delta.

Chapter 36

They queued outside for hours, streaming in when I opened the doors until no space was left. It's the end of a long day, but I have sold almost seven hundred charges worth, to the richest bidders. Tomorrow I will increase prices and book the surgery.

A droning buzz rang through the metal room, forcing Harl and Sonora from their restless dreams. Kane's voice sounded tinny through the speaker box above the door. 'If you are both awake you should eat and meet me in the library. The guards will guide you to it. Do not be long.' A click signalled the end of the communication.

'A library?' Sonora said and the excitement in her voice told Harl she would learn faster than he could ever hope to.

After using the cooker to heat some kind of oats Sonora had found in a cupboard, they sat in the smooth rigid chairs to eat. They discussed the plans for the day and agreed that they had to learn as quickly as possible if they were to integrate into Delta. It was vital if they held any hope of convincing these people about the Aylen shop.

The guards led them to a large wood-panelled room where books lined every wall on ordered shelves. The shelves rose higher than a man stood and the only access was from a ladder that slid on a rail along the base of the walls. The space was lit by electric lights which hung from the ceiling and shone down on scratched metal tables. A dozen or so people sat on benches around the room, deeply engrossed in the tomes.

As they walked past a central, stand-alone bookshelf that stretched to the ceiling, their guards took up flanking positions either side of them. The people deep in study at the tables cast wary glances at the newcomers. Their eyes would dart from their book to the guards, and then lock on to the strangers, narrowing as they scrutinized Harl and Sonora. Harl met the gazes one by one and they quickly continued reading.

'Ah, there you are,' Kane said, stepping from behind the stand-alone bookshelf. He wore the same white, knee-length jacket over his skinny frame as he had the previous day, and his eyes were full of excitement, like a child being offered a handful of sugary treats.

'I've been given permission to tell you something of our history,' he said. 'It's good to know something of us when we're asking so much about yourselves. But, as you can see,' he said, sweeping an arm around at the wary readers hunched over nearby tables, 'this is a place where many study. You are denied that privilege until judgement has been passed.' He rubbed a finger under his nose and then slid a small folder of papers towards Harl.

'This,' he said, pointing to the title on the first sheet, which read *Fundamentals of Electricity*, 'is a basic primer on Delta's history. You'll find it most interesting. Although,' he added, leaning down close to Harl and lowering his voice. 'I would suggest you voice any questions on this, um, history when we're in a more private location.' He winked and walked away humming to himself.

Sonora wasted no time and rushed to the nearest shelf. She pulled down a metal bound book and her eyes lit up as she flipped open the pages.

'It's in our writing as well, almost the exact same.' She beamed at the pages, running a finger lightly as if to inspect them as she scanned the words. 'Compared to the books at home, they're works of art. Even Grandpa could never get more than an armful for our own shelf.'

The guard closest frowned and stomped over.

'What's the name of the book?' he demanded.

'The properties of metal.' Sonora said, checking the scrawl on the spine.

What could the book show Harl in his own line of work?

The guard shook his head and snatched the book from Sonora and retreated to the side of the room, slipping the tome back on a random shelf as he passed.

Kane clambered up a ladder on the central pillar of shelves and plucked a thin volume from the top rack. He slid down and presented it to Sonora. It had a white cover emblazoned with a red cross.

'Perhaps you would be interested in this book,' he said. He sat down on the edge of the table and Harl noted that he was careful to check that the guard's eyeline was blocked. 'It is a textbook on healing. Perhaps some of the ideas are new to you, but you may have techniques that we are unaware of. I heard of your use of the herb you call banewort. Fascinating.'

He plucked a tiny notepad and pencil from the pocket of his white jacket and began scribbling, then popped it back and waved a frail hand at the table and cushioned chairs.

'Please,' he said, 'take a seat. I must teach you something about our ways so that when you do start to read you will be able to better understand the ideas of electricity and steam power.'

Most of the day was spent listening to Kane's enthusiastic lectures on the history of Delta. He told of how the hivers had repeatedly attacked the city, whittling the population down until it was smaller and smaller, before explaining how Delta had shrunk each time only to be rebuilt afterwards. During the worst attack the entire population had been segregated. They had split into Enlightened and Passives and lived independently for a generation.

'The Passives,' Kane said, 'left all of their technology and equipment here in Delta. When the hiver plague was first spotted, they grabbed what they could and fled in their hundreds. Those of us now known as the Enlightened chose to stay and fight. We managed to drive the hivers off, but at a great cost in lives.

'For years the Passives lived apart, over twenty days hard travel from Delta. Without the sun panels to generate electricity, they had to adapt to survive, relying solely on steam engines and the power they could provide.'

'How did you reunite?' Sonora asked.

Kane smiled. 'It was by the same sort of catastrophe that had separated us in the first place. We established contact again by distant trade and, when we learned that the hivers had regained their numbers and were swarming, we asked the Passives to return. This time, in a bid to redeem themselves, they marched back to Delta and supported their kin.'

'Did it work?' Harl asked, wrapped up the story.

Kane smiled at the eagerness on their faces.

'I'm getting there,' he said. 'Another great war against the hivers ensued and, with both groups working as one, the hivers were eventually defeated. The Enlightened forgave the Passives for their cowardice in the first battle, but the Passives never fully returned to the use of electricity as a main source of power. They feared another split and that the isolation would strip that power away. Steam had served them well, so they stuck to it.' He gestured around at those inside the library. 'Even now the rift between our two groups is as big as ever. The others on the council have decreed that the Passives are not as fit to learn as those descended from Enlightened, which, of course, has the Passives riled.' He shrugged. 'If I had it my way, it would be different, but as it stands, the Passives are strongly discouraged from learning and must stay in their roles until death or disease take them.'

'Roles?' Sonora asked.

'When each Passive comes of age they are assigned a job that they will continue until an Enlightened says otherwise. Which, other than myself, none have yet done. Few Passives have ever changed career.'

He looked over to Damen, who was sat at a bench on the other side of the library, deep in study with the help of a mentor. He was scowling as the mentor flipped through a stack of papers asking questions.

'Damen is one of our best students and he has progressed well,' Kane said, 'but it is hard for anyone to understand the full functions of electricity without learning from birth. I doubt any will ever mistake him as an Enlightened, but I believe, now more than ever, that we need as many educated minds as we can create. There are so few of us left that we can't afford to pick and choose who has the right to learn.'

'And the people?' Harl asked. 'They accept it?'

Kane sighed. 'There is little choice in the matter. I have tried, many times, to sway opinions to my own detriment, but the others on the council are not yet ready for change.'

'Why stop them learning?' Sonora asked.

Kane looked around as if to make sure they would not be overheard. 'Many Enlightened see it as a punishment for leaving the city during the first great war. Personally, I don't believe the Passives consider it so. For them it is just the way things have always been.'

'What about Damen?' Harl asked.

'What about him?' Kane asked, watching as the bearded man collected his books, grunted at the teacher and then stalked from the room.

'When we first met,' Harl said, 'he asked us what tribe we were from, but that seems odd now considering there are only the Passives and Enlightened.'

'I assume,' Kane said, 'that he was referring to those who live beyond Delta's walls, or those who hunt and gather for the city. He is not a true Passive, as we call those who use steam and who came back to us after the split. Some prefer to live a more primitive existence far beyond the city. Damen belongs to a tribe who recently came to Delta. They settled within the boundary of the caves and help the others who scavenge and hunt for our supplies. But there are still others who live far beyond the range of our patrols.'

'How many of these tribes are there?' Harl asked, surprised to learn of even more people than those left in the city.

'No one can say for sure,' Kane said. 'Some have come to Delta, as I said, but most still live in far off lands hidden from the Aylens. Who knows how far we have been scattered? It is a shame to say it, but apart from Damen and the hunters you met, most are unwilling to learn anything more than hunting and surviving. Most stay well beyond the city wall. They come in to trade meat and metal for weapons and clothing, then retreat back to small huts tucked away in the forest. Damen and his hunting group live inside the walls but are often away for long periods of time, like when they found you. Be glad it was not one of the other hunting parties that discovered you, or it might have worked out a lot worse.'

'What are they like?' Sonora asked.

'Simple people,' Kane said. 'If I had my way, I would have them join the city and learn all they can from us, but the rest on the council believe otherwise. They see them only as a means to get the food and the resources to build better technology, rarely considering them our brethren. Each human has a role in our future. Our city depends on it.'

It seemed odd to Harl that the city was so divided. There was no reason for it other than the council members' thirst for power and their resentment of the Passives. It mirrored his old land in a way. Perhaps all human societies developed a similar hierarchy, but did they all eventually rebel?

Chapter 37

The operation was a success and I returned to find a queue waiting for more stock. I need at least sixteen of these tanks if I am to continue this venture as my fame spreads. The extra tanks will be put to use to raise the other dependant creatures I found near their nest.

After the lessons, they were shown to the mess hall. Harl was wrapped up in his thoughts as they reached a fork in the metal-walled corridor.

'Turn right,' one of the guards behind said.

Harl was considering the rift between the Passives and Enlightened when he strayed left. An invisible hand choked him as a guard grabbed his collar and dragged him backwards to the junction. He fought to free the vice-like grip.

'I said right!' the guard yelled in his ear.

'Stop it!' Sonora cried, beating at the arm as a familiar face appeared further down the corridor.

'Free him,' Uman said, putting a hand on a dagger strapped across his chest as he started to jog towards them.

The second guard must not have heard and stepped in to assist, throwing Sonora aside. She hit the metal wall and collapsed.

Harl roared and clutched at the hand about his throat. He caught sight of Uman as he barrelled into the second guard and punched him full in the face. The guard crumpled to the floor. The choking stopped as the first guard stepped back from Harl and raised his hands. Uman drew his dagger as Harl helped Sonora up.

'He was running off,' the guard said, eyes on the dagger. His gaze then darted down to his unconscious partner. 'Not following instructions.'

'Next time you make a mistake in the training grounds, Yimil, and fail to follow orders,' Uman said, 'we'll see how much you like getting dragged back onto the right path.'

The guard stepped out of his way as Uman smiled at Harl and Sonora.

'I'll escort you to the mess hall,' Uman said.

'Thank you, Uman,' Sonora said.

Harl was sure Uman turned pink as he took the right fork in the path and led them to the hall.

They ate while Uman whittled a lump of wood, forming it into a rough replica of the flower they had passed when he fell against the Ripshrub.

'It's beautiful,' Sonora said between mouthfuls.

Uman beamed at her and slipped it back in his pocket. 'It is not yet finished, but thanks.'

Once they had eaten and said goodbye to him, two new guards escorted them to their quarters. Kane was waiting for them when they arrived.

'You will have to answer to the council soon,' he said, sifting through a selection of documents he held. 'You must explain how you came to be here at Delta and convince them your intentions are good. They will question you on your time in the sacred caves.' He glanced at the door. 'But their only real interest is information about the people inside your homeland. As one of them, I know they will be seeking to gauge the technology level of your people, so it will be better to claim ignorance.'

'We have no more of those weapons,' Harl said, 'if that's what they want to know.'

Kane shrugged. 'Like I said, ignorance will be your best bet.'

Harl had no idea what the council expected from him. If he failed to convince them to help in a rescue, would the Enlightened throw them out or would they be locked up in the city out of fear? Kane was little help. All he would say was that they should relate their story, but be vague on most details. The council would then decide what to do about those still trapped in the Aylen's home.

Harl knew he needed their help to get his people out, but he had no idea what he would do if they refused. Maybe they could find a quiet place among the tribes who lived beyond Delta's walls. Could he live out there? He guessed it had been their plan before Damen had found them and before he'd realised how harsh this new land was. They had left the tank in search of a cure for the blacking disease, but seeing Sonora's world thrown to the ground by the Aylen had put an end to that option. Could he face turning his back on the others inside the shop?

A light tap on the door made Kane jump. He had been going over a passage from the healing book with Sonora, but snatched the book away from her and slipped it inside his white jacket. He raised a finger to his lips to silence her.

'Yes?' he said.

Another Enlightened entered, bowing briefly to Sonora and Harl.

'I'm sorry to interrupt, Kane,' the man said, 'but a group has returned with new...' He glanced at Harl and Sonora then back to Kane. '...technology.'

Kane nodded and turned back to Harl and Sonora. 'Excuse me, both of you, but I will need to be there for the pricing.'

'Pricing?' Sonora asked.

'When new technology or objects are found,' Kane said, 'we haggle a price with the finding party.'

The newcomer frowned at his words, but Kane ignored the look and rose from his seat, drawing out his notebook as he took his leave.

Harl and Sonora were left to stroll around the corridors inside the caves. The guards grunted whenever they were about to take a forbidden corridor, which left them with nowhere to go except wander through the main corridors until they reached the entrance gate.

'Can't go that way,' the guard said as they stared at the imposing hinged doors of reinforced steel.

'Why not? Sonora said, rounding on the man. 'What gives you the right to cage us like this?'

'Because I said so,' the guard said with a cold grin as he fingered the hilt of his sword with one hand.

'Typical answer when you're not clever enough to justify your actions,' Sonora said.

The guard shifted at the insult, clearly debating whether he should hit her or not. Harl readied himself, but the second guard stepped up next to his friend and shook his head in warning.

'I'll take them out,' a voice said and they spun to find Damen striding towards them. The two guards took a step back not willing to argue with the imposing man.

The doors swung open with a hiss of steam at Damen's command and he led them down the steps to the main street. It was bustling with people, but the atmosphere was relaxed as people chatted in the middle of tasks or perused the shops brimming with a surplus of goods.

It was strange to watch it all. Everything seemed so familiar to Harl. People shopping, people talking, friends walking along and laughing, lovers holding hands as they dreamt of their future together – it could all have been taking place back in his own world. It was like a reflection of everything he'd known, but there was an effortlessness about it all. He watched two men as they worked a forge. Instead of one having to constantly attend the flames, they just pressed a series of buttons and the coals adjusted temperature in response. Another woman was hanging washing out on a strange circular line that looked like a toadstool made from metal and wire. She finished pegging the items in place and then pressed another button and the whole toadstool contraption began to revolve, the clothes whipping about in the wind. Everything seemed easier than his life had been back home. He saw no beggars or drunks shambling about and even those who looked like servants weren't running between tasks.

It was all a cold reminder of how backwards life was for the people inside the tanks.

'Thank you for back there' Harl said. 'I'm starting to feel like we should have taken your offer to go into the wild.'

'I said it'd be difficult,' Damen said, walking with them down the steps from the main entrance.

'Damen, what do you think of Kane?' Sonora asked as the three stepped off the roadway to let a troop of soldiers pass.

'He's a pompous ass,' Damen said, scratching the scar through his plaited black beard. 'But for an Enlightened council member, he's one of the better ones.'

'Better how?' she asked, stopping to let a child dash in front of her into one of the houses.

'Most aren't like him,' he said. 'They argue about teaching us - weather we are fit to learn or not - but all they really care about is their technology and their power over us. Kane isn't like that. I owe him a great debt for asking the council if he could teach me, which meant a home in the city. Without his aid I'd still be living outside. As for the others, they only care for us because we bring back supplies and sometimes find some of their beloved technology. They're far too cowardly to do it themselves.'

Harl remembered how Kane had said that it was the Passives who were considered the cowards. Now it seemed the roles had reversed.

Damen led them past a building that housed a loud pumping machine. Steam billowed from a vent in its side. He ushered them around the clouds of boiling vapour to a modest-sized, one story house built of wooden beams and rusted iron sheets all

366

amalgamated into a single solid structure. It was subtly coloured to match the dusty orange floor and, like every other building, the roof was a cascade of trailing plants and vines.

'You're welcome in my home, Harl and Sonora,' Damen said, opening the door to reveal a large living room.

The plaster walls were cluttered with the heads of hunting trophies, all lovingly restored to give a ferocious glare at visitors. Wooden furniture circled a central fire pit over which an empty iron pot hung. A single door led to another room from which a startlingly attractive, olive-skinned woman swept out.

She wore a bust-hugging grey and green dress patterned by leaves and carried herself with a dignity that a queen would envy. She twitched her smooth, dark hair aside as her brown eyes stared hard at the strangers entering her home. They flicked down to an iron poker beside the fire pit, but then Damen stepped through the doorway and her face lit up.

'Welcome,' she said, inviting them to sit down. 'I'm Yara, and you must be Harl and Sonora.' She beamed at them, plucking the pot off the hook over the fire. 'You must stay and eat. I'll put something on right away.'

She turned and headed in to the other room, her long dress swishing as she went.

They ate together and talked about the city. Yara was keen to question Sonora on her potion making and to have her relate the story of finding such a handsome young man, as she put it.

They left as night was drawing in, with repeated invitations from Yara to come back and visit echoing in their ears as they walked away.

'She's lovely,' Sonora said as they wound their way back to the cave entrance.

'Aye,' Damen agreed, 'she is. I know she's invited you to come again, and I would like it if you did, but tomorrow is the day you go before the Enlightened council, so it must wait a while. You can find your way from here?' he asked as they reached the entrance.

'We can,' Harl said, wondering if the man was giving them a subtle chance to leave before the meeting.

Too late now, he thought. Their fate hung in the balance and they were committed to seeing it through to whatever end these Enlightened deemed appropriate.

Chapter 38

The dependant creatures I found with them seem to be unlike anything else I have discovered. They share similarities with other species across the planet but they are so small they would have required an independent ecosystem to evolve at such a scale.

When they woke, it was to the harsh sound of a buzzer. Harl rolled out of bed and stumbled across the room to press the answer button on the wall-mounted speaker box. There was a burst of static and then Damen's firm voice filled the room.

'You must be up and at the council chambers soon. I'll be there to guide you shortly.'

When he arrived, Damen looked grim. They followed him through the narrow tunnels, passing curious onlookers and men performing maintenance to the pipes and wire that ran through the metal-lined passages.

'Do you think they'll believe us?' Harl asked.

Damen continued walking as he spoke. 'I cannot say for sure. The council are set in their ways. The balance of power in Delta is entirely in their hands. I can't see them wanting to give that up by admitting they'd overlooked thousands of people for years who were only a few days march away. I can tell you that no matter what their decision, many of the people in Delta are on your side. News spreads fast and the story you've told is now well known and has caused many people to hope for a better life.'

'What do you mean?' Sonora asked.

'Well,' Damen said, running a cupped hand down around his plaited beard, 'for a long time Delta's people, Passives, Enlightened and even some of the hunters, have known that we're on the decline. With less people to work and gather food, we are dwindling. Most of the Passives want to learn the ways of power that the Enlightened have partially shared with us. Even some of the Enlightened council, like Kane, believe that sharing is essential to our survival. But that knowledge is useless if we are a dying people.'

'What about the tribes?' Harl asked.

'Hunters are not troubled by such things, at least those outside of the city. It's only the will of the council that keeps us from true unity. If we were united, they might lose their hold over the power of electricity and thus their strict control of the people.'

The way Damen spoke at times confused Harl. When they had met he'd been a rough diamond, talking in harsh tones about killing. Then, as if the gem had secretly been polished, he would talk in an eloquent manner to Kane. Did he speak and act differently around the hunters?

He fell silent as they rounded a corner and found two guards either side of a large double door. Damen spoke into a speaker box on the wall and the doors creaked open. The guards stepped aside as the doors parted.

370

The room Harl entered was round and cavernous, with bricked walls instead of the usual metal plates. Half of the outer wall was lined with two tiers of curved benches that faced a raised wooden dais at one end of the chamber. The platform supported a semi-circlular table that seated eight wizened old men and two imperious looking ladies. Free standing electric lights were set at intervals on the table, illuminating a spread of papers and scrolls.

One of their guards stepped behind them and used the pole of his metal spear to shunt them both forwards to the centre of the room.

Harl shot the man a dark look, but Sonora gave Harl a warning frown and he turned his attention back to the room.

The scene reminded Harl of his trial back home. The old men presiding around the table cast imperious and hostile looks down at them as if they were unwanted bugs ready for extermination.

Damen entered behind them and took a seat on one of the benches. No one else was present. Harl noticed an empty chair at the far left of the high table. Kane was absent.

The central figure spoke into a small square device in front of him. Cables trailed away from it to a pair of speaker boxes set high in the room's bricked-lined walls on either side of the dais, making the sound amplify across the chamber. His long white beard muffled the sound and he tucked it under the table as he leaned over the device.

'You are accused of desecrating a tomb and have been brought here to explain your actions. We have been informed that in your attempt to explain your sudden appearance, you told a wild story

371

about thousands of people living inside the Aylen's lair. Do you deny this?'

To Harl the words seemed instantly hostile. Perhaps Damen was right and Kane was the only decent one among them?

'No,' Harl said, and just as he was about to continue, another man at the table stood and spoke.

'These claims have falsity written all over them. You claim that *people-*' He said the final word as though he knew Harl was delusional. '-are living in enslavement and without knowledge of even basic steam power.'

A woman at the end of the table stood and spread her hands with a shrug. 'Lies! How are we to believe even a word from this man?'

Straight after, a fat blubbery man rose from his seat to speak. 'I've checked with our quartermasters and over the course of the last four hundred days we have had equipment go missing from our stores, including items similar to those you possessed.'

Still standing, the bearded man at the centre of the table spoke again.

'Bring in their possessions,' he said, pressing a second button on the speaker box.

The doors swung open and an orderly strode in carrying their satchels and weapons. Harl frowned at the thought of him going to the room and taking their bags. The man took the dais steps quickly and upended the items unceremoniously onto the high table.

The fat man grabbed the sword.

'This could be one of the weapons taken,' he said to the others.

Harl couldn't believe that the council were treating them in such a way. He had not even been allowed to defend himself or Sonora. It was as if they had already been condemned.

One scrawny man, who had remained seated until now, jumped up, plucked a pair of spectacles from his breast pocket and stuffed them over his beady eyes. He snatched Gorman's book off the table and had a look of awe in his eyes as he unwrapped it. Gorman had told Harl that it was their most valuable possession.

It was a whisper when the man spoke, but it was picked up on the amplifier and they heard the shock in his voice.

'Can it be?' he asked. The others turned to look at him as he opened the book, his eyes wide behind his wire-framed spectacles. 'It is,' he said to himself, flipping through the pages.

'It's the Third?' the blubbery one asked. 'Truly?'

'Was this what Kane was searching for?' the bearded one murmured, turning the book over in his hands.

'It would explain his actions,' the councilwoman said, nodding.

The one holding the book scowled down at Harl and Sonora. 'Where did you come by this book?'

'It was given to us by my grandfather, Sonora said. 'He was a native of Delta. He also gave us the weapons. We did not steal them.'

The bearded councilman addressed the man holding the book. 'It does not matter. It's unimportant where it came from, only that we have it now.'

The others nodded.

'What do we do with them?' the spectacled man asked quietly.

'We don't need them,' the fat one said. 'They must not be able to spread word of this.'

What was so special about that one book? Harl looked around for Damen to see how he was taking it, but the hunter was nowhere to be seen.

'The council have decided,' the bearded man said, rushing the words, 'that you have defiled our sacred cave tombs.' His eyes flicked to the book, his fingers twitching as though eager to flip its pages. He scowled down at them. 'You are sentenced to death. You will be taken beyond the gate and your crimes read to the people before you are executed. Guards.' He shouted the last word and the speaker box amplified his voice until it was deafening. 'Take them!'

Chapter 39

Sales are down but consistent. So now I need to work on a breeding
program which means it's about time I made them feel at home.

Not again, Harl thought as four armed guards stormed
through the door into the council chamber. They split into
pairs and grabbed Harl and Sonora by the arms.

'You'll regret this!' Harl called as he was dragged out of the
room and the doors were shut behind them.

The guards held their arms firmly and marched them through
the metal tunnels and out of the caves to the main strip of Delta.

'You don't understand.' Harl said, tugging at the men. They
tightened their grip, half dragging him down the central road as
people poured from homes to watch the spectacle. He could hear
some of them whispering and shaking their heads at the guards.

'Wait!' a polite voice called. It was that of an Enlightened,
clearly marked by the white coat most of them seemed to wear.
He'd dashed from between two buildings, his arms up in protest.
'You cannot do this,' he pleaded to the man who Harl assumed
was the captain of the guards.

'And why not?' the captain asked, barely looking at him.

'You know as well as I that some of the council members are hasty in their decisions,' the Enlightened man said.

'So, you've been overruled,' the captain said. 'Tough luck.'

'They have found the Third!' the newcomer said, causing the captain's eyes to widen. 'You know of what I speak man - you have the training.'

The captain looked unsure, as though struggling with the decision.

He shrugged. 'I've got orders and if I don't carry them out, I'm as dead as them. Now out of my way.' He put a hand on his sword hilt.

The Enlightened shook his head in despair as he stepped aside and watched the guards pull Harl and Sonora further on through the main street.

More soldiers joined them as they passed the gate. Sonora looked from them to Harl, hung her head and wept. Harl didn't have the words to stop her tears, but he tried nonetheless.

'I'm sorry,' he said. 'I love you.'

It was all he could manage and it sounded pathetic. How could he have been so stupid and not taken the chance to escape when Damen offered it?

The captain stopped just beyond the gate as a small crowd drew close. He pulled a short roll of paper from under his leather breastplate. He unrolled the scroll and began to read.

'This man and woman,' he said, 'have been tried and convicted of tomb desecration by the Enlightened council. They are also guilty of threatening the lives of the Enlightened. The punishment for these crimes is death.'

'Lies,' Harl said, sickened that they had twisted his words, but the captain nodded at the guards and they were hauled further out beyond the gate.

The guards tugged them to a stop in an open area facing the forest of grass stalks on the horizon. The sky was a myriad precious colours as the yellow of sunset blended into the deeper red and purple of night.

Harl thought of the things they had seen since leaving their home and a single tear coursed down his cheek. This was how it was all going to end?

'You sure boss?' one of the guards asked.

'Kneel,' the captain said, ignoring the man.

Sonora sunk to her knees but Harl stayed standing.

'I said kneel, boy!' the voice came again, louder and impatient.

Harl roared in anger as the captain drew his sword and attempted to kick the back of Harl's legs out to make him kneel down. Harl turned around to stare at the face of his would be killer. His gaze travelled over the captain's shoulder to the entrance of Delta. It was crowded with people as they watched the horror and sheer brutality of the scene. Harl knelt where he was, daring the man to perform his so-called duty, while those from the city looked on. The captain shrugged as though it was inevitable and a humming sound pulsed from the sword as he raised the melting-blade.

Time seemed to slow as Harl waited. Everything came into sharp focus, the wrinkles in the captain's hands, the dust blowing softly over the ground, and the sound of his own breathing. The fact that the man chose Gorman's sword added an ironic twist to the surreal moment.

Just do it, he thought as he looked to his side so that his final vision would be of the woman he loved.

He had hoped to find Sonora looking back at him, but she was staring out away from the city. He looked up at the captain again, wondering why he was drawing it out, and saw that he too was looking behind Harl, the sword still held ready to strike.

Taking his chance, Harl twisted around to see two distant figures walking out of the stalks and across the bare ground. His eyes blurred from the tears as he tried to focus on the pair strolling towards them.

One of them was Uman from the gathering party, while the other shuffled along under a hood and cloak. Uman's nervous words carried on the breeze, attempting to urge the other on, describing how Harl and Sonora were on their knees in front of the captain. Harl tried to see who the cloaked figure was, but the face was covered by the cowl.

The pair stopped ten paces away and the hooded man whipped out a bow from under his cloak. A calm voice came from beneath the veil as he smoothly notched an arrow and aimed it straight at them.

'You have one chance to let them go, my lad,' the man said.

Sonora looked up from her kneeling position and let out a cry of wonder.

'This isn't your business, stranger,' the captain said, 'or yours, Uman son of Udal.'

378

The arrow loosed from the stranger's bow, puncturing deep into the captain's chest plate, forcing him backwards. The sword slipped from his grip and clattered to the ground as blood dribbled from the hole. He grasped the arrow shaft in both hands. A second arrow thumped into the back of one hand, pinning it to his chest. His screams turned to a bloody gurgle. Uman held his spear high, ready to impale the other guards as the hooded man spoke.

'Anyone else?' the familiar voice asked.

The rest of the guards, shaken by the sudden death of their leader and uncommitted from the start, turned to run, but only kicked up dust as they stopped mid turn.

Harl risked a glance back at the city and saw a large group of armed people standing in the gateway with Damen at their head.

'Grandpa!' Sonora shouted, standing up and running towards the hooded man.

She must have recognised Gorman's voice straight away, but Harl could not believe it himself. How could he be here? He knew he had not heard or seen Gorman die, but surely he could not have survived the destruction of the world.

The guards raised their hands in surrender as Damen led the mob from the gates to surround them. He then strode up to Harl and Sonora, sword in hand and the look of an exhilarated child on his face.

'They've locked Kane away in the cells,' he said, helping Harl to his feet.

Harl nodded his thanks to Damen, unable to find his voice after the turmoil of the last few moments. He turned to face Gorman and Sonora as they embraced

'I thought you were gone,' she cried into the old man's shoulder.

'Well, I'm here now,' Gorman said, stretching a mud splattered arm around her. 'It was hard going after you left, and there's much to explain, but from what I hear there are more pressing issues at hand.' He turned in Uman's direction. 'If it was not for this man, I'd have wandered until I could stand no longer.'

Sonora tore away from Gorman and flung herself at Uman. 'Thank you,' she said kissing him on his reddening cheeks. She let him go and moved beside Gorman again, linking an arm through his, as if they had never parted.

Uman looked around in stunned silence at the crowd and Harl smiled, thinking of Uman's description of his wife's terrible anger.

Gorman slumped against Sonora and rubbed his milky eyes.

'Thank you,' Harl said, placing a hand on Gorman's shoulder, grateful to have the old man to help guide them once more. 'You must rest, at least for a while.' He turned to face Damen. 'Is there time?'

'Some,' Damen said. 'Kane was taken to one of the cells just outside the caves. My men tell me that he found out about the book and attempted to take it before the meeting. '

'Damen?' a soldier called, breaking from the crowd as they headed back to the gateway.

'What is it, Forn?'

'The Enlightened councilmen have ordered their brethren to the caves and blocked themselves inside. They have the book.'

'We should help Kane first,' Sonora said, looking from Damen to Harl. 'He's been kind to us.'

Harl nodded. 'You're right. He risked his life for us, but there's more to it than that. He holds sway over the Enlightened, and he is one of the few who seem to care about the Passives. With him at our side we stand a real chance of uniting the people.'

'Then we'll help him first,' Damen said, 'and deal with the councilmen after.'

'So all we face is a group of heavily armed men with superior weapons?' Harl said, 'What could possibly go wrong?'

A nasty grin crossed Damen's lips and Harl didn't like it one bit.

Chapter 40

Many have paired up. It seems they are a monogamous species.
Maybe soon there will be eggs...

Harl, Sonora, Damen and Uman gathered outside Damen's house just as night was falling, while Gorman rested inside, fast asleep.

'There will be at least four men guarding the cells,' Damen said, testing the string of his hunting bow. 'If we can surprise them then we'll have the advantage.'

'Maybe they will give up,' Sonora said. 'No more lives need be lost than necessary.'

Harl looked at her. When she was called upon to fight she looked more beautiful than ever, like a sleek predatory animal. She had that look now. She stood differently, ready to spring into action and rend anything that threatened the ones she loved. Her eyes tracked every small bit of movement and her hands twitched as she prowled, pacing back and forth as she spoke. A short sword was slung over her back and a sleek fierceness in her face showed the changes that had come over her since she killed the first hiver. He found he loved her more when she showed such passion.

'They'll fight to the death,' Uman said. 'The ones in charge of the cells carry the pistols of light and have sworn oaths to the council.'

'So be it,' Harl said, picking up Gorman's sword from the porch and double-checking his quiver of arrows from the gifting so long ago.

It felt like an age since his times drinking with Troy in the Golden Spear. Waiting for such gifts had seemed like a blessing. In reality it was a curse, bare essentials given to sustain a living product in the hope of a profit.

No doubt Troy would be guzzling pints of foaming ale, perhaps remembering Harl, as he charmed the ladies. Had he slipped into a life of regret, using women and drink to mask the ruin that Harl had brought down on him? Maybe he would see him again one day, but Harl knew nothing came without a fight.

He walked down the steps and tightened his grip on the sword. The air smelled heavy with rain as though it was preparing to wash away the blood that was to come. He grimaced and walked on.

'Let's get this over with.'

Harl crept out into the night from the patch of shrubs. He was almost unrecognisable. Sonora had wrapped him in smelly rags and he hobbled along leaning on a makeshift crutch as he made his way towards the prison.

The only difference between the long brick building and the nearby houses were the criss-crossing bars that secured its windows and the two guards chatting in the darkness outside the heavy wooden door. Everything else was the same. Sandy coloured bricks made up its walls and a riot of flowers covered its roof and hung down the walls.

Harl took a deep breath, cursed himself for suggesting the plan, and then shuffled down the dusty road towards them.

'Right, left, left,' he murmured to himself, repeating the directions back to the others in his head.

The men took notice as he drew nearer.

'Halt!' the guard on the left ordered, drawing a pistol as Harl got within ten paces of the door.

Harl dropped the crutch and fled back down the street, his feet kicking the dirt into clouds as he sped away. As he had hoped, the guards gave chase. He ran through the directions in his head again as he dodged around the back of a building at the end of the street. Blue streaks of light burst from behind and slammed into the wall above his head. He ducked and twisted right, darting down a narrow passage. Another shot exploded over his shoulder, its light searing his eyes just as he took a sharp left. The men shouted curses as they rounded the corner into the long alleyway. Harl slipped left again just before a dense clump of bushes.

Uman and Damen stepped out from the shrubs and loosed arrows straight down the alley. The guards crumpled to the floor, each with an arrow embedded in their leg.

Harl stepped back around the last corner as Sonora slipped from the bushes, sword in hand, and checked each man's pulse.

'It worked,' she said, smiling at the two senseless men.

To Harl they looked like a pair of drunks sleeping off the ale after failing to make it back home.

Damen knelt and picked up a pistol, then plucked a key from the other's chest pocket.

'They're heavily armed,' he said, inspecting the weapon, before passing it to Sonora. 'This is not their usual equipment. Be careful.'

She took the pistol in one hand and then slid the sword into the scabbard on her back.

'They should be quiet for a while,' she said, stooping down to the guards and drawing the arrows out. She wrapped a thin roll of cloth around their legs to bind the wounds. 'The venom will last for a while before they come around again.'

'How did you make such a weapon?' Uman asked, staring at the two limp guards.

'Herbs are a wonderful thing,' Sonora said. 'Some can heal and others-' She gestured at the bodies. '-can be used to make life easier during an operation.'

Uman shook his head in disbelief and smiled.

'The ways of women,' he said.

They returned to find the jail door locked. Damen thrust the key into the keyhole and gently turned it, coaxing as much silence as possible from the lock. The click was barely audible when it came and he used a foot to ease the reinforced door open. He froze as it creaked, unwilling to continue for fear of more noise. Sonora slipped in beside him and braced her hands on the door edge, then lifted it up to take the weight off hinges as she swung it silently inwards.

Harl guessed that living with Gorman had forced her to get creative in avoiding detection.

Once inside, they swept the gloom with their pistols, but found the guardroom empty and abandoned. Only a battered table and chairs lurked in the darkness.

An open doorway led off into a long room lined with cells on either side. There was no sign of light in there, just a pitch blackness that smothered the furthest end of the room. All Harl could make out was the shadowy corners of some boxes stacked at the far end. The place was deserted.

'Maybe no one's home.' Harl said as he walked into the cell block. 'Have they moved him?'

'Our man said he was brought here,' Damen said. 'But it's possible.'

'Why the guards?' Uman asked.

'It's a trap!' Kane's voice screamed from out of the darkness ahead, just as the corridor lit up with twin streaks of blue fire.

Harl didn't have time to react as the shots hurtled towards him. A hand yanked him back, and as the blue light streaked past his head, Damen stepped in front to return fire with his bow. Sonora squeezed beside the hunter and knelt to fire her pistol. Her shots lit the hallway like a storm, splintering the boxes at the far end into a burst of flame.

'Behind!' Uman called as three guards charged in from the front entrance.

Harl spun and tore his sword from its scabbard. His heart began to pound as the closest man rushed him. The look in the guard's eyes was crazed with bloodlust. He slashed out with a melting-dagger, but Harl parried the blade and then launched a foot out to stop the guard from advancing. He felt the man's ribs crack and, as he thrust his sword out, the man sprang at him, snarling. Harl braced himself and thrust forward. The sword's tip punctured the man's armour, impaling him up to the hilt, Harl pressed forward but the weight of the body forced him back until his foot caught on a chair leg, and he toppled over backwards.

The body collapsed on top of Harl and he twisted, shoving it aside as he scrambled to his feet. He ducked as Uman launched a spear at the two men crowded in the entrance. The spear slammed into one of them and forced him backwards into the other. Harl leapt forwards and shoved the dying man aside, and then plunged his sword down into the guard pinned underneath.

He spun back to the cell block doorway. Sonora and Damen were on either side of it, backs against the frame as shots flashed through into the guardroom. Harl jumped aside as a couple of shots flashed towards him. He dodged them, barely, and they hammered into the far wall and dissipated with a hiss. Acrid smoke began to fill the room, growing thicker and thicker with each shot until it threatened to suffocate them.

Harl crouched beside Sonora as Damen knelt by the doorway, nocked an arrow, and then twisted around the door to fire blindly into the darkness where the last shot had originated.

'Sonora, shoot down towards the end,' Harl said.

She nodded, leant out and fired twice, lighting the walkway and cells on either side with blue flashes as her shots flew into the room. The searing blue shots rippled light past the bars until they struck the boxes at the far end, briefly illuminating the scene.

'There are more than two of them,' Uman said, lying flat on the floor to peer around the frame. 'They're hiding behind some boxes at the end.'

'Like cowards,' Damen growled.

Sonora fired again.

Damen and Harl leant out from either side of the doorframe and fired together, using the light from Sonora's pistol shot to guide them.

A cry came from the darkness at the end of the long room.

'Good shot,' Damen said, dodging behind the frame as a rogue blast whipped back through the doorway to scorch the floor beside Uman.

The scout growled and cursed as he tore off a piece of armour on his arm. The shot had glanced the metal to leave a reddening burn underneath.

'What now?' he said, pouring water from a waterskin onto the tender flesh.

'If they knew we were coming,' Harl said, 'there might be more outside. Cover the entrance, Damen.'

The big man moved to the front door without hesitation and peered out. He ducked back, dragging the bodies of the two dead guards to form a crude barricade in the doorway.

'Here,' Damen said, tossing a pistol from one of the dead men to Harl.

Harl kept up a steady stream of fire towards the crates as Sonora crawled over to Uman to apply a crude bandage around his arm.

It was a stalemate. Other than waiting for the men inside to die of thirst, Harl had no idea how to get Kane back. But it was a moot point. An electric light flicked on above the centre of the corridor and Kane was thrust out from behind the stack of metal crates.

Squinting against the glare, Harl raised one hand to shield his eyes and levelled his pistol at the crates concealing the captor.

'Drop your weapons and move into the cells,' a voice said. Harl recognised it. It belonged to the fat Enlightened council member who'd accused them of stealing the weapons.

'Walter,' Damen whispered.

Walter stepped out, but held Kane before him, pistol raised and pointing down the corridor. Kane was clearly terrified, sweat dripping down his face onto the arm around his neck.

Damn them, Harl thought. He hadn't practised enough with the pistol to be sure of hitting Walter; only a fraction of the man's shoulder and face were vulnerable. It was a near impossible shot with a pistol.

He hesitated, unwilling to risk the shot. The pistol seemed a wasted weapon in such a situation. The thought brought an idea to mind and his eyes were drawn up to the florescent tube set in the corridor's ceiling. He smiled. It was a small chance, but it might just work.

'Uman,' he said, keeping his voice low, 'pass an arrow to my left hand.'

Harl focused on Walter.

'Alright,' he called. 'We'll do what you want, but on one condition.'

'You're in no position to make demands,' Walter said, leaning out further from Kane's shoulder to get a good look at them. 'But I will humour you. What?'

'We'll surrender,' Harl said, spotting a second man peek out from behind the boxes, 'but only if we're given another trial. A fair trial this time.'

The arrow slid into Harl's hand, and, trying not to move his mouth, he whispered to Sonora. 'Shoot the light out when I say, then hit the floor. '

'Easy,' she muttered, but he couldn't tell if she was being sarcastic. 'Just be careful.'

'Fine,' Walter said and twitched the gun to Kane's head. 'Now drop your weapons.'

Harl stepped out, his pistol aimed at the ceiling, the other hand held the arrow behind the back of his arm, hidden from Walter's view.

He bent over, his gaze flicking from Walter to Kane's demoralized features, memorizing their positions.

'I also have a bow,' he said, placing the gun on the floor and starting to unsling the weapon from his shoulder.

'All of you,' Walter said, impatient. He pulled the gun from Kane's head and waved it at them. 'Your weapons. Do it!'

'Now,' Harl said.

Sonora fired, sending blue streaks flashing across the room. The shots disintegrated the light in the ceiling and they were plunged into darkness. Harl had the arrow on the string in a heartbeat and fired into the pitch black room before throwing himself to the ground. There was a scream and the darkness fractured as a flash of blue went wide into the cells.

Sonora rolled into Harl's view and stayed low as she unloaded her pistol into the far end of the boxes. Harl glimpsed a man edging out from behind them as her shots lit the room like a lightning storm. The man screamed and staggered in the shadows before crashing against a cell door. He grabbed his stomach and moaned in pain as he raised one hand to stare at the blood in horror. After a moment he slid down the cell bars to the floor.

Harl dived aside as a wave of blue raced towards them. The shot lit up Walter, the arrow embedded in his shoulder. A ferocious snarl twisted his chubby face.

'Die!' Walter cried, firing a storm of shots down the narrow space between the cells.

There was a muted thump and the firing stopped. A shrill scream rang out as a single shot was fired. Harl leapt up, terrified that Kane had been hit in the crossfire. He started to run, but stopped when Kane's silhouette stepped out from behind the boxes.

'I'm okay,' Kane said, stumbling towards them holding a pistol.

Light beamed in from the guardroom behind Harl as Uman found a switch. It illuminated Walter's body on the floor beside Kane.

Kane looked like he had been in a bout with a prize fighter. Bruises bulged from his head making it seem larger than usual. Somehow he had managed to keep his glasses on, but the wire-rimmed frames were buckled and twisted.

392

Damen stepped into the guardroom.

'A couple outside. Ran off when I went out. No spine in them,' he said and then nodded at Kane. 'Looks like you've hunted a scuttler. What happened?'

'I decided to have a look at your belongings,' Kane said, waving a trembling hand at Harl as Sonora dashed forward to inspect his bruises. 'When I found the book, I knew what the outcome of the meeting would be. The discovery of the Third would change our way of life. The other Enlightened would want to keep the knowledge to themselves, and that meant the removal of anyone who knew of its existence. But they sent someone to collect your bags just as I was checking them, and, before I could act, they locked me in a cell in the caves. They brought me out here during the meeting. Ha! Lynching is more appropriate. I guess they thought it wise to lock me up and teach me a lesson.' He rubbed the bruises on his cheekbone. 'So what's next?'

'The council are locked up deep inside the caves,' Damen said. 'The people are restless without guidance and I think some planning is in order before we try to pry them out.'

'And a bath,' Sonora said, dabbing a cloth against the blood coating Kane's face.

'What if they attack again?' Harl asked, thinking a counter-attack right now would be the end of them.

'I have men rooting out those still in favour of the Enlightened,' Damen said, 'So we need not fear a direct counter-attack.'

'They will be preparing for later,' Kane said. 'The longer they have to prepare their next move, the more people we'll lose in the battle.'

'Battle?' Harl asked, wiping the sweat from his brow. He didn't know how much more fighting he could take.

'They won't give up,' Damen said.

Kane nodded. 'We must organise ourselves. We need a base of operations.'

'What about here?' Sonora asked.

Kane looked around at the bodies and blackened walls.

'Anywhere but here,' he said.

'You can stay at my place,' Damen said. 'I'll give orders for a watch on the Enlightened inside the caves, but Yara will be pleased to have so much company.'

'I doubt she'll be so happy when we tell her we're having war meetings in her living room,' Sonora said.

Damen laughed.

'We'll see,' he said.

Chapter 41

If I am to keep a monopoly on the creatures for as long as possible I must ensure their habitats are are optimal for breeding. Unfortunately I do not know when their mating season is.

The six of them gathered inside Damen's house. The living room was far too small for everyone, so all the wooden furniture except the table and chairs were shoved to the sides. It was a tight fit. As he sat down, Harl found himself staring up at a ferocious hiver head mounted on the stone wall. It's dead eyes gleamed in the firelight.

'Okay,' he said, trying to pull his eyes away from it, 'before we hear from Gorman, I want to know what has happened. The book's discovery acted like a trigger. It caused our death sentence and now the whole town seems to have risen up against the Enlightened council members. People have stepped forward to act as our guards and, even now, a group seems to be waiting on us outside. What does it all mean?'

The question was addressed to Kane, who had been looking at Harl with an air of discomfort since Gorman's arrival. Maybe it was something to do with having another older and more experienced man in proximity. Had Gorman been the equivalent of an Enlightened before ending up in the tanks?

Kane cleared his throat, 'This might take some time to explain, but a little history is needed if we are to proceed. Before the separation of the Enlightened and the Passives, Delta was a place of technology and learning. For as long as we can remember there have been stories told of how we came to this planet from the sky above. The truth of these tales has been handed down through the generations, but only a handful of people know that they came from out of our own history books. Three books, to be precise.'

'Each of these volumes was special, teaching not just our history, but the rules of society, and the laws of science and technology. Each book was a manual showing the intricacies of the fantastic devices all around us. But each book held its own secrets. The complexity of ideas and schematics grew more advanced from book to book.

'The First Book was wide-spread with many copies. Half of the book was societal, the rest gave detailed use of metal working, smithing and steam power. These simple techniques allowed us to prosper without becoming savages again. They taught the basic skills needed for a life using science. The second was rarer than the first. It introduced electricity and how to combine of all the basic science from the First Book. It taught us how to build and repair all the equipment that our forefathers brought here, appliances, communications, even the weapons. The Second Book was the basis of our education for hundreds if not thousands of years. It is how we've maintained all the old equipment over the years and how we're able to keep Delta running. We have two or three original copies of the second book left over from the hiver attacks through the years and we guard these deep within the metal caves.'

He took a swig from a cup of liquor on the table as everyone waited, patient but eager.

'We've learnt everything from the first two books, but so many of the needed materials are unavailable that we can only use a fraction of that knowledge. The texts are studied only by the Enlightened and their descendants.'

Kane lowered his bruised head into his hands and was silent for a moment. When he looked back up, his eyes showed the glimmer of tears.

'Enlightened seems a misnomer now. What have we done for the people of Delta in recent years? The Enlightened have kept knowledge hidden away. Those of us trying to unite the factions are little better than the others. The histories hint that time and again mankind turned on itself and we fell into the same trap. The knowledge in the three books should have been free to all, not stashed away and hidden in the offices of the Council.'

'What about this Third Book?' Sonora asked.

Kane smiled. 'It is the missing link between us and our history. Let me explain. The Third Book's purpose is the same as the second. It's full of technologies and the details of how to use and repair them. In short, it's an encyclopedia of technology and advanced electronics.'

'Why is that so important?' Damen asked. 'We have everything we need.'

Kane was silent for a moment, as if collecting his thoughts.

'The Second Book told us about old technology. Most importantly it told us about the habitation modules left by the first settlers. These were lived in by our ancestors and, at some point, they were brought inside to hide them from the Aylen's discovery. Many of the rooms, like the one you stayed in, are modules that fitted together to make larger spaces to live and work in. They're in poor repair. Some have been scrapped, but others are still serviceable. The second book was vital in understanding all of this.'

'The Third Book is similar in nature, but it takes it a step beyond by detailing the ships that we arrived in.'

'Ships?' asked Harl.

'Yes,' Kane said. 'We had two originally, but over the generations we used one to repair the other.'

'But what are ships?' Sonora asked.

Kane raised his hands in apology.

'Forgive me. It's so easy to forget that you don't know any of this. Simply put, we are not natives of this planet.' Seeing their blank looks, he laughed. 'Let me see... At one time you thought that the tanks formed your whole world. You believed that you were natives of that land, correct? Then you discovered that there was a world beyond that. This world.' He stretched his arms wide to indicate the space around him. 'But we do not belong here either. We come from above, from the sky and the space beyond it. We travelled here in great ships, like carts built to transport people across the sky. This planet is like one of the tanks. We are from a different one and the ships allow travel between them. We have long hoped to use the ship to get back to our origin. The

Third Book contained all the details of the ships, how to repair them, how to fly them. It even traced some of the history of our journey here. Using those details we managed to salvage parts from one ship and use them to repair the other. We had nearly completed the repairs when the hivers attacked fifty years ago. The population split and the Third Book disappeared. Without it, the repairs ground to a halt. We just didn't have the knowledge to complete them without referring back to it.'

'You have hidden this knowledge from us,' Damen said, his fist crashing onto the table.

'True,' Kane said, hanging his head for a moment. 'It is just the way it has been since the split of our people. It was not my decision. The Passives knew about all this before abandoning the city. It was they who chose to forget.'

Damen grunted but let Kane continue.

'When the hivers attacked and the population split, the Third Book mysteriously disappeared and any work on the ship was halted. We know there is one key element left for us to be able to use the ship, something to do with the engines, but without the book it's impossible to complete the work. '

'The engines?' Harl asked, stumped by the word.

'They make it move upwards.' It was Gorman who spoke and as one they all looked at him.

'You know of this, grandpa?' Sonora asked.

'Yes my dear. My father worked on the ship, as did his father before him. Even back then it was in a poor state of repair. Much progress must have been made since then to be this far along.'

'That is true,' said Kane, a note of awe in his voice at finding this out, 'but without the Third Book it has been a guessing game. Although we're sure we have the right of it so far. You had the book all along?'

'Yes,' Gorman said, as though it was obvious. 'My father passed it on to me before he died. I've had it ever since, locked inside a box in a box.' He laughed sourly at his own joke. 'You say the Enlightened leaders have it now?'

Kane gripped the mug in front of him so tight his fingers turned white.

'Unfortunately so,' he said.

'And this ship?' Sonora asked. 'Where is it?'

'It's deep inside the caves in a hanger beyond the council chamber,' Kane said. 'The hanger doors open out into the plain beyond the mountain, but they can only be opened up from inside. The ship's still under construction so it's all a moot point, really; we don't even know whether the doors will open after all these years.'

Yara came in carrying plates of heaped meats and bread. Uman helped her to serve and silence fell as they became absorbed in the meal and their thoughts.

Damen was the first to break the silence. He paused with a fork of food halfway to his mouth and pointed his knife at Gorman.

'How did you end up in the Aylen's lair, old man? It's the one part of this mess that I can't figure out.'

'Only the one?' Kane muttered.

Laughter rippled around the table.

Gorman smiled, but then pushed his plate away as his face grew cold.

'When the hivers attacked us in the great battle,' he said, his blank eyes closed in recall, 'they drove a small group of us into a cave, separating us from the fighting at Delta. My whole family and about twenty other people huddled inside as the monsters fought to gain entrance, but being only a child I was unable to help. Men were dying at the cave opening, one by one, as they tried to protect us. Though we had good weapons, the enemy were too many in number and swarmed into the narrow opening. My father was defending the entrance when he was struck a hard blow and forced back into the cave. Others took up his place while my mother crawled over to tend to him. As he lay on the floor, blood flowing from a head wound, he bade me to bring his satchel over.

'When I handed him the heavy bag, he told me to take it and that I was now the man of the family. As he died, a hiver broke through the battle-weary men at the entrance and I stumbled backwards as it came at me. I tripped and fell. Thankfully a man skewered the beast before it tore into me, but he left the beast pinning me to the floor and it hid me from view. More foul monsters swarmed into the cave, slaughtering everyone in the cramped confines.' He stopped for a moment before continuing, as if gathering himself. 'I struggled free a long time later when the screams had faded. Picking up my father's satchel, sword and pistol, I had to roll my mother and sister's bodies from the pile blocking the entrance before I could get free.

'I assumed that the main plague of hivers must have made it to Delta, so I didn't return. Carrying the bag with the book inside,

I headed in the opposite direction. For two turns I wandered without food and water until I collapsed. I don't know how long I lay on the ground plagued by horrible visions, but, eventually, an immense shadow fell over me. In a daze I realised it was an Aylen. The next thing I remember I was inside one of those bloody tanks. It took me weeks to realise I had not imagined the Aylen and all that led up to it. I wanted to, believe me. I tried to forget and sometimes I wish I had...' He trailed off.

'I'm so sorry, Grandpa. I didn't know,' Sonora said, tears appearing in her eyes.

'Don't worry, my girl. I made it through.'

'How did you get out?' Harl asked, refilling his bowl. He wanted to reach over and take Sonora's hand but Gorman, sensing her sadness, put his hand on her arm.

'Well,' Gorman said, 'after you left, I dealt with those foolish friends of Felmar. I then made my way slowly to the house and used some of the old metal containers to forge a container big enough for me to fit inside.'

He pulled out his flask to take a swig, but stopped midway and placed it back inside his robe.

'At the time I was sure that the cube would be emptied by the Aylen. The disease had swept through the town killing everyone. What else could they do but empty the tank and start again? When I heard it coming, I padded the inside of the box and crawled inside. It seemed like an age before anything happened, but when the giant came, I held on as its voice boomed over the land. I could not be sure of surviving what was to come, but I wasn't ready to give in. When it clawed out everything inside the tank I

402

was bumped around, but I eventually felt a sense of weightlessness followed by a series of rolls and a final bang. I must have blacked out for a long time. I opened the container and crawled my way out. I lay there for a long time basking in the sun.' The last word was said with relish. 'I was lucky not to have been buried, but that is the way of things.'

'Fascinating,' Kane said.

Uman stepped closer to Gorman and placed a hand on his shoulder.

'I was sent to look into the ruins by Damen,' Uman said, 'and to my surprise I see an old, blind man lying face up on the ground, with a box next to him, half buried in soil.' He smiled at the strangeness of the sight. 'At first I thought him a dead man, like the rest, then I saw the old man twitch and I assumed he had crawled out of the box. I did what I could to help and we talked for a while. When he said his name was Gorman, I realised he was the same Gorman that Harl and Sonora had spoken of, the one who gave them the weapons. When I told him I had met you both he was jubilant. Then I explained that you were to be imprisoned.'

'Hearing that you were alive was all that I had hoped for,' Gorman said as he reached over and squeezed Sonora's hand, 'but I feared for you immediately. The book. I knew it would be of importance, but I had no idea that it would put you in so much danger. I asked all I could about the current state of Delta and, when Uman here had told me, I knew we would have to act quickly. I am glad we came when we did.'

'Me too,' Harl said, thinking of the guard at the gate and his narrow escape from decapitation. 'But what now?'

'Time to fight, I think,' Gorman said.

'Most of the population are on our side,' Kane said. 'They will act if we ask them to, but how far they will go, I cannot say. I have few friends among them, but most saw what the council condemned you to when they were at the gates.'

'So, it's a rebellion then,' Sonora said with a laugh, and Harl couldn't tell if she was being sarcastic or not.

'You're missing one thing from this rebellion,' Gorman said.

'What's that?' Damen asked, scratching his beard.

'A leader. Every uprising always needs a leader.'

'Alright,' Kane said, 'who?'

They all looked at him.

'Oh, no,' he said, throwing his hands up. 'I may be on the council, but I'm no leader. Anyway, if it came to it, many Passives would baulk at the idea for that exact reason.'

'He's right,' Damen said. He spun a knife on the table for a moment, flicking it round and round between his hands, frowning. 'Delta is split down the middle. Neither side trusts the other. How many Passives would follow an Enlightened after what they have put us through? But the reverse is also true. How many Enlightened would be willing to obey the orders of a Passive?' He laid his palms flat on the table and watched the knife spin to stop. It pointed away from him, at Harl. Damen raised his eyes. His frown deepened.

'What?' Harl asked.

'Deltans do not trust each other. So we need someone else, someone they know, someone like you.'

'Me?' Harl sputtered. He raised his hands in objection. 'I'm no leader.'

'And yet you led us in our rescue of Kane,' Damen said. 'You're a man I'd willingly follow, as would all around this table.'

Kane laughed. 'It seems that chance has chosen correctly.'

'I agree,' Uman said, slamming his fist down on the table. He punched Harl on the shoulder. 'He will be strong.'

'Then it's settled,' Gorman said. 'Harl will lead and, in time, learn all we can teach him.'

Damen pushed his chair back and stood. He looked at them all in turn. 'Our path is set. Get what rest you can. I will gather the men.' He walked to the door and paused to look back at them, fire in his eyes. 'Tomorrow we hunt.'

Chapter 42

They give birth to live young and do not lay eggs as I had imagined.

When dawn arrived the next day, a tension hung in the air. The sun crept above the horizon and cast its light on the entrance to the caves, but instead of the usual cloak of darkness from the overhanging rock, the fragile light threw ominous shadows against the cliff from the crowd of people waiting outside. The noise from the crowd bounced off the nearby brick buildings and reverberated around the square as if its echoes had somehow become imprisoned there.

The low rumble of voices faded out as Harl, Damen, Kane and Uman walked through the crowd. Faces looked at them from all sides as a path was cleared to the base of the weathered stone steps.

Harl looked up at the giant iron doors set back from the stairs. Rust had bled down them in places and there was a grim strength to them. It was the final barrier to the cave complex where the Enlightened had barricaded themselves.

They strode to the top of the steps and Harl turned to face the crowd. Hundreds of faces stared silently up at him in expectation. He swallowed, feeling his throat become suddenly dry.

'My name is Harl Eriksson. I have come from inside the Aylen's lair.' The words came out in a rush. He clenched his fists, annoyed with himself for being so nervous, then took a few deep breaths.

Slow and steady, he thought. *Calm.*

'It's a place where humans are kept as slaves for another race's amusement. I do not know your ways, nor do I know your technology, or you, the people. But I do know your struggles, your division and your hopes. I have lived under oppressive rulers all my life, so I can feel your pain. In time we will help free those I've left behind so humanity can come together again. But today we must throw aside three oppressions: the division of Delta, the gates before you, and the men who have ruled your lives. Arm yourselves and look to your leaders.'

He glanced at Damen smiling eagerly up at him, and then at Kane, who was standing there with a nervous grin on his face while scribbling notes in a small book.

'The time for peace is over. Raise your swords. Raise your shields. Free Delta!'

Harl thrust his sword in the air and the crowd roared and cheered.

He stepped down and moved into the throng of expectant faces. Some people slapped him on the back as he passed, but the majority were still either cheering or embracing their friends and neighbours.

Damen and Uman joined Harl as he moved up to the group of men who had been chosen as the main fighting force. Partially-armoured men, women and boys stood up proudly as he

408

approached, and he spoke to many of them as he passed, asking if they were ready, while Damen checked straps on armour, gave nods of approval, or stopped to tighten a loose cord.

Swords that had been kept above a fireplace for years or tucked away in a corner to gather dust appeared in hands, rusted and dull. Some men carried farm implements or hunting bows, while others waited for Uman as he moved down the line to hand out spears to any without a blade. When everyone was armed they headed back to the top of the steps.

Kane was rooting around in a control box next to the iron doors. He was engrossed in the tangle of wires, muttering to himself as he yanked them out and rearranged them.

He turned to Harl. 'The people at the front will need to crouch down when the gate is opened. There's a defence machine inside that will fire a wave of arrows when the gate is swung open, assuming those inside have enabled it.'

'Alright,' Harl said, steeling himself. He placed his hand on Damen's arm. 'Spread the word.'

Damen nodded and hurried away. He spoke to the host in a hushed tone, giving orders to those who he considered his lieutenants until the host were crouched down to await the attack. Damen was back in a moment and he raised his hand to signal they were ready.

Kane cried in triumph as a series of loud clicks came from inside the gates and they swung open.

A sudden whooshing sound came from behind the gates and a volley of arrows flew out. They sailed over the heads of the crouched warriors and clattered to the ground behind. No one was hit.

'Rise!' Damen shouted, waving his sword high above him.

The crowd of untrained warriors stood as one, and, with Harl, Uman and Kane in the lead, they surged inside the cave system. Damen joined them at the head of the newly-formed force.

'We should find the armoury further down on the right,' he said. 'I doubt they've had time to clear out all of the equipment.'

'Uman, take point,' Harl said, following closely behind Uman as the scout slipped into the lead.

They bustled into the tunnels, a hundred wary eyes scanning ahead for any hastily made traps. Small clusters of men kicked open doors and checked rooms as they passed. Uman raised a hand as he reached the armoury door and they halted, waiting anxiously for orders. He eased his head a fraction into the open doorway and then jerked back. His look of warning told Harl that the room was occupied.

Harl crept in front of him, crouched down and then peered inside, only to duck out the way as a blue streak of light shot past his head. It crashed into the wall behind him and dissipated in a flash, leaving a sooty scorch mark on the metal panelled wall.

'Trouble inside,' he said as Damen jostled his way through the crowd of anxious faces to reach Harl.

Another shot exploded into the wall.

'There's no way we can get inside against that pistol fire,' Harl said.

Uman clashed his sword against his metal shield. 'I can use this,' he said, raising the shield in front of both of them.

'How many are inside?' Kane asked.

'Only one,' said Harl. 'He's at the rear of the room behind the tables.'

'Rush him as one,' Damen said, looking to Harl for approval.

'As one,' Harl said, readying his sword. 'We go in behind Uman. Use the tables as cover. Go!'

Uman stormed in as the defender opened fired. His shield caught the blast, but Uman held steady as torrents of blue burst against the metal sheet. Harl ducked and ran for the nearest table, Damen close behind.

'It's getting hot!' Uman cried as shot after shot bored into the shield, which was starting to glow red in its centre.

Harl crashed into the table and kept low as another volley of rounds flew overhead. At his signal, Damen stood and fired his bow, and Harl darted to the next table, careful to keep out of sight as Damen ducked back down.

Harl peered around the table. He was close now and in a good flanking position. He recognised the shooter as one of the Enlightened Council. The man was focused on Damen and Uman, firing rapidly from behind a pile of armour stacked on a workbench. He crouched to reload his pistol with trembling hands, only to twist round in panic when he caught sight of Harl. Harl gripped his sword and leapt out into the open, rushing the man as he pivoted and raised the pistol to fire.

Time slowed as shots flashed either side of Harl's head, so close that he could smell singed hair. Fighting panic, he raised his sword into a two-handed grip above his head and screamed, slashing the sword down through the Enlightened's chest. The councilman's fingers twitched on his pistol, causing a few wild shots to flare across the room as Harl pushed in and down, twisting his sword as his enemy crumpled to the floor. He stepped back, breathing hard, and yanked the bloody weapon from the lifeless body.

Relief flooded the faces around him as he slid his sword back into the straps on his back and then bent down to retrieve the dead man's pistol. He passed the pistol to Kane and looked around the smoke-fogged room.

The councilman had been piling weapons into boxes on the workbench. Pieces of scrap metal lined some of the other workstations where they were being assembled into crude armour held together by leather straps. A pile of cables and rope were heaped in a corner next to a neatly stacked bundle of smooth metal spears.

'Hand out these weapons to the others,' Harl said. 'Make sure everyone is armed.'

Damen handed armour and weapons to Kane, who passed them back through the ranks of people in the corridor. Soon, nothing was left in the room but scorch marks and the dead man.

'I expected more,' Damen said as they left the room and stalked down the corridor, eyes scanning the gloom ahead.

'More?' Harl asked, thinking that if they had faced more men then they would likely be dead.

'More weapons,' Damen said. 'More armour. When we used to collect equipment from here before a hunt, there was always more than that.'

'Maybe they took it all,' Uman said. 'They're going to need it.'

'It's not the armoury,' Kane said, a guilty look on his face.

'What do you mean?' Damen asked as though he had just been told a spear was a fishing pole.

'There's a secret armoury deeper inside,' Kane said 'It holds far more weapons and technology than the spears and scrap metal we found back there.'

'More damn lies!' Damen said, banging a fist against the metal wall, making Kane flinch. 'It's past time they paid for their greed.'

'That's why we're here,' Harl said, hoping to calm him. 'There'll be no need to hold back anything from the people after this. The more they know, the better.'

He just hoped they lived to see it.

Chapter 43

At last count I have one thousand five hundred and eighty four individual specimens left. If my breeding calculations are accurate I will only be able to open the shop seasonally to allow time for their reproduction.

Uman led them deeper through the winding tunnels, stooping so his shield provided cover. The Enlightened had been clever and turned most of the lights off. The passages dark became tunnels where the threat of attack grew with each step they took into the gloom. A heavy silence hung in the air and, as Harl's men inched forward, the jingle and rattle of their equipment gave their location away as surely as if they'd been singing.

'Left at the next junction,' Kane said from somewhere behind Harl.

When they reached the junction Uman took the turn and then stopped. Harl followed and almost slammed into the back of the scout as he began to back-pedal around the corner.

Ten paces down the tunnel was a jumbled wall of crates and boxes with a small gap between the metal containers. Harl had just caught sight of movement through the gap when blue light burst out of it. He dived aside as Uman raised the shield to absorb the shots.

'Back!' Harl said, struggling to retreat as those behind blocked the way.

A man pushed past Harl from behind, eager to engage. A shot struck him in the head, knocking him backwards as he clawed at the burning light melting his face. Harl watched him fall as more shots hit the lifeless body.

Harl scrambled to get back around the corner, but there were just too many people crowded behind him. Abandoning the idea, he grabbed a spear from the man next to him and hurled it around Uman's shield towards the barricade. It clattered off one of the boxes and he cursed the feeble attempt.

Damen stepped out into the open and loosed an arrow just as a flash of blue streaked past his head.

'Back!' he roared at the men crowding the corner behind Harl.

The pressure of bodies eased and Harl was able to slip back around the corner beyond the line of fire.

Uman knelt in front, just out of sight of the attackers, letting the heat on the shield dissipate.

'Give yourselves up!' a man shouted from behind the wall of crates.

'No chance,' Damen said, letting off another arrow. It shot between two boxes and was followed by a cry of pain. Damen grinned as he stepped calmly back around the corner to safety.

'I doubt you can do that for all of them,' Uman said, ducking out from behind the corner for a quick peek.

Damen grunted. He knocked an arrow and leant out again, ready to take on the challenge, but a blue streak clipped his shoulder, sending him reeling back behind Uman's shield.

416

'Curse it,' he said, scowling down at the burn on his shoulder. The smell of seared flesh filled the air.

'We can't get past like this,' Harl said.

'Wait here,' Kane said from behind as he turned to push through the backlog of waiting men.

'Coward,' Damen said, half-heartedly. He winced at the fresh burn on his shoulder then set his face in grim determination.

Kane returned a moment later holding a metal tube that Harl remembered seeing stuffed into one of the boxes back in the armoury. Kane pulled the pistol from his belt and then reached into his white jacket for a small, cloth-bound tool set. He extracted a pointed tool, like a sophisticated lock pick, and deftly stripped the pistol, splitting it in half.

'Hey,' Damen said, 'we can still use that.'

'Its only got a few shots left,' Kane said, prising out a small metal cube from the centre.

Shots still flashed past the corner causing the metal plating further down the corridor to blacken.

'Hold this,' Kane said, passing the scrap tube to Harl. Harl looked inside and saw that one end was blocked. He turned it in his hands, feeling the pattern of criss-crossed grooves cut into the outside of the cylinder.

'When I drop the cube inside,' Kane said, 'throw it behind the barricade.'

Harl nodded.

'And don't miss,' Kane said, using the tool to depress a small button on the cube before dropping it into the cylinder in Harl's hands.

Harl stared at it as a high-pitched ringing noise began to build in intensity.

'Throw it!' Kane shouted.

Harl leant out over Uman's shield and lobbed the cylinder over the boxes. He choked as Kane yanked him back around the corner by his collar.

'Don't look,' Kane said, twisting away.

An explosion of blue and white light ripped through the tunnel, tearing the boxes and containers to shreds. The fragments of metal burst down the tunnel, battering Uman's shield from his hands and forcing him to take cover behind the corner.

Harl looked at Kane who was mouthing words to him, a frantic look in his eyes. It took a moment for Harl to recover his hearing. He massaged his ears, stunned that the blast had been so strong.

'Go!' Kane said, hustling half-dazed men around the corner.

Harl leapt over fragments of containers as he ran towards the enemy. His heartbeat drowned out the sound of his scream; it hammered in his head, it thundered through his body. He jumped the broken barrier with Uman at his side and then staggered to a stop, his breath gone, his mind reeling at what he saw before him.

Men lay scattered and broken amid a pool of blood and wreckage. No one was left alive. Each body was a mangled corpse. It wasn't like the cuts made by swords or even the broken limbs of a quarry accident, but sheer bloody gore. Shredded limbs had been scattered among the burnt faces and charred, smoking pieces of metal. Pale, fractured bones lanced out from inside the flesh and some had even been flung at the wall and were embedded into some of the softer earth showing between the metal plates.

Kane knelt down by one of the bodies, clearly knowing the man, and Harl read the shame in his tears as he closed the man's eyelids.

'I didn't think...' Kane said and shook his head as he stared in horror at the carnage.

Moving behind him, Harl placed a hand on Kane's bony shoulder.

'What happened?' he asked.

'An explosive charge,' Kane said, looking up, wide-eyed at the destruction, as if he hadn't expected so much damage. 'It was something we'd been working on. But we'd only done tests out in the open.' His eyes had a pleading look to them as if he wanted someone to absolve him of the death littering the corridor.

He raised a trembling hand and pointed past the destruction. 'That's the door to the armoury.'

Harl helped Kane to his feet and together they threaded their way through the blood-soaked bodies to the door. The only thing that marked it as special was an electronic locking system with a series of numbers on a keypad.

'It will take me a while,' Kane said, trying to compose himself, 'but I can open it as I did the first.'

'Good,' Harl said. He turned to Uman. 'Let the men rest, but send scouts down the opposite corridor to find out what we can expect as we near the main chamber.'

Uman nodded and turned to the men behind them.

'You three,' he said, singling out a group of hard-looking men, 'with me.'

The men fell into step behind him as he slunk back around the corner, scorched shield in hand.

Harl walked back through the crowd and crouched next to a groaning boy who was slumped against the wall and nursing a cut arm.

'It won't be much longer,' Harl said, looking at the boy's dirt-covered face. 'Another push or two and we will be at the council room. Here-' He handed the boy his pistol.

'Really?' the boy asked, looking from the strange weapon to Harl as if unable to believe it.

'Really,' Harl said. 'But remember that others will look to you to defend them now that you have such a weapon. Can you do it?'

The boy nodded.

'Yes,' he said, seeing the others around him taking note of the exchange.

'Good,' Harl said, standing. He walked back through the crowd as they stepped aside, some smiling, while others nodded.

It surprised him that they had already taken to him as a leader. The way they all looked at him was unnerving. There was still doubt in their eyes, but there was something else as well. Was it hope? He tried to think of it from their point of view. He wasn't one of the Enlightened or a Passive, and he'd never been forced to take sides. He was something new, someone different. He could sense something stirring in them as he walked by. They seemed excited.

Harl didn't know whether that was good or not.

He returned to the armoury door and found Kane talking to Damen. Kane was kneeling on the ground as he tried to rewire the control box, his fingers moving back and forwards over the lights and circuit boards.

'I had no idea the blast would be so devastating,'Kane said, sounding sounded guilty as he turned to face Harl. 'Nearly there. Just one last-'

The box sparked making Kane yank his hand out. The armoury door slid open and Kane led them inside. Damen gasped at row upon row of neatly-stacked weaponry.

Tables heaped with pistols and daggers stood in the centre of the long room. They were the same as Gorman's but with variations in size and design. Larger weapons were stacked along benches at one side of the room. Kane identified them as battle rifles. Shelves adorned with armour and shields ran the length of the other walls, along with heavy sets of armour and metal hunting traps.

'This is what I call an armoury,' Damen said, rubbing his hands together. He looked at Kane and then a frown creased his bearded face. 'You hid this from us?'

Kane stepped back and hung his head.

'It was not the right time,' he said.

'Not the right time?' Damen said, shaking his head. 'Do you know how many I've watched die because their spears were not good enough or their armour too thin? All this time they could have been saved simply by having...' He slowly raised his fist as though fighting the urge to unleash it and Kane took another pace back as the hunter slammed his fist down on the table, rattling the weapons on top. Kane raised his fists in a futile gesture, ready to defend against Damen's wrath.

'Stop it!' Harl said, moving between them. 'What you're talking about Damen, son of Terman, is in the past. You want to blame a single man for years of people dying? Then blame the leader of the council, not someone who has helped us every step of the way. If it wasn't for Kane we would still be waiting outside for the council to die of old age.'

Damen unclenched his hand and looked at Kane for a moment, saying nothing. He raised his hand again and, as Kane flinched back, the hand opened out to a waiting palm. 'You're right, Harl of no tribe, I judged one man on the actions of many.'

Kane raised his own hand, shakily, and clamped it into Damen's muscled palm.

'What's that?' Harl asked, noticing a long, open tunnel leading from the room towards a dead end.

'Firing range,' Kane said, releasing Damen's grip and shaking his hand to loosen it up.

Harl walked to the tunnel and looked down to the far end where a burnt and battered hiver statue hung on the end of a pole.

Confused, he returned to the table and picked up one of the rifles in front of him; it was rusted in places and bore signs of heavy repairs, but it felt formidable compared to the pistol.

'This,' Kane said, pointing to the small square box at the base of the rifle, 'is an ammo clip. It holds the power to fire the gun around fifty times before it needs charging with a new clip.'

'How do you refill them?' Damen asked, hefting one from a rack and admiring it from different angles.

'At the moment we can't,' Kane said with a hint of embarrassment. 'It should be easy – it should just recharge and be as good as new – but our last charger failed decades ago and our attempts to reverse engineer one have failed. Perhaps the Third Book will give us the answers to that as well.'

He shrugged and turned the rifle over to show them the clip.

'You remove it like this,' he said, placing his hand under the clip and then pressing a small button on the side, making the stunted square box fall out. 'Just place a new one inside and it's good to go again.'

'How many of these ammo clips do we have?' Harl asked as he watched Damen cock his head to aim down the sight, his beard scrunched up against weapon.

'Almost eight hundred,' Kane said, pointing to a closed door at the side of the room.

Damen moved over to it and opened the door. A smaller room stood on the other side. Dozens of shelves lined the walls and floors, each one covered in stacks of neatly arranged clips.

'That's more like it,' Damen said. 'It'll be good hunting from now on.'

'Thug,' Kane said.

'What?' Damen asked, turning and half-raising the new weapon.

'There's another door further back in that room,' Kane said as if nothing had happened. 'It's where empty clips are kept until we find a way to recharge them with electricity.'

Damen smiled and lowered the rifle.

'People will need to learn how to use these,' Harl said. 'They can practice here, but conserve as much ammo as possible.' He was thinking of the Aylens and how much fire power it would take to bring one down. It seemed an impossible task. 'Damen, select twenty men and give them a rifle each and some clips. We'll lead them towards the main council chamber. The rest can stay here. But have everyone try out these new weapons so that they're familiar with them. We may need reinforcements.' Damen nodded and marched back to the doorway leading into the tunnel. He waved people forward and they filed into the room, muttering as they took in the mass of weapons.

As they passed through the doorway, Kane showed them a rifle, explained its purpose and how to use one. Each man and woman moved up to the firing range, took three shots and returned to wait outside. Damen stood next to the shooters as they fired, and picked twenty from those that hit the target at the end of the range.

Uman returned and let out a chuckle of satisfaction when he found a thick rectangular shield tucked underneath a desk. He heaved it out and inspected the angled sides before peering through a slit of thick one-way glass set in the centre. It looked pristine, almost as if it had never seen combat. Uman saw Harl looking and beamed at him.

The armoury door burst wide open, knocking men back as they queued. Harl turned to see Elo, the woman he'd first met with Damen's hunting party, come barging in, her face twisted with worry.

424

'What is it?' Harl asked, noting the blood splattered on the woman's short hair and dented armour.

'A group of scouts are trapped in the warehouse cavern outside the council chambers,' she said, wiping her face with a bloody hand only to leave dark streaks across her cheeks. 'I don't know how many are left, but they're surrounded.'

'The old queen's chamber,' Kane piped in.

'How far?' Harl asked.

'Not far,' Elo said, 'but they won't last long.'

'Move out!' Harl called to Damen and the twenty men waiting for orders at the side of the room.

He snatched up a pistol and headed to the door as the group made a run for the cavern. He just hoped they weren't too late.

Chapter 44

I have solved the breeding dilemma. In order to slow sales to allow reproductive time I need to increase my prices until I find a balance of specimen to multiplication and steady profits.

Damen brought his rifle up to eye level as they reached the warehouse. He crept in front of Uman and Harl, then raised a fist to signal the soldiers behind them to halt. The reinforced double doors lay twisted and broken on the hard-packed dirt, revealing the carnage inside. Flashes of blue light lit up the smoke-fogged room.

Harl peered around the battered doorframe. The only things visible in the cavern centre were the shapes of men huddled behind containers and rusted machinery; everything else was hidden by the smoke. Closer to him, a large crane extended up to where a circular walkway ran around the wall. Brick pillars were the only things supporting it, but many had been blasted by so much rifle-fire that they looked as though they were about to collapse.

An air draft shifted the smoke above the crane and Harl caught a glimpse of what lay there. Holes impregnated the cavern walls like a honeycomb. There were hundreds of them, perhaps thousands. Kane had mentioned something about it on their way to the cavern. It was once a breeding place for hiver larvae, but now it was used for storage, with each alcove packed with boxes and crates. Harl shuddered. The thought of hivers crawling all over the walls and flying through the air made his skin crawl.

Some of the enemy had taken up position there. They were crouched in vacant larvae holes as they fired down on the helpless scouts. Others leant over the rail on the walkway, adding their fire to the assault. The sound of rifle-fire was deafening. Each shot screeched as it flew by, only to hiss and explode when it struck something.

Harl eyed the nearest stairs leading up to the walkway.

'Damen,' he said, 'take half the men over to the pillars and cover the scouts. Uman and I will lead the rest up onto that walkway. If we can take the high ground, you can help the men in the centre.'

Harl nodded at his men and sprinted into the cavern. Darting right, he made for the crane. The metallic beast blocked his view but offered cover, towering like an Aylen's skeleton over the fight below.

A man up on the walkway spotted him and shouted the alarm. Blue flashes streaked down, scorching the ground around Harl and Uman. Uman cursed and raised his shield to protect them both as more men joined the attack. Harl ducked behind the shield as another shot raced towards his head. Raising his pistol, he fired over the top of the shield as they closed in on the crane and then skidded to a halt behind it.

Harl glanced back and watched as Damen led his men into the cavern. They swept left below the walkway, and then ran from pillar to pillar, dodging fire until they reached a point where they could cover the scouts in the centre of the cavern. They were safe, for now, so he switched his focus back to his own attack as Elo slid in beside him.

'What now?' she asked, ripping off a volley of shots.

A man screamed above them and tumbled over the rail, landing with a thump on the dirt floor between them and the nearest set of stairs.

Harl pointed to a dented steel safety barrier at the foot of the stairs. 'There. That's our way up.'

He waited until the enemy focused on Damen's group and then broke from cover and raced for the barrier. Shots peppered the ground as he ran, their light blinding. He blinked to clear his eyes, staggering forward only to trip on a dead body and tumble to the floor. A strong hand hauled him up and he found himself being dragged along by Elo, even as she fired with the other hand. She thrust him forward and he stumbled into the barrier, collapsing to the floor behind it as Uman and Elo skidded in after him, their faces wild.

The shots pinning them shifted away as his remaining men sprinted across to the crane to provide covering fire. Three of them darted back out and raced to close the gap. Gunfire peppered the ground around them as they ran, light blazing through the air.

Then one of the men fell, arching his back as he clawed at a hole burnt into his spine. The sight of him writhing on the ground was sickening.

Harl sprang up and fired shot after shot at the guards perched on the walkway. Hitting one, he ducked back down, a cold smile on his face.

'Elo, Uman, there's a pallet of boxes up on the walkway. If we can get there we'll have a better position to take out the guards and protect our scouts. Take the stairs fast and fire. Keep low. Don't stop until we get there.'

Uman nodded and Elo grinned as she took sight along her gun barrel.

'Go!'

Harl launched himself over the safety barrier and bolted for the first stair. Uman followed, keeping the shield up with Elo at his heels.

A scream came from behind. Harl glanced back down as he began to climb the stairs. His remaining men had reached the safety barrier, but one had collapsed behind it, his rifle falling from burnt fingers as his companion gave covering fire.

Anger surged through Harl. The stairs rattled under his feet as he took them two at a time. Blood thumped in his ears as he ran. Every step was a strain, a waste of time. He roared and willed all his strength into his legs. He could hear Uman pounding along behind, impact after impact clanging into his shield, but Elo was lost in a battle frenzy. She rammed a fresh ammo clip into her rifle and raised it to her eye.

'Take that, hiver-bait!' she screamed as she shot one of the men on the far side of the walkway. He staggered back and toppled over the rail. 'Enjoy the ride, sucker!'

Harl pounded up the last few steps just as a soldier popped out from behind a crate on the walkway ahead. The man fired, but Harl dodged to the side and then squeezed his own trigger as the shots flashed by. The man dropped, clutching his stomach, and writhed on the walkway until his movements died away.

'Good shot,' Uman said, as he and Harl crashed into the metal boxes. They ducked down out of sight and Elo slid in beside them.

With Uman's shield blocking the group on the opposite side of the cavern and the boxes shielding them from those on the walkway ahead, Harl took a moment to look around.

Most of the remaining fire came from a group of guards across the cavern. Others were hidden in the honeycombed wall above and below the walkway. Their gunfire rained down around Damen as he finally reached the trapped scouts.

The men on the walkway began to creep closer together, edging their way through the gunfire to where their hulking commander barked out orders from a loading point that extended out over the centre of the cavern. It gave them a direct line of sight down to where Damen had joined the scouts behind the shelter of an immense water tank. Steaming water gushed from holes blasted through its thick metal sides.

Concern mounting, Harl traced the run of the walkway with his eyes. If the three of them could make a dash around it then they could hit the enemy from their blind side. He pushed past Uman knowing Damen had mere moments.

'I'm going around,' he called.

'Watch out!' Elo cried. She barrelled into his back and shoved him forward as a rifle fired beside them. She howled in pain as a shot blasted into her and then collapsed to the metal floor.

Uman roared with anger and dragged her back behind the shield.

Harl twisted around and spotted the shooter lurking in a larvae hole beside the walkway. He dived forward as the man fired again, then rolled to his feet and pulled the trigger, blasting the man half a dozen times until he was a crumpled, bloodied mass in the alcove.

Harl collapsed back against the railing and clutched it for support. He watched Elo's blank eyes for some sign of life, but there was nothing left of her soul. Her body was just slumped on the metal grating without any of the fire that had burned in it only moments before.

The guards on the far side of the walkway turned and fired. Blue streaks whipped past Harl to hit the railing, but he couldn't turn away from Elo, couldn't shake the horror of her death or the look of emptiness in her eyes.

'Go!' Uman yelled, tugging Harl from the rail as he wedged the shield between Harl and an incoming shot just in time to deflect it.

But Harl couldn't move. He just stared down at Elo in numb silence as the battle raged around him.

'Do something!' Uman roared as the shield began to glow.

Something snapped inside Harl. The paralysing horror turned to anger, then gave way to a simmering focus on the enemy. He shook his head, snatched up Elo's battle rifle and ran. The clunking of his feet on the walkway mirrored his heartbeat as he circled around the cavern, a wave of blue shots tracking him.

Damen must have seen what was happening as his remaining men stepped out and fired on the enemy just as Harl and Uman closed in.

With the enemy's attention split between the walkway and the soldiers below, Harl knelt and fired. He pulled the trigger and kept it down, unleashing a torrent of shots into the tight-packed group. The men on the flank died immediately. The next rank turned to counter-fire, but opened themselves to Damen's shots from below. They fell one by one, collapsing in a heap, or staggering over the railing to land, broken, on the machinery below.

Harl's rifle rattled and clicked as it ran out of ammunition. He forced himself to release the trigger as he stared at the pile of smoking bodies in horror.

Cheers came from below as Damen's remaining men thrust their weapons into the air and slapped each other on the back.

'We won,' Uman said, pride and disbelief spread across his grubby face.

Harl didn't feel the same. They had won. But at what cost?

Elo's body was wrapped in a white sheet and placed next to dozens of others. All of the bodies had been cocooned in the same way to signify their equality in death. They were arranged in a circle, giving the impression of a white flower, with each body symbolising an individual petal.

Harl stood alone on the loading platform as a forlorn silence settled over the warehouse. The bodies rested below him in a sea of broken crates and burnt machinery. Black scorch marks and drying blood coated everything. He had been a near stranger to Elo and yet she had sacrificed herself for him. He was distraught by it, and the guilt and pain shook his hands even as he gripped the railing for support.

He watched a weeping woman kneel and draw back a sheet as she searched for a child or husband. After several checks she let out a howl of despair and crumpled over a body, sobbing.

It was all so needless. If the Enlightened councilmen had just given up and surrendered then none of the pain would have been real. He wanted it over and done with. Why did people cling on to power like starving animals? He just wanted a simple life, to live with Sonora in peace instead of this constant struggle on the edge of bloodshed and war.

'They will be through there,' Kane said, joining Harl on the platform. His white coat was splattered with bloodstains and burn marks from the battle. He pointed down to a simple door nestled under the walkway behind a pillar.

Without waiting, Harl turned and jogged along the walkway, jumped down the stairs, and then strode over to the door, Kane in tow. Damen and Uman fell in behind them with a few other men.

The door was scorched from the firefight and slightly ajar, as if company was expected. A faint yellow light flickered through the gap. Holding his pistol at the ready, Harl eased the door open.

The room was a mass of shadow. There was no sense of its size because the only light came from a bonfire of books and broken chairs blazing in the centre. Everything else was lost in darkness.

The remaining council members were standing around the fire, apparently unarmed. They exchanged nervous glances as Harl led the others inside.

A long-bearded councilman stepped forward. His robe gleamed blood red in the firelight as he glared at the newcomers.

'You have come to kill us?' he asked. 'Or do you deny your interest in the Third Book?'

Harl wanted nothing more than to kill the man. He was horrified by the hatred burning inside him, but he couldn't do anything about it. He just wanted him dead. Breathing slowly, he stared into the man's eyes.

'No,' Harl said, finally. 'There won't be any more killing here, unless you threaten our safety. As for the book, it belongs to everyone. No one person or group should have control over it. Your reign over these people has ended, but you can still have a vital role. You could join us as equals and share your knowledge and wisdom.'

'Like the traitor?' the man asked, looking at Kane.

'I betrayed no one, Eltor,' Kane said. 'The people should know about the ships and the technology. We have no right to keep it from them.'

Eltor opened his mouth to reply, but Harl didn't want to get bogged down by another argument.

'Enough!' he shouted. 'We don't have time for this. We need to unite and free the people held inside the Aylen's lair. Everyone has to work together, to learn together.' He hoped that talk of learning would persuade Eltor, but he doubted it. Thinking of Elo he almost wanted them to resist.

Eltor shook his head. 'You're so righteous, boy, but you'll come to see that these Passives-' He spat the word and nodded at Damen, '-have stunted minds. They need a place in society and that is what we give them.'

Damen stepped forward and drew his knife. Eltor shuffled back and held a hand out over the fire. Damen froze. Eltor was holding the Third Book above the flames. The hands of some of the other councilmen twitched towards their coats, as though weapons were concealed there.

'Eltor, no!' Kane said, stepping forward.

Damen's men spread into the room from the doorway and raised their rifles, creating a semicircle that faced the councilmen.

'Please,' Harl said. 'You don't need to do that.'

He took a step forward, his hands raised to show he meant no harm.

It was a mistake. One of the councilmen panicked, drew a pistol from his coat, and fired.

Uman threw himself at Harl and knocked him to the ground as the shot blasted where he'd been standing a heartbeat before. Damen's troops opened fire and the air came alive with searing flashes and screams as shots lanced across the room.

'No!' Harl cried from under Uman's shield.

He saw Eltor open his hand and drop the book into the flames. The old man's smile was cold as he watched the book fall into the fire, but then shots slammed into his body and he was thrown back onto the floor.

The other councilmen were too slow to react. They reached for their weapons, but died within moments, their bodies tumbling to the ground in a tangle of dead weight and smoking ruin.

Kane ran into the middle of the room in an attempt to reach the book. He snatched it from the flames, but was too late, and could only stare in dismay at the handful of smouldering pages as they fell from his blistering hands.

They were only ashes now.

Chapter 45

After much investigation I discovered they are unable to reproduce between specific ages. Only certain male and females are viable to breed.

They trudged out of the council room after searching the bodies of the fallen Enlightened. At first Harl had thought it was a bluff. Why would men who revered knowledge do that to the real Third Book? But Kane's response showed Harl the truth.

When the battle ended Harl found Kane slumped on the floor with the ashes of the Third Book before him. His tears had rained down to splatter the wrecked pages. When Harl had laid a hand on his shoulder, he'd just looked up at Harl through the veil of his tears and shaken his head.

Little was said among the survivors as they left the cave system on their way back to Damen's house. Sonora ran to Harl as soon as he came within sight of the door. She threw her arms around him and listened with growing concern as he recounted what had happened. By the time he had finished, Gorman was stood quietly next to them.

'That's terrible,' Sonora said.

'It was to be expected,' Gorman said. 'Power had warped their minds.'

They ate together after Damen had dismissed his men to their homes and families. The sun bathed the distant forest in an unsettling blaze as it slid towards the horizon. Harl watched it all through the window as he toyed with his food. He could see the men as they trudged along, the elation of victory drained away to leave them exhausted. But it was the light, that hint of flame, that taunted him. All of the death and destruction had been pointless without retrieving the Third Book. He sighed, pushed his plate aside, and sat there in silence as the sun burned its way into darkness.

Gorman touched his arm.

'I think a walk would do us good, Harl.'

Harl nodded and let Gorman lead him outside.

'You seem lost,' Gorman said.

Harl breathed deep as they walked past a house coated with trellis and brimming with large flowers. It seemed the owners had gone a little too far in their attempts to camouflage the roof from an Aylen's gaze. Bright, delicate flowers trailed along the thick vines that grew over the side of the sandy-bricked house. Even a tree sprouted from the roof, its white blossoms raining down onto the gravel path as they passed. The garlands' scent lingered like a dream in the evening air.

Harl tried to imprint it on his memory, but it was too rich, too startling. He could only see the danger. The colours were a beacon beneath the rocky orange cliff that overhung Delta. How long until an Aylen noticed it?

He took a deep calming breath.

'I shouldn't have moved. Stepping forward... it was a trigger. If I'd stayed still, they wouldn't have destroyed the book.'

'Nonsense, my lad,' Gorman said. 'There's no need to blame yourself over this. I doubt they'd have let you take the book anyway. It was yet another measure of control. Possession gave them power over the people. And those people have suffered under Enlightened rule, Harl, make no mistake. No, losing the book is a sign that change is coming, and that thought is racing through Deltans like a firestorm.'

Harl watched the bustle of those nearest them. Even with the bodies not yet buried, women and men greeted each other warmly and called out across the dusty street to those leaving the caves from clean up duty. People hurried from building to building with a purpose Harl had not seen under the leadership of the Enlightened.

Gorman laid his hand on Harl's shoulder. 'These people need you to guide them. They don't care about the book; they only care that the divide is gone and that they face a different future. So you must lead them. You must show them what path to tread. But you have to show them fairness. It's something they've never experienced. Do that and they'll thrive. But it's just the first step. There are still those trapped inside the Aylen's cages. You have to free them and bring them back to the city.'

'But what hope have we got even if we succeed?' Harl said. 'All we face is the constant fear of hivers and discovery by the Aylens. That's no way to live.' He hung his head and sighed at his own folly.

'All is not lost, my lad,' Gorman said. 'I think I can be of some use.'

Harl looked up at this. 'What do you mean? You've done enough already.'

'Do you think that I sat on that book my whole life without reading it? After all, it was the one and only truth that proved my childhood was a reality.'

A slight smile crease Gorman's face.

'You've read the book? You know what was inside?'

'I do. My memory, unlike my eyes, is as keen as ever, and I believe I could recall the majority of it.'

'Why didn't you say?' Harl asked, thinking of Elo and those he had killed.

Gorman seemed to read his thoughts. 'Those who died are not dead in vain. Look around you. These people -' He pointed his walking stick at the nearest group of chattering women. '- know you did not recover the book, and yet they are happy. You did a great thing, my lad, by leading them in the fight to free themselves. They would not listen to you if the battle had not been fought.'

Realisation slowly dawned on Harl. After all of the fighting and loss they could still use the ship to escape.

'Come, we have to get back to Damen's house and find Kane,' he said, leading the old man around to head back.

'I will only do this,' Gorman said with a grin, 'if we can sample some of the local fruits on our return. I believe the market is that way.' He turned Harl in the opposite direction and shuffled towards the bustling stalls.

Impatient to get started, Harl left Gorman to enjoy his fruit on a bench in the market and ran back to Damen's house.

He found Kane sitting in a chair outside. His complexion was as pale as milk and the fresh lines on his face showed how hard the loss of the Third Book had been for him. He looked frail and beaten. People passed by in front of him, but he was oblivious to them. He just slumped there clutching a battered copy of the Second Book in his damaged hands as if it was the only thing that mattered.

'I have good news,' Harl said, grinning as he leapt up the steps.

Kane didn't look up.

'Does it matter?'

'It does if you want to know what was written in the Third Book.'

Kane swivelled around to face him, a suspicious look on his pinched face.

Harl took a deep breath and repeated Gorman's words.

It was like a change in the seasons. By the time he'd finished, Kane had jumped up from his seat and the look had changed from suspicion to utter disbelief.

'It's difficult to believe,' he said, his bony hands twitching as they gripped the book. 'But if it's true, then I must get someone to scribe for Gorman at once. I'm afraid to trust the truth of it, though. I don't want my hopes dashed again. It is true, isn't it?'

'It's true,' Harl said, laughing.

'Then I will find the scribe. We've wasted too much time already.'

He sprang off the porch, leaving Harl to head inside and tell Sonora.

They had not spent much time together since Gorman's return and he felt a twinge of guilt. There were so many things needing his attention that his time just slipped away and Sonora was the casualty in all of it. He longed to be with her, but he had to play his role. He had to live up to what people expected, what Sonora would expect of him. But now the weight of defeat had been lifted from his shoulders and he was here. He would make time.

'Sonora?' he called as he closed the door.

He turned round, expecting to see her. Instead he found Yara, feet up on a stool, stitching a child's play toy.

'She's out,' Yara said. 'I spoke to her earlier. She'll be treating the injured again in the medical centre. Spends most of her time there at the moment.' She raised an eyebrow as if having a brainwave. 'Perhaps she's met a nice man there, one who isn't trying to save humanity every waking moment. Don't panic,' she said, chuckling at his worried look. 'I'm just teasing. Now go find her. Shoo!'

When he finally found Sonora, she was speaking to an elderly lady outside the medical base. It was only a small hut, but it was packed with medicines and equipment. The two women were seeing to the wounds of a group of men, but Sonora noticed Harl and excused herself.

'Where have you been?' Harl said 'I was hoping to find you at the house.'

'I've been exploring Delta and speaking to the people. As the partner of their new leader that makes me a queen doesn't it?'

Harl laughed. 'Something like that. But you don't need to change, Sonora. You're everything that I need.'

She smiled and stroked his cheek with a soft hand.

His cheeks flushed at the touch, but he closed his eyes and savoured the moment, raising his own hand to cradle hers as he told her of Gorman's revelation.

'Typical,' she said, 'just like him to have something up his sleeve.'

'It's his way,' he said, 'How are things here?'

'Good,' she said, 'People are eager to help, bringing me every herb and piece of clean linen they can find. I was shown the healing facilities this morning, and they're better than anything we had before, but herb pickers and healers are in short supply.'

'Come on,' Harl said, taking her by the hand. 'We'll deal with all that in time. For now I think we should retire while Gorman's busy.'

'Retire?' Sonora asked with a sly smile.

Harl blushed and tried to stammer out some words.

She laughed. 'Are you afraid that Gorman will find out? I think he knows by now.'

'He does?'

She slipped her hand into his. 'Harl Eriksson, haven't you learnt by now that nothing slips by my grandfather's gaze? He probably knew before we did.'

445

He laughed, pleased to be back with her after so much hardship. The weight of his worries slipped away as he walked her home and then headed upstairs away from prying eyes.

Gorman was more than happy to lounge in a chair and recall all that he could of the Third Book, and for days he'd been sat in Damen's front room gorging on all the food and drink Kane could find, thoroughly enjoying himself.

Harl smiled as he passed the old man. One of the Enlightened was stooped over a table next to Gorman, rapidly scrawling on a parchment as he copied down the old man's words. Beside the scribe was a stack of finished pages covered with drawings and complex diagrams. It was a precious bundle and Harl touched it as he walked by. He wanted to pray that it held the secrets to their future, but praying meant the gods. He grimaced at the irony of it.

He met Kane and Damen outside the hunter's house. They were in the middle of a heated debate.

'It would be too many,' Damen said, the scar wrinkling under his beard as he shook his head. 'There's not enough space or food.'

'What's the situation?' Harl asked.

'Too many mouths to feed and not enough space to accommodate them,' Damen said. 'Assuming we rescue those held by the Aylen.'

'We must and we will,' Harl said. He turned to Kane. 'Surely we can expand the city to accommodate them?'

Kane shook his head. 'We can to support the current population, but any more and I fear we will start to struggle. We'll need to house everyone inside the cave system from now on. It will be too dangerous for anyone to stay beyond the walls if our plans go ahead. The same goes for food production. We need to move it all into the tunnels.'

'But how can you farm inside the caves?'

Kane looked excited by the question. 'You would think that most of our food is grown outside or gathered by the hunting parties, but we produce the majority of it in farms hidden inside Delta's cave system. It's a simple procedure, really, where beds of soil and overhead-'

'He doesn't need all the details,' Damen interrupted. 'This isn't another one of your lectures, science man.'

Kane gave him a dark scowl, but went on regardless. 'Overhead lights replace the need for sunlight. I've ordered them upgraded so that the farms can produce more efficiently, but it will take time.'

'Clever,' Harl said, 'but food and water must be a top priority. Have these cave farms work overtime to produce as much as possible. Even an excess would be preferable. But make sure the workers have regular breaks and are taught about the technology. Its been withheld for too long. For space, we'll expand the caves. What about the soldiers? Can we defend ourselves?' He directed the questions at Damen.

'We've one hundred and fifty men capable of fighting,' Damen said, 'but there aren't enough rifles to go around. We've plenty of bladed weapons and bows, and I've handed them out, but we're still vulnerable if hivers attack.'

447

'We have to do the best with what we have,' Harl said. 'Train the men to use blades. I'll leave the schedule to you, but make it daily if you can.'

'What happens if an Aylen finds us?' Kane asked.

'We fight,' Damen said.

'No,' Harl said. 'We run. That's why the ship is so important. We can't hope to stand against an Aylen. Our only chance is escape. Without that we'll just end up dead or back in the tanks as slaves. Kane, what about men to work on the ship?'

'Anyone not teaching will be employed to work on her once Gorman has told us more.'

'Her?' Damen said.

Kane shrugged.

'Good,' Harl said, 'If we're busy, we're productive. Can you draft a plan of action for the next few weeks and have it for me by tomorrow?'

'Of course,' Kane said, 'I have a few errands in the shipyard first, but then I'll get to it.'

'The shipyard?' Harl murmured and then slapped himself on the head. 'I haven't seen the ship yet! Can you show me?'

Kane grinned.'With pleasure.

Chapter 46

All attempts at forced breeding have failed, although I have noticed
hatchlings have appeared in the more established tanks.

Entering the caves, they found men busy opening up new tunnels under Uman's direction. Small explosions echoed in the distance, but, closer by, the constant clang of picks slamming into the rock walls made the air sing with activity. Workers pushed rock-filled carts through the narrow tunnels. Their faces glistened with sweat and rock powder, but they grinned as they passed.

The main council chamber had been renamed the Tactics Room. When Kane and Harl reached it, all signs of the slaughter had been cleared away. There was still a faint stench of smoke in the air, but at least the bodies were gone, and there was no sign of bloodstains on the ground. A large table stood where the fire had burned, and a crude map detailing Delta and its surroundings was spread across its polished surface. Several scribes were updating it from the reports returned by the scouts Harl had sent out.

A nondescript metal door stood at the rear of the chamber. Kane walked up to it and opened a small panel on the wall. He flicked a switch inside and stepped back as the doors swung open to reveal a set of stairs leading up into darkness.

'The ship is just below ground level on the far side of the mountain,' he explained. 'We stand almost directly under it right now. When our ancestors first arrived, the hanger was a sink hole above this section of the hiver nest. Once they took the tunnels, this passage was extended up to the depression and the remains of the ships were dragged down inside. A roof was then built over the crater to hide them from view.'

At the top of the stairs the narrow climb opened out into a huge chamber lit by wide spotlights. It was bigger than anything Harl had seen in the caves. Large, cream rocks had been squared into bricks and used to bolster the sides of the old sink hole. It gave the space a light unlike anything in the rest of the caves; it was clean and inviting rather than full of dead shadows as the tunnels usually were. Steel beams arched up to hold the metal roof high above the vessel squatting in the centre of the chamber.

Long and rectangular, the ship stretched far into the cavern. Two stubby protrusions extended from either side, giving the ship - top down - the look of a cross, where one line was much shorter than the other. Both arms were hinged and looked as though they could be swivelled around the central axis.

Engineers crawled all over the ship's exterior on a network of scaffolding as they poked, prodded, and worked away with tools that showered streams of angry sparks down to the floor. They looked like tiny insects scuttling around on the metal beast.

Harl stared up at what he presumed to be the front. A large pane of curved glass revealed a room inside. From his position on the ground the ship was too high above him to see more than the room's ceiling, but the window reminded him of an Aylen's giant eye watching the progress of the workers below.

Patched and repaired as it was, Harl had never imagined so much metalwork in one place. He'd envisioned a massive cart that could hold a few dozen people, but staring at the smooth, sleek beauty of the ship, he judged that it could hold hundreds with ease.

Kane led him across the chamber until they were walking beneath the vessel. Enormous landing legs rose like tree trunks around him, all gnarled and twisted where metal struts and immense hydraulic pumps bulged out like muscles. He could feel the vessel's weight pressing down on him like a giant rock.

When they reached the rear of the craft, he found a ramp leading up inside. Kane pointed a bony hand at it.

'This is the entrance. If you look above it, those wide slits house the main engines. It's difficult, but try to picture the ship when power is restored. We imagine something like fire blasting out from those slits to propel the craft up into the air and beyond. The two engines on the side-' He rotated his wrists around, demonstrating. '-swivel to allow changes in flight direction. As you can see, the ship is almost ready to go. Our only problem is the engines. Starting them requires a special fuel, but we don't know where the injection tank is concealed and we've no record of which fuel is required. We assume that the tank inlet is somewhere in the engine room or cockpit. At least that seems the logical place.'

451

The level of work that had gone into the machine was so complicated, it was amazing anyone could understand it. Harl had a sudden respect for Kane's immense knowledge.

As they walked up the ramp he saw a trail of cables running along the ceiling for the entire length of the corridor. They ran from light to light and darted off into holes and panels. He ran his fingers over switches and cables, admiring the complexity of it all.

'We've spent most of our time and resources getting the ship's lighting up and running,' Kane said, noticing Harl's interest. 'Most of the wiring had to be replaced, as well as whole banks of fuses. There's an insect that just loves the circuitry. It will happily strip wires and eat through circuit boards. They make little nests out of the material for the queen and she'll produce thousands of larvae. It's been a major problem with no obvious solution, but right now the bulk of our work is going on in the engine room, and we're hoping that Gorman will reveal the next steps.'

When they arrived at the engine room they found a group of men in grubby white coats working away at open metal panels in the floor. Desks stood against the walls around the room. Each one had a panel of black glass covering the work surface. Etched lines divided the glass into different areas. Harl had no idea what it all meant, but ran his hand over one. It was smooth and he got the tantalising feeling that it held secrets. He smiled, realising for the first time why Kane was so enthusiastic about it all.

At the centre of the room, the roof and floor arched towards each other. A hemisphere of metal was bolted to the ceiling with a matching one reaching up to it from the floor. They were

452

separated by a space barely large enough for two fingers. The whole construction reminded Harl of a giant metal hourglass.

'What's that?' he asked.

'That's where the energy should gather if we can start the ship,' Kane said, 'unless we're missing an important component. The control panel on the base is where we think the Third Book will come in handy. Powering it on shows that it's waiting for a code to be entered on the keypad. We've tried hundreds of combinations, but we've no clue what it might be. As you can see, there's a glass cover next to it that protects a bank of labelled switches. The labels have long since faded, but we assume that the code will trigger the lock and slide the glass aside. Or something like that. We won't know until we crack the code for the keypad.'

'So you have power to make it work?' Harl asked.

'We can provide power via a cable from the cave system, but it only seems to supply this one unit. The rest of the ship remains dead. We installed the lighting ourselves and run it all off a separate cable from the city.'

They moved through more corridors towards the centre of the ship and came to a double door which Kane pushed apart. The room beyond was enormous. Kane walked inside and opened his arms wide as he turned back to face Harl.

'This is the cargo area. We believe it's the best place for everyone to stay during the journey, although there's no telling how long that may be, or if we'll get anywhere at all.'

Harl frowned and walked over to Kane. He placed his hand on the man's shoulder. 'I have no doubt of your ability to get the ship finished. You've achieved so much despite the odds. Now, with Gorman's help, we've only a few steps left to tread before this ship flies again. I can only imagine what that day will be like, but I know that I'll be proud to stand at your side.'

As Kane beamed in pride, his cheeks pushed his wire-rimmed glassed up at an odd angle over his eyebrows. Harl laughed and slapped Kane on the back, and then stepped back to take another look at the room. He tried to picture it bustling with refugees. It would be like cattle crammed into a pen.

'If this is where people will live when we leave, then we must make it comfortable and equip it for a long stay. Stock it with as many provisions as we can spare, and set up partitions for families and supplies, but make sure everything is bolted in place. I don't know if it will be a bumpy ride like the carts my pa drove into town, but we should take precautions anyway.'

Kane's eyes widened in admiration of Harl's suggestion. He whipped out a small notepad and scribbled furiously, before sliding it back into his chest pocket.

'I will see to it,' he said. 'We don't really know what the trip will be like.' He moved his hand through the air quickly to mimic a ship flying past. 'The air offers so little resistance, but who knows what forces we may face?'

He looked around the chamber one more time and then turned back to face Harl. 'We should move on. I could spend all day telling you about the ship's operation, but perhaps the next room will give you a better idea of how it will all be controlled.'

Kane led Harl up a ladder to the corridor above and they entered a dark room with several seats arranged to face the window he'd seen from outside. Small glass-panelled workstations stood in front of each seat. They could be swivelled by turning the steel arm that connected them to the floor. Harl stepped towards the main window and tapped it with his knuckle. The glass had to be at least a hand thick.

Outside, half a dozen men carried a large container out of the hanger doors. They struggled to manoeuvre the container through the opening and wrestled with it until it tumbled through the gap.

Harl frowned and pressed himself up against the glass.

'How will the ship get out?' he asked as he peered from side to side.

'Look up,' Kane said, pointing out the top of the window. It curved back enough to give a glimpse of two enormous hinges in the hanger roof. 'There are two trap doors above us which, when sealed and covered with soil, are nearly impossible to see. They open outwards and we hope that the hydraulics are strong enough to push the soil and rocks away. Ideally we would clean the rubble away first, but if we have to leave in a hurry we'll just have to risk it.'

Kane walked to a central chair and caressed the screen in front of it. 'We've not been able to get power to this room, but we believe these glass panels light up to display information.'

'How do you steer the ship?' Harl asked, thinking of the reins needed to guide an ox cart.

'We don't know yet,' Kane said, sounding a little uneasy, 'unless it's done via one of these workstations; but we really don't know until we try. When we get the power up we'll perform a few test runs.'

'Well,' Harl said, 'let's hope we don't have to leave in a hurry.'

Chapter 47

I have catalogued each seed and seedling. If these can be cross-bred with

our larger species then a new branch of exotic flora will be opened up.

Even if they cannot be cross pollinated the potential for new medicines

means a vast separate income.

Harl returned to the Tactics Room and found Damen and Gorman in a heated discussion. They were standing beside the table debating the tactics needed in a battle against an Aylen.

'They will have a weakness,' Gorman said, tapping his stick on the floor. 'It's just a matter of identifying it before we engage them in battle. We must study them, somehow, with an eye to a conflict.'

'We should strike first,' Damen said, slamming his hand down onto the table, 'and take them out before they come for us.'

Gorman frowned at the sudden noise then sighed. 'Tell me, Damen son of Terman, how will you go about killing such a large creature with the weapons we have? Even a thousand men armed with rifles would fail.'

Damen raised a bushy eyebrow, causing his scar to crease. 'We can't just wait for them to find us.'

'That's exactly what we have to do,' Gorman said. 'This city has remained hidden for hundreds of years. Stealth has been our ally and until we can understand their physiology, we must be patient and prepare for what will come.'

'You use long words, old man,' Damen said, noticing Harl's presence. 'Haven't you got a book to dictate?'

'I do,' Gorman said, as he headed for the door, stick waving in front, 'and its got some very long words in it.'

Damen's frown deepened as he watched the old man leave.

'What is it?' Harl said.

Damen sighed and turned round. He shrugged. 'I don't know what to make of the old man. He irritates me.'

Harl laughed. 'Gorman's a good man. Too intelligent for the rest of us, though, except maybe Kane. But he has a caring heart and every move he makes is for the good of others. I'll admit his sense of humour does take some getting used to.'

Damen looked back at the door and grimaced. 'I'll figure it out if it's the last thing I do.'

'Figure what out?' Harl asked. 'Gorman's sense of humour?'

'How to kill an Aylen.'

'I doubt it'll fit on your trophy wall,' Harl said, sliding the map on the table until it was straight.

'Yara would never have it,' Damen grunted. 'She'd insist on a bigger home.'

Harl chuckled and then turned his full attention to the map. At the centre of the huge sheet was a detailed plan of the inner caves and the myriad rooms and tunnels. Further out, squares denoted the houses beyond the mountain and a series of lines represented elevation changes in the surrounding forest.

'How are things in the city? Harl asked.

Damen tapped a finger where a collection of new tunnels extended from the main cave section. 'The plans are falling into place nicely. We've made arrangements to house any people we bring back from the tanks and training is progressing fast for the soldiers going with us.'

Harl rubbed his chin. 'You've done well, but there's one other topic I'd like to discuss. It would be best for Gorman, Sonora, and I to relocate within the caves, maybe have somewhere we can use as our own. We appreciate the stay in your house, and Yara has been a kind host, but it's time we found our own home.'

'Of course,' Damen said. 'Sonora's been talking to Yara and they're already making plans. She wants to help grow herbs at the farms, so a room closer to them would make life easier for her and -' He broke into a grin. '- it would get the old man out from under my feet. Besides, Sonora is very knowing about plants. She helped me with a few personal problems which Yara has thanked her for.' He reddened, not meeting Harl's eye.

Harl knew that Sonora had been helping around the city while he was busy in his new role. Women would stop and present him with bunches of herbs and then give him polite orders to take them to Sonora immediately. Or a child would give him a gift of flowers in return for her help with a family problem. Men would chuckle when he passed them looking like a florist, but he was proud of all she had been doing.

Kane entered the room and came over to them. Two Enlightened were talking with him, but he dismissed them with orders to find Gorman and continue transcribing the book.

'Progress?,' Harl asked.

'Lots,' Kane said. 'We're close to figuring out how to start the ship. It's only a matter of time.'

'The usual story,' Damen said.

Kane ignored the comment. 'How are things away from electronics?'

'Crowded,' Harl said.

Kane seemed to understand and nodded as if deep in thought. 'If you need a place to stay,' he said, then you're welcome to one of the old councilman's chambers. Come, I will send for Sonora and we can go together.'

They met Sonora in one of the hallways. She was carrying a basket of herbs and scuttled around a corner towards them. Harl smiled at the sight of her. There was soil all over her dress and even some twigs in her long blonde hair.

'Look!' she cried as she ran up to him. 'The gatherers have returned and they brought some wonderful herbs back. See this? It's redwhelp. The leaves are so rare where we come from, but they've brought bundles and bundles home. They break even the most dangerous fever.'

Harl laughed. 'That is good news.'

She fell in beside them. He told her where they were heading and she looped an arm through his and beamed as they pushed deeper into the tunnels.

Kane led them through the dim maze until they reached a compact, round chamber once used as an Enlightened wash room. A large engraving of the Third Book covered the wall. Kane pressed a section of the diagram and his finger pushed a small circle of plaster inwards. A door-sized section slid silently to the side to reveal another round room. It had barely any furniture inside, just one small table in the centre supporting a stack of books. The only things of interest were the half dozen doors lining the walls.

'The council liked their privacy,' Kane said as he watched Sonora pick up one of the tomes and flick through its pages, 'so their personal chambers were hidden away. My own house is opposite,' he said, indicating one of the doors with a gesture before pointing at another. 'This will be your room from now on.'

He opened the door to reveal a luxuriously large room. Murals decorated some of the beige walls, depicting what must have been historical records of humankind. Some had ships on them, with people walking around underneath. Others showed the Aylens towering above crowds of people, their hideous faces twisted with rage as they glared down at the tiny humans. One even depicted a tunnel crammed with dead hivers. Groups of men with rifles were slaughtering a path through the few remaining insects.

Harl passed under an ornate arch into a kitchen. It was similar to their initial guest room, but the cooker and fridge were of a higher quality and much larger. Everywhere he looked he could see the touch of luxury. Plush rugs, dyed in exotic colours, covered the floor, and the walls were hung with paintings and murals. It was little wonder the councilmen had refused to step down. To give up such grandeur would be nearly impossible.

Another room led off from the kitchen. It was only small, with a bed up against one wall and a single armchair and desk. It would be a perfect space for Gorman, and it was easy to picture him sitting in the cushioned armchair next to the desk, smiling his secret smile. It was perfect.

When Kane left to continue documenting the Third Book from Gorman, Harl turned to Sonora as she relaxed on a sumptuous sofa and looked around. Exhaustion marked her eyes, but she was still brimming with beauty as she sighed and sunk deep into the thick, furry cushions.

'What do you think?' he asked.

'If it's ours for good then I'm a very happy woman,' she said, smiling at him.

'We won't be moving again until Kane has the ship ready, so it's ours until then. But there's still plenty to be done. Speaking of which, I promised Kane I would go see how the farms are progressing.'

'Don't be long,' Sonora said, running her free hand up a slender thigh. 'I'm not yet sure about the bed.'

'The bed? You look comfy enough right here,' he said. He let his gaze roam down her body and then traced the curve of her breast with his fingers. 'Maybe the farms can wait a little longer.'

Chapter 48

They have taken well to the new landscaped tanks. Some clearly danced or performed ritualistic acts when I placed them inside. I'm currently watching them divide up the land between them. Truly a unique species.

It was the first time that Harl had entered the farms. They were a series of long, sweltering rooms, about twenty paces in width. He followed Kane between two hollowed out platforms that ran in parallel down the middle of one room. They stood about half a pace high and were filled with rich, dark soil. Crops spilled from them and the stuffy air was full of the heady scent of soil and manure. There was enough room around the planting beds for the workers to move freely.

'We use electric lights to trick the crops into growing faster,' Kane said, grinning as he pointed to the lights hanging over the nearest bed.

'How?'

'Simple. We just leave them on all the time so that the crops can grow throughout the day and night. It's a simple trick, but it doubles our yield.'

'Kane!' A young Enlightened lad stumbled into the farm, waving a ragged piece of parchment triumphantly in the humid air.

Kane frowned at the intrusion, but waited for the boy to come to a stop. Harl recognised him as one of Gorman's transcribers.

'He's given us the code,' the boy panted, 'for the switch panel in the engine room. The keypad lifted out and the fuel pipe was right underneath'

Kane's face lit up as he turned to Harl.

'Go on,' Harl said, 'I'll be up there soon to see what the fuss is about.'

Kane said nothing, just turned on his heels and sprinted off.

Harl enjoyed the earthy smell as he strolled down the long rows of crops. In a strange way it reminded him of home, of running through head high corn fields when he and Troy were boys.

Freshly dug potatoes stood out against the dark, fertile soil in one bed, and stalks of corn filled another. Everything looked lush and healthy, there was no sign of disease or insect damage on any of it. He stopped at a strange, twisting vine that coiled up a stick framework and admired the small yellow fruits growing from the tendrils. Other alien crops grew in capped groups, like mushrooms, but were as large as a dinner plate. Beneath the frilled mushroom canopies, dozens of purple berries had dropped down and dotted the soil underneath.

Grey-haired workers were tending the crops. Some of them were hunched over the soil-filled containers as they watered and harvested, while others carried canvas bags from which they sprinkled a powder mix onto the soil.

Harl stopped by an old lady in a patchwork shirt and dress who was scattering fistfuls of the powder around the base of some small shoots. The dress looked almost as old as she did and, with her grey hair tied in neat bun, she looked like a stern school mistress.

'Can I ask what you're doing?' he said, making her jump.

She composed herself and turned to face him. Her eyes widened and she brushed the soil from her clothes, then stood up straighter, looking embarrassed. 'I - I'm on fertilizing duty, sir.'

Harl nodded.

'There's no need to be formal. I'm Harl.'

'Mary,' the old woman said, a kind smile playing over her lined face.

'What is it you're putting on the soil?'

'It's a mixture of ground bone and powdered blood to give the plants everything they need. The rest is mostly the leftovers from the communal kitchens.'

She grimaced as she heaved the sack down onto the seed bed, then wiped her brow on her sleeve.

'Oh, it feels good to put that down,' she said, winking at him.

He looked around and then picked up a small bucket from the floor, opened the sack and scooped some of the feed into the bucket.

'Carry some of it in this,' he said. 'I had the same problem spreading corn seed when I was a boy. The sack was bigger than I was.'

She rolled her eyes.

'You'd think I would've thought of that. Oh well, you can't have beauty and brains,' she said, laughing.

He chuckled and turned his attention back to the farm. There were plenty of other workers, all old and greying. Two men, who must have been three times his own age, were dragging a creaking trolley full of sacks into one of the far rooms.

'Are there no apprentices here? They could do the heavy work for you.'

Mary frowned, straightened her back and dusted herself off. 'I pull my own weight round here, sir.'

Harl raised his hands in surrender. 'No offence intended. I can see the farms are well-tended. I just think your knowledge could be put to better use. Why do the grunt work when you could be passing your gifts on to others? I wish I'd had someone like you to help me out when I was trying to work out which was a corn shoot and which was a weed.'

The frown vanished as she burst out laughing. 'Not a natural gardener, eh?' She pursed her lips and then took the bucket from him. 'You may be right, but we don't have apprentices. The young go out to hunt or gather supplies and the elderly are only assigned to the farms once they've gained enough knowledge and time to be useful. But with all the extra work more hands are needed.'

'How much additional food have we planted since the order was given to increase output?'

She paused for a moment as she looked around at the beds. 'We've set up more planting beds, enough to double the yield when we come to harvest.'

'How long until we see results?'

'I reckon sixty days,' Mary said. 'Maybe sooner if we don't run out of fertilizer. We ain't short at the moment, but I think we might deplete our stocks if we continue at this pace for much longer.'

'If we need more, how can we get it?' Harl asked. If his first one hundred days governing the people ended in starvation, it would be a disaster.

'Probably best to get it from people's homes as well as the community kitchen,' she said, turning to look at a clay flower pot on a shelf as it rattled against the wall. She frowned as it tipped off and crashed to the floor.

A grinding noise rose from the opposite side of the room and Harl assumed it was some piece of machinery, but a sudden look of terror came over Mary's features. Her eyes widened as she scanned back and forth along the wall. The brickwork bulged out as if someone had flung a huge steel ball against the far side.

'Borer,' she whispered. The bucket of powder fell from her grip and spilled across the floor. 'Borer!' she screamed and grabbed Harl as she hurried for the exit. The other farmers were already sprinting towards the door.

'What is it?' Harl shouted as the sound grew and the ground began to shake. 'What's a borer?'

The overhead lights danced on the end of their cables as Mary dragged him along, her grip like a vice. Powdered rock rained from a crack in the ceiling.

'A worm,' she shouted back as the rumble grew to a crescendo 'Quick. We must get out.'

'A worm?'

The far wall exploded out into the room, blasting the fleeing workers against the opposite wall as rocks and vast chunks of concrete rained down around them.

Harl froze. A mass of pink flesh and slime filled the hole. At first he couldn't make out what he was seeing. It was just a horror writhing its way into the room, no face, no sense of a body, just ten strides of oozing madness. But Mary was right. It was like a worm. An enormous worm.

The creature twisted in the hole then burst out, crushing workers beneath it as it crashed to the floor. Its razor-toothed mouth was big enough to swallow a man with ease, all pink and slimy, with rows of teeth reaching all the way back inside its cavernous throat. It launched across the room as fast as a runner, the bulbous body contracting and expanding in a grotesque way as it slithered from the hole. Hooks along its side propelled it through the open room as it crashed through the planters and smashed into the wall on the other side. The pink mass burrowed out as fast as it had come in, leaving a trail of blood and rocks across the floor.

Harl found himself shielding Mary as she cursed the creature. They were crouched on the floor, but he'd wrapped his arms around her and used his body to cover hers when the worm blasted concrete across the room. She stood up, quivering as she gripped a piece of rock in one hand. The rage seemed to boil in her for a moment and then she screamed and threw the rock at the rear of the borer as it disappeared.

'It's gone,' he said.

'It'll be back for the food,' she said and grabbed his arm and began pulling him towards the door. 'We must get out before-'

The closest wall shattered as the borer turned in the solid rock and forced its way back out above them.

They dived away from the falling blocks as the borer reared up over the planters, its circular maw opening to show hundreds of its small white teeth. It leaned over and slammed, mouth first, down onto the planters, swallowing the tallest crops whole.

Harl watched in horror as the borer reared up again and again, each time swallowing enough food to feed a family. He had nothing to fight it with, but an idea came to him as he watched it smash one of the dangling overhead lights.

He ran towards the writhing mass, leapt up, and used the borer as a quick foothold to boost up and grab the free-hanging cable, tearing it's fixings from the ceiling as he dropped. He pulled down hard until he had enough loose cable and then plunged the bare end deep into the creature's slimy pink flesh. Sparks flew from the live wire, lighting up the borer's insides as Harl was flung back against the wall by the creature during its final squirming death throes.

'Harl?'

He opened his eyes to see Sonora's tear-streaked face. She let out a cry of happiness at his feeble smile and flung her arms around him. He turned his head to see the beast lying motionless across a ruined section of planters, bodies of men scattered around it on the floor like rag dolls. Damen and an escort of armed men were standing around him, admiration on their faces as they glanced from Harl to the dead mass of blubber.

'Well, no one's done that before,' Damen said, grinning as he extended a hand to help Harl up.

'Disgusting,' Harl said, wiping slime from his clothes.

'A young one,' Damen said, tilting his head towards the borer. 'They dig under the soil, usually a lot deeper than this. I can't remember the last time they came into the caves. You're lucky to have survived such a fight.'

'Young?' Harl said. He walked over to the dead worm and paced along its length. Fifteen strides. 'How much bigger do they get?'

'Hard to say,' Damen said, eyeing the mass of blubbery pink flesh. 'Rumours from the old mines hint at some, fifty metres long, but no one has seen one here in a long time.'

'It's happened once before,' Mary said from behind Harl.

He turned to face the greying woman.

'Too many years for me to count,' she continued, shaking as she picked up a broken pot. 'I only remember it as a nightmare.'

Harl crouched down and brushed some of the soil from the face of one of the dead men before him. The man's face had been crushed in the attack. Harl closed the dead man's eyes and wished him peace.

'Did we lose anyone else?' he said to Damen.

'Six in total,' Damen said, 'including the head farmer. Probably more if you hadn't stopped it.'

Harl looked from Damen to the old woman.

'Mary, would you take charge of the farms? We need someone who knows what they're doing and I think you'd be perfect for the job. Will you take it?'

A look of surprise lit her creased face.

'I'm too old,' she said, then mumbled something as she plucked at her dress with her fingers.

'It will take days to find another,' he said, 'and you've already told me that you know more than most. I don't know anyone else who has the skills, let alone the courage to throw rocks at borers. You're perfect for the job.'

'Thank you so much, sir,' she said.

Harl laughed and leant down close to her ear.

'You're welcome, Mary. And remember, it's Harl.'

'Yes, er... Harl... sir.'

'How are you paid?' he asked.

'Food and shelter,' she said. 'I live on the outskirts of town near the main gate.'

'Take as much food as you need from the farms and I'll see if we can get you moved inside the cave system. It will save you a long walk.'

'Thank you so much,' she said. 'I won't let you down.'

Chapter 49

I have gathered some wood, stone and malleable metal resources and will place them in to see what they do with them.

The days passed and progress was everywhere Harl looked. Factories powered into overdrive, churning out new equipment, clothing and weapons. Food poured out from the farms until no one went to sleep hungry and an excess mounted, allowing them to trade outside of Delta.

The entire population had been relocated within the new tunnels and chambers. It had been chaotic at first with so many people trying to find their way around the unfamiliar passageways. Harl organised men and stationed them at strategic points to give directions, but many of the newcomers still wandered around lost. He worried about it for days, concerned that the confusion might breed uncertainty and resentment, but then he remembered how Gorman had set up markers to navigate and so he had men install sign posts throughout the city so that people could find their way around without fear.

Sonora found a friend in Mary. They sat and talked for hours about the plant life around Delta, both old and young sharing their knowledge while they helped those who'd lived outside adapt to the new regime.

Harl had ordered the deconstruction of Delta's perimeter wall and outer housing. He knew that if an Aylen found the rock, it would see the sprawl of buildings hidden behind the wall and attack. There was no way to hide any of it, so all they could do was destroy it. Damen had protested, but Harl had remained adamant.

'We can't hold on to it, Damen,' he had said as they walked through the outer streets of Delta one night. 'This is like a child's toy to them. They could crush it underfoot and hardly notice. We can't risk losing people like that. We've got to hide and that means it all has to go.'

Damen had walked away in silence, leaving Harl to worry about it through the night. But when they met the following morning, the hunter had given him a long, hard look and then nodded.

'If it has to be done, then I will do it,' he said, staring out across the buildings. 'I've known nowhere better than these streets, Harl. The caves and tunnels are for the Enlightened. Passives were never allowed to live in there and now that we're being forced to move in... It feels like they're controlling us again.'

'There is no you and them anymore Damen, and I don't want to force anyone into a life they do not want,' Harl said. 'But I do want to keep them safe.'

Damen nodded. 'It'll be done.'

While Damen saw to the destruction of the wall and exterior buildings, Harl turned his attention to the caves.

As part of their long-term expansion, parties of miners had been opening out some of the smallest tunnels. These tunnels had been ignored for years because they were barely large enough for a child to crawl through, but, with the growing demand for space, Harl had ordered the exploration of every nook and cranny in the hivers' maze. The Enlightened had mapped the tunnels years ago, but they had ignored all of the crawl-spaces that were now being explored. Most were just dead ends, small shafts bored into the rock, like the tiny honeycomb nature of a beehive. But there were others that led to larger caves, some still bearing the grisly ancient remains of hivers that had crawled into their cold, dark isolation to die.

Uman was fascinated by the skeletons. He broke them apart and laid all of their bones on the rock like a plan of the once-living creature. Harl had watched him measure and weigh each part in his hands, then move legs in joints, test their strength, find their weaknesses. He practised the correct way to slide a sword between their interlocked armour so that it could penetrate the creature's heart. And then, when he had done with them, he had the bones carted away to leave only a single skull behind, which he fashioned into a war helmet. Sonora was revolted by the sight of it, but Uman's eyes gleamed whenever he slid it over his head and he ignored all pleas to get rid of it.

The caves continued to be explored and even Kane was amazed at the vastness of the network. The miners had soon opened out enough space to double Delta's capacity, with a whole host of tunnels still to explore, but it was dark and dangerous work.

Harl was devastated when four miners lost their lives in a cave in, and kept waking in a sweat at night as nightmares of his own close call in the prison mines tormented him. All he could feel was the rock pressing down around him, the dust choking his lungs, and Troy's hands clawing at his ankles as his friend tried to drag him out.

But the nightmares were worth it in the end. The miners had been exploring the new caves for four days when Harl was sent an urgent summons. He scrambled through the tunnels, dragging himself on his stomach through some of the narrow squeezes until he reached the men. They were all talking excitedly around a small lantern and grinned as soon as he slithered through the last opening into the cave.

'We've found a place you should see, boss,' said the leader, Cooper, as he offered Harl a hand to drag him up. He was a small man, barely coming up to Harl's shoulder, but his grip was like iron, tempered by the corded muscles bulging in his arms.

He led Harl along a short tunnel that was thankfully high enough to walk upright in, and then raised one hand as they approached an opening.

'Kane has been tinkering with some technology of late,' Cooper said. He pulled out a small bottle and held it up. 'It's a combination of waxes that burn brightly when lit. They've been damned useful down here. I'll show you.'

He drew his knife and a piece of flint and soon had sparks showering down over the bottle. The wick caught and he held the bottle still for a moment as the flame steadied, and then moved up to the entrance.

'Prepare yourself for a shock,' he said, then pitched the bottle through the opening.

Harl had expected the bottle to smash against a wall or skitter across the floor. Instead, it sailed out in a huge arc through the darkness ahead and then dropped down out of sight. Harl hurried forward and peered down to where the bottle was still falling through the black expanse below. A moment later it hit the ground and smashed, splashing flaming wax across the rock around it. Harl teetered on the brink of the opening, stunned by the magnitude of the space before him.

'We figure it's at least two hundred metres deep and at least fifty up above the level we're on. It must be some kind of old colony space for the queen that was abandoned well before humans drove the last of the hivers out.'

Cooper dropped another wax bottle out, but it smashed only about ten feet below them. 'Looks like there are tiered levels, platforms, or whatever you want to call them, everywhere. We've used about twenty bottles so far - Kane's going to kill us - but it looks a right interesting place, boss.'

Harl thanked Cooper and his men, and then returned to the tactics room. Kane and Damen were talking over lunch when Harl walked in.

'Damen,' he said. 'Have you demolished the outside market yet?'

Damen nodded, chewed for a moment, and then forced the mouthful of food down. 'It's nearly complete. We're just carting the rubble away before a team of men begin transplanting saplings and grass to cover the more obvious signs that we've been there. Why?'

Harl took a seat and rolled out a map of the new tunnels that Cooper had given him.

'See this new area,' he said, tapping the map with one finger. 'I've just been down there and they've discovered a new cave. It's bigger than anything we've got already and so far down that even the Aylen would break a sweat digging down to it. We need space for a new market and this seems perfect.'

Kane peered at the map. 'It could be struggle to run power cables down there, even once the tunnels have been widened.'

Damen spun the map around to face him and traced the passages with his fingers.

'I'm surprised you missed this, science boy,' he said, a smile forming on his face as he tapped the map with one finger. He slumped against the back of his chair.

'Missed what?' Kane mumbled in annoyance. 'No one's been in those tunnels. How could I miss it if I didn't know it was there?'

Damen laughed.

'I don't mean the chamber. Look back at the map. The new chamber lies directly below the old council bedrooms. Some of our existing tunnels must run close to the new cave. If we could dig down to it, we'd need less of your precious cable.'

Kane agreed, muttering something about being too old for Damen to call him a boy, and set about organising the new space.

Shafts were dug down to it and spiral steps chiselled into the rock to allow access to the cavern. When they strung the first electric lights up across the roof of the cavern, they marvelled again at the majesty of the space. Tunnels and balconies wormed their way around the walls and into the rock, and they discovered a small spring of water at the bottom.

The market moved in soon afterwards and it became a hive of activity. Many moved closer to the new area as their houses outside the caves were dismantled after a week the market sellers clustered across the floor and spread all the way up the walls, using the ledges and alcoves as shops and stalls. Young boys swung down between the levels on ropes tied to counterweights, bearing messages and orders to the lower levels before hurling themselves back up with an answer. Hawkers' cries echoed from the roof and the constant chatter of voices and activity gave a life to the space that had been absent since the hivers had abandoned it so long ago.

Harl sat on a small bench near the entrance staring down at all the activity with Sonora. Night had fallen outside, but the market was still teaming with excited activity.

'Look at it, Sonora,' he whispered. 'Look at them. Passive and Enlightened arm in arm. Man, woman, and child working together.'

She hugged him and then kissed his cheek.

'It's all because of you, my love.'

Chapter 50

They seem able to craft ever more complex tools from anything that I put inside. But mostly they create weapons and throw them up at me if I hover over the top. Maybe when they realise they cannot hurt me they will use them for their own advancement.

Harl paced up and down in the Tactics Room while he waited for Kane. It had been three days since the new flight gyroscopics and electronics had been installed inside the ship following the book's guidelines, but fifteen weeks had gone by since the battle. He was pleased with the progress, but each day of delay felt like he was failing the people inside the tanks.

Kane was doing his best. Gorman had remembered a lot of what was in the Third Book, but a lot of guesswork was still involved. Kane made intuitive guesses for a lot of it and showed a level of genius and understanding that Harl could only marvel at. But progress was still painfully slow.

Harl had visited him in the hanger that morning to find him still engrossed in the work after a sleepless night. He looked haggard and worn, and passed Harl a single scrawled page without speaking that told him to arrange a meeting for later that day.

Harl had gathered Sonora, Damen and Gorman, and they stood around the map table waiting for the scientist to appear.

'No wonder the ship's not ready,' Harl said. 'If he takes this long to get to a simple meeting, it's a wonder anything gets done at all.'

He knew it was an unfair thing to say, but the constant delays were wearing him down.

Damen grunted agreement. 'Probably got his head stuck up the ship's ar-'

'Be patient,' Gorman said, turning his head to the door that lead up to the ship's hanger.

The door swung open and Kane bustled in. Two weary-looking engineers trailed behind him. 'Keep searching for a solution,' he said and they rushed back out the door.

'I am pleased to announce that the ship is nearly complete,' Kane said coming to a stop in front of them. 'There are still a few circuits to finalise and bolts to screw in, but thanks to Gorman, we have followed all the instructions from the Third Book and can see an end to the repairs.'

He looked at them each in turn, no longer jubilant.

'But we have come to a dead end. The engines need a special liquid to kick start them and we don't have any. The Third Book calls it petroleum and while we know the basic principles, we have no idea where to locate or how to refine it. It used to be a back-up for emergencies, but we now believe it's the only way to start the ship after such a prolonged period of neglect.'

'What makes it so special?' Harl asked.

'It's highly flammable and explosive,' Kane said. 'We've been working on this one problem for thirty days and made no progress at all. Finding some of the liquid would allow us to fire the engines, but without it we're at a loss.'

'Can't you light a fire inside with wood instead?' Damen asked.

Kane looked as if he was going to scorn the idea, but smiled wanly. 'It just won't work the same. It has to be the liquid. I'm sorry to bring such bad news to you all, but it looks as though the ship will never fly. The Third Book has shown us that if we managed to get it running and launched, the ship will automatically take us to a predetermined place without any input from us, but without the fuel...'

He fell silent and looked at each of them in turn, then slumped back in his chair and stared at the ceiling.

Harl didn't know what to say. Kane must have felt his life's work falling to pieces. Perhaps there was no way to start the ship on this planet? Was that why their ancestors had stayed?

'We have to go back,' Gorman said, breaking the silence.

'What do you mean?' Harl said, confused. 'Back where?'

'The Aylen's lair,' Gorman said. 'What you need is inside.'

'Grandpa, you're a genius!' Sonora shouted in triumph. She kissed him on the cheek before turning back to the others' stunned faces. 'Liquid fire.'

Harl laughed as the pieces fell into place.

'Of course!' he said, thrilled at the stroke of luck.

'What are you all on about?' Kane asked, clearly confused.

'When we lived inside,' Sonora explained, 'the Aylens gave us resources. One of them was as you described, a clear flammable liquid that we called fire liquid. We couldn't make it ourselves, but the Aylen always provided a lot of it. We used it for lighting fires and seeing at night. If this is what you need then we must go back and get it.'

Kane's eyes widened. 'It sounds like the right thing. How are we going to get it?'

The question was aimed at the group but Harl spoke up first, remembering the journey.

'We'll have to sneak in. Fighting our way past the Aylen isn't an option. There was no cover anywhere on the floor in the Aylen's lair. Sonora and I barely made it out without being spotted. Getting everyone across that space unseen will be next to impossible if the Aylen is there. But, even if we manage it, we'll still face problems once we get inside the tanks. I'm worried about how the people trapped inside will react. If they're as rabidly fervent in their religion as my own people, then we'll probably be hung for heresy if we burst in and start preaching about a life free from the gods.'

'We could just take the liquid and leave,' Kane said.

Harl shook his head. 'No. If we go in we rescue as many of my people as we can. The same for the others in there. I will not be part of this if we do not attempt to free them.'

Kane nodded.

'We could hunt the shopkeeper down,' Damen pitched in. 'I have a few ideas how we-'

'Our weapons will be useless against an Aylen, Damen,' Gorman cut in. 'But if those inside are as blinkered as you say, Harl, then the rifles will come in handy. Fighting other men will be easier.'

'We must not go in as aggressors,' Sonora said, frowning at Gorman. 'We should bring them peace and a chance for a better life, not threaten them with weapons.'

'Then it has to be covert,' Harl said. 'At least until we find the liquid. We can gather what we need from the tank I grew up in, but I don't know how they'll react to my return. They believe I'm dead and when I show up demanding they hand over their fire liquid and leave their home, it won't be all smiles and friendly faces. But we have to convince them to come with us. I want to free these people from their current lives, not leave them in slavery. They must know the truth.'

'What if they are happy?' Sonora asked. 'What if they don't want to leave their homes and fly away on a ship to an unknown destination?'

'Then they can stay,' Harl said, wondering if she felt that way herself. 'But I won't abandon them. There must be some way to free them. Perhaps, with time, we could slowly change their views.'

'How about a book?' Gorman asked, running his fingers across the cover of the newly-transcribed Third Book that rested on the table next to him. It was wrapped in leather with gold embossed writing stamped down the spine. 'We can produce a book that tells them the truth. It might be enough to convince them that life exists beyond their walls. Or we can just preach right back at them.'

'Grandpa,' Sonora said, 'I think you've adventured enough. Others will go instead.' Her tone was gentle but firm. Clearly there would be no arguing and Gorman accepted it with a sour grunt.

'What about the air changes?' Kane asked. 'Everyone who leaves will need the breathing devices that Harl and Sonora use. We've a fair number in the warehouse as they are not used anymore, but will it be enough? From what you've said there might be thousands of people inside. Not to mention the breathers we'll need to use for ourselves when we go in.'

'Can we make more?' Harl asked.

'There are details in the Second Book on how to make them,' Kane said, 'but the resources they use can only be taken from the rifles. Are we willing to sacrifice firepower in exchange?'

'We've no choice at the moment,' Harl said. 'How many can you make from a single gun?'

'Ten from each rifle and we have nearly two hundred rifles.'

'Then have the workshops scrap enough to make five hundred breathers.'

Harl had become so used to the breathing device resting on the roof of his mouth that he had not stopped to think how important it was in keeping him alive.

'What about getting inside the cubes?' Damen asked, looking at Kane.

'Well,' Kane said, scratching his chin, 'we could create a larger version of the melting blades by breaking them down to create a long, pole model. It will take some time, but I think we can manage it. The problem I can't get passed is how can we get up high enough to cut a hole into the tanks?'

'Why not use the melting blades to climb back up?' Harl said. 'We could climb up hand-over-hand by stabbing knives into the glass. Use them as anchor points to create a rope path from top to bottom, then use the pole to cut the hole and climb inside.'

'An excellent idea,' Kane said, 'but there's also the matter of resealing the cubes so as not to lose the air mixture within. And it needs to be done so that it remains unnoticeable by the Aylen. A large hole in the front would be easy to spot, even if they did not discover the one made by you and Sonora.'

'If it found the hole,' Damen said, 'then it might be on the lookout for more.'

'Either way, the tank was cleaned out,' Harl said. 'It might have seen the hole and then cleared the diseased interior, or found it after. It makes no difference. We still have to go in.'

'What about going in from the side?' Gorman suggested. 'You would leave less of a trace as the barriers to the side are black. You could paint a metal sheet and use it to cover the hole.'

Harl thought back to when he'd first looked down from the hole in the tank. The drop below had been terrifying.

'It would mean linking all the worlds via holes as we travelled across to the one we wanted, but we've no idea what to expect inside each individual tank, no clue as to the cultures or ideals of the people we'd meet. We'd have to convince them to let us pass, but they could just as easily try to stop or kill us. We cannot go into this with the intention of killing. They are prisoners and we will be there to free them.'

The group fell silent. Was it even possible? Either way they had to go through with the plan.

'How many lands are there?' Gorman asked.

'Seven across from what I can remember,' Harl said. 'Maybe more. But I don't know if all the tanks are the same size. It looked like it from a distance, but I cannot guarantee it.'

'How thick are the walls?' Kane asked.

'Again, I don't know about all of them,' Harl said, 'but the front was a pace thick when we cut through it. The other tanks looked to be the same as we dropped down, although I can only vouch for the front; the other walls may differ.'

They discussed how many should go into the tanks and agreed that twenty would be a safe number. Any more and the chances of being seen would be too high, but if there were too few then those inside the tanks could easily stop them.

But it all boiled down to secrecy. Conflict was a last resort. It was meant to be a rescue mission, not a battle. Avoiding casualties was vital. Any death would shatter whatever goodwill they might be able to foster, and their party would have little chance if the citizens turned against them. But, if they could remain hidden until they found a voice who'd listen to reason, then they might stand a chance of winning over the people in the various worlds they visited.

Harl didn't like the gamble. But what else was he to supposed do?

Kane grinned. 'Then we have a plan.'

The smile disappeared as a distant thunder shook the room. Springs and bolts rattled on the tables and Kane's eyes went wide.

'Aylen,' he said.

488

They raced out the door, twisting left and right through the tunnels until they reached the main entrance. Dozens of men armed with rifles had gathered before the huge metal doors. They stepped aside as Damen ran forward to peer through the crack.

'Damen?' Harl said, crouching behind him.

'It passed us without notice,' Damen said.

A hissing noise issued from the thick hinges as the gates closed, sealing the small gap. Damen stepped away.

'Why was it out here?' Kane asked between panting breaths.

'Morning stroll, probably,' Damen said.

'If this keeps happening,' Harl said, 'then it's only a matter of time before we're discovered.'

Chapter 51

I will resupply each tank at regular intervals with raw materials and see what they are capable of creating.

The community's spirit shifted after the Aylen passed. Excitement crumbled away to be replaced by a nervousness that crept into everything. Work slowed as people spent more time worrying about the future than focusing on the task in hand. The slightest sound would see men snatching nervous glances over their shoulders, while the women worked on in stony silence, their resolve undimmed, but their burden almost unbearable. In the end a brooding silence crept back into the tunnels and the choking weight of fear pressed around from every side.

Harl called a meeting in the market hall. People marched in, sullen and troubled. He watched their eyes and saw the doubt there. Divisions were creeping back, Enlightened and Passives drawing away from each other again as they reverted to their old beliefs. He stepped up onto a platform on one of the levels and raised his arms for silence.

'People of Delta,' he said. The echoes of his voice ricocheted off the dark walls. 'We are here because of the recent approach of the Aylen. It was a reminder. A reminder that the Aylen are a power that is beyond us, and the fear of that moment has infected our home. I see the dread before me and I've heard the whispers; There's no way we can survive. There's no hope for the future. What is the point of carrying on when the Aylen are so powerful and we live in fear of discovery? These are the words that I've been hearing. These are the dark thoughts choking the hallways of our home, but it is more than that. The passing Aylen has revived old enmities.

'I hear Passives ask how they can trust the Enlightened, but I also hear Enlightened worry about whether they can rely on Passives. It is the old ways reaching out from the past to cloud the future. But those days are done. They are just questions that fear has flooded your mind with. What you're scared of is the Aylen and you are right. They are deadly. They are terrifying. They can snuff out our lives with barely an effort. What's the point going of on when there's so little hope?'

He paused and watched as the crowd shifted uncomfortably. He laughed and shook his head.

'Where is Damen, son of Terman?' he called.

Damen shuffled forward and stepped up on the platform next to him. Sweat beaded on his brow as he faced the crowd. Harl reached to his side and slid his sword free. He tossed it to Damen who caught it and looked back, puzzled.

'If an Aylen broke through the roof now and peered down at us, what would you do?' Harl asked.

Damen ran a finger down the blade and grinned. 'I'd stick this sword in his bloody great eye.'

The crowd laughed.

Harl turned to where Kane stood next to Sonora and beckoned him forward. Kane clambered up onto the platform.

'Kane, you're one of the Enlightened,' Harl said. He pointed to Damen and then threw Kane a pistol. 'If this "Passive" faced an Aylen, what would you do?'

Kane studied Damen for a moment and then a nervous smile appeared on his face. 'He would not stand alone.' He raised the pistol and fired it at the roof. Blue light streaked up into the darkness above and exploded against the rock.

The crowd cheered.

'You would stand by this Passive?'

'Yes.'

Harl turned to Damen. 'And you would stand by this Enlightened?'

Damen nodded. 'I would.'

Harl turned back to the crowd and opened his arms wide as Damen and Kane stepped down.

'I will not belittle how frightened you are. I am afraid as well. We face an uncertain future, but I know that we stand strong if we stand together. I look down at you all now and see friends there. Mary,' he waved to her and the crowd parted around her. 'You have a wisdom that few possess. Will you stand with me.'

She nodded and stood straighter, the years dropping off.

'Cooper?' Harl called. The crowd parted again and the stocky miner raised an arm in salute to Harl. 'This is the man who led people deep into the darkness of the hiver tunnels to find this hall. It takes a special kind of courage to crawl into the depths of the world. Cooper, if an Aylen appeared now, would you stand with me?'

'Aye, boss. And I'd stick one of Kane's exploding bottles up his nose as well!'

Laughter filled the hall again and people slapped Cooper on the back.

Harl applauded.

'Fear is nothing to be ashamed of,' Harl called above the laughter. They fell silent, rapt to his words. 'Fear makes us strong. Fear bonds us like links in a chain until we are unbreakable. If anyone in this hall told me they were unafraid, I'd call them fools. The Aylen should be feared. They are a strength beyond imagining and they are clever. To survive we must respect that intelligence.'

He paused to let them take it in.

'Since I came here to Delta, we've grown strong as a people. But for us to grow as a community we must take action. Delta is now whole, but humanity is still held prisoner in the Aylen's lair. We plan to rescue our people, but when that rescue is discovered, I have no doubt that the Aylen will scour our own area. And yet we must be bold if we're to continue as a people. We have to strike. We have to step forward and stand against the fear of what is to come. The lives of those inside the lair depend on us. They are prisoners and slaves and we are their only hope. Their views will be as different from ours as mine were when I first came here. They will be scared and in need of support. You must welcome them as you have welcomed me.'

'But you must also stand ready to leave. When the Aylen finds us it will be terrible, a wrath unlike any we have ever seen. The ship has been fitted to accommodate all of us and, over the next few days, you must familiarise yourselves with it and the roles you must take up when it departs. As you know, we've no idea how long the journey will be, or even its final destination. If you want to stay, you may do so, but know that we may not be able to return. We've no idea what we will be heading into and the ship's systems remain clouded in mystery. It could be a one way trip, so you'll have to weigh your choice carefully. There aren't any easy solutions here. Every path poses a danger.'

He took a moment to run his gaze over the crowd, locking his eyes on as many of their worried faces as he could. But there was something more there now.

'We've all been prisoners, you at the hands of the Enlightened. The people in the tanks under the torment of the Aylen. This ship is the key that will finally unlock our lives, our potential, our hope. We are strongest together, even against a foe as great as the Aylen. No force is strong enough to defeat us if we stand with our brothers and sisters, our friends. We are unstoppable. Together we will win freedom!'

He stepped down from the platform and walked away to the sound of the cheering crowd.

Sonora was waiting for him. She took his hand.

'You are their hope,' she said.

'Unless we've got it all wrong and I'm simply leading the herd to slaughter.'

Chapter 52

As soon as I put more materials inside, the creatures automatically began construction. I didn't know what to expect – I foolishly thought that it might be nests. But after the holes they then raised a large communal structure, then smaller buildings popped up around it in parody of a city hall and surrounding town.

The men assembled before Harl on what was once Delta's main street, and they all looked ready for action. Each man shouldered a large backpack laden with food, water, air breathers, books and weapons. Two of the men carried a melting lance each, while another team looped large coils of rope over their shoulders. Harl was carrying much the same as the others, while his sword hung on one side of his belt and a pistol on the other. His mind wandered to Sonora as he watched the group preparing to leave.

She had understood that Harl needed to go and, to his surprise, she hadn't ask him to stay, or insist on going with him. It was like she'd known all along that he'd go back, but dragging her with him would be unfair. She had no home to return to, unlike Harl; everything had been uprooted around her and literally dumped. He was glad that, regardless of what happened to him, she still had Gorman to look after her. If the blind old man hadn't been around then, most likely, Harl wouldn't have had the heart to leave.

It caught him by surprise when he heard Sonora's calls from a distance. He had assumed that he'd not see her again after they had said goodbye, but now there she was, like a beacon of what he was fighting for shining out for all to see.

She walked briskly up to him, worry etching her features. He stepped forward into her embrace, wondering what had come over her.

'What is it?' he asked, starting to worry. She didn't reply for a time and Harl was about to prompt her when she spoke.

'I didn't want to let you leave before seeing you once more,' she said. 'There's something you need to hear before you go. I wasn't going to say anything until your return, but I have thought it over and I wanted you to have a reason...' Her voice trailed off.

'A reason for what?' Harl asked, wondering just what she meant.

'A reason for returning,' she said.

'I would return for you, alone,' he said. 'I'd walk under the foot of an Aylen for you.'

'You won't be returning for just me alone,' she said, stepping back half a pace and looking up at him to see if he understood.

He looked her up and down and shrugged.

'Men!' she said, exasperated. 'We're going to have a baby, Harl.'

It took him a moment for the words to sink in and, when he was sure he had heard right, he laughed out loud in joy, startling her. Instead of saying a word he moved in to hold her, just a bit less tightly around her waist than before.

'I don't have to go if you need me,' he said after a time. His voice was full to bursting with happiness as he stepped back to smile at her like an idiot. 'Someone else can go instead.'

'You must go,' she said, smiling right back at him, 'but come back for the both of us.'

'Of course I will,' he said, reaching out to hold her again.

For a short time they were rooted to the ground, oblivious to the world around them by the joy of what was to come.

Yara and Gorman appeared at the gateway into the city. Yara waved and escorted the old man over to them.

'Where are you, my lad?' he asked as he approached the group.

'Here, Gorman,' Harl said, touching the old man's arm gently.

'Ah, good,' Gorman said, coming to a stop. 'You remember the plan?'

'Of course,' Harl said having gone over it a dozen times.

'We'll have everything ready for your return. But be careful with those you find inside,' he cautioned. 'They'll be stubborn-headed about what you've got to tell them and it'll take a lot of effort on your part to remain calm, so take your time and use logic and reason. Oh, how I wish I could come with you,' he said and Harl felt for the old man.

'You'll be here for the next stage when we return,' Harl said, hoping to encourage him. 'Make sure the scientists and mechanics are ready with the ship when we bring the fire liquid, and keep people inside the caves. I hope we won't have to leave immediately, but in any case it won't hurt to be ready.'

'I'll make sure they know their business,' Gorman said. 'It's about time you left, I think.' He turned to Sonora. 'You will be going too?'

'No grandpa,' she said.

Gorman didn't seem to register the name.

'Definitely not,' Harl said, smirking. Sonora shot him a withering look.

Gorman raised an eyebrow at Harl's words.

Harl moved to Gorman and in a hushed voice said, 'Make sure you look after the both of them, *grandpa*. Or should I say, *great-grandpa?*'

Gorman took a second to react to the words.

'You, two... Three?' he said, stumbling over his words. He stepped close to Sonora, careful not to embrace her tightly. 'Wonderful,' he said as she returned the hug. 'Truly a blessing, my dear.'

'I'll see you when I return, Gorman,' Harl said, half skipping across to the soldiers waiting patiently for him. Gorman nodded and muttered to himself, a smile creasing his lined face.

'Bloody great-grandpa,' he said as Sonora laughed. 'The cheek of the lad.'

It was the last words Harl heard as he moved into his group of men, still smiling like an idiot to the bafflement of those waiting for him.

'Time to be going,' he said. 'I want to be back before my child is born.'

Raucous cheers burst from the men around him. They shouldered their packs and, as one, moved into the forest of giant grass.

A communications cable had been laid between Delta and the outpost nearest the Aylen shop. The outpost would be their last stop en route and was a final chance to turn back if anyone had a change of heart. Harl was sure that none of the men would back down, but he knew how much he was asking of them. There was only a slim chance of success, but as he looked around he felt pride in the look of determination on their faces.

They followed the cable through the forest for the better part of the day. It was a very different route than the one Damen had guided them along on their way to Delta, much more travelled. The grass stalks had been cut back to create a clearer path and Harl got the sense that there were other hunters stalking along at their sides just out of sight. It felt safer.

When they reached the wasteland created from the remnants of Sonora's tank, Damen led them confidently through. Unlike before, shoots pushed life up through the hills of soil, but it was still a horrid reminder of the casual way an Aylen could be so destructive. Buildings lay broken around them and decaying bodies sprawled in the sunlight, flies buzzing all over them. It was a chilling sight and silence weighed down on the group as they hurried through.

But Harl felt different as he plodded along. He had spent some of the happiest days of his life in Sonora's world, so he should have been sick with the horror of what was around him. Instead, he found each step get lighter as he walked. He wasn't running away any more; he was going back. He was returning to free people so something like this could never happen again. And the baby was like a shield around him, the joy of it lifting his spirits, hammering the horrors around into weapons that he would use in the battles ahead.

Harl found the trip fascinating. The world seemed so big and ever-changing. Kane had said that from historical documents they believed it to be so vast it would take thousands of days to run around it. It gave him hope. If it really was that big then maybe they could use the ship to get far enough away from the Aylen that humanity would have a chance to live in peace. With the baby on the way he wanted nothing more than to use the ship to find somewhere out of the way and to watch their child grow up away from the slavery of the tanks.

He knew it was a fragile dream, but he cherished it, nonetheless.

A high-pitched screeching broke his thoughts.

As one, they looked up. Three hivers soared overhead, wings beating the warm air as they dropped to the ground thirty paces away where the stalks opened up into a clearing. They hissed as they landed and then scurried towards Harl's group.

'Form up!' Damen shouted. The men stepped into a ragged line and raised their rifles.

Harl knelt to the side of the line, pistol shaky in his grip, all thoughts of the last few moments vanished to be replaced by sharp memories of the hivers attacking him and Sonora. The creatures were ten paces from them as Damen called out, 'Fire two!'

A scattered line of blue shots raced towards the hivers as each man fired twice. The hivers were hit simultaneously, changing from three hissing monsters into burnt limbs and droplets of gore.

The men waited calmly, eyes scanning the stalks.

'Good shooting,' Damen said.

Harl hadn't even fired.

'You two,' Damen said, picking out two of the soldiers, 'front and rear guard from now on.'

Harl was impressed at the display. Damen had trained these men into a precise force who followed orders even under pressure.

He said as much to Damen as they started off again, weaving around the broken corpses.

'All it takes is discipline,' Damen said. 'Enough disciplined men and one of those giants won't stand a chance.'

Harl wasn't so sure, but the hiver fight had been more than impressive. Not one man had suffered a scratch.

Kane slipped in beside them, almost tripping on a burnt abdomen. Damen laughed.

'I have yet to congratulate you on the good news,' Kane said. 'Another child is a blessing for the city. We need all the young minds we can get.'

'Thank you, Kane,' Harl said. He felt that he had a chance to get to know the man now that they were out and away from the ship. Kane's adoration of it had been the main reason for the progress, but it didn't make for easy conversation. 'How are you feeling about going into the shop?'

Kane cast a quick glance at Damen, who had crossed to one of the soldiers and was chatting about the fight, as if killing hivers had been a bit of fun sport.

'Nervous,' Kane said, 'but I would like to see for myself what has become of those inside. I don't think I can truly believe it until I see it with my own eyes. If it's as you say, and the Aylen are selling us for a profit of some sort, then it will be our duty to put a stop to it. But how many have already gone? Hundreds? Thousands? Even if we manage to free those held in the shop, how can we hope to free the ones who've been sold?'

'We must try,' Harl said. 'Once we've got most of them out then we can work out how to free others.'

He could not imagine where those who had been lifted went. How far away were they? What kind of lives did they lead? His parents' lifting still haunted him. He had thought them dead for years, but was there a chance that they were still alive somewhere? The thought was choking. It was something he couldn't face, couldn't think about. He forced it to the back of his mind and turned his thoughts back to the matter at hand.

'Have you heard of any other buildings similar to this one,' he asked, raising a hand to shield his eyes from sun so that he could examine the grey building that smothered the horizon ahead. It was a perfect rectangle, featureless as an egg, except for the doorway.

'When the Passives returned a long time ago,' Kane said, 'there were reports that they'd seen similar buildings in lands far beyond where they settled, although no one has ever confirmed the story. But it would make sense. There have to be other dwellings for these other Aylen that you spoke of, possibly in closer proximity, like in a town or village.'

Harl tried to imagine ten or even fifty Aylen in close proximity. They would block everything except the sky directly above, a wall of giant limbs and deafening voices.

'Here,' Damen said, turning off the animal trail they had been following into a gap between a tight group of stalks. He dropped his bag. 'We'll stay here the night and reach the outpost in the morning.'

'Why not press on?' one of the soldiers said, glancing down the trail. 'We could make it.'

Damen shook his head. 'Can you see in the dark, Krill? Men die in the blackness along these trails. I won't have us picked off one by one on our way to the scout post. Rest and have some peace.'

Krill didn't argue, but dropped his gear and began to gather logs for a fire.

'Trails?' Kane said, looking down at the narrow lane where the moss grew less dense. 'What uses them?'

Harl stepped inside the rough ring of stalks, hoping that whatever made the pathways was friendly.

'Sliders,' Damen said as he settled himself down against a log for a rest. 'like a borer above ground. They slither along the trails during the dark, picking off anything foolish enough to stray onto them.' He seemed to catch Kane's look of terror. 'Don't worry, clever man, the fire should keep them away.'

'Should?' Kane said. 'What do you mean "should"?'

Chapter 53

I have noticed that the creatures show signs of compassion when one is taken from the tank. Those in close proximity usually show signs of fear but at other times they seem to collapse from loss.

Harl had barely managed to find a comfy spot between the roots under his bedroll before Damen was shaking him awake.

'Time to be going,' he said, proffering a dried lump of meat to Harl. The hunter had his bag on and, with the exception of Harl and Kane, everyone was ready to leave.

When Harl stepped back out through the ring of stalks onto the trail, he found the men crouched around Damen as he studied something on the ground. Harl edged round to the front to see what was wrong. Yellow blood covered the ground in front of Damen. He looked up.

'We were lucky,' he said. 'Seems like the slider butchered something in the night. Best press on.'

Harl loosened his pistol inside its holster at the reminder of how dangerous it was out there. He had been lulled into feeling secure during their march the previous day, but death still lurked in the shadows.

They continued on as the sun arced overhead before Damen trudged off the trail between a series of tall, sandy boulders, five times the height of a man. They jutted up like Aylen fingers erupting from the soil, and were far too big for any group of men to move. The tops were dotted with small rock-hugging plants that trailed down the jagged sides.

Where the narrow path ran between two of the largest rocks, a figure stepped out, seemingly from the side of the sheer cliff. It was Uman. As they neared he called out a greeting and Harl could make out an archway to one side that led into a hollowed out boulder. Holes had been cut higher up in the rock and the tanned face of a watching guard eyed their approach.

As Harl's group entered the outpost, Uman grabbed Damen's hand and clasped it in both of his.

'So you finally made it,' he said.

'Not all of us are as sure footed as you, Uman, son of Udal,' Damen said, releasing the tight grip. 'We had to stop before nightfall or risk the sliders.'

'You'll be needing a meal before we go then,' Uman said, looking around at a pale-faced woman who dashed off only to return a few moment later with a tray of bread and meats.

Harl explored the adapted cave as the men threw off equipment and slumped in the cool interior. It had three small rock-hewn rooms and a ladder that led to an upper room where a single guard could look out from a series of windows. There was an armoury in one room, while small camp beds had been set up in another so that the soldiers could sleep when not on shift. The last room housed the communications equipment and a compact cooking area. A speaker box stood on a stone table against one wall and a bundle of cables snaked outside to lead all the way back to Delta. A solider was already in contact with the city about their arrival.

'Arla will alert us if we get any further messages,' Uman said. 'So I suggest you grab something to eat and have a rest before heading out again. I'll be travelling into the shop with you, but then I'll wait by the door. I can easily make the trip back here when I need to. People will want to know as soon as you're out.'

'Be careful though, sir,' another guard said to Damen as he and Harl ducked under a carved archway into the next room. 'Been a scuttler roaming those parts. Could be a nest near the door. Ain't had no luck trying to locate and block its burrow hole yet though.'

'What's a scuttler?' Harl asked.

'A nasty brute,' Damen said. 'Long, armoured beastie. Difficult to hunt. They move low to the ground and have got more legs than a pack of hivers.' He indicated the height just above his knees with a hand. 'They've tough segmented armour and can take a great deal of punishment before dying. Let us hope we don't come across it.'

Harl wasn't sure he liked the idea of meeting something Damen didn't want to hunt.

The weather turned when they left the scout post. Rain began to fall and the landscape was soon masked by the thunderous deluge.

As the storm grew in intensity the sound of hammering raindrops on rocks and soil drowned out everything. The ground became treacherous and moss turned into a slippery hazard as it absorbed the water.

Harl thought only of Sonora and the baby as he tried to fight off the biting cold that threatened to freeze him. He'd been soaked through plenty of times in his own world. When the dark cycle had come, he often used to step out into the blanket of dark and walk along enjoying the feel of the water coursing down over him. Out here it was different, though. The temperature varied day by day. He shivered as the wind whipped around him and rain lashed against his face. He found himself desperate to reach the doorway and slip back into the Aylen's lair, if only to get out of the rain. He laughed at the idea. How long ago had it been that he was desperate to leave? Not long. And now here he was longing for that grey world once again. It was a strange thing to realise.

After a time the forest came to an end and the giant door stretched up ahead of them into sky. Rain whipped down around them and clouds churned above the Aylen's lair. It made for grim forebodings.

Reaching the base of the door, Damen raised his hand to signal a stop and they craned their necks to take in the unnatural sight. It was a dull grey colour similar to the rest of the building, as if hewn from a single block. Stretching far on either side of them, it formed a sheer cliff the height of five hundred men one atop the other. Rain flooded down its surface until it almost looked like a waterfall.

A cracking rustle from behind made them all spin around. Some of the group must have known the sound as they spun and levelled their rifles before Damen could call out the order. Rain dripped from the rifle barrels as the men slowly shuffled into a line.

'Form up,' Damen ordered.

Harl didn't have long to wonder what was making the crackling sound.

'Scuttler!' Damen cursed as the group tightened up around Harl who, standing next to Kane, didn't miss the look of worry that crossed his face.

A long, sinuous body emerged from a clump of moss across the clearing and thrashed its way out between the last thick grass stalks of the forest. It was jet black and the height of a man's knee joint, with segmented armour plates running along the length of its body and then down its tail, which stretched back ten paces behind it. Dozens of stumpy legs scurried beneath the body, but the armour wrapped down so close to the ground that the creature's legs hardly showed. It wound its way out into the open and Harl noticed the serrated pincers at its mouth that curved like jagged sickles. The cracking noise had come from the pincers grinding against each other.

'Can you hold it?' Kane asked Damen, grabbing his pistol with shaking hands.

'I hope so. Depends how long it takes to cut through the door.' Damen looked meaningfully at two men with lances strapped across their backs. They dropped their rifles, unslung one lance, and then set to work on the door. 'The rest of you, slowly back up towards the door, eyes front.'

The scuttler didn't rush forwards, it weaved around in front of them as if probing for weakness from another angle.

Harl glanced behind. The lancers were levering the point under the door. They drew the lance upwards to carve a vertical line up from the base of the door. As they began to pull the lance sideways, Harl's attention whipped back to the front.

'Fire on! Damen called and the men unleashed a torrent of non-stop fire.

The scuttler reacted to the voice, somehow sensing peril. It dashed forward, low to the ground, and wound directly for the men surrounding the lancers. Blue shots flickered towards the creature, but each impact left only burnt patches on the creature's dark armour plates. One or two hit its legs, causing it to stumble, but with so many feet to support it there was little effect.

In a burst of speed the scuttler raced forwards. It moved so swiftly along the rank of men that they had little time to react. Pincers snapped at their legs as they stumbled back to avoid it. The scuttler caught one man's leg in its jaws and dragged him screaming from the line. His fingers clawed at the ground, leaving scratch marks in the boggy soil as the creature thrashed him from side to side.

'We're through!' one of the lancers yelled.

Harl glanced back at the door and saw the two men throwing their packs through into the shop. He had to buy them time.

Dropping his pistol, he pulled out his sword, activated it and shouted, 'Hold fire!' To his surprise the men obeyed, even as their comrade was flung left and right in the scuttler's pincers.

Harl ran out from the ragged line as the scuttler was busy with its prey. He slid past the creature's head as it swung its victim around. The soldier screamed as the scuttler's jaws tore into skin and bone.

Harl side-stepped the creature's head as it whipped past and then swung the blade down into its plated back. The weapon bit deep, melting through the armour plating as the beast screeched and thrashed around looking for the source of pain.

Damen pulled his short sword out and broke formation to join Harl.

Thinking the mouth was occupied, Harl had not accounted for the tail end. It whipped round after his blow and knocked him sprawling to the floor. The scuttler wasted no time in turning on Harl. It thrashed its head to send the mangled soldier flying and then reared up above Harl, its pincers clicking in rage.

He threw his arms up in a feeble effort to stop the razored mandibles, but, as the scuttler's head thrust down towards him, Damen swept his short sword in front, severing both pincers. Thick black liquid sprayed out, putrid droplets coating Harl, as the thing writhed away from him seeking safety.

Damen shouted again for "fire on", and blasts of bright blue trailed the scuttler back into the undergrowth.

'Cease fire,' Damen ordered and a silence descended. He moved over to inspect the broken, lifeless body of the soldier, before turning back to Harl. 'Quick thinking,' was all he said.

Kane moved to the fallen man, knelt and closed the eyelids. 'We should bury him.'

'Bury him?' Harl said, perplexed. 'Why? The scuttler will just sniff him out and dig him up, plus we need to get inside before it returns. We can't risk losing any more of us.'

Uman spoke up when Kane said nothing.

'It's our way,' he said, 'We bury the dead to honour them.'

Harl walked a few paces away while they went to work, sword clutched in hand. He didn't want anyone else to die, but he knew that it was an impossible dream. They were fighting an enemy far more powerful than they were.

Death was inevitable.

Chapter 54

They have societal tendencies and have organised into a structure of leaders and workers. They are not like queens and drone workers, instead they have much deeper individual traits.

After the man had been buried, they strode through the newly cut hole at the base of the Aylen door, while two guards kept watch for the scuttler's return. It was much dimmer inside the shop than Harl remembered. Perhaps he'd just got used to how bright the sunlight was outside? But whether that was true or not, the dim light made the place feel sinister and cold. The only light came from the long bulb high up in the ceiling. It was the same as the lights in Delta but on a scale a hundred times bigger.

Looking up at the distant roof, he felt a sudden sense of compression, as if the roof could fall on him at any moment. It was strange that after living under a roof for so long, he now felt oppressed by it. He couldn't understand it. All his life he'd been bound by walls and a roof, but now stepping into the shop had brought the weight and magnitude of those walls crushing down on him. His breath became laboured and he had to make an effort to calm himself.

They were standing in a short corridor to the side of the tanks. A bare wall ran ahead on their right to a corner that cut back in front. Harl couldn't see the archway from where he was standing, but the light from the tanks glowed from around the corner, like an eerie hint of the horrors they were about to discover.

The side walls of the tanks to their left were dark, the same black, featureless barriers as he had grown up with on the inside. He found it horrifying that people on the inside of those barriers had no idea what lay beyond them. They had no way of telling that life existed anywhere else and that there was someone on the outside trying to save them.

He craned his head back to look up at the tanks. How many lives were contained in those worlds? How much pain? How much suffering? He shook his head and lowered his eyes. He was here now though and if he could help those inside find freedom then it would not be a wasted journey.

Damen led the way along the base of the tank wall. There wasn't an overhang along this side of the tanks because the plinth came right down to the ground, so they had to jog along in plain sight and hope that they weren't spotted. Damen raised his fist when they reached the corner, signalling a stop. He stood with his back to the tanks and peered around the corner into the corridor beyond. Harl crept forward until he was beside the hunter and then inched his head out into the open.

The wall of worlds rose at their side like a giant cliff made from light. The archway opposite was a cavern of darkness in comparison. An Aylen stood at the far end of the passageway. It was impossible for it to see them in their current position, but just knowing it was there sent shivers down Harl's spine. The giant was staring into one of the tanks as it tapped a finger against the thick glass front.

Harl stared up at the tanks. There was no sign of movement up there, not that he'd expected any. The threat came from the Aylen. Everything depended on the creature staying out of their way until they were safely inside the tank.

Damen stepped away from the corner and signalled for the men to gather round.

'Safe for now,' he whispered. 'Let's get moving.'

Uman nodded and then tapped the nearest tank with his knuckle as if testing it for strength. He would be the first to scale the sheer wall. The idea was to climb up and plunge a melting-dagger into the side of the tank. He'd then attach a rope and drop the free end down so that the next man could climb up and repeat the process.

Harl watched as the scout dropped his pack and took out two blades. He then eyed the climb for a moment before selecting a length of rope from his pack and slinging it over his shoulder. Craning his neck, Uman took another look at the smooth black cliff, then shrugged and stepped up to the sheer face.

He turned the blades on and plunged one low down to use as a foothold. Stepping onto it, he reached up and dug a second blade in. He used it to grip and pull himself high enough to stick a third blade in before leaning down to retrieve the foothold.

He repeated the movements, getting more economical as each blade was pulled out and pushed in. After a time, Uman had scaled so high up the vast black barrier that Harl had to strain his neck to see him. A rope dropped down to where he'd set off, and a moment later Uman came sliding down to the base.

'Ouch,' he said, tearing off his leather gloves and blowing on his hands. 'It's in. Careful on coming down. It gets a bit hot.' This last remark was to another man who was about to make the climb.

Once all the ropes were set, the lancers climbed up. Harl and Damen followed close behind them to oversee cutting the hole. Harl tried not to look down. The drop was disorientating and, with only ropes to hold him up, he felt that any simple error would plunge him to his death. He doggedly clasped one hand over the other until the swinging lessened nearer the top.

He looked up and saw that the lancers were struggling to get the lance in at the right angle. They had to place a couple of knives higher up the wall and attach more ropes so that they could swing further out to add their weight to the lance. It slid in easily after that and they cut a small hole into the tank. It was barely big enough for a man to fit through, but the lancers were shaking with exhaustion by the time they had finished the rough circle. They strained at an awkward angle, but eventually the block slid through.

'Urgh!' the closest lancer complained as the block fell inwards, landing with a thud inside.

'What is it?' Damen asked, levelling himself with the hole. By now most of the team were at the top of the ropes, eagerly anticipating what lay inside. The hole had been cut a stride above head height and where the ground should have been was a mass of white and black. Thousands of cattle were spread between the walls, creating a sea of animal backs. There was barely any space between them. He poked his head through and gagged at the putrid smell. The ground was a foot deep with cow waste. He yanked his head out and gulped fresh air into his lungs before steeling himself and lowering himself down into the tank.

His feet squelched down into the muck as he landed. Cattle shied away from him, but there was little space for them to move around in as the tank seemed far smaller than his own world had been. The cows were packed around him so tightly that there was barely any space to move.

'Worse than a dead body,' Kane said as he dropped down into the tank. 'Food for the main product, I assume. There must be thousands in here. I wonder how they feed...' He stopped short, looking towards the back of the tank.

Harl followed his gaze and saw an enormous metal funnel clamped to the back wall. Its widest opening was close to the roof, while it narrowed towards the base before splitting into pipelines that ran along the floor of the tank towards the glass front. The pipes had their tops cut out to form huge troughs, and each trough was split into two lanes, one holding water, the other a few scattered slops of what Kane, after boldly dipping a hand in, identified as grain.

'Let's get through this nightmare,' Damen urged. 'We're too easy to spot among all these cattle.'

They barged their way through the narrow gaps between the cows, pushing against the distraught animals as they made their way across the tank. It was difficult and dangerous progress. The cattle were strong and skittish. Any sudden move and they shoved back or kicked out with a leg.

'So, if they have worlds full of cows,' Harl said, 'does that mean there are worlds full of corn?'

Kane looked thoughtful for a moment, but when he opened his mouth to answer Damen's gruff voice cut him off.

'What's the noise?'

'Cows,' Kane said, clearly annoyed at being interrupted.

Damen ignored the reply and turned to face the funnel at the back of the tank. A rumbling noise grew from the metal construction and the cows shifted round to stare at it. Movement rippled through the herd as they bumped and jostled against each other. At first it was a gentle heave then the press got tighter and the animals snorted in desperation to reach the nearest trough. Lowing erupted around Harl and the men, as the cattle struggled to move. A cow barrelled into Harl as they began to stampede. He tumbled into the muck and slid head first along the ground as hooves stomped around him. He scrambled to his feet, just dodging another cow as it charged him.

Damen yelled something to his men, but his words were overwhelmed by the lowing cattle. Harl spun in place, knocked and jostled as the animals rushed to get to their feed.

'Go,' Damen shouted as Harl was knocked to the ground again. He cried out as a cow's hooves crushed down on his legs, but all he could do was slip in the sludge as he tried to stand.

A hand gripped his bag by the strap and hauled him up from the muck. Harl found himself looking into Damen's dirty beard, but then Damen turned away as another man disappeared under the press of warm furry bodies.

Damen raised his rifle.

'Fire!' he shouted 'Clear a path.'

Someone must have heard him among the screams and lows as blue flashes lit up the space between the animals.

It worked fast. The cows raced out of their way, tripping in panic as Damen hurdled over one of the troughs and led the men towards the front of the tank. When they reached the glass, they turned and sprinted towards the far barrier. Kane slipped and went down under the cattle, but Damen fought his way back a few paces to haul him up as the last of the cattle fled.

'Thanks,' Kane said, wiping the grime off his once white coat.

Exhausted, they collapsed against the black barrier separating the worlds. Harl tried to clean himself as best he could while two men wrestled with the melting lance to push it through the thick wall. The lance kept slipping in their filth-covered hands, so it was slow going, but it lurched through, suddenly, as the tip reached the other side, and they began the careful process of cutting the hole that would allow them to escape the putrid smell of manure.

It was an anxious wait. When the circle was complete, Damen nodded to the two men and they pushed on the free section of wall to shove it through to the other side.

Nothing happened.

'It ain't going through,' one of them said. He braced his feet and heaved at the circle.

More men joined the struggle, putting all their weight into it but to no avail.

'Pull it towards us?' Kane suggested.

The lancers melted their way to a point in the centre of the circle and switched off the lance. They braced themselves and then tugged backwards. The block shifted in place and then slid towards them and dropped down into the muck with a sloppy boom.

As soon the block fell inwards, a cascade of yellow poured in from the other side. Everyone stumbled back as Harl stared in horror at a wave of cascading sand.

Chapter 55

A break in! Someone has entered in the night a stolen some of my stock.
I must find out what has been taken.

The sand poured in at an alarming rate as the group back-pedalled to keep from being swept up in it. One man was too slow. He stumbled and fell backwards as the sand rushed over him like a wave of yellow water. Harl leapt forward and grabbed the man's hand as his face was buried and his panicked scream cut off. Damen grabbed his other hand and together they yanked him free.

'Will it stop?' the man asked as more grains fell into the tank and the pile of sand grew into a mound. He coughed, spitting out a gob of wet sand, and rubbed the grains from his eyes as the flow eased to a gentle cascade.

Harl scooped up a handful.

'Sand?' he said, perplexed, but then remembered his decent with Sonora after leaving her tank. 'It's a sand world. Sonora and I saw something similar when we left the tank.'

'Fascinating,' Kane said. 'We have records relating to continents covered entirely with sand. It might not be as inhospitable as it sounds.'

The flow stopped after a moment, leaving a large mound that extended ten paces away from the hole in the barrier and two strides high.

'Clear the hole,' Damen ordered and a trio of men clambered up the mound, slipping as their legs sank down into the loose grains. They lay flat and used their hands to start scooping sand away from the hole, pushing it aside into the slop as more tumbled in after.

Harl stepped on to the sand. His foot sank a fraction into the grains as he struggled towards the hole. He waded through, sinking deeper as he climbed up. It felt like he was making no progress. The weight of it pulled at him and dragged him down. He struggled against it, sweat pouring from his body until, finally, he struggled to the top of the shifting pile and stretched out to grab the ledge and pull himself up and out.

He was blasted by a sudden, intense heat the moment he crawled through the hole. It didn't burn, but it was as though the air was sucking the moisture from his body. The air was heavy with a scent of salt as he wiped his arm across his forehead to stop a bead of sweat from dripping into his eyes.

He was at the bottom of a small hollow with sand all around. It reminded him of a funnel. His hands burnt from contact with the shifting ground, but he pushed on and reached the top of the funnel, only to sink to his knees as he took a look around.

A barren yellow landscape of rolling dunes swept away before him. A soft wind stirred against his face, bringing the sting of tiny sand grains with it. A few rocks dotted the scene and small plants clustered in their shadow as though terrified to step out into the light. Everything shimmered, the whole world seeming to shift before him as the heat distorted the air.

A valley nestled among the dunes at the centre of the tank. Small groups of trees grew in clumps at the bottom, but it was the sight of skin tents that drew Harl's eye. Hundreds of them were propped up around a large, domed hut as though it was the heart of their community. The hut looked to be made from sun-faded wood.

He shielded his eyes and could see people moving around down there. The men wore simple leather loin-clothes while the women wore longer coverings, but everyone had tan hoods that draped down over their shoulders to protect them form the fierce light.

'We had best keep going,' Harl said as Damen joined him. He could feel the heat delve into his skin. How could the people below them wear so little clothing and not shrivel up? Surely their dark skin would absorb the heat even more? His throat was already parched and the taste of salt flooded his mouth every time he opened it to speak. 'If we stay in this place too long, I fear for our water supplies.'

'It seems we have found something more than cattle,' Kane said, breathless as he joined them. 'Shall we go down?'

'Nothing else for it,' Damen said. 'We have to cross. Let's hope they're friendly.'

Harl stood up and half-jogged, half-slipped down the hot, sandy hill. The footing was treacherous and he had to keep his eyes on the ground as he slithered down the slope, but he kept glancing up at the tents as he descended. If these strange people decided to race out and attack them, they wouldn't stand a chance half-buried in sand. The sand rose like golden hills around them with only the path towards the tent village being open.

'We'll stop here and wait,' Harl said as he finished his own slippery descent and brushed the coarse grit from his clothing. He saw the dark men and women bustling around the tents in panic. 'We've been seen. Stow your weapons. We don't want to startle these people into a fight. We may well be the first outsiders to set foot here and I don't want to cause mayhem because someone's sweaty finger slipped.'

Damen grunted agreement and slung his rifle over his shoulder, but eased his hand down to rest on his sword hilt.

'I highly doubt they've seen weapons like ours before,' Kane said. 'Probably a futile gesture.'

Harl looked hard at him and the scientist shrugged.

'As you wish,' Kane said and reluctantly jammed his pistol into a holster on his waist.

By the time Harl had taken a swig of his rapidly warming water, a line of dark-skinned, half-naked men, women and children had lined up along the length of the outermost tents. A small huddle of men stepped closer. All of them were well built and had dark skin and hair. Most had belts around their waists that were covered in carved bones. Bangles circled their forearms and wooden jewellery hung down around their necks from under their shoulder coverings.

Although the distance was still a hundred paces away it was clear one or two of the men had more jewellery than the rest. They were dotted with gems and beads of carved bone. Some even had pieces of wood embedded in their skin like crude piercings. They gripped polished wooden spears firmly in their hands.

The group stopped about thirty paces away.

The largest, most ornately-clad of the men shouted across to them, 'Where have you come from?' His voice was deep and powerful and carried easily through the dry air.

Harl was surprised that they spoke the same language. It was more guttural and stunted, but the man sounded confident and looked them over with obvious curiosity.

Harl took a step forward and swallowed some more water to ease his dry throat. The man facing him eyed the waterskin, but Harl couldn't tell whether the look showed suspicion or desire. The man's face was a mask.

'We come from a land far beyond these walls and would tell you of the life you could live there. It is a strange tale and I beg that you listen, for it is a message of hope.'

The man was powerfully built. Muscles bulged under his leather shoulder covering and his arms were coated in dark tattoos. He seemed to be trying to convince the others around him to move closer to the newcomers, and kept jerking his head towards Harl, but they just shook their heads and muttered amongst themselves.

'Did the big ones send you?' the leader asked.

Harl found his deep voice fascinating. It had an earthy rumbling quality to it that was almost hypnotic.

Harl thought about the question and finally understood that he must be referring to the Aylen.

'We came for our own reasons. Nothing has sent us.'

This seemed to reassure the man. He moved forward a few paces, urging his men to follow, but they refused to budge, so he spat on the sand in disgust and strode forward alone. The others looked wide-eyed at the display.

'He's bold,' Damen said.

'He's big,' Kane said.

Now that he was closer, Harl studied his face. The man's dark eyes sat in sunken sockets that seemed to contrast with his puffy cheeks and wide mouth. It seemed that if he smiled he would look jolly, but the sunken eyes bore a gaze that was penetrating.

The man twisted to look at his people and growled something at them, then jabbed the butt of his spear into the sand in impatience. The others jumped in shock at the gesture and edged forward, but were still keeping their distance.

The leader slowed his pace as he neared, and then stopped several steps in front of Harl. He scanned them slowly from to toe to head, frowning at times as his eyes locked on to something they were wearing. He tightened the grip of his spear.

'We came through a hole in the barrier to help you,' Harl said, once more indicating the wall behind. 'My name's Harl Eriksson. We've come here to show you that you're not alone and to tell you that the world is bigger than this.' He gestured around at the walls in the distance and the vast see-through barrier that looked out on the shop.

The man was eyeing Damen with a peculiar look, as if weighing up which of them would prevail in combat. Damen glared back, but Harl noticed his fist tighten, almost imperceptibly, around his sword hilt.

528

'My name is Oscar of-the-well,' the man said. 'I'm leader of the tribe. How have you come here and where have you come from?'

Harl thought it a strange name. Was that his surname? Or was it where he'd been born? He had no way of judging it, but in his mind he could picture Troy sniggering at it. Looking at the man he had no desire to laugh. There was a dignity to him. The way he carried himself and the hypnotic rhythm of his voice conveyed confidence and strength. Those behind Oscar of-the-well sidled closer as he spoke and were following every word with rapt attention as if an order to kill or run might be buried in their meaning.

'We've come to free you and others from captivity,' Harl said.

'I am not a captive,' Oscar said, frowning. 'I am free to choose my own way.'

Before Harl could say any more Damen spoke up.

'You are trapped here by the big ones beyond,' he said, indicating the front of the tank. 'Your tribe and many others are under their rule.'

Oscar did not reply straight away, but those around him murmured amongst themselves..

'Do you bring water?' Oscar of-the-well asked.

Harl was taken aback at the oddness of the question, but replied anyway. 'Yes, we have water and food with us. May we eat and drink with you so that we can explain why we are here and where we come from? There's much you need to know.'

Oscar of-the-well looked thoughtful, but then eased his grip on the spear and began to smile. 'You will be our first guests,' he said and then turned to the men and women behind him. 'Prepare a feast!'

A cheer rose from all those gathered and the tension broke. The children whooped with joy as the adults darted off towards the skin-covered tents, calling out to those hidden inside.

Oscar led Harl, Kane, and Damen across the sands as the rest followed behind. They passed a field of low-lying crop as they headed for the village. It was a leafless plant where the crown of the root stuck out above the surface of the sand. The crown looked waxy and was like a giant carrot, but a pale yellow. The sand under them was a darker shade, indicating a recent watering, but the planting was sporadic and many of them had perished.

Oscar led them towards the village. It seemed strange to call it that because there were no buildings, it was just a shabby collection of dried animal skins propped up with sticks. But, as they navigated their way past the laughing children, they got closer and closer to the large central hut.

It was supported on solid timber beams with a round thatched roof, and was ringed with a well-trodden walkway made from weathered planks of wood that rose above the loose sand. An elderly man was slowly brushing the grains of sand from the planks with a broom, treading an eternal circle around the building. The hut walls were made from a lattice of woven fronds fixed to thick, sun-bleached beams of timber. Every now and then the old man would spot a few grains of sand on the wall and shift from his path to brush them away, muttering to himself each time he did so.

As Harl got closer he could see that curved lines had been carved into the beams. They reminded him of ripples on water.

People around the hut carried baskets laden with meat and fruit for the feast. They slowed to stare at the newcomers in fascination, their dark eyes tracking Harl and his men, before moving on along the well-trodden pathways between the tents.

Harl walked next to Oscar, and tried to peek around the man's hood. It was made from the same course material the rest of his people wore and, when the wind tugged it back, his inked bald head was revealed. The tattoos showed geometric patterns that curved like the water carvings in the building's beams. The bangles of carved bone around his arms and ankles rattled as he strolled through the encampment.

'Tell me more of your people, Oscar of-the-well?' Harl said, trying to keep up with the man's long, easy strides across the sand.

'There is not much to say,' Oscar said, stopping to let a child run past. 'Life is hard for us at times. We face a constant lack of water, even though our wells go to the bottom. Food is scarce. We must grow what we can with little water, but it is never enough for the children. Many sicken and die before they reach adulthood. It is a similar thing with our herds. They do not last long in the heat, so we must keep them under shade as often as we can. But, as you can see, shade is a blessing stripped from nearly all of our land.'

'Do the big ones not give you enough food?' Harl asked.

'They give us next to nothing and we have no love for them. They take our wives and children, and the strongest men.' A dark grin spread over his face. 'But only when they can catch us.'

'When they can catch you?' Harl asked as they stepped up onto the planked walkway around the hut, startling the sweeper from his reverie.

'We do not offer ourselves up freely.' Oscar said. 'When the hand comes, we hide as best we can, but the hands break our homes and pry us out, although they do not touch this wooden building for some reason. Maybe you can tell me why?'

'I cannot answer that,' Harl said as they reached a cloth covered doorway that led inside.

'But, if you accept what I have to say,' Harl said, as Oscar jerked the cloth aside, 'then you will never need to watch your people suffer again at the hands of the big ones.'

Oscar gestured for them to enter first and Damen turned to order the men to wait outside, then followed Harl in with Kane in tow.

The inside was spacious and cool, with a tiered row of worn, wooden benches to one side, overlooking a fire pit that was surrounded by mosaic patterned rugs. Several small torches were set in sconces attached to the beams that rose to the thatch roof above. A clay funnelled chimney extended down from where the beams met at the apex of the roof, directly above the fire pit.

Oscar walked to the rugged woven mats in the centre of the main room, crossed his legs and sat, nodding for Harl and the others to follow suit. The central fire had been lit and was being tended by an old bearded man. A cow was roasting over it on a spit, while people bustled in from adjacent doors to place wooden bowls overflowing with nuts and berries down on the mat. One woman carried a clay pitcher, which Harl assumed contained water, and filled small, carved wooden cups, before passing them around.

Kane had been talking to one of the men since they arrived and he leant over to whisper to Harl.

'We're rich,' he said.

Harl gave him a questioning look.

'They worship water, or at least treat it with a strict reverence. Those with a good supply are more influential in society. Why do you think he asked if we brought water.'

'Why would they do such a thing?'

'With it so hard to come by,' Kane said, picking a few nuts from a bowl and tossing them into his mouth, 'they have to rely on what the Aylen provides through the sprinkler system.'

'Sprinkler system?'

'The rain inside these tanks is artificial, Harl. It's provided through sprinkler holes embedded in the tank roof.'

Harl had never really thought about where the rain came from in the tanks. It had just been something that fell from the roof, but now that Kane had explained it, he marvelled at the ingenuity of it all. It seemed that the Aylen went to extraordinary lengths when they created their worlds. All of the lands, all of the animals, the lights and rain. He was sickened at the reason for it all, but he couldn't help feeling awe at what the Aylen were able to achieve.

'They have to dig deep wells to act as reservoirs and collect water from the plants and trees around the sand plain,' Kane went on. 'They regard trees as sacred, or at least the wood, as they take so much time and water to grow. They even recycle their waste through a filter system for use on the plants.'

Harl was fascinated.

'Give them some of ours,' he said.

Kane stood up and addressed them. 'Harl has asked me to give you some of our water. Ten waterskins will be a gift to the tribe.'

Oscar stood up.

'I, Oscar of-the-well, accept your gift to us. It is most generous.' He took a chunk of beef from the man cutting slices from the spit and sat down. 'Now you must answer our questions as you have promised.'

With that Harl, Kane and Damen related all they knew about the Aylen, the people inside the cubes, Delta, and the history of humanity. Eventually, once they'd finished explaining about the ship and the reasons for coming into the tanks, the crowd of dark faces around them showed a mix of emotions, but it was Oscar's face that held the one emotion that resonated with Harl.

Anger.

Chapter 56

Some of the creatures have been taken. I believe around ten individuals.
Not much in the grand scheme of things, but so far I have managed to
keep tabs on all of the ones I have sold. Having unregistered creatures
breeding could disrupt everything.

They ate in silence for a long time after all the questions had
been answered. Finally, Oscar stood up.

'My heart is filled with rage,' he said, his eyes flicking between
Harl, Kane, and Damen. 'For a long time I've watched my people
die from thirst and get taken away never to return. And now I'm
told it is for the amusement of these Aylen.' He struggled with the
new word. 'If all you say is true, then we shall join you and do all
we can to aid you in this war.'

War? Harl had never considered it a war. Had it really come
to that? But Oscar was right. They were at war with the Aylen and,
even though they had no way to kill such creatures, they could win
by freeing everyone, by taking away the Aylen's profit, pleasure, or
whatever humanity represented. He felt a surge of determination
and anger. Damen loved to fight. Perhaps it was time Harl
embraced it?

'Thank you, Oscar of-the-well,' Harl said. 'This is the news we hoped for. Although there are things you don't yet understand about the technology we speak of, I can see the strength in your people, and we would be glad to have you join us. If you send runners to the wall where we entered, You'll find a land filled with cattle. There's water inside as well, a constant flow of it.'

A muttering arose among everyone present.

'A constant flow?' Oscar asked. 'All this time there's been water close at hand and yet we've been forced to ration every last drop? Why? Why would they do this to us?'

'For profit. It's a harsh truth, but it's something we've all had to face. I'm sorry to bring such news, Oscar,' Harl said, seeing the resentment in the man's dark face.

'You hold no blame,' Oscar said, 'but despite the harshness of these truths, I see them as good news. No longer will we struggle to live. We will feast on cattle and the water shall flow forth!'

'I know you have suffered, but I must still urge caution,' Harl said. 'Don't take more animals than you need at one time as it's vital we remain undiscovered by the Aylen. The hole must stay open until we are ready to leave, but it needs covering. The Aylen mustn't know of our mission and everything should look as normal as possible. Some of my men will stay here with you as we might need to send someone back to relay a message to those outside.'

'I will come with you,' Oscar said. 'I want to see what you have said for myself and hold my spear next to your own weapons if a fight arises.'

'Very well,' Harl said. 'We'd welcome another to aid us, though I don't know what we will find.'

'Maybe,' Oscar said, 'if we meet more men, they will see that I have joined you and that they should do the same.'

He turned to one of his warriors.

'Send a group to fetch water from this other land. Do not spill any and return it to fill the peoples' wells.' He looked thoughtful for a moment. 'And send men to spread the word that we shall be leaving. Tell them to pack, but nothing should appear out of the ordinary. They should carry on with their work until all is ready.'

The man headed off to do Oscar's bidding.

'And Grower,' Oscar said. The man stopped and looked back at Oscar, 'Tell the guards camping in the far dunes that the order to kill these men when they leave is to be disregarded.'

Grower nodded and ducked out into the chill night.

They talked and feasted long into the dark cycle. When Oscar's men returned with the water after the light came on, the festivities rose up again as it seemed the promise was true. Wrestlers were brought forth, a circle made in the sand, and encouragements shouted as the two muscle-bound men battled each other.

Half way through the fight, two of Oscar's men stumbled drunkenly over to where Damen was sat. One of them slapped him on the back and turned to the crowd.

'What about the bearded newcomer?' he shouted. 'Let's see him fight.'

'Not today,' Damen said, taking a long swig of some potent spirit from a skin.

'Didn't take you for a coward,' Kane muttered, glancing around innocently at the men as they began to move away, disappointed.

A low growl came from Damen's throat and he threw the skin at Kane's feet, making him jump.

'What?' Damen asked.

Kane didn't meet his eye, but the nearby warriors grinned at the sudden change in Damen and started to form a circle around him and Oscar. The hunter looked around for Oscar and met his eye. Oscar nodded curtly and Damen tugged off his leather jerkin, revealing a criss-cross of scars and bite marks decorating his thick muscles.

One of the men slapped Kane on the back in thanks for making the fight happen and tossed a bangle at a heavily inked warrior. The man caught it and nodded. 'Oscar to win?'

Kane's new friend shook his head. 'The new one will take it.'

Had they just made a wager? Harl didn't know who he'd back in such a fight.

Kane grinned and pulled a water skin from his belt. He held it out to the bet taker, 'Oscar of-the-well to win.'

The man raised an eyebrow as if weighing the chance of such a steep bet, then nodded.

An aged man hobbled out from the crowd and used a crooked stick to draw a fresh circle in the sand.

'First to either give in or be pushed from the circle will lose the bout,' he said

'What happens to the loser?' Damen asked as he handed his leather jerkin to Harl.

'They will be drowned in the well of ruined water,' Oscar said, his face grave.

Kane went pale at what he'd initiated and Harl and Damen started to protest, but the crowd burst into laughter and a grin spread across Oscar's face. It turned into a hearty laugh as he slapped Damen on the back and ushered him into the circle drawn through the sand.

The bout started as Oscar and Damen moved in towards each other. A tense quiet spread through the spectators with one or two men breaking the silence to urge them on. A cheer rose as they collided and interlocked, their huge muscles bulging as both men fought to keep the other from toppling him. Oscar had a well-practised technique and after a moment he flung Damen down to the ground. The bare sand powdered out from under them as Oscar manoeuvred himself on top. He caught Damen in a strong lock around his shoulders, levering one arm up into an unnatural angle.

Harl couldn't see how Damen could resist much longer, but the hunter manoeuvred his legs slowly to the side with a strength and flexibility Harl hadn't known he possessed. He brought one leg up and over Oscar's shoulder to wrap it around the man's neck and then levered Oscar down. He rolled on top of him, and ended with an arm lock which had Oscar straining to free himself.

The Deltans shouted encouragement at Damen as both men struggled to gain the upper hand, tumbling over and over in the sand until they eventually rolled out of the circle.

The old man overseeing the bout shouted, 'Draw!'

Both men released each other and climbed to their feet, grinning as they tried to work feeling into their tired muscles.

'You fight well,' Oscar said, a look of pleasure on his face at the unexpected outcome.

'And you,' Damen said.

'Come,' Oscar said. He stepped forward and put an arm around Damen's shoulder. 'We must eat more and talk. Tell me of your fighting, of your "hunting", as you put it.'

Both men sat next to each other during the meal and to Harl it seemed as though they could have talked with relish of fighting and battles forever.

Eventually, Oscar gave them all leave to rest, promising that he would be ready to join the expedition in the morning.

Harl curled up on a rug inside the hut and used his bag as a prop for his head. It was like trying to sleep before a gifting when he was a child. The prospect of adventure and the dizziness from drink kept him up and he imagined the different people they would meet crossing the tanks.

A dark thought struck him before sleep conquered the excitement. What if they found enemies as tough as Oscar's people on the other sides of the barriers? Only a small group had entered the tanks and if they met a population of even a few hundred who were armed, they would have to abandon their search for Kane's petroleum.

It was a chilling thought.

Chapter 57

I have increased security to prevent another break-in but I neglected to

secure the tanks. Some have escaped into the shop.

Harl woke to find the tank's false dawn beaming under the cloth that covered the door. The fire had gone out but the chimney glowed in the artificial light as if it had stolen the flames away. Faint wisps of smoke coiled up through the clay funnel and the sound of his men's snoring filled the stuffy air.

He stood up and stretched his muscles awake. Pain hammered in his head. It reminded him only too well of nights spent with Troy.

An old man, who'd been cleaning the hall, looked up sharply as Harl muttered a few chosen curse words. He smiled.

'You like fire-drink?'

It took Harl a moment to realise he meant the potent spirit Oscar had produced.

'Lovely,' Harl muttered, massaging his temples.

The man chuckled and continued to sweep around the snoring soldiers.

Damen and Kane were beyond the curtain discussing the need for them to get moving. Harl's throbbing head made it hard to focus on what they were saying. It was like the hot air subdued the sound. Their voices fell silent as he picked his way through the sleeping men, but then light flooded the room as Damen dragged the curtain aside and stepped into the wooden hut. Harl raised his hand to shield his eyes against the glare.

'Right, you lot!' Damen shouted. 'Move and get ready!'

Harl watched Damen limp across to the nearest man and give him a kick to wake him.

'How are your muscles today?' Harl said.

'They'll recover,' Damen said. 'They sure know how to fight. I think these people will be a great help to us. I can't believe they've lived like this for so long.'

'We may find worse before the end,' Harl said, thinking of all the ways a confined world could change its people.

He couldn't believe how lucky they had been stumbling across Oscar's people. The chances of finding someone so open to their story had to be tiny, and yet Oscar had accepted their words with good grace and directed his anger towards the Aylen. Harl couldn't picture his own people being quite so amenable.

As the men stirred, Harl ordered one of them back to the entrance to meet Uman and tell him about the discovery of their new allies while the rest made ready to depart.

Oscar, dressed in slightly more clothes than usual, knelt on the sand for a few minutes as if in silent prayer. Was it a prayer or just some kind of meditation to prepare him for what was to come? When the big man rose to his feet the calm determination in his eyes seemed to steady all of those around him.

Food was handed out and Oscar made sure that each man carried an equal burden even though his own pack bulged more than the others. When he saw the books being piled into one of the bags, he strode over and picked one up, opening it upside down to flick through the pages.

'These contain records?' he asked as he poked his nose close and inhaled sharply.

'Yes,' Kane said, switching to his teaching voice. 'Others contain stories or instructions.'

Harl had to smile as it made Kane sound more than a little pompous

'Instructions on fighting?'

'Most contain more...refined things. But yes, some do describe the arts of war.'

Oscar tilted the book to the light and squinted at it as if trying to get a glimpse of the fighting techniques hidden inside.

'Not in this book,' Kane said, plucking the book from Oscar's hands and then sliding it back into the bag. 'I'm sure Damen would be happy to lend you some of his. They have pictures.'

Oscar missed the sarcasm in Kane's voice.

'Pictures?' Oscar said and then marched over to Damen.

Kane shook his head in puzzlement.

At Damen's insistence the troops had given Oscar one of the small melting swords. Oscar spent ages cutting through everything he could find, bowls, bones, even the steel blade from an old sword.

Before they left he'd badgered Kane for every bit of history about the blades, how they worked, how they were crafted, how they gained power. Kane was in his element, giving lecture after lecture on the history and technology involved, while Oscar issued a stream of profuse thanks at Damen for the mighty gift.

Oscar headed back into the domed hut and returned with a pair of carved bone daggers. Each was a work of art and must have taken him hundreds of days to carve.

'On the handles is a carving of this land,' Oscar said. He gestured around him with a hand. 'I hiked to the heart of our world and carved what I could see around me. One dagger shows the landscape towards the back of this world while the other shows the front. When you hold them together you can see the entire world in the palm of your hand.'

Damen clearly was moved by this gesture and he stared at the tiny details on the handles, then traced them with the tips of his fingers, before tucking the daggers into the belt around his waist.

They left the small town with the peoples' blessing and trudged over the sand towards the pitch-black wall that shot up to join the roof of the tank high above. The bright light beamed down on them and only Oscar and Damen showed no signs of feeling the heat. Harl was soon sweating and taking regular sips from his water bottle as his feet sank into the searing sand. When they reached the base of the wall, the lancers set to work while the rest of the group sat under the shade of a few trees that grew close by.

Oscar stared in wonder as the lancers cut a hole through the side of his world. They cut at about waist-height and then heaved the large slab back into the tank when it was loose. Oscar ordered two of his people to wait by the hole and then relay any news back to the others who would pass it on to Uman, but his eagerness to see what lay on the other side of the hole infected the whole group. With excitement mounting, they gathered around the opening to peer inside.

Beyond the barrier lay a world of darkness. It was a black gulf in comparison to the light of Oscar's world. Harl ducked into the hole and looked around, confused by the blackness before him. His eyes took a moment to get used to the darkness, but then he found that he was looking down about ten paces to a bare black floor and that a small amount of light filtered in through the Sight. Peering further inside, he could see that the tank was completely empty. It was just a smooth, giant cube. There was nothing to hide them, no shelter, cover, or landscape at all.

He crawled back into Oscar's world and shielded his eyes from the glaring light above.

'It's empty,' he said, the shock of it echoing in his voice.

'What?' Kane asked. He scrambled into the hole and crouched there in silence before crawling back out. 'It's a dead space, an unused tank.'

'Can we cross without being seen?' Oscar asked as he leant through and glanced right towards the clear glass front.

'We'll have to run or we risk everything,' Harl said. 'If the Aylen spots us then it's over.'

'We should wait until the shop is quieter,' Kane said.

'We can't waste any more time,' Harl said. 'We must risk it. We need to get the fire liquid and make our way back. The longer we wait, the more chance one of the holes will be noticed.'

Kane agreed, reluctantly, and, after tying a rope to one of the trees, they threaded it through the hole and climbed down.

Harl waited as the men slid one by one down the rope. He was impatient to get across. His eyes had adjusted to the light and the vast empty space was not as dark as it had first appeared.

As soon as the last man was on the ground, the rope was pulled up and they started off, their equipment rattling as they raced over the suddenly flat ground. When they reached halfway the sight became shrouded in darkness. Harl twisted round in panic.

'Aylen!' he yelled.

An Aylen had stopped in front of the tank and the metallic weave of its clothing blocked their view like a second wall beyond the glass. It was only the Aylen's midsection, but it's rippling silver clothes flashed reflected light throughout the tank.

They skidded to a halt, frozen in the middle of the barren world like a row of statues. Harl's heart pounded in his chest and it was only by force of will that he didn't pray to a god for deliverance. What would happen if the Aylen ducked down to peer inside the tank? His muscles had seized up. There was no way he could run. The fear of the creature was just too overwhelming.

'It must be looking into the world above,' Kane said, panting.

'Go!' Damen said. 'Run!'

Damen sprinted past and grabbed the strap on Harl's bag, dragging him forward into motion. With packs bouncing against their backs, they raced ahead and tried to force more speed from their tired limbs. Harl was already winded and gasping for air, but the numbing fear shattered and he thundered along, his footsteps like drumbeats against the floor of the tank.

Kane spoke through heavy breaths. 'We need to cut the hole higher in case there's land on the other side and we hit soil.'

'Or sand,' Oscar chimed in. 'If it's sand then it'll pour in and any passing Aylen will notice.'

Harl's mind raced as he tried to figure out how to overcome this new problem. He had an idea, but he wasn't sure if it would work. He reached into his bag for a small coil of rope.

'Oscar,' he said.

Oscar turned from staring at the giant form outside. 'Yes?'

'I need the blade that Damen gave you.'

Oscar didn't hesitate to part from his new weapon. Harl took the blade and activated it as he approached the wall. Holding onto one end of the rope, he dropped the rest and then tied the rope to the hilt of the blade. He stopped at the base of the wall and turned to Oscar.

'Will you to let me get on your shoulders?'

Oscar knelt down facing the barrier. Harl climbed on to his broad shoulders and balanced there while Oscar pushed up off his knees. Harl braced himself against the wall until he was confident of his balance and then reached up with the blade and pushed it into the solid barrier. He switched the weapon off and tested that it was stuck firmly into the smooth wall.

He climbed down from Oscar's shoulders and turned to the two lancers. 'Climb up the same as you did on the outside of the tanks,' he said. 'The ground on the other side will be high.'

The first lancer gripped the rope and planted his feet against the wall before starting to climb. When he reached the dagger he used it as a handhold and plunged a second blade in further up, and then began a slow climb up the side of the tank, locking each blade in place before moving on and repeating the process to climb higher and higher. He stopped when he reached about forty strides above the base and then tied a loop of rope around the top dagger. He tied the rope around his waist and then propped himself away from the tank with his legs and used the lance to cut a slow circle.

Harl glanced at the Aylen's midriff as the creature shuffled this way and that beyond the front glass. Why hadn't it moved away yet? Was it working on one of the tanks above or was it a shopper looking for fresh specimens?

When the lancer had managed to cut the hole, Harl grabbed another short sword and coil of rope from one of the soldiers and tied them together. When the lancer came down Harl scurried up and pushed the blade directly into the middle of the loose block, then turned it off to fix the short sword in place. He slid down and wrapped the rope around his wrist. Oscar and Damen joined him and together they pulled on the rope. The block slipped free and they dived away as it crashed down. To everyone's relief no soil, mud, or sand flooded through the hole. But then the relief turned into horror.

Blood was leaking in through the hole.

Chapter 58

I have found the escapees after weeks of searching. They have been living in the kitchen, stealing food from my stores. They have been returned to their original tank.

'What is that smell?' Kane asked. He held his sleeve across his nose and had one hand propped against the wall as though he was afraid to step away from it.

Oscar sniffed the air and then knelt at a line of blood slowly trickling down from the hole. 'Death.'

Damen nodded 'I fear this is a charnel house, but what kind of horror we face I dare not guess.'

'We must hurry,' Kane said, glancing to the glass front where the Aylen's body still shifted.

Harl was the first up. He crawled into the hole and gagged as the smell engulfed him. Light was visible on the other side of the barrier, but he couldn't make out any details from where he was. He pushed forward on his hands and knees and poked his head out beyond the wall.

He was a step above a landscape of reddish, wet mud. A copse of dead trees stood directly ahead. They were torn and scarred as though raked by a thousand claws. It was an ominous sign, but

Harl hopped down into the mud and clambered between the trees to get a clearer picture of what lay beyond. The ground was even more slippery than he'd imagined and he slid the last few steps until he sank up to his calves in the mire.

The land was smaller than the other tanks and it curved down to a shallow pit in the centre. The blood-red mud looked as if the Aylen had used its giant hand to scrape it to the sides to form one giant valley that filled the entire tank. To his left, on the back wall of the tank, a gigantic funnel scooped down to a huge metal building that took up a full quarter of the tank floor. The funnel was similar to the one from the cattle world, but the building was bizarre. Dozens of metal doors were lined along the front of it. Some were small and set midway up, but others were built at ground level and were wide and imposing, like barn doors.

Scanning from the back of the tank to the front, Harl noticed huge red symbols stamped across the lower half of the sight. He couldn't read the strange curved markings, but he was stunned by them. Was it Aylen writing? He had never considered them capable of writing even with all that he'd learned since his arrival in Delta. Now he was staring at the alien scrawl and it fascinated him. What did it say? Did they write books as well? He pictured what an Aylen book would look like. It would have to be massive. What kind of stories would they tell?

But then cold realisation hit him. He'd seen Aylen holding books before. They would walk up to the tanks holding the massive tomes and stand there flicking through the pages as they eyed the world inside each tank. But his perceptions of the scene had changed now. He had grown. He knew more. Now, when he thought back on those memories, he saw the books for what they were. Catalogues. The Aylen were checking stock and selecting the humans they wanted to buy. The thought was horrifying. They were picking humans to lift from the tank. Were they selecting families to rip apart and lives to ruin, or were they reading a list of bare facts, like the ingredients of a pie? They had no empathy for those inside, they only had a thirst for profit and an insatiable appetite for their own entertainment.

He had seen them as gods once. He had been a fool.

He stared around at the alien landscape. Something was different about this cube compared to the others, something artificial. It seemed like the Aylen had played a big part in its making instead of leaving it to the inhabitants. The red writing on the wall and the blatant lack of flora made it seem unnatural.

Movement snatched his attention away from the markings. He had been so overwhelmed he had failed to spot a battle raging in the centre of the tank. A dozen armour-clad men had surrounded a green, spindly looking creature in a crater that was pooling with blood. A collection of metal buildings were perched halfway up the crater, but the men were ignoring them as a possible defensive position.

The monster towered over them on six stalk-like legs. It had a stubby tail and long body, with a neck that jutted out in front of it. It's small head seemed out of proportion as it twisted left to right on the end of its neck, eyeing the attackers as they surged in to strike then retreated back. Raising its legs, the monster would spear them down at the men or sweep the front pair out in arcs to batter its enemies aside. Rows of curved spikes ran up the back of each leg. The men kept dodging in and out of its reach as it jabbed its legs down at them like a crude fisherman with a spear. Each thrust punctured the earth and sprayed blood up into the air around it.

Every time the creature thrashed its legs at them, it forced the group to widen and contract around it as they struggled to contain it. The creature was revelling in the gore around it. Blood and mud erupted into the air whenever it moved or skewered the ground with a leg. A man already lay dead at its feet, but the others were playing a dangerous game. Spearmen would force the creature to rear up and then the men armed with sword and shield would dash in under its body and hack at its spindly legs.

Harl watched, fascinated, from the valley rim as the men slowly gained the upper hand. They worked in rhythm, spears and swords taking it in turn to clash against the creature's hard exoskeleton. Every now and then one would slice the soft underbelly and dart away before the spiked legs swept them up.

Before Harl had a chance ask what the others thought of the scene below, Oscar bellowed a war cry and sprinted down to join the men in their struggle.

'Come on then,' Damen said, seeing Harl's shocked look. 'Let's get down there and help them.'

They pelted down the hill after Oscar, half running, half sliding through the sticky red mud.

The fighting men spotted Oscar at the last moment and turned to engage, but he paid them no attention and charged through to the heart of their circle as they leapt aside.

The creature saw the threat and turned, swiping one of its long legs at Oscar in the hope of pining him against the wet ground, but he dodged around it and rolled underneath to come up under the beast. He plunged his new weapon up into the monster's pale underbelly and twisted it in place to open up the wound. The creature shrieked in pain and tried to side-step away so that it could strike the man who was causing it so much pain, but Oscar was too quick. He ran along underneath, jabbing the sword up again and again, leaving the creature no chance to retaliate as it skittered left and right, craning its neck to see him.

The creature reared up in desperation. Oscar darted forward and sliced his melting-dagger through the nearest leg, severing it completely. He rolled away from the falling body and stood to one side as the thing collapsed, screeching in agony. The strangers, realising their opportunity, swarmed around the creature and stabbed the flailing monster until it ceased twitching.

When it was over, the men turned to Oscar, a mixture of fear and awe on their faces. They raised their weapons, hesitantly, and formed a line facing him. Every eye was locked on Oscar until one of the men caught sight of Harl's group jogging towards them. He shouted a warning and half the men pivoted to face the new threat, levelling their spears. They were a ragged bunch. Their armour was rusted and dented but they held their ground and the spear tips didn't waver.

One man stepped forward and the men lowered their spears at his approving nod. He had a suspicious look in his eyes, as if trusting the newcomers was a luxury he couldn't afford, but he sheathed his sword and stood there with his arms folded while he waited for them to approach.

Harl ordered a halt about twenty paces away and studied the man facing him. He was short and rugged-looking, with every exposed patch of skin covered in thick scars, as if he'd been fighting since birth. Blood splattered his dented light armour and sweat had stained the red cloth band he wore around his forehead. His arms were bare and covered in the slick, blood red mud. He scratched at one of the fresher scars as Harl spoke.

'My name is Harl Eriksson,' Harl said. He raised a hand to Kane and the others beside him. 'We've come from beyond the walls and are here to help you.'

'No one comes from outside without being put here,' the man said. His eyes flicked down to Harl's sword and to each of them in turn.

'What is happening here-'

A blaring siren cut Harl off.

Some of the shabby men scanned the ground at the rear of the tank while the others looked at each other in disbelief. The leader sighed and flexed his fingers as if to force them to keep moving. He clicked his neck left then right and his shoulders sank as he turned from Harl to face the rear of the tank.

His men glanced around as if expecting something dreadful. One of the group, a boyish youth who seemed to have the cleanest armour, trembled as he turned towards the metal building, as if weighing up his chances of escape.

The leader noticed the boy's glances and placed a blood-encrusted hand on his shoulder.

'Peace, Zane,' he said. 'If we work together we'll survive this.'

The boy looked up at him, confidence returning at the man's words.

'Twice so close together?' he asked. 'Can't we rest? I'm so tired, Drew.'

The helplessness in the boy's voice was heart breaking. Harl had never seen someone so close to giving up on life.

'Not yet, but there's more of us now,' the leader said, nodding towards Harl and his men. He placed a second hand on Zane's shoulders and looked directly into the boy's weary face. 'Stay close to me this time.'

He turned and addressed his men. 'Stay together, live together.'

The group raised their weapons and shouted in unison, 'Stay together, live together!'

'Will you fight with us?' Drew asked, glancing from Harl to Oscar and then towards the line of doors at the back of the land. Without waiting for an answer, he hefted his sword and shouted orders.

'Make a line! If it's another bloody strider, then surround it and keep the circle intact.'

His men obeyed, metal weapons clunking as they trudged to his side to form a row facing the back of the world.

One of the smaller doors high up in the metal building opened and a group of five hivers flew out. They shot up and circled once, as if to get a better view, then spotted the humans and let out a chorus of hideous screeches before heading directly for them.

'Pointed rank!' Drew called out and Harl watched as the line of men contracted into an arrowhead formation pointed directly at the incoming hivers.

Damen reacted as usual when dealing with the winged creatures.

'Form up!' he shouted and hefted his rifle up to eye-level.

Their soldiers stepped into two lines, weapons pointed skywards. The front rank dropped to one knee while the second rank remained standing.

A couple of the tank dwellers glanced to the side at the men with strange weapons.

'Eyes front,' Drew said. 'If you're too busy looking away and the man beside you is killed, then it'll be your fault.'

The hivers soared to within twenty paces and circled once overhead before darting down to attack

'Fire two then two!' Damen's order rang out above the growing buzz of hiver wings.

Blue light seared the air as the first volley of shots flew from the weapons. Drew's men jumped and twisted round to see where the blasts had come from. Panic etched their faces and one even dropped his spear, but Drew barked out orders and the man snatched it up, then steadied.

The second burst of shots exploded from the rifles and flashed through the air, hitting their targets. The hivers split apart as the lancing blue light smashed into them, raining yellow gore down into the blood-soaked mud. Even Oscar was shocked and turned to stare at the riflemen in awe.

Damen turned and grinned at Drew.

'Not bad, eh?'

Chapter 59

I have a competitor. Already another shop has opened but without buying direct from me they are unable to produce the same level of stock.

'**W**hat was that?' Drew asked, wide eyed. 'Specials...' The last word was said in a whisper as if to himself. Harl stepped forward as his men shouldered their weapons. They were looking smug at the display and one or two of them had sniggered at Damen's comment.

'We'll be happy to tell you about all it,' he said, 'but why don't you start by telling us what's going on? Where did the hivers come from?'

Drew seemed to regain his composure now that the threat was dealt with.

'Don't know what you mean by hivers, but I'm Drew,' he said. 'Drew Bronze. These are the men who choose to follow me.' He gazed around at the blood-streaked and weary men with a look of pride. 'Each of us was put here by the Watcher, naked and alone. We do not belong in this place, but it seems fate has dropped us into this nightmare. That and the Watchers. Every fifty times the light comes and goes, the Watchers place food and supplies according to whatever we've slain. If we do not kill these monsters-' He kicked the nearest piece of shredded hiver. '-then we do not eat fresh food and have to make do with the rotting carcasses of what we've killed.'

'Should we expect more?' Damen asked.

Drew shook his head and Damen nodded to his own men and they relaxed, stepping out of line to reload or drink from their waterskins.

'What about your weapons and armour?' Harl asked.

'They are put inside,' Drew said, banging his sword against his rusty armour. It was an angular breastplate, unadorned except for a line of neat scratches, like a tally around the bottom. 'But only if we've piled the corpses of our foes at the front.' He waved a hand at a large pile of rotting creatures heaped together near the front window of the tank. A trickle of yellow and red blood was seeping down from the corpses into the mud.

There must have been dozens, Harl thought.

'When do they come?' Damen asked, eyeing the dead hivers.

Drew shook his head. 'We never know. They come any time, dark or light. All we know is that if we don't want to eat beast flesh then we must kill them. Every now and then one of us will be taken and another who needs training will be placed among us.'

He looked at the young boy and then back to Harl.

'But now you must explain yourselves. How did you enter this place and where did you get these weapons?'

Harl waved to the collection of buildings nearby.

'Shall we sit, eat and talk?' he said. 'We've plenty of food and will tell you all that we know and our reason for coming here.'

Drew agreed and led them towards the small metal buildings.

The buildings were simple boxes of metal. They were scored by scratches and covered in ancient layers of dried blood. It seemed nothing in the harsh tank could escape the violence. Stepping inside the largest building, Harl found bundles of rags heaped in a circle around a dirty firepit.

Drew noticed him looking at them. 'They're for sleeping on. The Watcher doesn't grant us the luxury of beds.'

The firepit looked as if it had barely been used. How often did they have any wood for it? Harl hadn't got a clue, but, as he stared at the empty hearth, he began to shiver. At first he was surprised and assumed that it was a reaction to the battle, but then he noticed that most of his men were shivering as well. Oscar had even wrapped his arms around himself against the cold. Harl cursed to himself. Had the Aylen forced this cold on these people as another hardship, another test?

His breath steamed in the air before him as he took another look around. The one thing in the building that seemed out of place was a weapons bench in the far corner. It was covered in whet stones, ball-pein hammers, and pieces of armour. It was the only thing that looked new.

Kane spoke to Harl while Drew was praising Oscar for his efforts in the fight.

'I believe these men are being bred as fighters,' he whispered. 'I think they're sold to Aylens who use them for sport, although what kind of sport I can't say.'

'I thought the same,' Harl said. 'Whatever is happening here is barbaric and we'll put an end to it.'

Drew uncovered a hidden plate on the floor and pulled out a few twigs and sticks from a stash underneath. He made a mound in the fire pit and soon had a small blaze going. His men huddled around the fire as if it was a rare treat.

As they ate, Harl told their story and repeated the information he had told Oscar of-the-well about their purpose and mission. Drew took it well, as if he knew more than those in Oscar's tank.

'I believe you,' Drew said. He bit into a piece of cold meat and chewed in silence, anger scrawled on his face. He looked out the door to the Sight. 'And you can get us out?'

'Yes,' Kane said, 'but first we need to cut through the next wall and travel on until we can find the petroleum. Then we can get both our people away from the Aylen.'

'We'll join you,' Drew said walking to one of the piles of rags. He almost collapsed into the bundle. 'Sleep first.'

The alarm sounded, blaring the dreaded sound throughout the tank as if the Aylen themselves were screaming in through a hole in the barrier.

All of the fighters had slept in their armour with weapons close to hand, as if expecting such a wake up call. Damen spoke as the tank-dwellers rolled over and snatched up their blades and spears.

'The sentries will sort it,' he said.

Harl led them outside to join those on duty. Drew was already outside, his sword drawn but unbloodied. Hivers lay dead all around and the sentries were kicking the burnt and broken bodies to check they were truly dead. It looked as though Damen's men had dispatched them easily enough. No one seemed to be injured.

'We're lucky it was not a more grievous foe,' Drew said, sheathing his sword as he stared at the multitude of gates as if recalling worse times.

'What type of creatures come out?' Damen asked.

'The hivers are the most common,' Drew said, 'but we've faced much worse.'

'Like the one attacking you when we arrived?' Kane asked.

'No,' Drew said, 'the worst was a swarm of low, many-legged creatures. Ten in all.'

'Ten scuttlers?' Damen asked, his interest piqued. 'You fought ten of them?'

'Yes, although we don't have the same name for them, but that fits them well,' Drew said. 'We lost double that number during the battle and had to set traps to triumph in the end, but it was still too many men to lose. Good men. Their blood stains this soil like so many others. But we remember their names and their sacrifice and they shall never be forgotten.'

The way he said it made Damen look at him in a new light.

'You must tell me of this great battle,' Damen said, 'and the names of those you lost.'

'It would do them honour,' Drew said. 'The fighting has been hard for too long.'

'You don't need to fight any more,' Harl said. 'You'll come with us?'

'We will,' Drew said. 'We've discussed the wonders you speak of and agree that even if it's not true, any place is better than this.'

Oscar grinned at Drew and stepped forward to place a hand on the man's shoulder.

'It's the right choice,' he said, his rhythmic voice was deep and gruff as Drew nodded.

'We've been neighbours for a long time,' Drew said, 'It's about time we become one people and start a new life.'

'One tribe,' Oscar said.

Harl looked around as they talked about what to expect from the outside world once they made it beyond the Aylens' door. He could feel the death in the place. Blood had trickled from the dead bodies to form ruby puddles on the muddy ground. Years of fighting had impregnated the soil with it and he could smell disease in the air. Sonora would've been horrified. The Aylen had inflicted so much suffering and murder on Drew's people. The weight of that pain had to be unbearable, but when he looked back at Drew and saw the strength of his posture he felt proud of the man. Horror after horror had been thrown onto his shoulders and yet he still stood tall and proud, and the men around him looked on with love and respect shining in their eyes. It was an example for all.

'We should not linger here,' Kane said, joining Harl outside. 'Feels like death will return here until it claims everything within these four walls.'

'Then we leave now,' Harl said. 'Unless Damen wants to hang around for another ten scuttlers to arrive.'

564

Kane shushed him.

'Don't say that,' he said, glancing at the hunter. 'He might hear you.'

Harl chuckled and headed to where Damen, Oscar and Drew were standing.

The three warriors looked up as he and Kane approached.

'We'll leave immediately,' Harl said. 'Pick six good men to stay behind and keep the way clear for our return.'

'If the Aylen see a build up of creatures,' Kane said, 'they will surely investigate. It is vital that our mission and escape are kept hidden until the last possible moment.'

It was a grim and dangerous task, but as Drew and Damen picked out soldiers, the chosen men stood taller, clearly honoured to have been given the task. They took a rifle each and headed for a more defensible position.

'We will have to act fast from here on,' Kane said. 'No more stopping. We need to press on and get back home as soon as we can.'

Harl explained to Drew about the melting lance as they waited. He accepted it as he had everything else, quite calmly and with little scepticism. He was an understanding man, clearly placed in a difficult situation.

'Where did you all come from?' Harl asked as the men gathered their meagre belongings.

Drew didn't answer. Instead the young boy spoke up.

'A dark place,' Zane said. 'Don't remember much of it. Don't want to. But I had a family there. We didn't all grow up together if that's what you mean.' He glanced at Drew. 'No one knows where he came from, but a few of us knew of each other before we were brought here.'

Drew looked around as if he'd overheard and the boy broke into a light jog to catch up with the other soldiers. Harl didn't want to provoke the man and so he let it lie.

Reaching the barrier, they cut through with no trouble this time. The two lancers managed to pull the block free and Harl stepped through into a new world.

The view was astonishing and he knew immediately that this world would be vastly different to any place he would ever see again.

Chapter 60

*With all the creatures I found near their lair I could create a self
contained ecosystem. It would not be an entire ecosystem but there's enough
for predators and prey at a basic level.*

The tank was split into two levels. The first was the ground
level, as flat as a board and covered with fields and ditches.
The other was a giant-sized shelf halfway up the tank that was set
against the rear wall. At ground level, the sprawling farmlands
were dotted with small, single-story hovels and a grid of gravel
roads that spread towards the shadowy area underneath the shelf.

But what amazed Harl was the shelf. It hung out over a third
of the farmland and blocked the light from above to leave the
small dwellings underneath it in perpetual shadow. A heavy block
wall ran along the shelf edge. It rose at least five times the height
of a man to form a solid white barrier unmarred by blemish or
defect along its whole length, except for where a huge ornate
archway sat in its centre. The archway was big enough to
accommodate three carts side by side, and a multitude of spires

and rising turrets poked above it, hinting at a vast city behind. Each spire seemed to compete for space as they grew taller and more grand, only for the competition to end in the furthest corner of the tank where a single white tower rose to dominate those around it.

The only way into the city was via a long stone ramp that led from a crossroads in the middle of the farmlands up to the archway high above. All along the ramp, carts pulled by long trains of cattle trundled up and down under the relentless cracks of whips. People hauled baskets back and forth, heads bowed under their loads, but they were very different to look at. Their skin had a deep bronze tan and their eyes were hooded under jet coloured hair. They looked more alien to Harl than anyone he had met so far

'Soldiers,' Damen said, pointing out armoured men walking along the length of the ramp.

One of the cloaked soldiers thrashed a whip at a scrawny figure who had spilled a basket of produce. The man cowered as the whip lashed him, but he still managed to scramble around under the onslaught as he tried to stop the contents rolling back down the ramp.

'They don't look friendly,' Oscar said.

'They look like slaves,' Kane said.

Harl had to agree. Everyone looked underfed and weary as they carried their burdens or ploughed the fields behind a team of malnourished cattle.

'We should stay here and not risk being discovered,' Kane said, looking behind them at a hollow in the ground where they had entered.

The flat ground sloped up towards the barriers on either side of the world as if the farmlands had been created by levelling the soil with a giant trowel before the excess was piled near the walls. By sheer luck they had entered close to a hollow in the hilltop where they could remain unseen. They might be spotted if someone used a looking glass to peer down at them from the shelf, but most of the taller towers were on the far side of the shelf, and there was no one patrolling the parapets along the length of the imposing white wall.

Kane winced as the distant man was whipped again and again until he hunched down into a ball. 'Something tells me that we won't be unwelcome if we go striding down there preaching about freedom,'

'We should send scouts out,' Damen said. He pointed up at the vast city perched on the shelf.'I want to know what's going before we decide on anything. I don't like the look of that place. It stinks of privilege.'

'It won't work,' Kane said. 'These people don't resemble us. We'd stand out among them like a candle in darkness.'

'Then this is an ideal place to make camp for the night while we send out scouts,' Harl said.

'What happened to pushing on as fast as possible?' Kane asked.

'I'm not in a rush to get caught and whipped,' Harl said. 'If we-'

'Down!' Damen said, throwing himself to the ground just as two labourers came out of the nearest building. They were still a long way off, but if they happened to glance up the slope they would easily spot the newcomers.

Harl lay on his belly in the grass tufts that covered the ridge as he observed the two labourers. One slung a basket over his shoulder and knelt down so that the other could fill it with wood from a pile beside the stone hut. Then they turned away and headed along a dirt track towards a cobblestone crossroad.

'Can we hide out among them?' Oscar asked, rising again to a crouch.

'If a few of us can head down to those farm buildings,' Harl said, looking at the squat stone buildings on the edge of the nearest field. 'They might accept food and supplies in exchange for information.'

'Or report us and have us whipped until our spines turn to powdered chalk,' Kane put in.

'I'll go,' Damen said.

'And I,' Oscar said. 'I haven't seen anything like this before.'

'Couldn't let you have all the fun,' Drew said, seemingly unwilling to let others have all the action.

'Take some of the books with you,' Kane said, 'that way, even if we do not find a way to free these people, we can leave evidence that there is more to life than what their masters tell them. We should head out soon afterwards so that we can continue our search for the petroleum.' He rubbed his hands as if eager to find the fuel and get on board the ship.

'I won't leave these people to suffer,' Harl said.

'And if the Aylen discovers what's going on before we can recover the liquid?' Kane asked.

'Then so be it,' Harl said. 'You haven't known oppression.'

Kane shrugged an apology.

'We should split into two groups,' Harl said. 'Damen, Oscar, and I will make for the houses out in the open.' He pointed to the building where the two men had loaded the firewood and swept his arm out to indicate the buildings closest to them across the fields. 'Drew, take two of Damen's men and head under the overhang. Careful in there. It's much more densely populated.'

Drew looked at him, his scarred face weighing up whether he wanted to take orders from a stranger, but then he nodded and looked at his own men, who were still staring in wonder at the giant city hanging in the air.

'I will take one of my own as well,' he said, choosing a grizzled-looking man whose beard was split into a fork.

'Can I come, Drew?' Zane asked, looking hopefully up at him.

Drew shook his head. Too dangerous for a large group Zane. I need you to keep an eye on the other men for me and keep their morale up.'

Zane seemed to grow taller with the sudden responsibility.

'We'll wait until night comes,' Harl said.

'Night?' Zane asked.

'Darkness,' Kane said as he looked back at the hole they'd cut in the tank. 'I will send someone back to Uman before we cover the hole. He'll want to know our plan and I'll wait here until the messenger returns.'

'Coward,' Damen said as he walked over to his soldiers to explain the plan.

'Thug,' Kane murmured.

When the lights shut off, Harl was surprised to see that flickering flames still came from the city on the shelf. The lights were scattered up the towers like the stars in the sky outside. It was a stunningly beautiful sight and a part of him just wanted to sit there and admire the view. What would Sonora think of it? He pictured them living in one of the towers to raise their child and he had to admit that it was an enticing prospect. But when he looked down at the landscape below the shelf he knew that he could never accept such a life. There had to be fairness. He could never abandon those who were suffering.

Harl wished Drew all the best and arranged to meet back at the camp before day came, then he, Oscar and Damen split from the group and headed for the farms.

His own plan was to place the books near buildings where they'd easily be found, scattering the others in the fields to be discovered in the morning. The more inhabitants knew about them before they were discovered the better. It was a risk, but he didn't know of any other way to proceed without increasing the amount of danger they were already in.

They crept into the darkness, crouching low over the ploughed fields as they crawled through the ditches that lined the sides. The land was empty of people and cattle, as if they had been eaten by the thin sheen of mist that had risen from the fields to hover at knee height above the fertile soil.

When they reached the house where they had seen the two men, light flickered out from the only window beside the door. The window didn't have any glass in it, just a rotten lattice of wood with a veil of cloth drawn across it. The diamond shapes of light between the wood lit up the gravel path that led to the door.

While Damen and Oscar kept an eye out, Harl ducked down under the window frame and slipped out a book from the bag around his shoulder. He placed it on the stone doorstep and paused as voices drifted out from inside. The voices were hushed, but he was relieved when he understood them. Kane had warned that each world might have it's own language, something that Harl still couldn't get his head around. It would have made their task almost impossible.

He hesitated at the door. He didn't have the courage to peer inside for fear of being seen, but perhaps on the way back he would risk it, so he crept back to the edge of the nearest field and headed deeper towards the centre of the tank. Time was slipping away.

Chapter 61

In order to best access the tanks, I have built in airtight flaps at the top of each, front and back. Being able to reach in from both ends will be a great help, especially if the tanks are stacked.

The silence was eerie as they skirted a wide path around the ramp in the centre of the tank. Harl had lost count of the number of houses they had stopped at along the way and he was covered in soil and debris from all the fields and ditches they'd crawled through. All the houses they had visited were built in a similar fashion, single story rectangles made from grey stone, with a simple door and window at the front.

'That's the last one,' he said from the shelter of a rickety lean-to at the side of one house.

They were ready to work their way back across the land to their camp. It would be easier going because they could cut straight across the fields on the return trip. Harl knew they had been far too exposed dropping off the books and his shoulders relaxed when it was done, as if he'd been carrying a burden heavier than just the books.

He began to edge out from the lean-to when a woman's voice broke the silence. It came from inside the house.

'Fetch some wood, Argus,' the shrill voice said. 'Fire's out again.'

Harl glanced down at the feeble pile of logs stacked under the lean-to beside him and cursed. The door clattered open and footsteps rounded the corner. Damen and Oscar scurried along the side of the house and ducked around the corner. Harl turned to follow them, but his foot snagged the pile of wood and he was sent sprawling to the floor.

'Hey!' a man's voice called.

Harl scrambled to his feet and looked up. A short skinny silhouette stood glaring at him.

'I'm sorry,' Harl said quickly, not wanting the man to draw attention or call for help.

When the man took a step closer, he froze. Shock was written all over his face as he looked at Harl.

'I am not from here, Argus,' Harl said, hoping the name might ease the tension. 'I mean no harm to you.'

'And yet you're creeping around my house?' Argus' eyes flicked to the lean-to. 'Stealing my wood?'

'I'm not stealing,' Harl said. 'I have something to give you.'

'Are you alone?' Argus asked, looking at the dirt on the ground near Harl. Oscar and Damen's footprints stood out clearly.

'No,' Harl said, relieved that the man had not run off in fear.

Argus sucked in a breath to shout.

'Wait!' Harl hissed. 'Please, Argus. Hear me out. Then I will leave.' The words tumbled out before Argus could call for help and, instead of shouting, Argus let out a long sigh.

'Tell me,' he said, simply.

'I have two companions with me,' Harl said. 'We-'

'Bring them out then,' Argus said, cutting him off. His eyes roamed over the small shrubs and tufts of grass lining the field beside his house.

'Be warned,' said Harl. 'They don't resemble me. You may be startled at their appearance.'

Argus frowned. 'You're not exactly normal looking yourself.'

'Damen, Oscar?' Harl said. 'Come out.'

Argus looked hard at Damen as he came round the stone corner, but took a step back when the large, dark form of Oscar followed.

'Don't be alarmed,' Harl said, quickly, seeing the confusion in the man's face at witnessing someone so different in complexion for the first time. 'We're here to help you.'

'You are not with the Callers?' Argus asked.

Harl shook his head. 'I do not know these Callers, but no, we are not with anyone by that name.'

Argus' demeanour changed and he stayed silent for a while until Harl thought he had frozen in fear. Should he have said he was with these Callers?

Argus glanced over his thin shoulder at the gravel path that led to an empty main road.

'You must be quiet,' he whispered. 'You may come inside, but first wait a short time. My wife must be told what to expect. If she was to cry out, the Callers would come, and that would mean death for all of us.'

Argus slipped inside and after some low murmurings, a woman's concerned voice replied.

'You can't,' she said. 'If they're strangers or out of bounds then we must report it to the Callers before it's too late.'

Argus talked in a lower voice and Harl couldn't catch much. He just hoped he had done the right thing. They could slip away now and head back to camp before morning. He turned to tell the other two that they would leave but the door creaked open and Argus reappeared around the corner.

'Inside,' he hissed. 'Quickly now.'

He beckoned them to follow and scanned along the road before ducking inside.

It was a small house, lit by sputtering candles and divided into rooms separated by bedraggled curtains hanging in the doorways. The three of them stood on a tattered woven rug in the main living room as Argus poked his head out the door, looked both ways and shut it, throwing a rusted latch across.

The white-washed room was sparsely furnished, with a pair of worn timber chairs standing close to a small table. To their right, a smooth clay fireplace arched over a large, dented cooking pot. It stood on a bed of dying embers that threw out a last whisper of warmth into the room. A large painting of an imperious-looking man hung in a polished wood frame on one of the walls. The stern face that peered down at them was so expertly drawn that the eyes seemed to follow Harl as he shifted position. Two curtained doorways led from the room and the ageing woman standing in one of them let out a muffled gasp when she saw them come in, and then slapped a hand to her mouth to stifle the sound.

She had the look of a piece of knotted rope. Her thin arms were wrapped in tight muscles as if she had worked the fields since birth and the greying streaks in her hair shone like silver.

She eyed the three strangers from the far side of the room as Argus bustled Damen and Oscar away from the window.

'You can't stay long,' Argus said, peering out through the lattice in the window. 'It is death to harbour people or speak to strangers without permission, so explain yourselves. Where have you come from and why were you sneaking around my house?'

Harl noticed a pitiful heap of vegetables by the side of the fire. They were wrinkled and withered but apparently waiting to be thrown into the pot.

'May we eat with you first?' he asked, thinking it the best way to the ease tension. 'We've some food and it'd be better to explain over a meal.'

The woman stopped examining Oscar and looked up sharply.

'You got food?' she asked. It was the first time she had spoken since they came inside and her eyes scanned the three of them, lingering hopefully on their bags.

'Yes,' Harl said. 'And we'd like to share it with you. But while we eat I would tell you of a message we have for your people.'

'Our people?' she asked. 'Or the Callers? They rule here.' Her voice had a slight hint of distaste at the word "Callers".

'The message is for everyone here,' Harl said and looked at Oscar who was now eyeing the darkness beyond the small window. 'Oscar get out some food, enough for us all to eat well.'

As Oscar heaved off his pack, Harl took the chance to ask more about these people before he started his now well-practised speech.

'Tell us everything you can about this place,' he asked, looking from the woman to Argus.

'There ain't much to tell,' Argus said. 'We're ruled by the Callers, the ones in contact with the gods. Together we strive to build a city worthy of their favour, or at least that is what we're told.'

'By the gods?' Harl asked.

'By the Callers,' the Argus said, his eyes flicking to the woman as she scowled. 'In reality we're their servants and slaves.'

'Shh!' The woman hushed, but Argus went on regardless, as if he had wanted to say such things for a long time and finally had a willing audience.

'As the lower people, we're forced to grow crops down here. Others are put to work mining the rocks and making stone for the city. We build the city to the Callers' will,' he said, looking around the bare room and dirt floor. 'But we see little in return.'

Oscar unpacked the food he carried and the two became fixated at the sliced chunks of salted meat and lumps of bread he placed on the mat.

'Will you cook for us?' Harl asked the woman and before he could finish, she was picking up the meat and placing it straight into the cooking pot.

She made for the door.

'Where are you going?' Damen asked.

'I go where I like in my own house,' the woman snapped, but her gaze drifted to the food Oscar was unpacking and she sighed. 'Firewood,' she said before unlatching the door and ducking out.

She returned a moment later and heaped an armful of brittle logs on to the embers before blowing into the pile. She actually started to eat the bread as she tended the growing flames. Argus looked at her and then at Harl, almost in apology, as she forced the bread down with some water from a clay jug.

'You must excuse us,' Argus said. 'We don't have the luxury of much food and often go without.'

He looked embarrassed at his words and Harl felt a surge of pity for the man and the people of the tank.

'Please,' Harl said, pushing the loaves to him. 'Eat what you like.'

Argus snatched up some of the bread and bit away a chunk. It took him a moment to wash it down before he continued.

'As I was saying,' he mumbled, mid chew, 'the Callers rule us. They use whips and worse things when someone doesn't obey. There are strict rules for all the low people and death is more common from Callers than from hunger or weakness. We're made to bring all our food to the city every few switches and if we do not meet our quota we're punished. Jo,' he said, looking at the woman as she stirred the pot and continued to stuff bread into her mouth, 'was cautious of bringing you inside because us low are often checked on by the Callers to make sure we don't steal any of the produce not rationed to us.'

'Who is the painted man?' Oscar asked.

Argus glared up at the painting on the wall.

'That man,' he said, 'is our most gracious host, The One, and it's for him that we do all these things. He is a god himself, and under his eye we're kept in line so that the building of the great city can continue. We're made to keep his picture on our wall as a reminder of his benevolence, and to thank him when we wake and before sleep or sustenance. Few have ever seen him 'cept when he comes out on his throne to make a rare speech about how well we're doing, but it seems our efforts are never enough.'

The man drifted off as Jo declared the food was ready. She began dishing some stew into a pair of splinter-riddled bowls.

'I am sorry,' she said. 'We've only two bowls.'

'No problem,' Harl said, pulling his own copper bowl out and watching Oscar and Damen do likewise.

They ate in silence and Harl had to avert his eyes from both their hosts. Their faces switched between greedy haste and guilty pleasure as the meal disappeared from the bowls as quickly as it had been ladled in.

He waited until they had finished, both resting hands on swollen bellies, before he outlined their mission, where they came from, and the books they'd left at the other houses.

Argus looked concerned when he heard about the books and, after flicking through one that Damen had passed to them, he spoke.

'These may help,' he said. 'But just as likely people will suffer if the Callers find them with one. It'll be considered heresy for anyone to read them. Many will be left where you placed them.'

'I understand,' Harl said, 'but we have to spread this message. Your people, more than all of the others we've found, need our help the most. This is the only way to spread a message fast enough.'

The man nodded, still hesitant, and Harl decided to continue with his story, finishing it with the revelation of taking the ship away from Delta. By the end he saw hope in their eyes, mixed with worry and the expected disbelief.

Jo jumped up, knocking her empty bowl to the floor as she rushed to the front window.

She turned, wide-eyed with fear.

'Callers!'

Chapter 62

It's a matter of tests from now on. Each tank will be isolated from the others, so they must be almost self-sufficient. Of course, I will have to set up agreements with manufacturers for precision supplies.

'**O**ut!' Jo hissed as she attempted to shove Oscar's huge bulk to the door. 'Get out!'

'Too late, Jo,' Argus said as his face turned ashen.

The woman cupped her hands over her face. 'I told you Argus. It was a set up-'

'Hush woman,' Argus said, looking around the house as if an exit would present itself. 'No,' he hissed, seeing Oscar and Damen reaching for their weapons 'You must hide. Go to the back room; take your things. Move!'

They were bustled through a curtained partition and in a moment all three were cramped in a small, dingy bedroom as blandly furnished as the living room.

The footsteps crunched on gravel. There was more than one. Guilt wracked Harl for placing these innocent people at risk, but what else could he have done?

'The bowls,' Oscar said and Harl cursed. They'd left them on the floor in plain view.

Harl didn't waste any time. He thrust aside the tan curtain and crouched low, moving into the living room. The couple looked startled and attempted to usher him back. He grabbed the bowls and scampered back as someone began pounding on the door.

'Open up!' a commanding voice said from the far side of the door.

'Open up or we break it down,' another said.

'One moment,' Jo said, suddenly sounding more frail than before, as if to mollify the unwanted visitors.

The front door squeaked open.

'What's going on here?' a man's voice asked. 'You're up late and there was a sighting of strange folk near here earlier this-What's that smell?'

The man sniffed over the sound of the crackling fire. The smell of cooked meat must have been a rare occurrence in the hovels and the man had picked up on it.

'We're eating,' Argus said, innocently.

It was not innocent enough. The crack of a whip was followed by a small cry.

'Are you suggesting I don't know what food smells like?' the Caller asked. 'How did you come by meat?'

'They must have stole it,' said a second, high-pitched voice.

'Did you steal it?' the first Caller asked.

'No, master,' Argus said. 'We've saved it for a special occasion.'

Harl could sense Argus flinching back from the whip as he said it.

'And what is special about this occasion?' the Caller asked, clearly not believing the explanation.

'Our daughter Alina was given fifty switches ago,' Jo said, her voice getting more nervous as she spoke. 'And we are honouring her.'

'Did I ask you?' the caller said. 'Do not dare speak to me unless spoken to.'

Harl's eyes flicked to Oscar as the man clenched and flexed his meaty fists at the words.

'It's all lies!' the other Caller said in his high, snivelling voice. 'No meat has been given out recently, least not to the low born.'

'Where did you come by the food, bitch?' the first asked.

'Most likely slaughtering cattle,' the sneering voice said.

Harl was filled with shame and anger as the whip cracked again and Jo cried out in pain.

'Leave her alone,' Argus said, but a thumping noise came from behind the curtain, cutting off his protests.

'Please,' Jo pleaded 'We have done nothing wrong.'

'You're lying!' said the first again.

'And if you want to stay living then you'd best do as we say,' the whiny voice said.

Someone landed hard on the floor and Harl risked a look, twitching the cloth partition aside a fraction. He saw, to his horror, that one of the men, whip in hand, was holding Argus back as the other leaned over Jo, attempting to remove her clothing. Argus's protests were cut off with another knuckling crack from his captor as Jo begged the man to stop.

Harl glanced at Damen and Oscar as he levered the pistol from his belt, ready to pull the cloth aside and teach the Callers a lesson.

'Take her to the back room,' the one with the whip said.

Harl stepped back from the cloth partition as the man indicated it with a hand. Harl stayed still, anger boiling inside. If his prey came to him, then all the better to give them a surprise.

'We don't want her cries to bring more,' the Caller said. 'I've enough bloody trouble without twenty men trying to mount the shrivelled wretch.'

The sound of the attackers footsteps were laboured as he dragged Jo towards the curtain. Harl took a quick look around. There was nothing to hide behind, so he tensed, ready for action.

Oscar moved to Harl's side and touched his shoulder, indicating that he wanted to be first to encounter the Caller. When the partition was tugged aside, the Caller backed into the room, both arms wrapped around Jo's waist as he struggled to pull her in. He swung Jo around and let go. She tumbled to the floor and cried out in pain.

Shock split the Caller's face when he looked up and saw Oscar's dark, muscled form in front him. He froze, completely speechless as he stared at Oscar, his hooded eyes blinking rapidly as though he couldn't quite believe what he was seeing.

Before the man could say a word, Oscar thrust his large hands out and grabbed the man's neck as silent rage stormed across his usually calm features. Shock turned to horror on the Caller's face as Oscar twisted violently, snapping the man's neck as if it were a chicken's.

Oscar held the limp body up and dragged it further into the room, where he eased it to the floor.

Harl helped Jo up and put a finger to his lips. She nodded.

'What is it now?' the other Caller asked as if bored. 'Ardy? Come on man, she's only an old low woman.' When no voice came in reply, footsteps came towards the small room but stopped in front of the curtain. 'Ardy?' The man waited a moment and must have sensed something was wrong. The ring of a sword being drawn vibrated through the curtain.

Oscar tore the blade Damen had given him free and reached a hand out to grab the cloth. He ripped the curtain down and stormed through the gap with Damen and Harl behind him.

The Caller froze in the face of what must have looked like a tattooed daemon surging towards him. He held his sword limp in one hand, terrified of the alien men who had stormed from behind the curtain.

Oscar kicked the man squarely in the chest, sending him sprawling onto the floor. The man's curved sword and whip tumbled from his hands as Argus leapt aside. The Caller scrambled to his feet and, instead of grabbing his weapons, he turned and ran for the door.

Damen reacted first, stepping around Oscar as he drew out one of the bone knives Oscar had given him and hurled the blade towards the Caller. Harl watched it spin, tumbling over and over through the air to land with a light thump into the man's back. The Caller arched, a short cry escaping his lips as he crashed through the door and sprawled on the gravel.

'Good shot,' Oscar said, moving quickly across the room to check outside. He froze.

Standing in front of the door was a cloaked figure staring down at the body. The man looked up at Oscar.

'Wait!' Argus said as Oscar raised his short sword.

Oscar stayed the weapon and both men faced each other like statues.

'Cheng?' Argus said, hurrying to the door. He slipped past Oscar and grabbed the stunned man, tugging him inside.

'This man is not an enemy,' Argus said. 'What are you doing here, Cheng?'

'I-I was coming as usual,' Cheng said. 'What in the name of the One is going on?'

Oscar grabbed the Caller's ankles and hauled him back inside, closing the door behind. He turned the groaning man over. Blood streamed from his mouth as he stared up at Oscar, gurgling and choking on the liquid before shuddering to stillness. The man's hooded eyes and tanned complexion were similar to the owners of the house, but fleshier, as if they lived a life of excess in comparison to Argus and Jo.

Harl now saw that the Callers were dressed in a leather and light scale armour. Patches of red cloth showed underneath, darkened by blood.

'I'm sorry,' Cheng said, blowing alcohol fumes at Harl. He stared, aghast, at the bodies and raised his hands as if he might be next. 'I won't say a word.'

'These men,' Argus said, looking at Harl, Damen, and Oscar, 'might be able to help us. Do you still have contacts in the city?'

Cheng nodded.

'Yes,' he said, 'but things are difficult up there at the moment. Food for the masses is almost non-existent. I would've brought the usual supplies, but even I go hungry nearly every switch.'

'The food is not important,' Argus said to an astonished look from Cheng. 'I owe these men a debt. As you do me. Can you get them into the city?'

Cheng looked as if he wanted nothing more than to run and pretend he'd not seen the dead Callers or frightening strangers, but reluctantly he nodded.

'Possibly' he said, then, at a look from Argus, shook his head up and down. 'Yes, I can get them up there. But only if we meet under the city in two switches time.'

'Two switches?' Argus said. 'Why so long?'

'It's not a matter of walking up the ramp,' Cheng said. He staggered slightly as the drink took hold, and then steadied himself against the wall. 'They must get up a different way.'

'Fine,' Argus said, turning to Harl. 'I hope that will satisfy you. Sorry we cannot do more.'

'I would prefer to leave sooner,' Harl said, 'but it's more than we'd hoped for.'

'I must go,' Cheng said, still staring at the bodies. He fished a flask from his jacket, shrugged an apology, and then took a swig.

'Cheng?' Argus said, raising an eyebrow.

Cheng looked up, focusing again.

'Two switches,' he said, 'under the city, left of the ramp, after dark.' He opened the door, peered around, and then scurried out into the darkness towards the city.

'I hope that will be enough to repay our thanks,' Argus said. 'He'd better be there.'

'Why does he owe you?' Damen asked, watching Cheng through the window as he stopped halfway up the path to be sick in the ditch before disappearing into the dark.

'When our daughter was taken-' Argus swallowed hard. '-she was with him. When the hand came down, he ran, leaving her in the open. Later, he admitted he was drunk, but by then it was too late. Maybe the God would've taken her anyway, but maybe not. He blames himself for it every single switch and brings us food from his job up in the city. Although lately I hear he began drinking hard again at the city tavern after swearing off it for so long.'

'Clearly,' Damen said.

'We're going to need him if we're to get inside the city.' Harl said

Argus nodded.

'Why is getting into the city important?' Oscar asked. 'We could just cut through to the next place.'

'The more we can spread the book the better,' Harl said. 'And perhaps this leader can be persuaded.' He looked at Damen, 'or assassinated?'

Damen nodded.

'Either way,' Harl said, 'we don't need enemies at our back on our return.'

'I don't know how to thank you all,' Argus said, looking round at his wife, who had regained her composure.

'There's no need,' Harl said. 'Just spread our message and we'll meet Cheng in two days. But now we must go.'

As Harl opened the door to leave, the world lit up as the lights above switched on. It illuminated fields, houses, and people heading out to work.

Not good, Harl thought, not good at all.

Chapter 63

By tweaking the interior lighting I can achieve better plant growth. I've released my reports on this to the newly-formed hobbyist societies which have sprung up around the globe.

'What do we do?' Oscar asked as he peered around the doorframe at the people marching to the fields, and a stream of guards coming down the giant ramp, ready to start another day of whipping and torment.

Harl had an idea.

'Take their clothes off,' he commanded Argus and Jo as they automatically readied themselves to join the others in the fields. They seemed to shake off the lifelong habit and obeyed, stripping the Callers' clothes and then handing them up to him. He passed one set to Damen. 'We need to put these on,' he said.

'What about me?' Oscar asked.

'You're going to be a prisoner,' Harl said.

Oscar frowned at the mark of treachery, but Harl chuckled.

'Our cover will be we are taking you to be executed,' Harl said. He waved a hand out the window towards the crossroads at the base of the ramp. They would need to pass the front of the giant ramp if they were to rejoin the others at the camp.

'If they follow us,' Damen said, 'we'll lead them straight to the camp.'

'We have to risk it,' Harl said looking from the bodies to Argus. 'You'll be alright taking care of the bodies?'

'We can bury them before more come around, and Jo will take care of the mess inside. She's most grateful and I'm beholden to you,' Argus said, smiling. 'You're welcome here any time, Harl, and all your friends. Especially if they're as tough as those two,' He looked from Oscar to Damen, who was now dressed in a tight-fitting, but serviceable, Caller uniform.

'Be ready to leave with us Argus, if you're both willing,' Harl said. 'Here, take this.' He passed Argus a bag containing some food and a couple of small daggers Damen had slipped inside, not needing them because of Oscar's gift.

Jo seemed to have recovered from the shock and she handed Damen a short coil of rope. 'For his bonds,' she said and suddenly threw her arms around him and then Oscar. 'Thank you.'

'If you need to leave,' Harl said, 'then we're camped over the hill on the far side.' He pointed in the general direction and they both nodded.

'Farewell,' Harl said, feeling the uniform start to itch as he and Damen escorted a loosely-tied Oscar along the road. They had made sure to cover as much of his skin as possible and Damen went so far as to put a sack over Oscar's head to disguise his appearance.

It was a tense walk, but they were not hindered along the gravel path. As they passed the crossroads, a Caller patrol started up the ramp and, in a stroke of luck, the men had their backs to Harl's group. Some of the passing slaves glanced towards Oscar in his role as prisoner, but no one stared. They just assumed a submissive stance when they walked by, and bowed their heads towards the ground as they struggled along under their burdens of baskets and sacks.

'Seems to have worked,' Damen said as they trudged along the road towards the hill at the edge of the tank.

Harl nodded and then scurried up the hill when they reached it. Oscar almost tripped as they led him over the crest. They ducked down on the other side and looked at their camp. The men were sitting in a circle around their belongings while they ate.

Oscar yanked off the sack and his eyes shot wide open as he looked along the ridge of the hill. Harl snapped his head round at the sound of a sword being drawn. One of Damen's men was running at them with his blade held ready to strike.

'Wait you fool!' Damen hissed 'It's us.'

The man skidded to a halt and stared hard at them before apologising.

'It was the uniforms, sir,' he said.

Of course, Harl thought. They looked the same as all the guards over the hill.

'Why did you not see us approaching?' Damen asked.

The man looked crestfallen. 'Was eating lunch sir.'

597

'You're on double duty from now on until you learn how to keep an eye out,' Damen said. 'And make sure you use a bow next time.'

'What took you so long?' Kane asked, tucking away a small notepad. He stood as the three of them trotted down the hill into the natural gully. He squinted as he looked at their clothes, then sniffed. 'Did you go shopping for clothes? They suit you.'

'It's a long story,' Harl said. 'But let us eat and rest first, then we'll tell you what we found out. We're in for a bit of a wait.'

Harl outlined everything that had happened, from killing the two guards to meeting Cheng. Drew and his men had returned well before the light came on and had delivered all the books to houses they found on the way. They had learned that the ramp up to the city was closed during darkness.

'We'll meet the man and he'll show us the way,' Harl said. 'Once we're up there we can leave the rest of the books.'

'What then?' Kane asked. 'I don't think all these people will come with us. These Callers will try to stop them.'

'Can we pass word around that anyone who wants to leave should meet at a certain time?' Damen asked as he quietly scraped a sharpening stone up his sword. 'Or we could just fight these Callers. Looks like they need teaching some manners.'

'With an army of malnourished peasants?' Kane asked.

Damen stopped the stone and tested the blade with his thumb. 'And what would you do instead, clever one?'

'Sneak them out somehow,' Kane said.

'I don't think there is a way we can get them out without trouble,' Harl said. 'If there's to be fighting, then we must make sure the Callers and this One are dealt with before we continue.'

'It'll be a tough fight,' Damen said and resumed scraping the stone. 'But maybe we can use some proper weapons.' He placed the sword down and picked up his battle rifle as an example.

Harl realized they had a huge advantage over the Callers, even if the Callers had the numbers.

'Send word back to Uman,' Harl said, 'and those we passed on our way here. Have them send as many as are willing to come. They must be ready to fight.'

'It might take some time for them to reach us,' Kane said. 'Until then, we can spread more of the books. We can meet Cheng and scatter them in the city. Maybe find out more about this One they talk about.'

Harl knew time was against them and he hated that they must wait for Cheng.

'By now the Callers will know about the books,' he said. 'They may even try to find us before our forces arrive.'

'What will we do?' Kane asked.

'Keep a good lookout and get some sleep,' Harl said.

No soldiers came marching up the hill during the next day and night, and they passed the time by guessing what they would find up in the city and the tanks to come. Harl was fascinated by some of the ideas the men came up with. One suggested a tank filled to the top with soil where the people lived like rodents in tunnels and warrens beneath the surface. Kane had hopes of finding a tank brimming with lost technology, where humans had transcended martial combat and lived in tranquillity and peace.

But it was all dreams, really. Harl knew the reality of living inside the tanks in a way that most of the men could never understand. Only Drew, Oscar, and the people from their worlds shared that curse. It was something Damen and Kane would never see as clearly, because they had never lived through the pain and never woken each day to the walls and roof constricting their lives.

And yet he envied them. They had known freedom. Yes, they had lived under the yoke of the Enlightened, but they had an endless world to explore and the ability to fight against the monsters that came to claim them. It was the freedom to roam, the freedom to face the risks life had to offer and know that you had a chance.

Harl's people had nothing.

When the specified dark cycle came, Harl, Kane and Drew crept out beneath the shelf to meet Cheng. The shelf formed a low ceiling that seemed to press down on Harl. It was a reminder of the quarries, except, instead of dust, the air was heavy with humidity as moisture rising from the soil became trapped between the two layers.

Cheng was waiting for them beside a small farm house nestled at the tall end of the ramp where the shelf began.

As they approached, Harl noticed he was leaning on the wall for support. He looked drunk.

'You're ready to go into the city now?' Cheng asked.

'Yes' Harl said. Something felt wrong, but he couldn't put his finger on it.

'Follow me,' Cheng said as he pushed off the wall and began to walk deeper into the darkness.

'Cheng,' Harl said and the man stopped. 'Argus told me about the accident.'

The pop of a bottle cork broke the dark silence around them. 'So?' Cheng said.

'It wasn't your fault,' Harl said.

Cheng looked startled even in half-light.

'What do you care?' he asked and took a long swig from the bottle.

'My parents were taken,' Harl said. 'I've seen it happen too many times. No one can hide when they come to take you but, if we succeed in our plans, then no one need fear them again. Your help won't be forgotten.'

Cheng stopped mid-swallow. Maybe no one had spoken to him about the events before and he stayed silent, not moving.

'Are your people willing to fight against the Callers?' Harl asked.

Cheng seemed put out by the question and shifted uncomfortably, looking around as if someone was waiting in the shadows beside them.

'Most of us want to be free,' Cheng said. 'But it's not possible. The One is too powerful.'

'You're wrong,' Harl said, knowing how he felt. It had been the same with the Eldermen and the council at Delta. 'We'll put a stop to it.'

'Come on,' Drew said, 'or we'll be here when the light comes and be easy pickings.'

Cheng hesitated, looking back into the darkness, then strode off.

They followed his silhouette deep under the shelf towards the rear barrier of the tank. Darkness encompassed everything the further back they went. What if they lost Cheng? Or the shelf collapsed down on top of them? Harl tried to relax and stop hunching over like an old beggar. The shelf held the weight of a hundred towers and must have been there since the tank was made.

Cheng stopped, finally. Only a thin sliver of light showed above them.

'Up there,' Cheng said, pointing at where the shelf joined the tank.

Harl strained his eyes in the darkness, looking for whatever Cheng was showing him, then he spotted it. The light was coming from a gap near the base of the shelf where it met the back of the tank. It ran from a tiny crack at one side of the tank to where it widened out into a man-sized opening further along. Most of it had been bricked up, but there was a small section where the bricks had obviously crumbled and fallen away.

'Fascinating,' Kane said as he stared up at the faulty joint. 'The Aylens must have made it out of alignment.'

'That is what you call the gods?' Cheng asked.

'Yes,' Kane said simply. 'They are not gods, just large creatures who have captured humanity, as it says in the book.'

Cheng hesitated. It was clear he hadn't read the volume. He bent over and picked up a small stone and threw it up towards the widest point of the crack. It knocked against the corner and ricocheted off the wall, landing with a light thump in the damp soil.

A small light flickered into the crack and a shadowy head peered down at them. Cheng pulled two small objects from his ragged black jerkin and struck them together twice. The pieces sparked and flickered. It must have been a signal. A knotted rope dropped down from the widest part of the opening and hung loose next to them.

'I'll go first,' Cheng said, steadying the rope in his grip. 'When I'm up, follow quickly, but be careful not to hit the wall and bounce off. Watch,' he said as he grasped the rough fibres and heaved himself up. He placed his feet against the black barrier and, using them to balance himself, half-climbed and half-walked up the wall and rope.

Harl followed next, heaving himself up, hand-over-hand, focusing on placing his feet in the correct place against the wall. When he reached the top he glanced up and saw several faces between the crack glaring down at him. None looked friendly.

Uncertain, he looked back at the ground ready to slide down to safety, but two strong hands clasped his wrists and hauled him up. When he stood, he was not only facing a nervous Cheng but several men in the same uniform he had borrowed two days before.

Callers.

He cried out as a sword flashed up to his neck, but the sound had been enough; he could hear Kane and Drew's distant footsteps as they ran.

'Scum!' a Caller holding a coil of rope shouted as he hit Harl in the stomach. The air rushed out of him and he doubled over, winded.

'They got away,' the Caller said, turning his fury on Cheng, who stepped back, fearful.

'I tried,' Cheng said, raising his hands to placate the man. 'I couldn't help it. I did as you asked.'

'You get a third,' the Caller said, indicating a lumpy sack at his feet.

'I couldn't help it' Cheng said again. He looked at Harl, opened his mouth, and then snapped it shut again.

'Just take it and get out of my sight,' the Caller said, kicking the sack. A mud-covered carrot rolled out.

Cheng grabbed the sack and swept it up over a shoulder, and then ran off into the city.

'Hope this one's enough,' one of the men said, scrutinizing Harl. 'Should've been all of em. How'd you get him to do it capt'n?'

'Easy,' the captain said, 'The scum had been stealing food from the kitchens. Caught him last switch pinching a joint of meat 'an he starts blabbing about foreigners. Didn't believe a word until now.' He eyed Harl, pointing his sword at Harl's chest.

'Bloody cattle,' another said, 'I'll never understand them.'

'You've some explaining to do,' the captain said to Harl, 'and you'll do it in the dungeons.'

Despair coursed through Harl for trusting Cheng as the guards took his weapons, tied his hands, and walked him into the city built for the gods.

Chapter 64

General Valrich came into the shop today. A general! He asked how easy it was to train them. I hadn't a clue what to say. Training them for the military makes no sense. What use could something so small be?

Harl finally saw the full splendour of the city as he was kicked and shoved along the street. The buildings were the biggest man made objects he had ever laid eyes on, dwarfing the homes and buildings from his own world. Even Delta seemed tiny by comparison. Each building was taller or wider than the next in a series that stretched to the back corner of the tank. It was as if each generation of builders had wanted to outdo the last.

At street level, pale stone was used in everything from the cobblestones underfoot to the statues of the One that stood outside every other building along the road. The statue's strong, set jaw, soft eyes and wide shoulders gave the impression of a firm but benevolent ruler.

Unlike the ghostly stillness of the farms below, the city was bustling with people moving about the streets. Some were obviously slaves carrying wide backpacks and walking with hunched spines under the heavy loads. Others must have been off duty guards as they called out to his captors with queries about their strange prisoner as they passed. Several times the guards shoved him aside as a group of wealthy men staggered past, moving from tavern to tavern, but mostly they just prodded him along with their swords. It didn't seem to matter that it was night. Life just seemed to carry on.

The Callers had roughly disarmed Harl of his equipment when they bound him and one carried his sword, bag and pistol. Harl saw no way of taking it back without ending up either wounded or dead on their jagged swords. If he could get hold of the pistol then they wouldn't be a match for him, but it was no use wishing for what he couldn't have. He just had to hope that some opportunity presented itself.

They marched him deeper into the city until the captain halted and held his sword across Harl's path. Harl staggered to a stop and sucked in his stomach to avoid a slice across his belly.

They had stopped in front of the tallest building and, up close, it was even more impressive than seen from the farmlands. Its pale stone walls were so ornately etched with pictures and words that it was a marvel that anyone could have spent the time to carve it. It spread out far to either side of him, taking up the entire back corner of the city. The only entrance was a tall, pillared archway that was guarded by two armoured guards, their polished suits gleaming silver in the light.

His captors hauled him roughly through the archway and past the silent soldiers on duty inside.

Harl found himself staring down a straight corridor lined with tapestries and gold embossed portraits of the One. The floor was cushioned with a deep red carpet that stretched all the way to a set of ornate stone doors covered in sparkling jewels.

The captain led the way along the carpet and then knocked twice on the jewel-encrusted door. He yanked Harl backwards as both doors hinged open and a small man stepped out. He was wrapped in a bright ruby robe and wore a golden-domed hat. Peering at them through delicate glasses, he made a tutting noise as he looked Harl up and down.

'You have one of them?' he asked the guard. His voice was like a reedy wood instrument, high and imperious. Somehow it managed to convey boredom and interest at the same time.

'Yes, master Lou,' the Caller said, shoving Harl forward a step.

'And the rest?' Lou asked, smiling as he surveyed Harl for a long time.

'We were unable to catch them, sir,' the guard said, swallowing and bowing his head in submission.

The thin framed Lou frowned and clenched his jaw before the smile reappeared.

'I'll send for my personal guards to collect him,' he said. 'Then he may be presented to the One. Guards!' he turned, and called back into an opulently furnished room.

Three beautiful and finely-armoured women marched forward at the small man's orders and snatched the equipment from Harl's captors, while another grabbed Harl by the shoulder and stood waiting for further orders.

'Take him to the top room of the dungeons,' Lou said to the leading woman. 'Leave his things here with me. I'd like to examine them before interrogation. Go.' He spoke the last word to the captain who had brought Harl.

The Captain and his men bowed and backed away, before turning to hurry off.

Lou turned to one of the female guards. 'See that that captain does not fail me ever again.' She nodded and crept off after them, a dagger appearing in her hand from up a sleeve.

Harl was led up a circular flight of stone steps that ended in a thick, wooded door. Beyond the door was a windowless room with four dirty, unoccupied cells, and he was thrown unceremoniously into one. The cobblestone room was split between two cells on either side of a walkway. The door stood on his left and ten paces away on the opposite side was a rack of torture implements covered in dried blood.

The guards left without a word and Harl stood alone in the silence. He found himself thinking of Sonora and their unborn child. He had promised to return to them, but looking at the damp, blood-streaked walls, he thought he might end up breaking that promise. He gripped the cell bars in both hands and pressed his head against the metal. He'd just wanted to help everyone inside the tanks and the shame of failing bit at him deeply. He had assumed humanity to be made up of good people willing to accept his help, but he should have known better. Corruption was everywhere. He'd seen it in his own world, in Sonora's; he'd even seen it in Delta. Why had he continued on blinkered by his misguided belief?

Footsteps rang on the stairs. The door flew open and a fat, shaven-headed man came in flanked by two of the female guards.

Lou stepped in behind, a twisted grin on his pinched face as he paced the length of the room. The fat man waddled over to the rack and unhooked a leather whip.

'Before I ask you any questions, Lou said, smiling pleasantly as he walked back to Harl's cell, 'I must make sure you understand who is in charge here. I will not be lied to or cheated.'

As if on cue, the fat man looked at Lou and, after a nod from his master, he produced a ring of keys from his rotting leather belt and quickly unlocked the cell. He reached in, grabbed a handful of Harl's jerkin and hauled him out. Without a word he spun Harl and kicked at the back of his legs, knocking him down.

Hot pain seared through Harl's back as the fat man lashed out with the whip. It ripped his shirt, scoring lines into his flesh. Another crack and he arched his back as the cord drew blood. The rope bit into his skin again and again, slicing deep into him as he tried to squirm and avoid the pain.

Harl screamed for mercy, not understanding why he was being punished. No questions had been asked and he knew in his heart they didn't expect an answer. There was no way to make it stop. He cowered under the relentless blows, telling them he would do anything for them, babbling, hoping to say the right thing. No one listened and he begged for mercy until, after what seemed an eternity, they left without a word. Only the torturer stayed to kick him back into the cell. The foul man eyed Harl's boots and chuckled. He nodded at them.

'Give me,' he said.

Harl was too weak to take them off, so the torturer lumbered into the cell to yank them off, then locked the iron bar door and hurried after Lou.

'Curse Cheng!' Harl said, forcing both hands out to clutch the bars, hoping to distract himself from the pain.

He had blacked out as soon as the fat torturer had left, but he didn't know how long for. When he came round, all he could feel was fire burning its way down his back from where the whip had cut deep into his flesh.

Was Cheng even the traitor's real name? Harl cursed him again, not quite believing it all. Betrayed for a bag of vegetables? Was that all he was worth?

It seemed obvious that humans were flawed. Maybe even as bad as the Aylen. Everywhere he turned there was greed or the expectation of power. Greed and power, he thought. It was the greed for power that drove his people towards evil.

A single torch mounted on the wall above the rack cast flickering light into Harl's cell. He turned from the cell door and let his eyes roam over the cell. He hoped he might find something useful, a way out, or even a crude weapon, but the floor was bare and the bars were solid. When the burning from the wounds on his back calmed, he curled up on the old, hard floor and slept.

He woke to the sound of footsteps beyond the bars and scrambled across the floor in panic until his back was against the cold wall. He'd not leave it exposed for another lashing.

A hooded man in tattered clothing passed a bowl through the bars into the cell, followed by another sloshing with water. The man's face was covered and, with the room so gloomy, Harl couldn't make out any features among the shadows. The man said nothing as he turned from the bars and walked out, closing the door behind him.

Harl moved to the bowls and sniffed at the sloppy brown substance inside the first one. He tilted it back like a drunk downing a beer, barely registering the taste of beef and vegetables. Well at least the food's not bad, he thought, finishing it off.

The day passed and nothing happened. Very little sound made it up to the top of the tower and, with no windows, there was nothing to see. Harl could think of nothing but the child within Sonora and his fading hope of rescue. Another beating or two like the last and he'd be dead in a day. He just wasn't used to such punishment.

Surely Damen and the others would come to get him. He strained to hear something other than the crackle of the torch, but there was no sign of a commotion through the wall or from down the stairs. It was just the silence and the faint drip of water.

Harl didn't know how many times he drifted into sleep. The pain in his back seemed to flare and drain all his strength away, leaving nothing but sleep's deep, dark embrace to comfort him. Finally, footsteps bounced up the stairs. When the door opened, he saw it was the hooded jailer bringing food again and, as he stepped in, he bowed and held the door for Lou.

Lou strode in.

'Leave,' he said and the jailer placed the bowls down and scurried out the door.

Harl stood up to face the man beyond the bars. Lou's glasses glinted in the flickering light and Harl watched the man's eyes as he took in the fresh blood streaks in the corner where Harl had slept. Lou's smirk became a toothy grin.

'I've read this book of yours and the absurd claims inside,' he said, producing a copy from inside his red robe and waving it. 'Although I believe it to be nonsense, there must be a grain of truth to it, for you are here, are you not?'

Harl did not know whether he should answer, so he stayed quiet and let the small man continue.

'How did you get here and what is your purpose?'

'You said you've read it,' Harl said. 'The answers are inside.'

Lou clenched his fists.

'This is nonsense,' he said, flicking through the pages. 'You are causing rebellion. The people are reading this and trouble is flaring among the slaves.'

'So what do you want me to do about it?' Harl asked. 'You've done it to yourselves. You cannot imprison people and expect no resistance.'

Lou nodded as if agreeing with Harl, then his face twitched and turned bright red in anger. 'Then people will die, until they resist no longer!' He threw the book at Harl and it rattled off the bars.

'The One will speak to you and, when he does, you will see how much innocent death you have caused. He will crush this rebellion before it has a chance to strike. At the end many will lie dead, and it will be because of you.' Lou kicked the bowls over and stormed out, slamming the door behind him.

Harl waited, taking heart from the words of rebellion, but the feeling of hope fled as footsteps pounded up the stairs and the door flew open. The fat man came first, flanked by the two female guards. Lou came in behind holding a whip. He stood in front of the cell door and smiled a nasty grin.

'Get him out,' Lou said.

Harl forced himself back against the wall as the fat man tugged the door open and stepped inside. Harl ducked as the man tried to grab him and managed to slip under the burly arms. He twisted, feeling the scabs on his back tear, and slammed a fist into the man's pudgy face.

The fat man roared as his nose dripped blood onto the hard stone floor. Harl felt satisfaction simmering away inside at inflicting injuries on the man who'd hurt him so much. He was about to throw himself at him again when the point of a blade rested on his neck. A hand turned him slowly around until he was stood, face to face, with one of the guards. The fat man stepped forward and cracked a meaty fist into Harl's face, knocking him over.

Lou, seeing the will to fight leave Harl, bore down on him. He stood above Harl and thrashed the whip down on him again and again. The hits were weaker than the last time, but this time they struck his face and head. He tried to cover the vulnerable areas with his arms and wished for blackness to take him.

After an age it mercifully did.

When he woke, the jailer was staring in at him and, before the figure came into proper focus, another two bowls slid under the bars. The jailer turned to leave.

'Is all of humanity so ruthless?' Harl asked himself aloud.

The jailer stopped, his hooded face turned away from Harl.

'Not all,' he said, 'and some need only to redeem themselves.'

He bent and picked up the book from the stone floor, then walked out the door, closing it softly behind him.

Chapter 65

When I enquired about using them in the military it was suggested that they could be utilised to fix machines from the inside during combat and unblocking weapon jams. Needless to say I have refused to sell them for that purpose. Although the prices offered were extremely tempting.

Harl lost all sense of day and night as time stretched and all he could think of was the pain. No matter how he sat or lay the agony of his wounds was there. It dogged his steps as he paced the cell during the day and engulfed him during darkness. He'd never known anything like it. It chipped away at his spirit until he dreaded footfalls on the stairs and ended up cringing in the corner whenever the jail door swung open.

It couldn't have been more than a cycle since the last meal when footsteps sounded on the stairs. His hopes for more food were dashed as the door opened and once more the two guards marched in followed by Lou. He didn't have the strength to resist if it was another beating. He didn't even know whether he could endure it again. Maybe he could throw himself on to one of the guards' blades?

The two women unlocked the cell and hauled him out on his knees, each holding an arm. He looked up at Lou's mocking smile.

'The One would like an audience with you,' Lou said.

The guards dragged him down the spiral stairs and then through a maze of corridors. His hands were tied and he could feel the prick of a sword point at his back, urging him on, until they reached a massive door guarded by two burly soldiers. Lou ordered the two men to open it and the sword forced him forward.

Lifting his head, Harl took in the opulent room. A red carpet split the room down the middle, separating rows of empty benches on the left from those to the right. The carpet ran the whole length of the room to where a set of steps led up onto a silver dais crowned by a rough wooden throne. It looked as if it had been carved by a child a long time ago. There was no artistry or skill to it, just the coarse shaping of someone with no experience.

A pale ghost of a man sat on the ancient wooden seat. He must have been only a few dozen giftings older than Harl and was wrapped in a white robe made from the pelts of some exotic animal. Harl could see veins running down the man's bald head to his colourless face and piercing red eyes. He sat upright, feet slightly apart, with his hands resting on either arm of the throne. His ruby gaze fixed on Harl.

There was something familiar about the pale man that reminded Harl of a litter of rats he and Troy had discovered in the barn when they were children. All except one had been dark furred. The loner looked as if it had been dipped in white paint and its eyes flecked with blood. Could it be a similar thing or was it completely unrelated?

618

Lou strode past Harl, wafting a floral scent past him. Lou bowed, and then walked up the dais steps and stood next to the One. He leant over to whisper in the One's ear before standing aside and smiling down at Harl.

The two men were in complete contrast. Lou's tanned skin colour bore no similarity to the ghostly translucence of the One. Even though he was young, The One looked like someone hovering on the edge of death.

Was the One from a different tank? Harl had been surprised by Oscar's dark skin, but Oscar was a picture of health. This man was the opposite. Could he have come from a world of eternal darkness?

A huge glowing sphere was wedged into the throne between the One's legs. It gleamed as though it was made of glass, but colours swirled and twisted inside it. One moment they were like molten gold tendrils licking at the glass, then tongues of red flame snapped and flickered angrily, before twisting and curling back into the depths, where they spun together into a glowing ball of light. It was mesmerising.

A guard slammed his sword pommel into the small of Harl's back. He stumbled forward until he was ten paces from the pale figure.

The floor and steps surrounding the throne were all made from polished metal. It extended out to the edge of the red carpet where Harl was standing, and he was careful not to step onto it. He'd lost his shoes during the torture and didn't like the idea of standing on the cold surface. Lou beckoned him forward but, in a moment of defiance, Harl stayed put, staring at the One.

'Water,' the One said. His voice was creaky and frail.

A servant scurried forward, head bowed, and held a delicate bowl up to the One's mouth for him to sip.

To his horror, Harl realised why the man looked uncomfortable. Both his feet and hands had been nailed to the throne and blood was seeping out around the golden nails. Blood stains marked the timber as if he'd been there for years, with the wood so deeply tainted that all previous attempts to clean around it had proved fruitless. Even as Harl looked at the horrid sight, a thin trickle of blood seeped from the One's foot, across the wood, and then dripped down on to the polished metal floor.

Dozens of servants lined the walls. They clasped a variety of items, towels, flagons of liquid and heavy smelling food. One of the attendants noticed the blood and rushed forward. He fell to his knees before the throne and pulled a silk cloth from a pocket to gently wipe the blood away.

The other servants looked wide-eyed at the man, one even attempted to pull him back, but missed and snapped to attention, eyes front, staring at nothing.

'During an audience?' Lou screamed at the servant on the metal floor in front of the throne, showering the cowering man with spittle.

Lou lurched forward, but stopped as the One shook his head and gazed down at the servant. His red eyes narrowed. Lou hurried to join the men at the side of the room and bowed his head as if in expectation.

'Die,' the One said.

The servant looked up at his master, horrified, then convulsions wracked his body and his eyes rolled up into his skull as he crumpled to the floor, twitching in agony.

The smell of burning hair hit Harl as he watched the man writhe, before one final shudder twisted his tortured form. He fell still and his eyes glazed over. He was dead.

The servants and guards standing around the room prostrated themselves on the floor. Others knelt or bowed in worship.

Now Harl knew why these people considered this One a demi god. How had he done it? All it had taken was a simple word and the servant had dropped dead. That kind of power was impossible and yet the One had managed it. The lifeless body on the floor was ample evidence.

The One waited for the body to be removed, then stared at Harl for a while before he spoke, taking in Harl's cuts and bruises with apparent relish.

'Do you know how I came to be on this throne?' he asked. The voice was frail, but it still sounded imperious and strict, like a general commanding his troops. Harl could feel the menace in it. 'I can see it bothers you, which I find amusing.

'This throne was carved by the god beyond the world, when that god was young. And the god deemed my family worthy, so he gifted the throne to us. But the gift came at a price, for our own ascension to godhood meant binding to the chair. As it was with my father before me, and his father before that, my body and soul are bound to this throne. We are connected. Nails pierce my flesh and I am one with the divine essence. Dark or light, waking or soaring through the dreams of my people, I am doomed to never leave this chair. But I see more, I become more than any other man alive.

'It is only right that my family honoured this gift by becoming part of it, for we have been chosen by the Divine. My food, my wine, the excretions of my body are things beyond me, for I am bound. I am tended by my loyal servants,' he said as he glanced at the body as it was dragged away from the throne, 'when they observe the proper formalities.'

What did the man mean when he said "when that god was young"? An Aylen child? Harl had never heard of anyone seeing one, but it proved, once again, that the giants were as mortal as any other living thing.

'How many generations have you had the chair?' Harl asked, wondering if he could glimpse the lifespan of the Aylen.

'Four.'

'Perhaps, your highness,' Lou said, trying to reel the topic back, 'we can find out more about the rebellion and the scum behind it.'

The One nodded but shot a warning look at Lou, who bowed his head.

'You and your friends have caused much trouble for me,' the One said. 'My people are whispering to each other that you have come to save them. This book you have spread is being hailed as a new future, but it is as a disease. You have already poisoned the minds of so many. They will have to be culled, of course: we cannot have them infecting others with the blasphemy of your words. My men are already searching for how you came to be here. What have you to say?'

622

Harl watched as they dragged the dead servant from the room. He tightened his fists until his fingernails bit deep into his flesh. No man should die like that. No one had the right to take a life without reason. Harl raised his head and stared at the One until the man blinked, but stayed silent. There was a strength to it that gave him new hope. To refuse to speak was about the only way he could be defiant.

'Speak, you impudent scum' Lou shouted.

Harl avoided the gaze of both men by staring at the glowing sphere set in the base of the throne. Metallic lines ran from the orb to the metal platform covering the floor. They reminded him of the cables Kane used to run electricity around the ship. The sphere was almost identical to the ones handed over to the Aylen in exchange for the humans. It was nowhere near as bright, though, but the patterns and colours were the same. His eyes were drawn deeper into the globe while he considered it.

He knew he'd seen something similar before, but it was only when he looked back at the lines that everything fell into place. Kane would have noticed it straight away.

The orb was a power source.

The One, or more likely his great-grandfather, had somehow tapped into the orb and fed electricity down into the metal plate using the cables. But how had The One electrocuted the servant with a single word? Harl wrestled the pieces of the puzzle around in his mind. The power was not on constantly so the One must have an on off switch. Then it dawned on him that there must be connectors on the chair, possibly under his hands, allowing the

One to connect and disconnect a basic circuit, turning it on and off.

Did anyone else know the truth? Perhaps Lou would. But the One would want to limit that knowledge. It was the source of his power over the people. Anyone who knew the truth posed a threat to the One and whatever twisted legacy he wanted to leave behind. What had he said earlier on? As it was with my father... Perhaps the knowledge only passed from father to son?

It gave Harl an advantage.

'What is the tradition when you are connected to the throne?' Harl asked.

Anger flashed across the One's ghostly face. Some of the servants whimpered.

'Your mind is plagued with questions,' the One said. 'You are here to answer for your crimes, not show the deficit of your intellect.' He laughed, coldly. 'But I will show mercy and answer your question. The son releases the father and the father fuses the son to the throne. It is a reverent moment that you cannot begin to fathom. That you would even ask shows how low you have fallen below the eyes of the gods. Enough,' he said. 'Extract the answers from him.'

Lou thrust a finger at him. 'Where did you come from? Who sent you? What is your purpose here? Answer or you'll die as well!'

Harl sighed.

'These people are slaves,' he said, waving a hand at the servants and guards. 'They should be free.' He stared into the red eyes knowing that his words would mean death. The One was powerless against him provided he stayed away from the metal part of the floor. It still left the others though. Lou would kill him if this pretend god-king ordered it, the same with the guards around the walls of the room. Harl didn't quite know what the servants would do. Were they in such terrified thrall of this beast that they would kill another? He didn't want to test the theory.

'You've no right to enslave and kill these people. I came here to free them, but if I die, others will complete my work. There's nothing you can do to stop it.'

'There is something I can do,' the One said whipping his head sideways at the nearest guard. 'Kill him. Take him outside and make it visible to all who dare oppose me.'

A guard marched to Harl's side and grabbed his shoulder.

'If you're so powerful' Harl yelled, 'then why haven't you killed me as you did your servant?' He glanced meaningfully down at the metal plate and shuffled forward so his feet were almost touching the metal. He stared at those around the chamber.

'Your god-king is a fraud,' he said.

The servants bowed their heads or turned away from him, avoiding being tainted as he looked around. Then he spotted the hooded jailer standing at the edge of the room. He had edged to the front and was holding his black cloak to one side. A flash of silver revealed Harl's pistol and sword concealed beneath the dark material.

The jailer nodded and held five fingers at his side. The One was paying no attention to the people around the room as he issued orders to the guard. A second guard stepped up to Harl's other side as the jailer tucked a finger in to his palm, followed by a second, then third.

It was a countdown.

Chapter 66

I have brokered a deal to sell the remains of the vehicles and machinery I found alongside them. I no longer need to worry about funding.

Harl's mind raced ahead as he watched the jailer. No one else seemed to have noticed what was happening. The jailer nodded one more time and then tucked the last finger into his closed fist.

Harl interlocked his fingers and spun around, landing a doubled-handed blow to the side of the nearest guard's face. The guard's eyes rolled up into his head and he slumped to the ground. Harl kicked the other guard in the chest, forcing him backwards, and then charged towards the jailer with his hands out, pulling the rope tight between his wrists.

'Kill him!' Lou screamed.

'Not the sword!' Harl cried.

The jailer tugged out the pistol and threw the weapon to him. Harl just caught it in one hand as the jailer pulled the blade free and stepped forward to slice down between Harl's hands, severing the cord.

Harl swung around to face the room. The guard he'd kicked was sprinting towards him, sword swinging mid-slice. Harl raised the pistol and fired. The wave of blue light incinerated the man in a blast that made the hairs on the back of Harl's neck rise. Guards all around the room rushed them. Harl spun and fired, killing three more before two others closed in on him. He levelled the pistol at them and they froze, their eyes fixed on the weapon.

Twitching the pistol, he ordered them to put their swords down. Transfixed on the gun, they lowered their weapons to the ground. The hooded jailer slipped around Harl and kicked the swords aside, then held the melting-blade up at neck height ready.

Harl turned to the One and Lou. Both their mouths hung open in astonishment. It was obvious that Lou had meant to run, but awe had held him.

'What is this power?' the One asked.

Harl ignored the question.

'You will free these people,' Harl said, holding the weapon level with the One's head as he prowled along the edge of the metal flooring. 'Then you will step down as ruler. Your hold on them is broken.'

Lou was shaking with fear, his eyes flicking from Harl to the end of the pistol, but the One stared without fear. He seemed more curious than scared, and clearly believed either Harl would not or could not hurt him.

'I will free no one,' the One said, his voice full of authority. 'You cannot overcome me. You are a mortal; I am a god.'

'Your power is false,' Harl said. 'You can only kill those who step on the metal and even that is not your own power. It is the power locked inside that orb in your chair.' Harl turned to the few servants who hadn't fled in terror. 'Do you think this man is your god? Has he struck me down for blasphemy? Has his godly might reached out to smite me even as I killed his loyal men? No. He is powerless against me. I could shoot him from here and he would die. His strength is a lie. Even now he sits there, pitiful and wretched in the face of my words. Look at the face of this, "Your God". He is nothing but a man. He is nothing but a fool.'

'Kill him!' the One screamed, a red hatred flooding his pale features.

Soldiers charged from the far sides of the room. Harl spun to face them.

'Look out!' the jailer shouted.

Harl twisted as Lou leapt on top of him, dagger in hand. Harl dug the end of the pistol into Lou's chest as they fell to the floor and fired point-blank. The blast threw Lou off him, practically incinerating the thin man in a rain of ash and blood.

Swords rang out behind him. Harl scrambled to his feet then twisted around. The jailer was on the floor as the soldiers above plunged blades down into him. Harl stepped forward and fired at those standing over the jailer, killing both before he reached the dying man. The jailer moaned within the pool of his spreading blood.

Harl knelt over the man and eased his hood back. It took him a moment to realise that he knew the face of his saviour. It was the man who had betrayed him for a bag of food.

'Cheng?' he said, looking into the man's eyes as the light started to leave them.

'I'm sorry,' Cheng choked, blood running from his mouth.

629

'It is forgiven,' Harl said, placing a hand over Cheng's heart. 'You've saved me and redeemed yourself. We all make mistakes.'

The light was leaving Cheng's eyes as he stared blankly up at Harl.

'Free them,' he said, his voice fading as his eyes went still.

Cries and footsteps came from somewhere far off. Running, screaming, a wave of it was rushing closer and closer. But all he could focus on was Cheng. His death was a last desperate act in a tragic life and the One was to blame. But Harl had to shoulder some of that blame as well. Cheng would still be alive if they had never met. That guilt would fester away inside him as yet another burden. It had to have meaning though.

Harl rose and turned away from Cheng's broken form. A group of guards surged into the room intent on protecting the One. But a cold fury exploded inside Harl. He snatched his weapons from the floor and roared. Light scorched from the end of the pistol as he fired, dropping the guards one by one before they could close the gap. He tightened his grip on the sword and turned from their smoking bodies to face the throne.

The One's face was a mask of fear now that his subjects lay dead around the room, their killer stalking towards him.

Harl held the sword out as he advanced towards the wooden throne, stepping onto the metal floor and then walking across it to The One. The ghostly man squirmed against the chair, held fast by the nails as blood seeped from each wound, then his red eyes flicked to the metallic floor and he smirked. But Harl was too quick. He raised the sword and sliced it down to sever the cables leading from the side of the chair to the polished surface. The One twisted his hand towards some kind of hidden switch built in to the arms, but nothing happened. The smirk turned to a snarl as his eyes locked on to the humming sword as it inched towards his chest.

'How long can you last without your servants to tend your wounds?' Harl asked. 'With no one to administer treatment I would say seven, maybe ten days. Without water, three days?'

'The gods will come for me,' the One said straining against the nails. 'My men will come once you are dead.'

'No one will come,' Harl said 'because no one wants to be ruled over. If you want to live you will have to stand up and leave your throne, but I don't think you can. It's been too long.'

He turned for the door, leaving the rotten king to decompose.

Chapter 67

Could genetic change be possible? We breed other species by artificial selection to gain the best genetics, so why not this one? Can they be made to breathe our atmosphere?

Harl padded through the tower corridors searching for a way out. Panic reigned around him, with servants scurrying around in fear and guards running past, clanking under the heavy load of their weapons. No one seemed to pay him any mind.

He had no idea how he was going to escape from the city. His pistol would run out of ammo long before he reached safety and he was not a good enough swordsman to battle his way through. And he had no idea what he might find out there. Even if he managed to fight his way through the city, would things be any better down in the farmland? What if all of his friends were dead or captured?

He forced the thoughts aside and ploughed on. Running out from the tower, he found the streets were in chaos. Slaves yelled and dropped their burdens as they fled to their homes. The guards had abandoned their posts next to the tower, but some ran past toward the top of the ramp at the city entrance, shouting at the slaves to move out of the way. It was the first sign of meaning in all of the chaos, but Harl didn't know what to do. Should he follow them and risk a fight or would it be better to find a safe place to wait it all out?

Flinching back against the nearest wall, he tried to make a decision, then a familiar sound soared overhead as a streak of blue light shot over the top of the nearest parapet. Grinning, Harl dashed between two towers and rushed up a set of stone stairs to the ramparts that overlooked the farmland below. He could make out figures scattered across the fields firing rifles as they headed towards the ramp. Damen was at their head and Harl watched as the group of around forty men fought their way to the base of the ramp. Callers dropped their weapons in surrender and stepped aside as Damen led his team up.

Running down the stairs from the rampart, Harl made for the ramp. When he arrived he found Damen ordering men into a defensive position under the great stone archway. A few bodies lay scattered in the street, but there was no more resistance.

'It's Harl!' Zane cried as he spotted Harl running across the smoking battlefield.

Damen stepped out of the circle of men and grinned.

'We thought we'd be avenging your death,' he said looking at Harl's blood-streaked jerkin. 'What happened to you?'

'A disagreement with the leader of these people,' Harl said. 'He's no longer a problem.'

'Good,' Damen said 'And what of the traitor?'

'He is dead,' Harl said feeling the guilt come back to his stomach.

'You got him as well?' Damen asked.

'No. In the end he gave his life for mine. He should be remembered as a hero.'

Harl looked at the smoke rising over the fields below them. Some of the smaller buildings had been set on fire where Callers had used them as defensive positions. More bodies were scattered across the land. Slaves and Callers alike. So many dead. He felt sick. He drew a breath and turned back to Damen.

'What's next? You seem to have overwhelmed the guards.'

'It was easy enough when we started shooting,' Damen said. 'Most of the slaves helped us, but some fled in terror. It took a while for Oscar's men to arrive, but they're below now securing the farms and rooting out survivors. We were planning on attacking the main tower as we assumed you'd be there, or at least this leader of theirs would be.'

'For the time being we'll take up a position down in the fields,' Harl said. 'Order the men to regroup and then set about distributing food to the slaves. They're free now, but will need time to recover and adjust to being their own masters if they're to join us when we leave for Delta.'

'Will do,' Damen said. 'I'll have the houses and towers searched one by one. The last thing we need is some crazed Caller getting the jump on one of our men.'

'Leave the main tower,' Harl said, 'Put a guard on it until we leave. No one is to enter unless I say so.'

Damen frowned at the instruction, obviously curious, but then nodded and started giving out orders.

They discovered huge warehouses stuffed with food and provisions, and, as per Harl's orders, Damen set up a street wide kitchen and gave the underfed and malnourished crowd a feast beyond their wildest imaginings. Kane found a large quantity of petroleum amongst the supplies and ordered it sent back to Oscars' people in case Harl's land had run dry.

Anger bubbled up inside Harl as he paced the battlements of the white wall.'Like I said before,' he said. 'We're not leaving people behind.' He leant through a crenelation and stared down at the farmlands below as the wind blew through his hair.

'Then perhaps I can return with the shipment?' Kane said moving to the crenel next to Harl's and staring down at the fuel shipment as it was carried across the fields towards the hole. 'I can load it into the ship and be prepared for when you come back.'

'No,' Harl said, 'It's not part of the plan.' As much as he trusted Kane he didn't trust him to not attempt something foolish where the vessel was concerned. 'We go on until my old land and only then do we turn back.'

'And what about the tanks above and below us?' Kane asked. 'Will you leave them behind?'

The anger in Harl boiled over. 'At least I'm not trying to abandon people every chance I get, Kane.'

Kane's glasses steamed up as he turned red from frustration.

'The longer we wait,' he said, 'the less chance we have of ever leaving this forsaken place. These tanks are filled with death, Harl and I do not want to end up trapped inside like some caged animal to be squashed whenever an Aylen chooses.'

Harl put a hand on Kane's shoulder 'Then help me to free those who have lived like that for generations, so they suffer no longer.'

Kane sighed and turned to look out over the land. 'For so long I have been wanting to fly away from my own life that I have not stopped to think of those who are unable to jump on a ship and get away.' He plucked his glasses off his nose and rubbed the lenses on his stained white coat. 'Very well, go on if you will, but when you reach your land, head to the quarry you spoke of and cut a hole to the tank below. You can drop books and one of the melting lances. Perhaps that will give them a chance to free themselves and those in neighbouring tanks. I'll stay here, as we planned and prepare everyone for the journey out.'

Harl slapped him on the back.

'Knew you'd come around,' he said and headed down from the wall to the streets of the city.

The cobblestone roads were in a constant bustle, not muted as before but full of excitement and energy. People would thank him in passing, pointing him out to others as the saviour of the people. Laughter and the constant chatter of voices filled the air. Almost all the slaves had belongings waiting by doors in expectation of leaving. Some even shouldered their burdens and began following Harl wherever he went, afraid that they might get left behind. Oscar's booming laugh would explode whenever this happened. He would smile, wrap his arms around the strangers, and steer them away.

'None will be left behind,' he would say. 'You're free now. Have no fear.'

They reached the barrier shortly after Kane's farewell and the lancers set about cutting a hole once more. Harl knew that they had to be nearing Sonora's old tank and he expected to find an empty tank, similar to the one after Oscar's sand world. He and Sonora had watched the Aylen scoop out the contents and then carry it away to be discarded between the Aylen shop and Delta, but he wasn't prepared for what they found.

Once through the hole in the barrier, it was almost as if the destruction of Sonora's world hadn't happened. Had he miscalculated and there were still more tanks to go before they reached Sonora's? It took him a moment to see that the ground was not fully covered with established grass and foliage. New shoots coated the soil and hundreds of trees had been placed where forests had once stood.

'I thought you said it'd be empty?' Damen said, plucking a small sprig of fresh grass from the ground to inspect.

'I assumed it would be, unless this isn't Sonora's home,' Harl said. 'It must have been replanted and set as new for more people to inhabit.'

'Where do they get the plants from?' Oscar asked.

Harl thought about it but no answer came to mind.

'I don't know,' he said, though the thought nagged at him. How were the Aylens able to get the supplies on a micro scale? To them the grass seed must be minute, like a powder, and the seeds for trees were not easy to grow even for those small enough to pick and plant them. Perhaps they scavenged from other tanks, a few trees here and there?

As they reached the middle of the tank, the memories hit Harl and he stopped. Life had been a dream in Sonora's world, perfect days with the woman he loved. If he could have it back, would he? He didn't know. So much had happened since then. His world had changed and he'd had to change along with it. But now standing in this tank he didn't know what to think. Was it the same place? The difference was overwhelming.

The town had been in the centre of the valley. He turned around and looked at the bare expanse of ground surrounding him. There was nothing here. No sign of the buildings. No sign of foundations and pathways leading from the villages to the outlying homes. He closed his eyes and pictured the scene. The main gate had faced the sight and as you walked out under its archway, Sonora's hill rose in the distance to the left. When he opened his eyes, there was no sign of the hill. Everything had just been wiped away.

He clenched his fists and shuddered. There was nothing left here. It was barren. The only part left was Sonora and she was so far away from him.

'Let's hurry,' he said to Damen. 'This place fills me with dread.'

'Down!' Damen cried as an Aylen strode into the sight and began peering in at the growing landscape. Its yellow eyes scanned the fields and bore down on them.

They all dropped. From their position, some small trees blocked the view to the sight. But it might not have been enough. The Aylen might still have seen them. Harl risked a glance at the enormous face as it scanned the inside. The Aylen let its eyes rove over the infant landscape and then lumbered off after what must have been a cursory check on the tanks' growing progress.

'We need to cross fast,' Harl said to the group. 'If the Aylen checks the other tanks thoroughly it will know that things are changing.'

'Kane will keep everything looking normal,' Damen said.

'If not, we're all done for,' Drew said, tightening the straps on his armour.

The land rose, meeting the black barrier that had separated Harl's first home from the one Sonora had been in. His coming had changed both their lives, ending up with this adventure to free hundreds of slaves and power a flying vessel. The oddity of it, strangely, did not shock him. He'd come to accept that vast creatures ruled their lives and that they could fly away. It could have all been a child's dream if it were not so real. He thought of the child inside Sonora, would it live life as a human should, free from slavery, with Sonora and himself to guide it?

He didn't know, but it was a dream worth chasing.

A cry from one of the lancers caught his attention and he looked up to find that they were through.

The next tank would be his own.

Chapter 68

The more I study them and create a world around them, the more I see how clever they really are. It's more than just independent intelligence; I can see signs of their society and traditions.

Harl found himself getting more and more nervous as the lancers got to work. Even after living on the other side of this barrier for most of his life, he had no idea how the people beyond would take his return.

The lance team seemed to take an age to cut the barrier and, when the free section was pushed loose, the smell of his homeworld sent a wave of nostalgia jolting through him. The scents of his childhood wrapped around him, Troy's farm, the forests, Gifting Square; he even caught a hint of Harkins on the air. He wouldn't have guessed there was a particular smell to a world, but he knew it immediately. He didn't even need to look through the hole to let the others know that they'd arrived.

Harl clambered through first. He stepped down onto an overgrown field full of ripe, golden corn. There was no one in sight. He waited as Damen led the other men through. He took his bearings quickly and knew that if they headed Sightwards, keeping close to the barrier, they would walk straight to his old home.

He doubted the old house would be empty, but it seemed his best chance at finding somewhere they could stay for the duration. Treading through the corn he spotted a small collection of houses next to where he had once lived. Three more buildings had been erected beside his own, creating a small grouping of thatched timber buildings. People sat on benches around the new houses, while a gaggle of children raced around, sword fighting with sticks.

He looked up at the Sight beyond them and again nostalgia filled him. For so long, that had been his view. All the other walls had offered nothing but the same black mask and yet the Sight had hinted at the great beyond. It was unchanging, eternal, and the only hint of life beyond his own walls had been the Aylen as they walked by or stopped to peruse life inside the tanks.

Harl's focus snapped back to the field as some of his men walked past.

'Wait here and keep low,' he said.

The soldiers crouched down in the field as Harl moved towards the rear of the houses and then headed right to where his old home stood apart from the other buildings. At least twenty grazing cows wandered around the fenced paddock, which meant the new owners were far more wealthy than he had ever been.

A pretty woman with shoulder length hair walked into view around one of the houses and started throwing seed out to the chickens. She spotted him and stopped, cradling a baby in one arm as she stared across the paddock at him. He made a beeline for her and, as he got closer, he recognized the woman immediately.

'Emily?' he said.

The dark-haired woman gave out a small cry when she recognised him. Some of the children ran into sight around one of the buildings, laughing as they carried on their swordplay.

'H-Harl?' she stammered.

'Yes, Emily,' he said. 'It's me. Please don't be afraid.'

'I'm not,' she said, although she took an involuntary step backwards. 'Where have you been? And how did you get here? Troy swore you were alive. He stormed into one of Eldermen meetings just after you were lifted and caused quite a stir with his claims.'

'Did they believe him?' Harl asked.

'Of course,' Emily said. 'He felt more responsible than anyone else for your death and no one doubted him.'

Harl felt bad that Troy had somehow known about him being alive but hadn't been able to do anything about it.

'How is he?' Harl asked.

'After you left he began drinking more at the Golden Spear,' Emily said. 'But the last I saw him he was well and back to his usual self.'

'Emily,' Harl said. 'There's a reason I'm back. I've been through so much that I can hardly believe it myself, but I've come back with a mission to accomplish.'

'Go on,' she encouraged.

'Can we stay at your place for a while? When we have a place to stay I'll explain everything.'

She looked at his old house.

'I live here,' she said, 'But who is we?' She glanced around for the others, but the men were too low in the field for her to see.

'About fifteen of us,' he said, not wanting to overwhelm her but left with little choice.

'Fifteen!' she said, causing some of the nearby children to stop as they ran past.

'Go on with you,' she chided and the three children dashed off.

'We can feed ourselves,' Harl said. 'We just need a place to stay for a few cycles.' He pointed to the field. 'They're over there. They may seem strange to your eyes, but if you put us up for the night, at least, we can tell you our story.'

'Night?' Emily asked.

'Until the next cycle,' Harl said. 'Then we'll go to the Eldermen and explain the same to them.'

'And what about Troy?' Emily asked.

Harl was nervous about seeing Troy again. It played on his mind that so much had changed for him and yet Troy's life had carried on the same. Well, he thought, that wouldn't be the case for much longer.

'I'd like to see him again,' Harl said. 'But I don't know whether to go to him or send a message first. The last thing I want to happen is for him to think he has seen my ghost and go back to the drink to cure it.'

Emily smiled and looked thoughtful. 'I can get a message to him if you want. One of the little ones can go.'

'If you'd do that, I'd appreciate it. Erm...' He looked at the house. 'Is there a man? I don't want him to come home to find his living room full of strangers.'

Emily looked forlorn and stared at the baby in her arms.

'Lifted,' she said. 'Two giftings ago.'

'I'm so sorry, Emily,' he said, reaching out to touch her. 'We have come to put an end to the liftings.'

She looked up. 'Truly?'

He nodded and waved a hand to beckon Damen and the men to join them. Emily stared in shock as the group of men stood up from the corn and trudged across to them.

'Emily, I'd like you to meet Damen, Drew and Oscar,' he said, pointing to each in turn. She lingered for a long time on Oscar, obviously startled to see someone with a different skin colour and a tattooed head, but she straightened and smiled.

'Pleasure,' she said eventually, her gaze shifting to Drew and lingering until he broke eye contact. 'You're all welcome to stay with me. Although you will have to feed yourselves.' She looked at Oscar's large frame and Harl could tell that she was wondering how much he would eat in a sitting.

Emily led them inside the cottage and while she was settling the group, Harl took a moment to walk outside to the bench and grove of trees he'd cultivated. It was still the same, with the exception of a few more weeds and a lack of wax on the bench. He sat on the bench and breathed in the scent of the climbing roses he'd planted so long ago at the base of the trees.

The Sight in front of him was the same and he suddenly felt like he had wasted so much time inside this prison without even knowing it.

He glanced at the trees beside him. Someone must be tending it, he thought, spotting the pruned stems. His thoughts wandered from his childhood and loosing his parents, to the baby still growing inside Sonora. He couldn't tell how the child would grow up. Would it be in a time of constant flux, or even war? For a fleeting moment he considered letting the child grow up inside the tank. It was a perfect playground, safe and plentiful compared to the world outside, but it was still slavery and he couldn't go back to that.

The choices that lay ahead of him now were complete unknowns. What would happen after they left this slave shop? He knew there was little hope for his people if they stayed in Delta. It was only a matter of time before either another swarm of hivers attacked or the Aylen found them again. He'd set in motion a series of events that would inevitably end up with them leaving Delta and heading out into the unknown to start a new life somewhere. It was a terrifying gamble.

Only if the ship actually works, he thought.

He trusted Kane immensely, of course. There was no one better at tinkering with things, but it worried him nonetheless. He could leave half the people behind in case the ship failed mid-launch or blew up, then at least there'd be someone to carry on, but in reality it had been everything or nothing ever since he left the tank. All he could do was keep fighting.

A voice came from behind him, snapping his thoughts away from the future.

'I've been tending this place ever since you faked you own death.' It was Troy's voice and Harl spun to see his old friend standing behind him with a huge smile on his face.

'It is you, isn't it?' Troy asked when Harl didn't speak.

'Of course it is, my friend,' Harl said, standing and embracing him.

'Where in the Sight have you been?' Troy exclaimed, standing back to view him. 'I saw you move when you were lifted and now Emily's boy comes telling me you've returned. There's not been a god's hand in sight and yet here you are sitting on your bench as though you never left. The boy said you'd sprouted up in a field behind your old house, but I'm a professional farmer and I know better than that.'

'Professional?' Harl said and chuckled as Troy broke into laughter.

'You look like you haven't had a bath since you left,' Troy said, 'and your clothes...' He pinched Harl's shirt between his thumb and finger and rubbed the material between them.

'I think "where in the Sight have I been" is the perfect question,' Harl said, sitting back down on the bench. 'I've seen more than we could've imagined, Troy. Sit down and I'll tell as much as I can before we head to Emily's and get some food.'

'She's a terrible cook,' Troy said.

'I know,' Harl said. 'Thankfully, she's not cooking.'

Harl took him through the events since his "death" leading to meeting Emily behind his old house.

647

After breaking out into laughter at the tale Troy suddenly turned pale. 'You're serious?'

Harl nodded.

'Bloody crazy,' Troy said. 'But looking at you, somehow I can believe it.'

'Come on' Harl said, standing. 'Better get you back and make introductions.'

'To the golden-haired beauty?' Troy said and started to straighten his top.

'She didn't come,' he said, 'but there are others.'

'Other golden-haired beauties? Does she have a sister?'

Harl shook his head and laughed as they headed back to the house.

Chapter 69

I guess age catches all of us sooner or later. If only I had discovered them sooner, I could really understand them, even communicate.

Fire blossomed under the chimney. The flames were licking the sides of one of Emily's biggest pots., casting a delicious smell of stew up into the air. Emily and the men had been throwing in food from their own packs in anticipation of the feast to come. Drew stood over the pot, stirring it gently, and proved to be a skilled cook when Harl tested the mixture.

Troy had taken well to all the men. He was fascinated with their weapons when they explained that one shot could kill from a distance. Like the others who had encountered him, Troy was taken aback by Oscar when the huge man stood to introduce himself.

'I could use a strong hand on the farm,' Troy had said, giving Oscar's bicep a light squeeze. 'If you need a job...'

'Troy?' Harl said.

'A jest!' Troy said, quickly throwing his hands up. 'Just a jest.'

Oscar seemed amused by Troy's antics.

'How about a drink?' Troy asked, 'I'll have one of the lads bring a cask over from the farm. I'll pay him well for the delivery seeing as credits will be useless in a few days.'

Oscar had not drunk ale before and, in no time, he was singing its praises as food was slopped into bowls. Troy and Harl stayed up long in to the dark cycle staring out into the blackness of the Sight and talking of what had happened in his absence and what was to come.

'Rufus has been pushing things,' Troy said, swigging at a mug of ale.

'He's not rotted from the inside out yet?'

Troy chuckled then his voice turned sour. 'Two of the Eldermen died suddenly before the last gifting. Both were against Rufus's latest vision of building his sculpture.'

'Sculpture?'

'Of the One True God. To appease the almighty. Think he was hoping to get a bigger gift and to take a portion as a reward.'

Harl shook his head. 'Mad,' he said and stood up. Even having been outside the tanks for so long, he could almost tell when the light would switch on, so he headed for bed, knowing the day to come would be a long one.

Harl woke to find Damen sharpening his sword, while Oscar rubbed his sore head, classing ale as a terrible drink, one that places a foggy curse in the mind after sleep.

His first orders were to send a man back through the tanks to find Uman and have him prepare to receive a lot of people on their return. A message was also relayed to Oscar's people instructing them to build extra tents around the large hut in their sandy tank. It would be the only stopping point where they could stock up on supplies before finally exiting the tanks. Drew led a small group to the quarry to cut down into the tank below and drop a book and one of the melting lances through.

Harl imagined Drew meeting Queeg, the brutish whip master of the quarries. It would be an interesting encounter. He could picture Drew putting Queeg in his place as he forced his way into the quarry. Whether Queeg would survive the encounter was difficult to judge.

Harl thought it best if only he, Troy, Damen, and Oscar met the Eldermen, to avoid anyone misinterpreting it as a show of force.

Dozens of townsfolk ran ahead of the four of them as they walked to the meeting hall. There was no doubt the Eldermen were expecting him. People he knew greeted them with questions and he had repeated the words "I'm back to free you all" about twenty times before they reached the Elder chambers.

Two guards stood in front of the ornate entranceway and Rufus walked out from the door behind them as soon as Harl arrived. The thin, hawk-faced man stopped and sneered at them as they approached.

'What's this all about?' Rufus said.

Hearing his voice, the guards snapped to attention and stepped to the side. Rufus strolled out between them and raised his hand. The guards saluted and then lowered their hands to rest on their sword hilts.

'Rufus,' Harl said keeping a pleasant smile on his face in the hope to pacify the man's constant scorn.

'You?' Rufus said. He frowned and his eyes narrowed. 'It seems even the gods reject you, Eriksson.'

The guards tightened their grip on their weapons as Damen and Oscar filed in either side of him.

'I'm here to speak to the council of Eldermen,' Harl said. 'It is urgent.'

'An Elderman is already before you,' Rufus said, laying a hand on his own chest. 'State your business and I will consider its import.'

'You don't represent the council, Rufus.' Troy said. 'Move aside.'

It was the wrong thing to say. Harl could have sworn Rufus growled in his throat. The guards noticed it too and stepped forward, half-drawing their swords.

'Things have changed since you left,' Rufus said.

Harl sighed. If Rufus was in charge then they'd get nowhere.

Troy laughed.

'If things had changed that much,' Troy said, 'then I'd have died and left, the same as Harl.'

Rufus, clearly not used to such outright insults grew red in the face.

'I'm still an Elderman,' he screamed. 'Take them!'

The guards stepped forward to arrest them, but Harl was thrust aside as Oscar roared past, grabbed the nearest guard and hauled him off the ground with one-hand. He pinned the guard against the door and snarled as the man's feet kicked the air.

At the same time, Damen lunged passed Troy and seized the other guard, choking off any protest by pressing his forearm against the man's throat and pinning him to the wall.

Perhaps Rufus had been too distracted by Harl's reappearance to notice the two alien men, but his eyes shot wide open as they wrestled his protectors into submission and then turned to him, grinning like savages.

Rufus took a step back, throwing his hands up in surrender.

'As you can see,' Harl said, stepping right in front of Rufus, 'I too have changed.' He thrust a hand out to grab the man's white robes and pulled the wretched face closer. 'I've seen more than you know, Rufus. I have fought battles and ridden on the heels of God. I've killed kings and monsters, vermin and filth, and crushed petty little men who think nothing of others. Men just like you.' He shook Rufus with each word then released him.

Rufus staggered back, his hands shaking.

'I will speak to the council, Rufus,' Harl went on, 'and, as an Elderman, you are entitled to join us, but push me and I'll have you kicked out into the dirt.' He looked at Oscar and Damen and they released the guards. Oscar even patted his man down, as if to clean him of dust.

Rufus spun on his heels and raced ahead into the building.

'Are they all like that?' Oscar asked.

'No,' Troy said. 'Just Rufus. I don't think anyone likes him. He probably even hates himself.'

Harl laughed and then walked inside, but his amusement crumbled away. It was time to tell his story. He just hoped they believed him.

The council room was large with thick wooden beams running along the roof. Three sides of the room had tiered benches that all faced the raised platform at the back. A semicircular table on the dais at the back of the empty hall seated the nine Eldermen, and Rufus had taken a place that was closer to the centre of the table than Harl remembered. The nine looked dishevelled, as if summoned in haste.

Arlet, the wizened Elderman in the centre of the half circle, stood up to address the four of them and to possibly get a better view of the man who had come back from the dead.

He glanced from Harl to Oscar and then Damen in a moment of silence. When he'd apparently satisfied his curiosity, he spoke in a raspy but confident voice.

'Harl Eriksson,' he said, almost a question. 'Where have you been since you were lifted almost six giftings past? How have you returned?' He took his seat again, waving a hand for Harl to begin.

'This will be a long story, Elderman Arlet,' Harl said. 'There's much to relate and it'll take some faith and time to believe what I have to say.'

Rufus stood up to interrupt him.

'Faith,' he said, 'is for the gods.'

This is going to be difficult, Harl thought as he cleared his throat.

'Rufus,' he said, staring the man down, 'you will be the least likely to believe what I have to say, and so I ask you to refrain from interrupting me until I have finished. As you have seen, I have living proof.' He looked at Oscar and Damen pointedly.

Rufus grunted as he sat back down. Harl lifted his gaze from Rufus and focused on the others at the table. 'I'll start my story from when I was lifted after the mining accident.'

He retold the tale that would seem as unbelievable to these men as it would have to him if he'd never left the tank. All throughout, the Eldermen struggled to contain their astonishment and outcries. Harl knew that the idea of their gods being nothing of the kind outraged them the most. He was throwing away all their lifelong beliefs and attempting to replace them with the truth about the outside world.

They could not dispute what he was saying as the evidence had walked in with him. The fact that Oscar and Damen were with him and had never been seen before immediately proved most of their beliefs wrong, and they could not disregard his words without looking foolish.

There was stunned silence when Harl had finished. He knew that it was his chance to convince them once and for all.

'The people of this land have been getting less in number each and every gifting. There are too many being lifted; eventually there will be no one left. Would a benevolent god let his people die out?' He let the words sink in. 'But things do not have to continue like this. There is new hope for our people. I won't deny that it will be dangerous on the path ahead. We're stronger now than ever before and, by the time we get back through the tanks to Delta, we will number close to a thousand, more than enough to live comfortably.' He looked at each of them in turn. There was doubt there but also something else, perhaps a craving to explore the possibilities now open to them.

Rufus was the first to react and, by the look on his pinched face, Harl knew it was not going to be acceptance.

'This is ridiculous,' he said jumping up and pointing an accusing finger down at them. 'You want us to believe this wild story about cities, flying creatures, and some form of giant self-propelled cart to take us away.' He paused, breathing heavy. 'The gods will strike you down for this-'

He was interrupted as Arlet stood up and cut in.

'Sit back down Rufus,' he said and waited patiently until his orders had been followed before turning back to Harl.

'Harl,' he said, 'as much as my mind wants to tell me otherwise, I believe you. But if we're to uproot and leave then we will face many problems. Who will lead this group? Once we've integrated with each of these other lands, and those beyond, we will not be in charge any more. As you said, these other tanks have leaders like this Oscar,' he said, indicating the big man.

Oscar spoke up at this, 'I will have Harl lead my people.' His rhythmic voice carried easily to the men above. 'He has brought us this far without trouble.'

Harl was touched by the man's words. He hadn't known that Oscar held such a high opinion of him.

'The people of Delta trust him, and so do I,' Damen pitched in.

Harl had nothing to say except to mutter a 'thanks' and turn to the Eldermen again.

'It is not a matter of leadership,' he said. 'I take no appointment unless it's agreed by all, and I will step down to any who'd be willing and accepted in my place. We don't need to debate these small matters. Much more is at stake here than leadership. The Aylen have kept us long enough and we either need to fight or flee from them. Assuming we choose to leave, the ship might take us somewhere else without these giants. We should go while we still have the knowledge to plant crops, taking our seeds and livestock with us. Whatever happens, survival is key and, to do that, we need to unite together and make a life worth living. A life without oppression and reliance on so-called gifts.'

Feeling that he had said all that he could, he knew that it was now up to the Eldermen to decide if they would let go their hold on power and follow him. If they did not, then it'd be up to the people to decide individually if they would return with him.

'This window of opportunity to escape will not be open long,' he said.

The Eldermen argued among themselves, but eventually broke apart. Apparently a decision had been made. Arlet stood to speak.

'Harl Eriksson,' he said. 'We do not understand much of what you tell us of this outside, but you speak truth when you say that we're dwindling as a people. We'll follow your lead beyond the barriers. You understand that we're giving up our leadership to you, at least as far as this journey is concerned, but if the people want us to continue to lead, we will. You may spread copies of this book among the people after we have addressed them all and told them of our decision. We'll require at least three cycles as we prepare to leave, and we must think of the elderly and the children. This will be an arduous journey for them. Food will need to be stockpiled and possessions limited to what can be carried on foot. From what you say, there will be no way to get more than a satchel per person to Delta.'

'That's correct,' Harl said. 'We'll also need the strongest men to help the elderly and children when we reach the ropes that lead down the side of the tanks towards the door.'

Arlet nodded his acceptance and the four of them were excused from the chamber, leaving Rufus in a heated argument with the High Elderman as they made their way back out to the streets.

'You're welcome to stay at my place, unless you plan on sleeping in Emily's bed?' Troy said as they walked back through the town to the house.

'Certainly not,' Harl said.

Troy nodded. 'She's a terrible cook anyway.'

'I'm going to have a baby, Troy,' Harl said.

Troy looked down at Harl's belly as if some new technology had allowed genders to be reversed.

'With Sonora,' Harl said.

Troy beamed in delight and punched him in the arm.

'Well done,' he said. 'What's the bet?'

'Bet?'

'Boy,' Damen said from behind.

'Girl,' Oscar countered.

Troy shook his head. 'I don't care about that.'

Harl was confused. Had the drink finally addled Troy's mind. 'What then?'

'Black or blonde hair?' Tory announced with a flourish of his arms.

The two warriors behind burst into laughter.

Chapter 70

Their perseverance and ability to adapt to any climate has led me to create fantastic works of art in the landscapes. I have begun to see why some hold competitions based solely on the aesthetics within.

'I'm surprised the Elders agreed with you,' Troy said as they walked through the streets. Eyes tracked them as they passed and an excitement hovered in the air that Harl had never known before. 'Even Rufus must have given it some credit. Although I expect he'll be trouble before the end. I doubt he enjoyed being put in his place. People were watching, and as you know, news spreads fast.'

'I'll deal with him when I must,' Harl said. 'There are more important things than Rufus.'

'The people will expect you to speak to them at this announcement,' Troy said.

Harl had guessed as much, but he felt more comfortable this time, having grown up among these people. If he could speak at ease with anyone, it would be them.

'Well,' he said, 'we'd better be ready to answer a thousand questions.'

'Then perhaps a drink first?' Troy asked as a man stumbled out in front of them from the Golden Spear. He stopped to gaze at them before doubling over and throwing up in the street.

'Welcome home,' Troy said with a smile.

'Perhaps a drink somewhere a little less populated?' Harl said.

One drink at Troy's farm later and news came from the town via an overly-excited Bren Pewter that everyone had gathered in Gifting Square. They were waiting for Harl to confirm the rumours.

When he and Troy arrived, they took their place on a makeshift podium that had been set up. Arlet, the head Elderman, was in the middle of a passionate speech about how the people would be migrating to a new land.

Harl was glad the old man had taken it upon himself to explain everything Harl had told him about the Aylen, giving a brief overview about what Harl had witnessed. By the end of the speech there was little else for Harl to do other than tell the people that he was grateful they were willing to go with him and what to expect on the journey to come.

When the time came for questions, a roar of shouting arose from the crowd as each person fought to have their question answered first. When would they go? Where did they come from? Who were these new people?

Harl could only explain that most of the answers were in the book.

'Who are you to call our god a mere creature?' one of the priests called out from a small group of robed figures.

662

'You must decide that for yourself, Holyman,' Harl said. 'I can only show you the door. You must choose to walk through it. Let your own eyes decide what is real and what is an illusion.'

'What about our things?' a woman called out.

'There is no way to carry them out of here,' Harl said. 'The journey is treacherous and long. You won't be able to carry all that you wish. In order to live a free life you will have to give up the material chains that bind you to this place.' He glanced at the richly-robed priests. 'We will all start anew as equals.'

The crowd barely dispersed that night. The majority of the townspeople were still milling around the main square or gossiping in the Golden Spear long after the light switched off. Harl stayed with Troy and walked out of town to the barrier where they'd cut the hole.

'So I've been thinking,' Troy said.

'Oh dear.'

'When the baby comes,' Troy carried on,' I'm convinced it will have striped hair, half and half.'

Harl chuckled. 'As long as it's healthy then I don't mind what it looks like.'

'Unless it comes out looking like Rufus,' Troy said.

Harl smiled. 'I just hope Sonora is alright. They've been preparing the ship for a long time and, with so much food and water to load on board, I doubt she has been idle.'

'She seems like a strong woman,' Troy said as they stopped in front of Damen's guards by the hole. The guards had moved the black wooden cover to one side, leaving a view through the barrier into the growing tank beyond the hole.

'Blimey,' Troy said, stepping forward and running his hands around the inside of the barrier, marvelling at the world beyond. 'You managed to escape that tank in a similar way?'

'Yes,' Harl said. 'We had to cross the ground under the eye of the Aylen. Luckily we weren't spotted. But I'll admit I'm worried about so many people moving back through the tanks on our way out. If we do it during the dark cycle, we'll need to bring a lot of fire liquid to traverse the tanks safely. If any Aylen see it burning, it will be obvious what's happening.'

'Was it dangerous coming through the tanks then?' Troy asked.

'The only real threat was in the tank Drew came from. The rest were dangerous simply because of the people we found. I've no idea what the purpose of Drew's land was, but something horrible was going on, and I can't let it continue any more.' Harl looked back at the glowing town. 'I wonder how everyone will react to each other when they meet along the way. The first time they see the sun and stars will be worth it alone.'

'One more cycle,' Troy said, 'and you can find out. All this makes me glad I didn't find a permanent woman.'

'And why's that?' Harl asked.

'Just think,' Troy said, excited. 'In a cycle's time I'm going to be meeting hundreds of women more exotic than I could imagine.'

'And?'

'And with me being so handsome I should get pick of the crop. It's going to be an extremely interesting harvest.'

Harl laughed. 'Just be careful you don't suffer the jealousy of the men who have lived with them all their lives, or you're bound to find trouble.'

'Trouble? Me?' Troy said, feigning innocence.

They both laughed and then headed back to town.

The buzz of talk the following morning was a ripple of excitement and fear. People had read the books by torchlight during the dark cycle and word of mouth had spread quickly to the rest.

A mass of packing was being done within homes, so as not to attract unwanted Aylen attention. The shops were emptying their shelves in exchange for people's word that they would help the owners in future times of need.

Harl believed everything to be well with the other tanks. A couple of Aylens had peered inside with their usual interest, but nothing to cause alarm. He had also made a point to wander about the town, speaking with old friends and reassuring them about what was to come. It seemed like a simple gesture, but the warmth with which he was received gave him fresh hope for the future.

Damen had also been going around town. He and Oscar gave out the air breathers and instructed people how to use them by placing them on the roof of the mouth and taking slow, steady breaths. There had been some resistance to the men at first. The oddness of their looks made people nervous and it was only when

Troy joined them that people began to take note of what they were saying and show gratitude.

'Strange men approaching,' Troy would shout as he marched ahead of Damen and Oscar. 'Hide your daughters and then place your bets on which one gets the pox first!'

Just before the darkness came, Harl had everyone line up by the hole, ready to move. It was a risk, but attempting to organise them by the light of liquid fire would have been a disaster. Children ran amok between bags and carts, while some of the adults kept returning to their home to bring out fresh bags full of possessions that would be useless beyond the tanks.

Damen kept them in check and soon a pile of reluctantly discarded items stood beside the hole. He had taken to walking the length of the line shouting that if they did not organise themselves then people might be left behind.

Troy clutched a bundle of torches and strode up and down handing them over, before lighting the rags on the top with his own torch. When all the torches had been lit there was no part of the line left in darkness.

The light above the world shut off, leaving only the orange flickering torches to illuminate the crowd's terrified faces. A silence more profound than any Harl had ever known descended over the world.

'Time to go,' he said.

Chapter 71

I have experimented with the cultures inside. Some live with the bare minimum and face a harsh existence, while others are given excessive resources. They seem to adapt to any circumstance, but are mostly affected by changes in temperature for long durations.

Damen kicked one of his heavy boots at the fake panel covering the hole and it flew into Sonora's old land, bringing the scent of freshly-tilled soil and planted crops through the hole.

They made fast time across the sprouting valley of grass. Damen's men had gone ahead and placed torches along the route. The torch line stretched to the opposite side of the tank and, with the Aylen not expected until morning, they had a good window of escape. The torches were being lit one after another by a runner sent ahead with a torch. The fiery glow blossomed out, lighting up the landscape around it with a flickering yellow hue.

Harl was the first through. When he reached the second hole on the other side of the tank, he looked back to see the long line of blazing torches and the shadowy mass of three hundred people moving across the terrain. It was a staggering sight to see and it gave him a nervous thrill greater than anything he'd experienced to far. This was where their defiance started. This was the moment when they stopped believing in gods and made a stand. This was a moment of history.

As they passed into the next tank, the overhanging shelf loomed to their right, like a shadowed Aylen mousetrap waiting to snap shut and catch them. The flames lining the fields below the city reflected off the underside of the shelf, casting the tall spires above in eerie shadow.

'By the gods!' Troy exclaimed as he walked in front of Harl. He looked up at the city and the long ramp that led to the giant archway above.'Is that what I think it is?'

'It's a city,' Harl said.

'I think we got it bad judging by the looks of this place,' Troy said. 'They must have lived like kings.'

'The people who built it were enslaved,' Harl said, putting a damper on his friend's remark.

'Still,' Troy said, 'maybe we could've done better if we had worked together more in our own land.'

'Maybe,' Harl said. 'Perhaps the Aylens gave them more to work with. There were more people in this land than ours.'

'Where are they?' Troy asked, stumbling on a clump of mud as they trudged across the field.

'Some were unfriendly,' Harl said. 'They didn't take too kindly to us upsetting their way of life. The rest will meet us on the other side.' He saw the smile on Troy's lips in the torch light. 'And it'll be too dark to talk to the women.'

'Perhaps they'll need a hand across all this difficult terrain,' Troy said, flicking a lump of mud from his boots.

Harl smiled as Troy's pace quickened.

Damen jogged up and down the line to keep stragglers moving in the right direction and thinning the crowd wherever the train bunched up. He was having a particularly challenging time with the bogging soil as it tripped the unwary and sucked boots off those without decent footwear.

It took longer than Harl had hoped to cross the soggy fields and treacherous ditches that made up the ground floor of the tank. The mud clung to his boots, slowing the entire train as families stumbled in the quagmire. When Harl finally saw the hill where the hole into the next tank lay, he could make out a mass of torches lighting up a crowd of chattering people.

'Harl?' It was Kane's voice coming from somewhere on top of the hill.

'It's me, Kane,' Harl said, holding up a hand so Kane could spot him.

Kane trotted down to them, relief on his face.

'Kane, this is Troy,' Harl said, pointing to his friend.

Kane put a hand out in the Deltan gesture of greeting, but Troy was paying him no attention. Instead he was eyeing a group of women, giggling among themselves in the light of a small fire.

'Troy?' Harl said, digging an elbow in Troy's ribs.

'Ouch,' Troy said. 'Oh, yeah, nice to meet you, Dane.'

'Kane,' Harl said, but Troy was already ogling the women again.

'Have you sent a final group to extinguish the torches?' Kane asked, staring back at the line of flames running away into the distance.

'Damn,' Harl said. He should have remembered. If they left a line of bright lights, the Aylen would figure out they'd escaped a lot more quickly, possibly before they could make it to Delta. He cursed his stupidity.

'Don't worry,' Kane said. 'I can find a volunteer group to go back, stamp them out, and check for stragglers once we get through here.'

Harl looked at the hole Kane indicated. Just on the other side was Drew's tank. Men were already lined up inside with weapons pointed towards the back in case the alarm went off and the creatures let loose.

'There could be trouble during the crossing if something is released,' Damen said, joining them. 'I'll need Oscar and more men to guard while you cross. If anything comes we'll slaughter it.'

Harl nodded. He didn't want to risk a rampaging animal tearing into the train of already fearful people.

'I'll stay as well,' Harl said, 'perhaps patrol the flank.'

'What about me?' Troy asked.

'Stay here and let those coming up behind know that they can rest here until their turn to go through, but don't let the line of people break. Keep them flowing through the hole.'

Troy glanced at Harl's sword as if to imply he wanted to be more than a herder, but a woman's voice distracted him. One of the ex-slaves was asking how long they were to be left waiting and Troy's face lit up with a cheeky smile.

'They're beautiful,' he said in a daze.

Harl gave him a look that he hoped would convey caution.

'What?' Troy asked, innocently. 'If it's as dangerous as you say in there, then someone should protect them.'

'They're tougher than you, Troy Everett,' Harl said, looking to Kane who was smiling.

'I'll keep an eye out here,' Kane said, giving Harl a quick wink, 'and send a party back to extinguish the flames.'

Drew led his ragged band of soldiers in front of Harl as they stalked towards the doors at the rear of the tank which housed the creatures. They spread out and formed a watchful line, rifles and torches at the ready. The dozen or so men waited as the sound of feet trudging through the blood slick mud behind them wore on and on. Harl glanced back as he led men to the side on a patrol. The stream of people reached the exit and began to file through without incident.

The alarm suddenly blared, echoing inside the tank as Harl's heart sank. The doors flew open and pure fear gripped him at what emerged. Dozens of doors had slammed open at once and the dim lights just beyond them revealed the shadows writhing inside. It was not just one creature, or even a group, it was a deadly mixture.

A dozen hivers swarmed out from a hatch far above the ground, wings flapping at their sudden freedom. Then, from a short wide opening further down, two scuttlers raced out. Their low, many-legged bodies weaved across the ground towards Drew's men. The largest door wrenched free as a ferocious strider burst out, its six, spindly legs covered in spikes, and supporting its long, green body high above the ground as it thundered out. It was the same kind of creature that the soldiers had been fighting when

Harl had first entered the tank, but this one seemed far bigger. It hammered its razor-spiked legs into the mud as it screeched a horrible sound of pure rage and galloped at them.

'Fight together, live together,' Drew said, hurling his torch out toward the strider and raising his sword as the monsters closed the gap.

'Form up!' Harl said to his own group of men. 'Throw your torches out to light the area.'

He hadn't anticipated so many hostiles, and knew that his small group of men wouldn't be able stop so many. His only hope lay in getting back to the barrier and sealing the hole behind them. He turned to see the column of lights had disappeared, leaving a small group of men behind to guard the hole.

The soldiers rallied around Harl and he was suddenly flanked by Oscar and Drew on either side. The hivers were the first to reach them and they landed hard in the sticky mud. Their mouths opened wide as they hissed in unison.

'Fire and retreat back to the hole!' Harl called.

The soldiers fired and a wave of shots slammed into the hivers. Four died instantly, turning into charred husks that filled the air with the putrid smell of burning. Several others took to the air again and swooped down mid flight, knocking a man over before he could turn to run. As the hivers dived at them again, Oscar broke from the circle and hauled the man back as the hiver's pincers snapped at empty air. He kicked the hiver hard in the face, forcing it back, and dragged the man to his feet and towards the hole in the side of the tank.

Twice more the hivers dived at them, but Damen and Drew stopped as Harl rushed past and the two men held a line, firing up at the diving creatures. Their concentrated fire brought more hivers down, covering the pair in gore. A final one landed as Drew's rifle clicked on empty. He tossed the gun aside and drew his sword, side-stepping the hiver's lunge as he hacked down through its neck with several well-aimed blows. The creature crumpled and stilled.

'Scuttlers,' Damen called.

The two scuttlers weaved towards them, closing the gap fast.

'Run!' Harl cried, hoping the two wouldn't try and fight.

He turned for the exit and found himself a hundred paces away, but then a man screamed at the back of the group and Harl glanced back to find that a scuttler was crawling over one of the men as he tried to fight it off. The second hiver joined in the frenzy and together they pinned the man to the bloody ground and tore his limbs off.

Drew and Oscar separated from the group as the six-legged strider scurried down the hill along the side of the tank, making for the hole. They raced to meet it, giving the others time to make it closer to the exit hole. Damen let off more shots but stopped as the creature reared up over Drew and Oscar and then slammed down around them, encaging them inside it's legs. They stood back to back underneath its pale belly and Oscar fired his rifle up as Drew attempted to sever the spiked legs with his sword.

The scuttlers discarded the soldier's mangled carcass and wound towards the strider. Harl stopped to fire at them, then dropped his rifle as the trigger clicked and tore his sword free. He pressed the button and stepped from the cluster of retreating men and ran, full pelt, at the two scuttlers who were homing in on Oscar and Drew.

Harl screamed like a madman, drowning out the constant noise of rifles as the pair of scuttlers closed in on him instead. He jumped aside as the leading beast lurched forward, and then brought the sword down in a sweeping arc to cut a deep slice through the thick armour. He was forced backwards as the second scuttler turned, snapping its pincers and weaving towards him. He swung the blade down in panic and it bit into the side of the creature's head. It flipped over, screaming in pain, but its tail smashed into his chest, knocking him to the ground. It writhed and screeched as Harl scrambled to his feet and ran.

A heavy thump drew Harl's attention. The strider had collapsed to the ground with most of its legs severed. Oscar and Drew jumped back from the creature as it spun uselessly on the reddened ground, thrashing its remaining two legs in an effort to reach them.

Suddenly, the alarm sounded again and a chill seeped into Harl's bones. Twisting around in the mud, he saw two of the tall-legged striders scamper from the doors and rush straight for them. Another pair of scuttlers wove from the shadows.

'Run!' Drew cried, and Oscar and Damen broke formation, turned, and raced for the hole.

The striders' long legs covered the ground so fast that Harl barely had time to turn and run. A man stumbled in the mud as Harl overtook him and Harl slowed to loop an arm through his and heave him up again.

'Move!' Harl yelled, but the man slipped again, threatening to drag him to the ground as well.

The man let out a hideous scream as the injured scuttler raced up his back and sank its teeth into his neck, throwing him forward into the mud.

The hole was close, promising safety, but the striders had caught up. The slowest soldier was Zane. The young boy turned and fired up at the long-legged monsters as they cast him in shadow. Their hooked legs swept into the panicked boy as he fired up into the soft bellies.

Drew roared and rushed forward, grabbing Zane by the arm and then hauling him out from underneath the beast. The boy fled towards the exit hole as Drew severed the creature's nearest leg with his sword, but the creature spun in place and knocked him over with one of its flailing limbs. It tore a gash in his shoulder and Drew roared with the pain. Harl could see the rage in his eyes as he looked up at the creature from where he was sprawled in the blood-soaked mud.

Drew pulled himself into a tight ball as the second strider barrelled into the first. Their spiked legs clattered together and they hissed, biting at each other in a frenzy as they fought over the nearest carcass. Drew lay forgotten beneath them, but it was clear that he would be left behind and probably killed if he didn't get up soon.

Harl stopped, ready to help, but Oscar ran past him, fighting through the sticky mud until he dodged under the battling striders and reached down to haul Drew up. Both striders screamed in rage and disengaged when they saw the two men rush out from under them, then thundered after Oscar and Drew as they sprinted for the hole.

The first soldiers to reach the exit dived through as though it was a swimming competition. Harl readied himself to jump as well, but the men behind the divers skidded to a stop as screams echoed back from the opening. Harl was about to shout at them to hurry, when he realized that there was a drop down to the hole into the empty tank beyond. Those who'd dived through must have landed head first on the floor below.

'Use the rope to get through!' he yelled as he turned back with the rearguard to face the incoming striders.

Drew had snatched a wooden spear from one of his men and was thrusting it up at one of the striders in an attempt to skewer it. Oscar was next to him, waving his sword at any leg that came close.

One man was firing at the second strider. His gun suddenly clicked on empty as the creature reared up and thrust a leg down at him, piercing him through the chest. He screamed in agony as the creature lifted its leg and flicked him off into Oscar with such force it knocked the big man down.

Harl cried out as the strider rushed in and raised its leg above Oscar, ready to strike, but Drew stepped underneath and thrust his spear upwards, burying it deep in the strider's belly. He pushed his full weight and strength into the weapon, forcing the strider to stagger backwards. It screamed and reared back, dragging the weapon from Drew's hands, but the move gave Oscar enough time to scramble to his feet.

'Go!' Drew shouted, shoving Oscar towards the hole and then stooping to pick up a sword as the strider hissed in rage next to him, but the scuttlers had finished with their prey and snaked towards him, ready for a fresh meal, as the last few soldiers slid down through the exit hole.

Harl and Oscar turned back to help Drew. He screamed with a savage blood lust and drove the creatures further back as he hacked at their legs with his sword, but then the alarm sounded for a third time and another group of hivers erupted from the doors and flew towards them.

'Go!' Drew cried, slicing down to hold the first scuttler at bay.

No!' Harl roared as he skewered scuttler. 'We go together.'

'Go, dammit,' Drew yelled and looked back at Harl, his eyes ablaze. 'Someone has to stay.'

Harl froze as the reality hit home. Someone had to keep the creatures back until the others could seal the hole. There was no way the three of them could kill all of these creatures and there was no telling how many more would be released. Drew was right.

Harl made his decision and clamped a hand on Oscar's shoulder as the big man started to head back towards Drew.

'Come on,' he said. 'We can't win this. Drew has to stay.'

For a moment Oscar stood rooted to the blood slick ground.

'Quickly!' Damen called from the other tank.

Oscar half turned towards the exit, but he seemed unable to tear his gaze from Drew. After a moment Harl felt the shoulder relax and the big man headed for the hole.

They both slid down the rope into the empty tank as a team of men heaved at a second line that was attached to a crude

677

wooden frame. They hoisted the block up to re-seal the hole, while men directed it with their spears.

Drew stayed behind.

Chapter 72

It sickens me that some would train them to fight. The price of a trained fighter on the market is exorbitant but I refuse to sell them. How can one creature treat another in such a way?

Harl fell to his knees inside the next tank and dropped his head into his hands. What had he done? Drew was probably dead by now, torn apart in a frenzy of claws and razor sharp pincers. It had been his own choice, but Harl still felt responsible. It should have been him.

'Damn it,' Harl said.

'We should've stayed,' Oscar said, staring up at the hole as the block was forced back into place.

'Should we take down the frame sir?' One of the men asked, dropping the hoisting rope.

Harl didn't respond at first. It just felt like the final step in abandoning the warrior.

'Get rid of it,' Harl said at last.

Oscar roared, lifted his sword, and hacked repeatedly at the frame, taking huge chunks out until it collapsed. The men jumped back as the timbers tumbled to the ground. Oscar stood panting with effort, his eyes transfixed by the block above them. After a moment he turned away.

Harl looked at the dark front glass of the Sight. It wouldn't be long until the Aylen returned and, if they were still inside, then they'd never get out again. He needed to make Drew's sacrifice count.

'Come on,' he said, rising and then breaking into a jog. 'We have to keep moving.'

They sped across the bare ground, eventually passing a group of cloaked men who were waiting to extinguish the flickering torches that lined the floor. Harl could see people making their way up a ladder and into Oscar's tank and redoubled his efforts to reach them. He wanted out of the tanks. They'd taken too much from him.

His thoughts strayed to Sonora. He pictured her helping people to prepare for the unknown journey once the ship was ready to leave. She was his future. She was all he cared about, her and the child waiting to be born. Their child was the first step to a new life, one of the first children conceived in slavery yet born to the freedom of a life beyond the Aylen. They were what made the pain worth bearing.

A tremor of anger filled him as he reached the next hole. Someone had built a ladder between the tanks. He placed a foot on a rung and scrambled up. As he reached the top he glanced back across the dark void. Why had no one thought to do the same on the previous side? Drew could still be alive if only such a simple thing had been done.

He wished he'd taken the time to get to know the battle-scarred man. He had been too caught up in the race of getting back to his old homeland, too focused on the next part of the plan to reach out to those around him. He knew that Oscar and Damen had spoken at length with Drew. How had they managed to find the time and yet he had just stumbled on ignoring those around him? Was he shallow? Did it show that he cared less than them? He knew that he was being ridiculous. It was just the pain speaking, but the raw feeling twisting inside didn't care. These people were his responsibility now. If he didn't feel pain for them then he was no better than the Eldermen or the Enlightened; he was more like the One.

He hoped Oscar would be the one to tell Damen of Drew's sacrifice. He didn't know if he could find the words.

Anger flared up again at the thought of how the Aylens toyed with the lives of humans. How many other tanks were spread out across this vast new world? How may humans in prisons? He doubted that the tank Drew and his men had come from was singular and knew that there were probably far worse out there. Just how much suffering could humanity take without breaking?

He hoped that somewhere there was an Aylen that took an opposite view to those of its species. What an ally that would be, he thought, to have that same strength standing with them against the enemy. But it was a ridiculous dream. There were only humans. It would be like him protecting and aiding a bone beetle all day. He had other things to deal with. No one else would stand with them.

As the last few men climbed the ladder down into Oscar's tank an exhausted silence fell over everyone. The torches flickering along the train of people cast a yellow hue over the whole landscape. There were hundreds of them milling about in a buzz of excited talking. Harl was pleased to hear people from different tanks talking together about their common goals and fears; a couple of women were even exchanging beloved family recipes.

Oscar caught sight of Damen and Harl watched the big man lumber over to tell Damen the bad news. He didn't feel like joining them, so he squeezed through the crowd of men, women and children in the hope of finding Kane.

He found him inside the large circular hut, surrounded by a mixture of Eldermen and leaders from the other tanks.

'We've only enough for three days at most,' Kane said to the group. 'If we wait any longer we'll be caught. We must consolidate our supply now and take only what we can carry. There is much more at Delta.'

Kane looked up as Harl shuffled closer.

'Everyone's accounted for as best as possible,' Kane said, glancing at his notepad as if to check figures. 'And I've given orders for food to be distributed before we leave. Uman has informed me that the hole to the outside has been expanded under the door and my pulley system idea has been installed to lower groups from the tanks to the ground.'

'A pulley system?' Harl said, clapping him on the back. 'Kane, you're a genius.'

Kane spluttered and continued talking to the assembled leaders.

'We'll start the descent immediately. We'll need men to guard a gathering area outside the Aylen's lair and, once we've regrouped, we can lead them all to Delta.'

'How long will it take to get there?' an aged man asked, as if worried he could not finish the journey.

'A day,' Kane said, maybe less if we cut through past the tree.'

'What about the breathing pieces?' Harl asked.

'I've handed them out,' Kane said. 'A few will be placed by the exit for those who forgot or were overlooked.'

'Then we're ready,' Harl said, amazed at how smoothly it had gone. There had been no fights or arguments between the different factions. He guessed they must still be in shock, never having seen a stranger until he'd arrived, but, in all honesty, he'd never actually expected to get this far in the plan.

Now all they needed to do was stay alive until Delta.

They left shortly after the meeting. Crossing Oscar's world seemed to strain almost everyone. The way the sand shifted under each footfall sapped the strength, and nearly everyone was exhausted by the time they reached the cattle world. But it was easy after that. Most of the cattle were asleep and a brief walk brought them to the hole that led to freedom. Oscar's people had slaughtered a large number of cattle and each person passing through the tank was given an extra portion of beef to add to their supplies. It lifted the mood and boosted everyone's strength after leaving Oscar's tank.

Harl thanked Oscar, but the big man just nodded and then leant in to whisper, 'It seemed only sensible. There's much hardship ahead and the people are afraid already. Any hope for the tribe is good hope.'

Harl climbed up the rope ladder that had been rolled down into the tank from the exit hole. This was the final hurdle. He looked back at the people waiting below him. They seemed nervous again now. None of them quite realised what they faced beyond the tanks, despite what the book had told them and Kane's lectures along the way. He smiled at them and stepped into the hole. If they could do this smoothly, then it was a major obstacle out of the way.

The hole hadn't been expanded, chiefly because it was still a danger to enlarge it in case the Aylen looked in, so it was a bit of a scramble to get through. He stepped out onto a square wooden platform on the other side and looked around, impressed.

The platform was five steps across and made from sturdy wooden planks. How Uman had arranged it all amazed Harl. He had assumed that the scout was just going to wait at the hole to relay messages back, but together with Kane's plans, he seemed to have worked miracles.

A rough wooden railing surrounded the platform on the three sides that faced away from the tanks. A huge pulley was suspended over it and ropes ran down from it to four metal rings tied to the platform. The pulley was attached to the tank wall by a series of ropes tied to melting swords embedded in the tank wall. It was an ingenious solution.

Kane and Oscar climbed up and stood beside Harl as Damen positioned a few of his men around the edge of the platform to balance the load. They would head out of the door as soon as the platform reached the ground and then move through to stand guard outside the door. Harl hadn't forgotten his first scuttler encounter and he didn't want to risk one attacking the host of people when they stepped out into the world for the first time. The whole trip back to Delta would be dangerous. The people from inside the tanks had no idea what the world beyond looked like and, in the darkness, people could go astray or fall foul of the nocturnal beasts that hunted among the maze of grass stalks. But if they were attacked so soon, chaos would erupt and all their plans would be in ruins as the people scattered in terror.

Oscar looked over the railing towards the grey floor hundreds of paces below. His eyes widened in wonder.

'It seems impossible,' he murmured.

One of the soldiers picked up a small ball of hay from a pile on the platform and dropped it over the edge.

'What's that?' Oscar asked.

'A signal to those controlling the winch to begin lowering us,' Kane said. After a moment the platform gave a shudder and the ropes groaned as they were lowered slowly to the floor.

Uman was waiting at the bottom surrounded by the bags of food that had already been sent down to bolster their provisions. Beside him a team of sweating men were braced against the rope that controlled the platform's descent. Harl nodded his thanks to the men and then turned to Uman.

Uman's face lit up as the platform thumped to the floor and he grasped Harl's hand. 'It's good to see you again, Harl. I've already spoken with Delta and Sonora is fine.'

'Thanks for letting me know,' Harl said, grateful.

'We must hurry,' Uman said, turning to look at the Aylen door and the dark gap underneath. It had been widened to an opening big enough for a row of tall men to walk through. 'Light will come soon.'

'We need everyone out there before the Aylen returns,' Harl said. 'The next group down will be armed and can secure the area. Then we must move.'

Harl watched the dark gap under the door as teams of people were ferried down. By the time that most of them were down a faint light was creeping under the gap.

'We need to leave,' he said to Kane as he strode over to the platform. 'First light has arrived.'

Kane nodded as a group of haggard-looking men on the platform were lowered to the ground. 'That's the last of them.'

Harl glanced again at the gap under the door that led to the outside. The light was coming fast. They'd better go soon or risk an Aylen walking in and scooping them all back inside.

Looking at the people huddled together on the floor, he realised how strange it had to be for them. Most were staring around, wide-eyed, and he knew it was because they had never seen such a large open space without a window in front of them. He remembered his own wonder and fear at being out of the tanks for the first time. Perhaps it would be easier for them? They had guides, people who had been out here before, people like himself, but it was Kane and Damen's people who were the key. They were the ones who could help the most. They could shoulder the burden of knowing what to do. All these people had to do was follow along and remain strong. Everything else would be taken care of.

It was still dark inside the Aylen's shop, but the distant walls were just visible. The scouts around the door had scattered torches close to the base to light the way.

Harl was about to order everyone to move on, when he saw the group of people who had just stepped off the platform. Something had caught his eye, but he didn't know whether to trust his instincts. He nudged his way through the press of bodies and spotted Rufus among the last group. The hawk-faced man was talking to the others in a hushed voiced. It was odd that Rufus had been so quiet since they left the tank, but Harl had just put it down to fear of the unknown. Thinking about it now, he hadn't seen the man at all since the council agreed to follow him. The two men he was with were also familiar. They had been the guards that Damen and Oscar had pinned before seeing the council.

'Why are you last?' Harl asked, making the three men look up sharply.

Rufus steadied himself and his look of loathing returned.

'Fire clearers,' he said and the other two nodded, not meeting Harl's gaze.

Kane, who had not been with Harl when he had gone to the council and had no idea what kind of man Rufus was, came over from the lift.

'What is it?' he asked seeing that something was wrong.

'These are the men who volunteered to put out the torches in the tanks?' Harl asked.

'Yes,' Kane said, baffled. 'Is something wrong?'

Harl looked at the three men.

'You volunteered?' he asked.

'We did,' Rufus said, looking to Kane for confirmation with a smile.

'Harl?' Kane asked, ignoring Rufus, clearly sensing that Harl was suspicious. He looked at the three men in turn and glanced at the gap under the door. 'Is there a problem? We have to get going.'

'This man,' Harl said, stepping up to Rufus, 'has never volunteered for anything in his entire life, and I don't see him suddenly changing his ways.'

'I don't...' Kane started.

'Get back on the lift,' Harl said quietly to Rufus, moving forward and forcing the grubby man to step backwards onto the wooden platform.

'Take us up,' Harl said and watched as the team of men who had been about to dismantle the system took the strain of the rope and began to haul them both back up.

Harl said nothing as they ascended, but stared hard at Rufus, who was shifting his hands from his pockets to the wooden rail that edged the platform.

The lift levelled with the hole and, as it did, the line of burning torches stretched far into the tank. Even the golden glow in Oscar's tank shone through the distant hole. Harl sighed as the lift shuddered and came to a stop.

Rufus, knowing his plan had been discovered, snarled like a cornered animal and yanked a dagger from his robe pocket. He thrust it straight at Harl's stomach, attempting to disembowel him.

Harl, half-expecting the weapon, stepped to one side and almost fell over the low railing. He gripped hard to keep his balance, and then turned as the blade came at him again. He ducked as Rufus lunged out and the dagger whipped through the empty air where he had been standing. He grabbed Rufus' hand with both of his own and tugged down, pulling Rufus off balance to smash his hand into the railing. Rufus cried out in pain and the knife tumbled from his hand, lancing down through the air to stick upright in the wooden plank with a resounding thunk.

'No, please!' Rufus said, throwing his hands up as he stepped back to where the platform met the hole.

'Why?' Harl asked.

Rufus shrugged as if it was obvious.

'Respect,' he said simply.

Harl shook his head.

'Not from you,' Rufus spat, 'or those sheep below, but from the gods. If they realized I was worthy enough to lead the council and those beneath them, then they would've let me leave that bloody prison. I was so close...' He trailed off before laughing, his voice growing in intensity. 'Then you come along just before I took full control of the council, promising a new life and all of your usual rubbish. A life where everything I've worked so hard for would be cast away. And for what? For a sense of stupid adventure!' He spat on the floor. 'Now the gods will see what you've done and they'll know I stopped you. There's not enough time for you and your flock to get away now. In ten strides, the One True God will be above you and stamp you into the ground for your heresy against him.' His eyes flicked down and Harl followed his gaze to where the knife was stuck in the platform.

Rufus lunged forward but Harl slid a foot across the floor, sweeping the knife over the side, and grabbed the man's shoulders, hauling him back up.

Harl stepped forward, shifting Rufus closer to the hole. The strength in Harl's grip came from a sickening anger at the man. Harl sighed, but said nothing. There was nothing to be said now. He raised a foot and kicked hard, releasing his grip.

Rufus screamed as he fell through the hole down into the tank.

'Now you can be your god's only pet,' Harl called down. He tugged the rope ladder up and tossed the last clump of straw over the side. 'Just as you wanted.'

Harl's sense of satisfaction drained as he descended. Time would be against all of them now. As soon as the Aylen saw the line of torches across the tanks, it would be a race, one he was sure the Aylen would win.

Chapter 73

I guess the fighting can be the same as Gruble wrestling but the difference is in the intelligence of the species. I assume that's the draw for someone wishing to fight them.

'The Aylen will know we left as soon as full light comes,' Harl said, as the platform touched the ground. He leapt off and hurried to where Oscar, Damen and Kane were shouldering their packs.

'What?' Oscar asked. He glanced at the bright gap under the door, where the row of people started. All of them were packed and ready to leave.

'It's here?' Kane asked looking around as if the giant had snuck up on them.

'No, not yet,' Harl said. 'Rufus betrayed us. There's a line of torches stretching through nearly every tank. As soon as an Aylen sees the tanks, the torches will lead it directly to the hole and it'll track us down.'

'That man?' Kane asked looking up at the side of the tank stack.

'A traitor,' Harl said. 'He left them lit. Without a way down, he'll stay to enjoy his loneliness until the Aylen arrive.'

'Bastard got what he deserved,' Damen said.

'As for us,' Harl continued, 'we have to go now or we'll all be captured and thrown back in the tanks before nightfall with no way out.'

Troy, laden with a pair of bulky bags that clearly belonged to a couple of chatting women trailing behind him, fell in beside Harl. 'Rufus?'

Harl nodded. 'Betrayed all of us. So I let him stay behind.'

'He'll have everything he wants now,' Troy said. 'Except people.'

'He never got on with them anyway,' Harl said. He turned to Kane. 'Break the scaffold and pulley. No more stealth. It's now a race.'

'Move out!' Damen shouted, waving his hands at the soldiers beside the gap.

Harl slung his satchel over a shoulder and made for the head of the column. Troy lugged his self-imposed burden along, puffing to keep pace with Harl.

'Uman,' Harl said, after he'd ducked under the hole beneath the door and seen the man on the other side. Uman was watching the light rising on the horizon.

'Sir?'

'Send word to the outpost that we're coming straight for Delta,' Harl said. 'Have them relay to the city that the ship must be ready to go immediately. Time's against us now.'

'Yes, sir,' Uman said, nodding to Harl before running into the nearest patch of grass stalks.

'Bloody hell,' Troy said, shielding his eyes. 'Is it always this bright?'

'It gets brighter,' Harl said, waving the first group out from under the door. 'You'll get used to it.'

Like a tide smashing against the rocks, each wave of people coming under the door staggered to a stop and collided with the one before it. They were stunned by the brightening sky, shading their eyes in wonder as the sun climbed up above the giant foliage ahead of them.

Harl remembered when he had first seen it himself. The world so big, so overwhelming, and the colours of dawn spreading across the horizon and sweeping up to paint the sky with light was truly awe-inspiring. It made the heart leap. All of these people were seeing it for the first time, they were feeling that same strange mix of wonder, fear, and hope that he and Sonora had felt all that time ago. The memory of Sonora holding his hand made Harl smile. She was his hope. She and the baby.

'It's unbelievable,' Troy said, taking in the vista of giant grass stalks and the back drop of the great tree spreading out above the world in the distance. He held his hand out in front of him, sighting between his pinched fingers as if testing far off objects for scale.

More groups followed, ushered out by pairs of men tasked with keeping the train moving. When they numbered into the hundreds it was hard to keep them all in the vicinity. Some wandered off to inspect the plants as others stood on the flat plain, staring up in awe at the sky and the horizon. Guards kept rounding them up and bringing them back together.

'Bit like sheep,' Troy muttered as yet another group was brought back into the fold

When everyone had come through the door, Damen stepped out from the shop and Harl moved through the press to meet him.

'We won't be stopping to rest at the outpost,' Harl said. 'We can't afford to lose any time en route. Can your men stay to the sides of the train and keep people from straying?' Harl asked.

'We'll be stretched thin, but we can do it,' Damen said.

The day was going to be hot and, with the exception of Oscar's people, the tank-dwellers were unused to any strong fluctuation in temperature.

The exodus was a catastrophe. People were terrified, but if that had been the only problem it would have been easier to manage. Curiosity was the danger. People kept stepping away from the path to investigate the strange sights and sounds despite their fear. It was a maddening confusion. Damen's men had to race up and down the column to fend off curious creatures or to find lost children and straying parents.

But as the novelty wore off, the fear of what lay around them began to build. Those who had felt the pull of curiosity now huddled closer and closer to the main train. The forest stifled the breeze and became more menacing as the sunlight fell into shadow and the train of people plunged deeper into the swaying grasses.

When they finally reached the outpost, the sun was just above the horizon and Harl sent another message to Delta informing them that the train of refugees had arrived.

To Harl's surprise, Arlet, the old Elderman approached him as the line started off from the outpost. He gestured for Harl to step into the shelter of the archway that led through the sandy boulders into the outpost.

'Harl,' Arlet said, looking around at the small outpost carved into the rock as he led Harl inside.

It was more chaotic than when Harl had last seen it. Supplies were scattered across the floor and piles of timber were stacked against one wall. Probably remnants of the wood used to create the lift platform.

'This is unreal,' Arlet continued. He looked weary but invigorated, as though he couldn't walk any further physically, but could wander for years in his mind. 'So beautiful.'

Harl felt pity for the man. Arlet had believed in the gods for all of his life and only now, near the end of his days, did he see the truth. He wouldn't even have the time to fully understand it all.

'You'll adjust,' Harl said. 'Just as we did.'

'I'm afraid not,' Arlet said, slumping into a wooden chair by the radio. 'I can't go any further.'

'I'll have the men carry you,' Harl said, looking around for some of Damen's troops. 'All we need is-'

'No, my boy,' Arlet cut him off. 'My legs are weak and you need speed. You will be lucky to make it as it is.'

'You want me to just leave you here?' Harl asked.

'You said you can contact this Delta from here?'

'Through the radio, yes,' Harl said, pointing to the speaker box that had scared him half to death when he'd first heard it. It had been talking non-stop since they arrived, informing Kane about the status of the city and the ship.

'Show me how to use it and when the god-' The old man sighed. '-when the creature comes, I can at least send you a warning and be useful.'

Harl didn't know what to say. He was touched at the sacrifice this fragile old man would make to save hundreds of people he'd never known.

'I'll have Kane come and show you how to use it before we leave,' he said.

'I'm sorry about Rufus,' Arlet said, standing and putting a bony hand on Harl's shoulder.

'It's no one's fault, Arlet. Rufus was bad from the beginning. He was planning to take down the Eldermen. Told me as much before he tried to kill me.'

'If we'd had any sense, we'd have made you a councilman,' Arlet said. 'When you saved those boys from Rufus, it showed your true self, but I was blind to it.' He glanced out through a hole in the rock to the forest beyond. 'Like so much else.'

'You knew about that?' Harl asked.

Arlet nodded. 'There are a great many things that we Eldermen knew of that were kept from the people. Many were just tales from long ago, things we believed to be superstition. But now I can see that our own minds were too weak to grasp the truth, and for that, I am truly sorry, Harl. You have carried many burdens through your life, but I thank you for it. You have given us hope, Harl. Your parents would be proud of you, as am I. Now, send this Kane to me and be off. I will do this last task for our people and be glad of it. We're wasting time.'

'Thank you,' Harl said.

He turned and walked from the outpost, a single tear running down one cheek. He didn't look back.

They pushed on through the growing light. The grass forest and the tree above it cut out most of the light and only the flickering torches kept the line together. They had to reach Delta. If they were found out in the open, the Aylen would catch them. Delta and the ship were their only chance.

Harl glanced over his shoulder at the building as a loud bang sounded like distant thunder. He broke into a run, making for the front of the line where Damen had taken the lead.

'Urge them on faster, Damen' Harl said. 'Something is happening. I sense the threat, and if we don't get them home soon, it'll be too late.'

Damen grimaced before racing down the line of people.

'Move! Move!' he shouted. 'Pick up the pace!'

A man's scream cut through the air. Harl spun on his heel. He could glimpse a tiny bit of sky through the tangle of grass stalks above, but there was no sign of the Aylen. He couldn't make out anything further back. Everything was far too tangled and dense. He ran back along the line, but stumbled to a halt.

The man who'd screamed was writhing in pain on the ground, blood gushing from a wound on his leg. A woman was kneeling next to him, horror written all over her face as she clamped her jacket down over his wound. Blood soaked through it immediately.

Harl waved everyone on and then knelt down next to her. 'What happened?'

Her eyes were locked on the spreading bloodstain.

'He was just running along and then he fell down clutching his leg,' her voice trailed off.

Damen arrived and lifted the jacket away. Blood sprayed out as he tore the man's cotton trousers open to reveal the wound. His face was grim.

'Ripshrub,' he said. He looked around and then pointed at a large plant nearby. It had a faint metallic look and gleamed in the shadows. When he turned back to Harl, he shook his head.

'No!' the woman wailed. She grabbed Harl's shirt. 'You've got to do something. Please, I can't lose him.'

Harl pried her hands loose and then ripped his belt free.

'We aren't losing anyone,' he said. He wrapped the belt around the man's leg, pulled it tight, and then snatched a sheathed dagger from Damen and used it to wind the belt tight, cutting off the blood flow and clamped the man's hand over it.

'You two,' Harl said to a couple of council guards nearby.

Both had been holding bows up to the shadows, in case it had been a creature, and they looked around at him.

'Get him up and help him to the city. It's not far,' he said and watched as they scrambled to pick the paling man up.

Damen furrowed his brow as the man was helped away.

'I know,' Harl said, 'but if I tell everyone we're only halfway then some will give up.'

'Leave them then,' Damen said.

'You can't leave them to wander out here,' Harl said, trying to keep his voice low. 'You've no idea what it's like. It'd be cowardly.'

'I do,' Damen growled, glaring at him, but he turned as a series of shouts came from ahead, followed by the buzzing of wings and gunfire.

'Hivers!' Damen shouted, raising his rifle and storming towards the commotion.

Harl sprinted up the train of scared faces and headed for the neon blue flashes off to one side of the line.

'Move,' he yelled at a family who had stopped to watch, holding up those behind them.

He broke from the line, dodging between stalks as he followed the flares of gunfire. He stumbled into a small clearing where a line of soldiers were attempting to form up as a row of hivers sprung at them. The men were firing wildly. Some hit their targets, but most were getting picked off from above as more hivers dived down from the stalk tips to land on top of them.

Oscar was stabbing at anything coming from above with a long sharpened stick, while Damen calmly knelt and fired, yelling commands at anyone who would listen.

Harl fumbled for his pistol and watched for Oscar to lunge upwards. The shadows made it hard to see anything solid but, as Oscar's spear jabbed up, he aimed for the tip and fired.

The shot hit its target and Oscar looked around at him, grinning, but then his eyes grew wide and, in a moment of utter madness, he drew back the makeshift spear and launched it straight at Harl. A heavy weight fell on Harl, knocking him to the ground. He rolled aside and lay there staring at a dead hiver. Oscar's spear had gone straight through its head and, as the creature twitched, he had a moment to take in the carnage.

Several men were dead and the others were grouped up, holding their own against the remaining winged monsters. At Damen's command, they stepped back and fired in a neat line until the last hiver retreated back into the forest.

The buzzing stopped and sporadic shouting filled the air as people who had broken away from the line tried to regroup with loved ones. Harl climbed to his feet, still shaken by the hiver that had almost got him.

Another loud bang echoed in the distance.

'Keep moving,' Damen called out, running back to the column. He turned to Harl, 'If we keep making this much noise, every living thing in the forest will be on our heels, if it's not already. We must go faster.'

He grabbed a worried-looking soldier who had been casting furtive looks into the dense stalks.

'Get to the front of the line and tell Kane and Uman to start running. Let those you pass know we're going faster and if they lag they'll be left behind.'

The man nodded and Harl looked at Damen.

'How many can you spare to speed up the old and young?' Harl asked.

'We'll all be dead if we don't leave some behind,' Damen said.

Harl tucked his pistol away and pointed at a family huddling together. Their young daughter was clutching her mother's hand and looking around in fear while the mother attempted to soothe her.

'Think of it as an adventure,' the mother said, kneeling to get level with her child. 'We won't let anything bad happen to you.'

'Tell them that,' Harl said, sickened by Damen's selfish attitude. 'Tell them that we're abandoning them.'

Damen just grunted and pushed past him, heading to the back of the line.

People began to collapse from exhaustion. Some stumbled away from the ever-widening column, while others just dropped to the ground, unable to continue. They were hoisted up by a group of soldiers, and half-stumbling, half-dragged, were forced forward.

Harl jogged along behind one ragged group. One of the men being supported slipped, knocking his helper into a huge, rotten branch. It crumpled as the man tried to push himself off, fighting tiredness. As he stood, the branch wobbled, then a section of the log tore open, splitting apart as a fanged mouth whipped out and wrapped around the man's entire arm. It yanked him off his feet and into the rotting mass. His scream cut off as his comrades scattered.

Pistol in hand, Harl backed away and turned to run. He caught up with Oscar, who was struggling with an angry man attempting to scramble back the way they had come.

'But my daughter's back there,' the man said, trying in vain to push Oscar out of the way. It was like a child struggling against a boulder and, after a moment, fatigue made the man stop.

'We'll send someone to look,' Harl said, stepping between them. 'But you have to keep moving. Someone will have picked her up.'

'I'll go and make sure.' Oscar said.

Screams erupted at the back of the line. Harl turned and froze. Far behind them a titanic shadow rose into the sky. It was the Aylen.

Chapter 74

Another must carry on. The work I have started was lost and corrupted by my own selfish greed. The communities inside the tanks represent something much deeper than mere financial gain. Culture.

Harl heard the screams from the people around him as they saw the creature. It looked even more titanic out in the open, rearing up against the skyline as if it really was a god. It was stood by the giant door, its head turning slowly from side to side, scanning the ground at its feet. A roar echoed out towards them, like thunder, and it took a huge step closer.

It was coming for them.

'Move. MOVE!' Harl yelled.

People were frozen in place, cowering and hunched down. Every eye was trained on the monstrous creature as it took another step forward, its gaze surveying the ground where they had entered the forest.

Harl grabbed the nearest man by the shoulders and spun him in the direction of Delta.

'Run!' he yelled and propelled the man forward.

He did the same for three more, shouting at everyone in hearing distance. They stumbled the first few steps and then, as the fear took hold, they ran. Possessions were thrown aside as they fled. A trickle of people moved at first, then a flood of them, all staggering along, tripping over each other and the uneven terrain. Some fell to the ground, then scrambled to their feet as a wave of terrified cries rolled back and forwards through the people as they gave in to their fear and fled.

Damen staggered up to Harl, a child under each arm.

'Get your men to guide them, Damen,' Harl shouted at him. 'They'll run right past Delta if we don't get them under control.'

Damen began calling the names of his men and bellowed orders as the children in his arms wailed.

Harl raced along the rough paths until the ground dropped away ahead of him into a small valley. The giant blades of grass opened out ahead and he saw Delta gleaming in the distance. He staggered to a stop and collapsed against one of the last blades of grass.

Why was Delta sparkling like that? He'd never noticed it before.

'What are the lights?' he asked as Damen crashed out from the undergrowth next to him.

'The energy panels!' Damen cursed. 'We've got to get them covered before the Aylen sees them.'

By the time Harl reached the doors, most of the refugees were already outside. They were being funnelled up the stairs and through the narrow entrance and, as a result, the crowd had nearly stalled. The gates were wide open, but there press of people was just too much. Panic was breeding along the line, everyone pushing and pulling against each other. Harl saw more than one person stumble and fall, only to be trampled over as the line lurched forward.

Damen's braided head was just visible above the crowd next to Oscar at the top of the stairs. Both were shouting orders at those who blocked the door although, the hunter was being much less diplomatic than Oscar.

'Move it!' Damen roared, hauling men and women through the doorway one by one as if he was swimming through them.

'Damen,' Harl called and the big man pushed himself up on tiptoes at his name. He waded down into the bodies and forced a path to Harl. He grabbed Harl and dragged him back through the crowd to the door.

Harl stopped just before he was through and glanced back over the panic-stricken faces.

The Aylen was towering far above the stalks, its monstrous legs devouring the distance left to Delta as it ran towards them. It must have seen the light reflecting off the panels on top of the mountain because it didn't hesitate, it just churned its way through the forest in a nightmarish display of power.

Had it noticed the crowd still struggling to get into Delta?

The people around Harl thinned and Damen roared as he dragged the last man inside.

'Seal it up,' Harl yelled, but then turned as a small voice cried from the nearest stalks. It was the girl he'd seen with her mother, alone now, and running for the base of the mountain.

'She won't make it,' he said.

She was two hundred paces away and slowing. He didn't know why, but he looked at Damen.

Damen, the faster of the two of them, sighed and burst out the door. He sprinted full pelt down the stairs, closing the distance fast. Harl had never seen someone cover so much ground so quickly. It was a clear run and Damen soon had the girl over his shoulder as the Aylen stomped down from the fringes of the forest. It stared down at the running figure running ahead of it, cocked its head and roared.

As Damen rushed past, Harl pulled both doors inwards. The gates slammed shut in a pathetic attempt to seal the city from the wrath of the giant.

Harl leaned against door and looked at Damen as he lowered the girl to the ground. An eerie silence descended on the people behind the door, then the vibrations rumbled into Harl's back as the giant stomped towards the city.

What had the plan been? What were they supposed to do? He held his head in his hands and tried to still his thoughts, but they just scattered as the floor vibrated under him.

'Harl?' Kane asked, stepping through the silent crowd and laying a hand on his shoulder.

Harl lowered his hands. 'It's coming, Kane. It's too big, too fast, and it knows we're here.'

'We stick to the plan.' Kane said. 'Everyone has to take shelter in the ship while we fire up the engines.'

'Move along!' Damen roared at the expectant faces. 'Push deeper into the city. Follow the soldiers to the ship.'

Harl nodded, glad to get moving again. Troy skidded in next to them, panting.

'There's no time,' he said as the crowd surged down the tunnel. 'That thing will destroy this place within moments when it chooses to.'

'Then we'd better move,' Kane said, a sad smile on his face.

'The fire liquid?' Harl prompted as a shudder rattled the metal panels against the walls.

Kane slapped a hand against his head. 'It isn't loaded!' Without saying another word he barged past Damen and raced into the city.

Troy scrunched his shoulders up, cringing, as another roar echoed from outside. It sounded close.

'I'm out of here.' Troy said and ran off after the crowd.

'Harl?' It was Sonora.

She squeezed past the last stragglers disappearing round the corner and threw her arms around him. He breathed in the scent of her and closed his eyes against the chaos. It was only a single moment, but when he stepped back and looked into her gleaming eyes, the weight and horror of it all slipped away. He kissed her.

'Are you okay?' he asked.

She nodded and laid her head on his shoulder, then stepped back and punched him in the chest.

'Don't worry me like that,' she said.

He squeezed her hand as another roar shattered the moment. He pulled her along in a racing blur through the tunnels.

'We have to get to the ship,' he said, taking a short cut through a narrow utility tunnel towards where the where the ship was waiting.

707

'Gorman is already on board,' Sonora said as they came out the other end. She forced her way around a pair of soldiers shooing the last people deeper into the cave system.

A giant hand crashed through the ceiling, spilling light onto the screaming people as they dropped to the floor. Everything around them shook and vibrated as debris rained down, cables sparked, and the walls buckled. The grey face of an Aylen leered in through the hole.

The hand plunged in again, shredding the corridor as it forced its way in. Harl put his arms around Sonora to shield her, and saw half a dozen terrified people snatched away as the Aylen's huge fingers closed around them. Others tried to reach out, grabbing the flailing limbs of their loved ones as they were lifted away, but it was no use. They were just yanked up to join them. Some even fell back down as the hand gained height and ended up impaled on the jagged edges of metal that formed the broken sides of the tunnel walls.

Looking up through the jagged hole, Harl could see the Aylen as it stuffed the people into a clear jar. Many of them had been crushed, but even the survivors looked to have broken, mangled limbs.

He needed to get Sonora out of sight.

They scrambled over the broken timber and rubble from the roof, and then ran off down the corridor. Harl could hear the injured moaning behind them as he dragged Sonora away, but he focused ahead and tried to ignore her protests. *Just this once*, he thought. *No one else matters, only Sonora.*

The Aylen's hand smashed down through the roof again. Harl staggered as the floor buckled and then smashed into a wall as the impact shook the corridor. Sonora fell on top of him and they both tumbled to the floor. Harl shrugged a beam off his back and struggled to his feet, pulling Sonora up with him, before racing off down the corridor. They soon caught up with groups of people who were running around in panic. They were tank-dwellers, and it was obvious that they had no idea which way they had to go to reach the ship. Only a sense of self-preservation had pushed them deeper into the heart of the city.

They found Damen at a junction several corridors further on. He was ushering people into the hanger although he wasn't being too polite about it.

'Get a bloody move on!' he kept roaring as people scurried forward.

The hanger lay under the plain in front of the city. Harl hoped it was far enough away from the Aylen to remain undetected. The ship was too precious to lose and he doubted the roof was strong enough to support an Aylen stomping around above.

'We need to get up there and fight,' Damen said when he saw Harl barging through the crowd towards him. He surrendered his post to one of his men and led Harl and Sonora into the hanger. 'It can't end like this. We must do something.'

Oscar ran down the ramp beneath the ship as Damen, Sonora and Harl got underneath the sleek vessel.

'There's not enough time for Kane to get the ship out,' he said, waving his arm at the vessel.

709

'Let's buy him some time then,' Harl said, looking at Sonora. She nodded.

'I'll tell Kane to leave the ramp down,' she said and gave him a tight hug before scampering up into the ship.

Damen, Oscar and Harl ran for the armoury while, in the distance, the sound of tearing rock rent the air.

The lights in the empty tunnels flickered as they took the twisting corridors. Whole passageways were flooded; the Aylen must have ruptured the water storage units and the torrent drained down into the lowest levels. Damen opened a door and a surge of water almost washed them back down the corridor. Only Oscar's firm grip held the three of them in place, his muscles working against the current until the pressure eased and the water levelled to knee height.

'Up ahead,' Damen said, pointing to a reinforced door at the end of the corridor.

'What's that?' Oscar asked as a steady rumble grew louder.

It was hard to pinpoint the sound above the noise of rocks raining down from above ground, but it was familiar.

'Borer!' Harl shouted. He grabbed their shoulders and forced the two huge men down into the water, and then dived under as well.

The rocks split apart ahead of them in an exploding shower of jagged blocks. A soft pink mass crashed through after, throwing more rubble and fragments out into the tunnel.

They scrambled to their feet as the tail end of the giant worm disappeared into the opposite wall. A second rumble built up behind them and they raced for the door. The wall burst apart and the borer plunged out into the tunnel. Instead of forcing its way through the other side, it turned into the tunnel and writhed towards them. Its mouth was a circle of sharp teeth, opening and contracting in anticipation of an easy meal.

Damen reached the door and gripped the handle. It didn't open. He launched his shoulder against it but it still refused budge, so he gripped the handle again and strained to wedge a knife in the split and slide it open before the monster reached them.

Oscar put his strength against the door as well and it inched open wide enough so that he could get his fingers between it and the frame. The borer slithered closer and, as Harl prepared to kick out, the door split open and they tumbled through.

The borer slithered past the doorway, ignoring them. Damen grabbed a rifle from the wall and stepped out behind it, gritted his teeth, and then fired at the rear of the creature.

It was dead before he'd emptied the clip.

Chapter 75

Using tools from my old lab I have discovered the hidden potential inside

these creatures. The power within them must be kept secret.

Harl moved to the nearest rack and pulled down two more rifles. They were battered but serviceable, and he tossed one to Oscar who looked at it as though it was about to explode. Seeing Oscar's fear, Harl had an idea and scanned the tables for what he wanted.

The water in the room rippled and sloshed as the Aylen continued its hunt for humans somewhere above.

'Sir?' a voice said from the doorway. It was a soldier, one of the men Damen had trained. Half a dozen other soldiers stood behind the ragged figure, peering into the dim room.

'Grab something with a trigger,' Damen said, 'and follow us.'

Harl found what he was looking for in a metal container. Explosive cylinders. Kane had used one when fighting the Enlightened and they'd proved to be devastating weapons. Harl shoved them into his pockets and tucked ammunition into every other crevice.

The soldiers looked like they had barely escaped capture. One had his arm in a sling and another had part of his scalp missing and a gash down one cheek. Harl could see the man's teeth glinting through the wound, but the soldier just spat blood on the floor and nodded that he was ready.

Damen checked that everyone was loaded and then led them through the maze of broken passageways towards the surface. The sunlight was blinding when they reached the upper levels. Harl's eyes were slow to adjust, but it was almost worse when they had. They were standing amid a ruin of broken tunnels and piles of rubble. Parts of the city were completely open to the sky and everything in sight was twisted metal and piles of stone. The only thing truly recognisable was the face of the Aylen, leaning over the city through a hazy cloud of acrid smelling smoke and powdered dust. It was like a fruit picker rummaging through the debris as it hunted for treats.

The tall, transparent cylinder for transporting humans was placed to one side of the city. It was almost half full of people who had been stuffed inside like sweets in a jar. Harl felt sick as he watched them squirm out from under each other.

Damen had led them out through a tunnel near the main entrance and, sticking to the shadows, they were able to slip past the Aylen as it continued to sift the wreckage. Eventually they came to the open plain above the ship. It was overlooked by a long ridge topped with grass stalks that marked the boundary of the forest.

'Stay out of sight and get to the ridge,' Harl said. 'I'll join you in a moment.'

Damen looked puzzled, but nodded and led the crouching group in behind the Aylen towards the tree line.

Boulders littered the flat plain. Whole sections of the city had been torn out from the rock and casually discarded in the Aylen's search for victims.

The jar was only fifty paces away. People inside squirmed against each other and hammered on the glass in a futile attempt to get out. Harl waited for Oscar, Damen, and the men to reach the ridge and then watched as they disappeared into the stalks before he ran towards the jar.

The poor souls inside – those still standing or close to the side – pounded on the glass when they saw him. He pulled an explosive cylinder from his pocket and just before he flicked the switch to activate it, an explosion rent the air above him. The cylinder flew out of his hand and clattered down a hole in the rubble. He cursed and thrust his arm down the hole, fumbling blindly in the gap as rubble rained down around him, followed by a wave of choking dust.

The Aylen had ripped out a steam engine, but it had burst apart, tearing chunks from its hand. Yellow blood fell through the cloud like a mystic rain. The Aylen roared in pain and grabbed its injured hand.

Harl tried to ignore it all and grasped the cold cylinder in his fingers. He pulled it out and sprinted the last few paces towards the jar, then flicked a switch on the cylinder and launched it up at the jar. The mechanism inside activated and the air around the glass was engulfed in a blinding explosion. When the smoke cleared, he could see the glass had a thin vertical crack. Harl cursed and ran closer to the jar. He had one more cylinder left which gave him another chance to shatter the container.

The Aylen roared and whipped its head down at the noise. Its yellow eyes widened in anger as it spotted the crack, then the evil gaze locked on to Harl and his heart skipped a beat.

The Aylen swiped its hand down just in front of him. He skidded to a stop just in time and the hand flew by, scooping the ground out in front of him to leave a trench carved in the dirt. He jumped the hole and hoped he was close enough to the jar.

Flicking the switch, he lobbed the cylinder as hard as he could and watched as it hit the clear wall and dropped down to the ground beside the container. Hands on ears, he flung himself backwards into the trench as they Aylen's other hand swooped through the air where he'd been standing. Time slowed as the dust around him rose, kicked up from the giant hand's movement. Then the salty particles blew back in his face as the cylinder exploded.

The jar broke under the pressure and shattered, leaving a hole big enough for the prisoners to escape.

The Aylen bent over, barking sharp guttural sounds that, to Harl, sounded like curses as the people inside made a bid for freedom. The Aylen started to swipe them back in, impaling one man against the broken edge as the others tried to scramble out of the way.

Damen's men opened fire from the ridge line and the blasts struck the Aylen, making the giant spin around to search for the attackers. The Aylen clawed a section of what had once been the marketplace out of the ground and threw it at Damen and the soldiers, before stomping over towards the ridge.

Oscar had run down from the ridge towards a section of the city that had been cast aside. He made a beeline for a tumbled heap of containers that had spilled open and snatched up a muddy bag, stuffing handfuls of items from the containers into it.

Harl was too far away to see what he was doing. Why had he left the ridge?

Oscar hunkered down as the Aylen strode over him towards the ridge where Damen's men were still firing. He then leapt up and ran through the city's debris, dodging between broken tunnel sections and ancient metal modules until he reached the mound of rubble Harl was hiding behind.

'Harl,' he said, holding out the bag.

Harl peered inside. It was full of the metal cylinders.

There were enough explosives inside to do some serious damage to the Aylen. He tried to count them but Oscar grabbed his shoulder.

'The ground!' he said, pointing across the plain further around the broken city.

The hanger doors were hinging open on the far side of the city and, from Harl's point of view, it looked like the ground was slowly angling up like a hill. If they could keep the Aylen distracted then Kane could get them away.

The huge doors eased open, slowly pushing up and outwards to reveal the hanger and the sleek vessel inside. Harl could only just make it out from his position, but if the Aylen spotted it then all would be lost. All it would have to do is stamp down on the ship before it could rise from the crater.

717

Oscar seemed to understand Harl's thoughts and drew his sword.

'We must distract,' he said.

Harl nodded.

The Aylen was standing on the ridge, kicking at the ground where Damen had fired from. Both Harl and Oscar would need as much speed as possible to get to the Aylen before it killed everyone. Several blue shots flew up from the grass forest, signalling that Damen and his men were still alive and trying to keep the giant occupied.

'Let's go,' Harl said, breaking into a sprint across the plain towards the ridge. They dodged between rocks and broken sections of tunnel as they clambered up the ridge behind the Aylen, then rushed in close to its feet.

The Aylen soared over them like a moving cliff face of flesh and metallic clothing. It was still busy stomping a foot through the forest as sporadic shots fired up at it. All of its weight was on its back foot, closest to Harl. An idea sprang to mind.

'Go right,' Harl said, pointing to the forest on their right. 'When it turns, move past and get Damen down to the plain.'

Oscar nodded and broke right, heading into the stalks.

Harl took a deep breath to calm the thudding in his chest and rummaged inside the bag. He pulled out a trio of cylinders, flicked the metal latches, tossed them at the foot and dived into the nearest stalks.

The Aylen screamed as they blew, threatening to deafen Harl. The mesh that covered the foot shredded until a cascade of yellow ran from the hole.

The Aylen turned, its glare fixed on Harl's location, the golden eyes scanning the stalks. Oscar was just visible, creeping through the foliage to get behind it. The face tilted down towards Harl and an evil gleam entered its eyes as the Aylen spotted him.

Harl's throat turned desert dry as he stared up at the craggy grey face. His legs refused to move and he felt like an insect under the gaze of a cruel child. He willed himself to action, broke cover, and ran.

The giant lashed out with a foot, stamping down at where he'd been to miss him by only a pace as he raced down the ridge towards a boulder. The ship began to rise up out of the hanger, dust billowing around it as though it was caught in a storm.

Harl skidded to a halt at the boulder, only to realise that it was a chunk of the city that had been torn away by the Aylen. A section of tunnels led through it. The Aylen raised its foot above him again, so he flicked a switch on one of the cylinders inside the bag and dropped it. He counted one heartbeat then dived aside as the foot slammed straight down into the ground beside him.

The foot crumpled as the cylinders exploded underneath it, and tore apart with a sickly wet pop. Harl threw himself into the tunnel as hunks of flesh and yellow ichor splattered around him. The Aylen's roar was blood curdling and the world shook as the giant toppled to the ground.

The tunnel saved Harl's life. The Aylen fell on top of it, a mountain of flesh crashing down on to the ground like thunder reverberating through the soil. Rock fractured around him, but the metal panelling held it at bay. Harl cowered there, not quite able to believe that he was still alive.

For a moment there was silence, then the downed Aylen went berserk. It rolled over and thrashed out at anything around it. A fist connected with the tunnel section, flinging it away with Harl trapped inside. The world tumbled over and over until the boulder shattered fifty paces from the Aylen, throwing Harl out on to the dusty ground.

His vision blurred, but then the sunlight turned to silver. He rubbed at his eyes trying to clear them. Was it the Aylen? He didn't know, so he scrambled on his hands and knees to get away. The silver light seemed to track him until his vision cleared. He turned back and shouted with joy when he realised that the silver light was a reflection off the ship as it skirted around the Aylen's flailing limbs.

The silvery mass slowed as it drew close to where Damen had been, and then, instead of rising up and flying away, it floated towards Harl. He rubbed his eyes again and saw that the loading ramp was hanging open just above the ground.

'Dammit,' he said, trying to roll over and get up. Pain surged through nearly every part of his body. It felt like the foot had actually landed on him. He tried to push himself up, but his hand slipped and his face slapped into the soil.

As if in a dream, he imagined he was rising, and then, in a moment of bewilderment, he was. His feet hit the floor as he felt a tight grip on his waist. He looked to his side and found Oscar there, ducking underneath his arm to half carry him towards the ramp as the ship glided over them.

Troy was leaning out from the ramp, his hand stretched out to help him in. The ship didn't slow and, instead of letting Harl

720

try to jump on, Oscar roared and heaved him up. Troy grabbed his hand and yanked Harl inside to sprawl on the ramp.

A billow of dust blew into the ship as the Aylen tried to stand, but it collapsed, its mangled stump unable to support the weight. The creature roared in fury and started pitching huge fistfuls of soil and rocks at the craft.

Oscar leapt up, grabbed one of the struts that connected the ramp to the roof of the cargo bay, and swung himself inside.

Troy's face turned pale as he stared out the back. Harl looked around to see the Aylen on its knees and lunging for the ship with both hands. In a moment of horror the grey hands wrapped around the ship and jolted the vessel to an instant stop.

Harl was flung back towards the hideous face beneath them.

Oscar gripped the strut with one hand while his other shot out to catch Harl's, jarring Harl's shoulder from the socket. He was left dangling from the ship like bait on a fishing rod.

The Aylen roared and dragged them back towards it, a malicious grin spread across its face.

Harl closed his eyes and waited for the end.

Chapter 76

An apprentice! There might just be time. Time, no matter the species, is never enough. One hundred and forty thousand oscillations, and I'm only just seeing how similar we are, regardless of size.

Troy grabbed the second strut and gripped Harl's free hand. The ship lurched again and together he and Oscar held Harl from plummeting out of the ship.

The Aylen was battling against the power of the engines to drag the ship closer, but it was a stalemate.

Harl scrambled up, but his feet were swept out from under him again as the Aylen tilted the ship and peered in through the open ramp. Harl swung above its leering face as Troy and Oscar strained to hold him.

One of the crew had opened the interior cargo bay door and the woman tumbled out, screaming as she slid past Harl. Troy's grip weakened, as if he was going to grab her, but as the Aylen shook the ship again, Troy's fingers tightened around Harl's hand

and the woman shot out the back of the ship. The Aylen didn't flinch as she bounced against the face.

The ship tilted further over as the Aylen started to shake it. It peered through the opening again as though hoping something else would fall out.

Oscar's feet slipped and he staggered, letting go of Harl as he grabbed the strut with both hands to save himself from falling. His feet swept out from under him and he dangled there next to Harl as they stared down into the Aylen's face.

Troy's arms were giving way under the strain of holding Harl in place. His fingers started to weaken and slip.

'I'm sorry,' Troy said. 'I can't... hold... us.'

Terror rippled through Harl, but then it ebbed away, leaving only a cold sadness. He would never see his child or watch it grow up. There was no way Troy could hold them both. He nodded as he looked at the anguish in his friends eyes. Oscar was still holding on to the strut and staring down at the face as if calculating the drop.

'You've done enough, my friends,' Harl said, peeling his fingers free from Troy's grip.

'What are you doing?' Troy yelled. His eyes widened. 'No. No! I won't let you do that!'

'Tell Sonora I'm sorry,' Harl said.

'Its not your time,' Oscar said. He tilted his head back and roared with a savage fury. Dropping one hand to the scabbard at his waist he drew the sword Damen had given him. He pressed the button on the hilt and fixed his gaze on the Aylen below.

Without another word, he let go.

Oscar dropped straight down, both hands gripped the pommel of his sword and he slammed into the eye socket of the Aylen. He drove the tip of the sword in first and plunged down through the cornea deep into its yellow gaze.

The Aylen screamed a deafening cry as Oscar sliced left and right, gouging out chunks. It snatched its hands away from the ship to clamp them down over its injured eye. The fingers missed Oscar as he jumped aside, but the impact broke his grip on the embedded sword and he was catapulted free, sailing out into the air.

The ship's engines roared as it swept up into the sky. Harl watched his friend fall, tears streaming from his eyes as Troy dragged him up the ramp. Low clouds engulfed the ship at the instant Oscar hit the ground and Harl dropped to his knees on the cold metal ramp and sobbed.

The clouds parted for a brief moment to reveal the Aylen as it toppled backwards to the ground covered in its own blood.

Harl knelt in silence, unsure what to do. The clouds shifted over the world until the dead Aylen was nothing but a tiny speck on the ground below. It was as if their roles had been reversed, Harl had become the giant while the Aylen shrank away to nothing.

Troy stood behind him and, when Harl finally turned around to thank him, the buzzer droned on a wall-mounted radio beside the door.

'Anyone there?' It was Sonora and he raced across the cargo bay to press the reply button.

'I'm here,' he said.

'Harl?' Sonora said. 'You're alright, I thought...' She broke off.

'I'm fine,' he said, almost choking on the words, 'but we lost Oscar. Tell Kane we're on our way up to you.'

Kane's voice came through a moment later. 'I'm sorry about Oscar. We're on autopilot at the moment. The ship should take us from here. No need to rush. Other than a few bruises, everyone's alright. The ramp will close momentarily, so make the most of the view.'

The radio clicked off.

Harl looked around at Troy who was perched on the end of the ramp staring out at a spectacular sight. Harl didn't care what was out there – the shock and pain of losing Oscar was too much – but his feet seemed to drag him over until he was beside Troy.

A vast blue sky spread out around them as the ship climbed up into the higher wispy clouds. Below them, vast areas of the planet were sectioned off, not by a fence, but by two colours. The land masses were divided into black and green rectangles. It looked like someone had taken a plough to most of the surface, slowly turning lush vegetation into barren soil one square at a time. Was that how the Aylen grew their crops?

The two tone plains were broken apart by white-tipped mountain ranges and long, stretched out lines that resembled roads. Buildings lined the roads, some much bigger than the shop. The lines intersected from every direction, but seemed to converge at a grey smear on the horizon. It could only be a city, a city of giants.

The ramp lifted, and Troy jumped up, blocking the view as it closed.

'Kane,' Harl said, moving quickly to the radio. 'Keep it open.'

'I can't,' Kane radioed back, 'It's automatic from here on.'

'From here to where?' Harl asked, hoping the man might know where the ship was headed now it was actually flying.

'You'd better come up and see for yourself.'

Chapter 77

I was too late to train another to take my place. I lie here, in the health centre, and I realise that from the start I made the wrong choice. I know I'm thinking like one of the Compassionates, but the creatures should not have been caged. I have only myself to blame and I will answer to the One True God when I pass from here.

Harl met Damen coming back from the cargo bay and the hunter had darkened at the news of Oscar's death. The two men had only know each other a short time, but it was an instant friendship, one that would have blossomed over time. Harl let Damen lead him to the cockpit, unwilling to see whether or not the hunter had tears in his eyes.

The cockpit was crowded and, when Sonora saw him, she ran into his arms. She kissed him deeply.

'I was so worried when you were down there,' she said, holding him tight as tears flowed onto his bloodstained jacket.

'I couldn't leave you two,' Harl said, stepping back and touching her stomach.

'Sorry to interrupt,' Kane said, his hands flickering over the control screen. 'But we seem to be going a little high.'

'What do you mean?' Harl asked, looking out the window as the clouds whizzed by.

'Well,' Kane said, 'I expected us to go up a bit but to eventually level out.'

'And?' Harl prompted.

Kane cleared his throat nervously. 'Erm, we're still going nearly straight up.'

It was true. The ship was gaining height at an alarming rate with the window tilting up to a darkening blue sky.

'What happens if we keep going up?' Harl asked. 'Can we stop it?'

'I don't think we need to panic,' Gorman said, stepping into the room and tapping his stick on the computer consoles to feel his way forward. 'This ship is well built and the chances for it to head directly upwards on automatic and not be designed for that purpose would be unlikely.'

The words had a calming effect on all of them and even Kane seemed to relax a little. He punched buttons on a comms box and started to get the engineers busy again, before ordering status updates on those in the community room, where over a thousand people waited expectantly.

Reports came back that the ship's engine core was working as well as could be expected and, after the rough handling from the Aylen, the ship was in remarkably good condition.

The distance from the surface was immeasurable now. The once flat land below them had transformed into a curve. For some bizarre reason Harl had imagined the world to be cubed, like the tanks, but if they kept going up it would surely be round.

'Help!' Gorman cried, and Harl turned to discover what could make the blind man so unnerved.

He felt and saw it at the same time. Gorman rose up from floor at the same instant as everyone else. They were floating in the air. Only Kane, who was clipped into his seat, did not rise. Small items floated past them across the room, spinning through the air as if they were in a peaceful dance.

'Hold on to something,' Kane said, keeping a firm grip on the console in front of him.

Harl had risen from the floor like everyone else, but then – as if reality had snapped back into place – they all dropped back down. A noise came from the ship itself in response and Harl guessed, somehow, that it was countering the effect.

'What was that?' Sonora asked.

'I would guess,' Kane said, 'that we have left the pull of the planet and the ship has engaged something to reverse it. I should have expected it, but with so much to concentrate on I forgot.'

'Forgot?' Troy said, incredulous. 'That we might suddenly start flying around?'

Harl gripped the back of one of the seats and watched the window in awe. The blue sky kept darkening until it went black. Pinpricks of light studded the void ahead of them in a dazzling display.

Gorman must have sensed the change.

'Tell me Kane,' he said, 'what do you see?'

Kane looked up from his console and gasped. 'I see... I see the darkness of night is all around us, but the ship is coming around.

It's so beautiful, Gorman. I see the sphere of the land below. I see the planet.'

'And the stars?' Gorman asked.

'More than I can count,' Kane said.

Gorman smiled to himself. 'What now then?'

'We're safe,' Harl said. 'Wherever we end up now is a new adventure.'

Epilogue.

I have left my entire wealth in a trust to the Compassionates in the hope they can help, but life is slipping from me. My story is ending, but my work will go on... must go on. As soon as the truth about them is known, the world will change. Energy, currency and politics, they will be altered forever. But that is for another generation to deal with.

'What's that?' Troy asked, pointing at where the haze around the world met the darkness.

Harl scanned the area, but saw nothing other than the countless stars scattered at random.

'Right there,' Troy said, leaning against Kane's console so he could jab a finger on the glass window.

'I see it,' Kane said, unclipping his belt and scrambling over the controls to get closer to the window. 'Fascinating.'

Harl followed Troy's finger and saw a star, or what seemed like a star. It was larger than the rest and pulsing gently.

They waited, anxiously, as the object lost its shimmer and grew in size until it was distinguishable as another ship.

All of them, except Gorman and Damen, had pressed themselves against the glass, eager to get a good look.

'Judging by the proportions, it must be enormous compared to our ship,' Kane said.

'How is it up here?' Sonora asked.

'Two possibilities,' Gorman said. 'Either it came from below, as we did, or we came down from it. Either way, it's been up here for a very long time.'

'A ship of that size,' Kane said, 'would be difficult to launch from the surface.'

They were coming up behind the grey vessel and Kane had been right when he said it must be bigger than their own. It was far bigger than even the tanks the Aylen had made for them, more on the scale of the room the tanks had been kept in.

At the rear of the grey ship, a huge bell-shaped section housed what Harl guessed was the engine. The bell alone was big enough to easily swallow their own ship. The hull was pockmarked as if struck thousands of times with an Aylen hammer until no surface was smooth. Some of the dents were enormous, not breaking the hull but bending the metal deep in on itself. A scaffold of metal struts shot up mid way along the top. The ends were bent and twisted, as though someone had driven the ship through a tunnel that was too low for it and torn a section off.

'We're changing direction,' Kane said, looking down at the panel in front of him. 'And slowing.'

'Look!' Sonora said, as two square sections of the huge ship parted along one side to reveal a dark opening.

'It still responds after so long,' Kane murmured in awe. 'It must have some source of power inside.'

'Can we go back?' Troy asked.

Gorman laughed. 'Not until we reach the end of this journey. Maybe we can take the ship back down if we need to. I just wish I could see it for myself.'

Their ship turned into the opening and glided into a huge hollow within the larger ship. It was like a dimly lit corridor for Aylens, long and narrow, with square sections cut away along one side. Each cut-out was big enough for a ship to dock inside, like a harbour where boats could offload their wares.

'I guess we're the only ones who returned,' Kane said, eyeing the empty bays in the docking area.

'Maybe not,' Harl said, looking at a row of windows and doors that lined the end of the bay they were heading for.

Sonora moved up next to him and raised one trembling hand to point ahead of them.

A thrill of excitement surged through Harl as he stared at what lay ahead.

There were people looking back.

Thank you for reading The Humanarium. Please forgive the small cliffhanger. I haven't the skill to write all the books in one go, but it doesn't end here.

Continue to read this series right now.
Humanarium book 2: Orbital

Reviews are so powerful when it comes to getting attention for a book and, without the huge budget of a giant publisher, I am unable to advertise in the special spots reserved for the cream of the crop. But I do have something so potent that all the main book publishers would shed blood for it:
You and other Committed loyal readers who understand how a few words can spread what they enjoy to other readers.

Wherever you bought this book from please leave an honest review behind for others and fuel the life and future of this series.

About the author.

Thanks for reading the book. I thought you might like a few details about me and to find out where the idea for the book came from.

I live in Cambridge, England and work as a gardener so I have plenty of thinking time when it comes to standing behind a lawn mower and walking up and down to make stripy lawns.

The idea for the book came several years ago during a phase of keeping tropical fish. I always enjoyed rearranging the landscapes inside the tank and one day, I realised in some bizarre way that I could be considered a god to the fish inside.

I was the only one who fed them, cleaned them and looked after their well being, all in a non god-complex way, of course. But it was because of me that their quality of life was so good.

I chuckled to myself and said "I wonder what it would be like if I was one of the fish inside." Perhaps with a fish on the outside being the sole provider...

From then on I could easily imagine a group of humans living inside and a small story began to form.

When I finally couldn't hold all the details in my head I had to put it somewhere and a crude story formed on a ragged piece of paper.

I had no intention of writing a story but was intrigued by the idea, the concept seemed almost unique. To be honest before the thought hit me, I couldn't write at all and it has been a long learning process to get even close to something readable.

Thinking back on my childhood I realise that I was heavily influenced by "small concepts" I think it started with ants (they still fascinate me), watching them scurry back and forwards in a world that must have been overwhelming in size to them. A single foot or child's hand could destroy days of hard graft and murder their comrades instantly.

I remember watching the borrowers by Mary Norton every week on TV and it held me enchanted with the little people living like mice in a human's house, sleeping in matchboxes and "borrowing" everything they could. I guess it was 50-50 that I could have become a thief.

How the Humanarium blended into science fiction rather than solid fantasy? I have no idea, I guess a love of the stars and trying to make it seem plausible were key ingredients.

Anyway, there's plenty more ideas of where to take the series, so I guess we'll take the adventure together.

Chris.

Printed in Great Britain
by Amazon